THE CHILDREN'S HOUR

School and Sport

A BOOK TO GROW ON

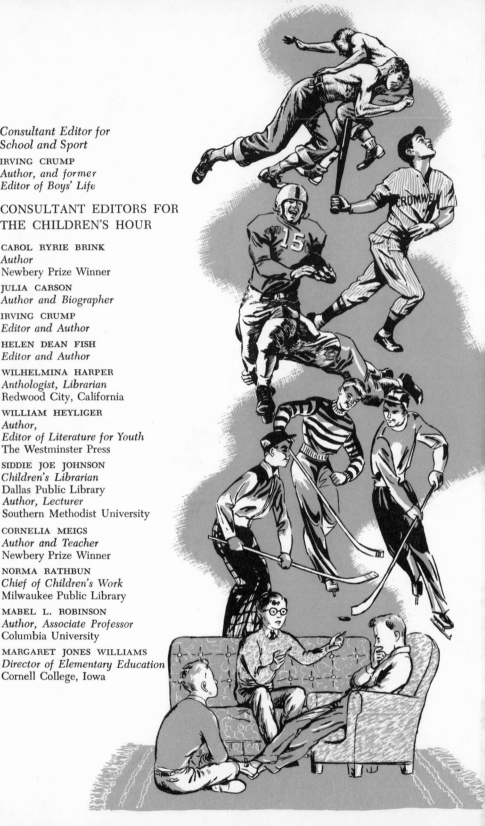

MARJORIE BARROWS, *Editor*

School
and Sport

MATHILDA SCHIRMER
Associate Editor

DOROTHY SHORT
Art Editor

THE CHILDREN'S HOUR

PRINTED IN THE UNITED STATES OF AMERICA

Acknowledgments

The editor and publishers wish to thank the following publishers, agents, authors, and artists for permission to use and reprint stories and illustrations included in this book:

HEDWIG M. BARBOUR for "'Hoot!' Said the Owl" by Ralph Henry Barbour, first published in *American Boy*.

THE BOBBS MERRILL COMPANY, INC., for "'The Prize" from *The Jennifer Prize* by Eunice Young Smith, copyright, 1952.

THOMAS Y. CROWELL COMPANY for "The Gawk" and "Knights of the Red Rose" from *Varsity Letter* by Franklin M. Reck, copyright, 1942, by Thomas Y. Crowell Company.

HARCOURT, BRACE AND COMPANY, INC., for "Ginger on the Fire Escape" from *Ginger Pye* by Eleanor Estes, copyright, 1951, by Harcourt, Brace and Company, Inc.; "The Cutter Race" from *Red Horse Hill* by Stephen W. Meader, copyright, 1930, by Harcourt, Brace and Company, Inc.; "The Pass" from *All-American* by John R. Tunis, copyright, 1940, by John R. Tunis, and two illustrations by Hans Walleen from this book; "Two-Mile Race" condensed from *Iron Duke* by John R. Tunis, copyright, 1938, by Harcourt, Brace and Company, Inc.

LITTLE, BROWN & COMPANY for "Beauty's Sister" from *The Prodigious Hickey* by Owen Johnson, copyright, 1938, by Owen Johnson; "The Third Round" from *Stover at Yale* by Owen Johnson, copyright, 1912, 1940, by Owen Johnson.

LONGMANS, GREEN AND COMPANY and the author for "Caricature" by Ernie Rydberg, from *On My Honor* edited by Marjorie Vetter, copyright, 1951, first published in *American Girl*.

JULIAN MESSNER, INC., for "The Most Wonderful Thing in the World" from *Melindy's Medal* by Georgene Faulkner and John Becker, copyright, May 29, 1945, by Georgene Faulkner and John Becker.

WILLIAM MORROW AND COMPANY, INC., for "Marshall at Bat" from *Starting Pitcher* by Duane Decker, copyright, 1948, by Duane Decker.

L. C. PAGE & COMPANY, INC., for "The Holiday Cup" from *Beacon Hill Children* by Elizabeth Rhodes Jackson.

THE VIKING PRESS, INC., for "Big Moment" from *The Fair Adventure* by Elizabeth Janet Gray, copyright, 1940, by Elizabeth Janet Gray.

HOWARD M. BRIER for "Yogi's Dark Horse," first published in *Boys' Life*.

B. J. CHUTE for "Anybody Can Ski" and "Master Mind," first published in *Boys' Life;* "Denny Puts in His Oar," first published by *Boys' Life* and later by The Macmillan Company.

RUTH H. COLBY for "Horse Mackerel."

IRVING CRUMP for "The Little Guy," first published in *Boys' Life*.

HELEN GREGUTT for "Jam Session at Abby's," first published in *American Girl*.

WILLIAM HEYLIGER for "Hit or Error" and "Clutch Man."

OLIVE BURNS KIRBY for "The Iceboat Race."

HELEN DIEHL OLDS for "The Basketball Mystery," first published in *Child Life Magazine*.

RUTH GIPSON PLOWHEAD for "Josie's Home Run," first published in *Child Life Magazine*.

JACKSON V. SCHOLZ for "Hoop Hokum," first published in *Boys' Life*.

MARGUERITE DAVIS for illustrations for Elizabeth Rhodes Jackson's "The Holiday Cup."

KEITH WARD for illustrations for Olive Burns Kirby's "The Iceboat Race" and Ruth H. Colby's "Horse Mackerel."

Great pains have been taken to obtain permission from the owners of reprint material. Any errors that may possibly have been made are unintentional and will gladly be corrected in future printings if notice is sent to the Spencer Press, Inc.

Contents

Part I: FOR YOUNGER READERS

Eleanor Estes

GINGER ON
THE FIRE ESCAPE

ILLUSTRATED BY *Ruth Van Tellingen*

IT WAS during these October weeks that Ginger discovered the enemy dog. It was lucky that Ginger did find out about him, for whom else could he play with? School had started, but what did Ginger understand of school? All he understood was that, for some reason, Jerry and Rachel now abandoned him for a great deal of each day. Therefore, in whom could Ginger take an interest if not in the enemy dog, and for a while he was obsessed with the very idea of him.

The enemy dog lived in the tall pier glass mirror, at least that was where Ginger first saw him—the tall pier glass mirror that stood between two windows in the horsehair parlor. This mirror had been a wedding present to the Pyes; and the three large vases that stood in its marble base were also wedding presents. One day Ginger was reaching up for his orange duster that happened to be lying on the marble base, and it was then that he made his amazing discovery.

There was another dog in this house, and he was in the shiny mirror! Yet, all along, Ginger had mistakenly thought he was the only dog in this house.

Ginger Pye gave this new dog a friendly woof for he did not realize all in a second that this was his enemy dog that was going to torment him and stay in shiny places. The dog gave Ginger a friendly woof too, only Ginger couldn't hear it. Ginger Pye then barked loudly at the new dog, and the new dog barked

1

back at Ginger, only still he made no sound. His woofing and his barking were silent and, because of this, rather exasperating.

Ginger made a dash for the dog in the mirror, and the dog in the mirror made a dash for Ginger. They growled at each other, Ginger in his loud fashion and the new dog in his silent fashion. Their noses were plastered right close together, so close Ginger couldn't even see the other dog any more. But the cowardly dog stayed inside where he was good and safe, and he wouldn't come out. It was infuriating and it made Ginger Pye frantic.

It was then that Ginger realized that this dog in the mirror was an enemy dog and not a friendly companion.

Moreover, it turned out that the dog did not stay inside his pier glass mirror after all. He cropped up in other places, in other mirrors, in the windowpanes, even in Ginger's own eating pan, eating up Ginger's dinner. And outside the house, he might be met up with too. For he was also a water dog, staying in puddles, the reservoir, the harbor, and the Sound.

Once Jerry and Rachel took Ginger for a walk over to Gramma's. They went by way of the shore instead of the street, and it was a most interesting excursion. The tide was low. Periwinkles and horseshoe crabs lay on the beaches, and clams were spouting here and there in the wet mud of low tide. The children crawled under every little red boathouse, smelling the wonderful stale sea smells there. They walked out on every wobbly little wooden pier. And everywhere Ginger delightedly frisked ahead of them.

It went to Ginger's head to be with Jerry and Rachel on such an unusual expedition. He picked up dry chunks of wood for them to throw and he tried to nudge the horseshoe crabs into getting a move on. He had no thought of the enemy dog. He was a carefree happy dog and he was always the first one out to the end of the little piers. There he barked at the water endlessly stretching, at the sky, the singing gulls, the bobbing buoys.

At the end of one weather-beaten, shaky old pier, to which a little boat was tied and placidly rocking, Ginger happened, for the first time, to look straight down into the queer green water.

2

And there, looking up at him, was his enemy, the dog!

Now Ginger was the dog of Jerry Pye. The enemy dog was not. Yet here he was, right here in the green-blue sea. Apparently he had tagged along, sneakily, all the way, hoping to become the dog of Jerry Pye. These were Ginger's thoughts as he dived into the water, with Jerry and Rachel shouting earnest instructions to him from above. Ginger had never before been in such deep water and could he swim, they wanted to know.

"Ginger, can you swim?" yelled Rachel.

"Of course he can," said Jerry. "Look at him. Swims like he's swum all his life."

It was true. Ginger could swim, and he managed to get back to dry land in a very accomplished and intense fashion. He felt refreshed from his brisk salt-water swim and he rolled over and over in the warm sand happily.

"He's always thinking himself in mirrors, and water is his enemy," laughed Rachel.

"Um-m-m," agreed Jerry. "I'd hate to meet the real enemy, old Unsavory, along here in one of these old boathouses."

"O-o-o-h," gasped Rachel, stunned at such a prospect.

But they didn't. And neither did Ginger happen to have any further encounters with the enemy dog on that trip. He enjoyed a pleasant relaxed afternoon with Uncle Bennie and Jerry and Rachel, and he chased Gramma's chickens, getting a pecking or two, and he tasted Gramma's homemade peach ice cream,

3

spitting out the hard cold lumps of peach as Rachel and Jerry were doing, likewise. He really never expected to see the enemy dog again, having jumped on him in the water that way, scaring him out of his wits.

But of course, he did. When he got home the enemy dog was right there again, in the tall pier glass mirror, tongue hanging out thirstily, ears drooping tiredly. Secretly Ginger was glad to have the other dog back so he would have him handy for future bouts when life at home, without Jerry and Rachel, became too tame.

Soon after this wonderful expedition along the shore, however, Ginger began to suspect that the enemy dog was himself. He gave up pursuit of him in preference to the pursuit of cats. Cats certainly did not stay inside shiny things, and they really came out to fight. They were a more satisfactory type of enemy than the enemy dog had been.

During the time when everyone had been worried about the unsavory character, Ginger had been kept in the backyard unless he was with some person. Now, however, he was allowed in either the front or the backyard. It was impossible to keep Ginger from slipping out of the house with Gracie-the-cat anyway, for Gracie had the knack of opening the front door by leaping up and undoing the latch.

So Ginger now had the run of the land. Naturally, he preferred the front to the back of the house. From the front he could survey the entire neighborhood, get into other yards besides his own, and chase all the cats.

There was a matter that had begun to bother Ginger, however, and it had nothing to do with cats or the enemy dog. It was this. Where did Jerry disappear every morning and afternoon with his tiresome, "Go home, Ginger!" And Rachel, too. Where did they go?

Ginger's feelings were hurt, being deserted this way, even though Jerry patted him and gave him fond scratches behind the ear and such attentions before tearing out the front door saying, "I'm late again, by jiminy."

"Where could he go, anyway?" puzzled Ginger. Today he in-

4

tended to find out. Ginger was a purposeful dog. Once he had decided to do something, he did it, provided he was not obstructed by some person. Now was the time, he felt, to investigate the constant goings away and comings back of his master, Jerry Pye, and of the master's sister, Rachel Pye. They had something to do with the goings past the house and the returnings past the house, twice a day, of all the boys and girls in Cranbury, practically. Wherever they all went, it might possibly be more fun than chasing cats, more fun, even, than going up to the reservoir.

At this moment Ginger happened to be lying opposite the tall pier glass mirror surveying himself with a thoughtful planning look. He arose, stretched, and gave himself a challenging yap for old time's sake. He made a dash for Gracie-the-cat, leaped over her imploring crouching form, and went into the kitchen. After a few laps of water he looked around for something of Jerry's to smell, to get the scent well fixed in his scent department.

He found Jerry's sweater slung over the back of a kitchen chair and he pulled it to the floor and thrust his nose in its folds. Thoughtfully and earnestly he breathed in the essence of Jerry until it permeated his entire being, down to his toes and the tip of his short tail. His heart thumped with delight, and he thought excitedly, now, now he was going to find Jerry. "Jerry, Jerry, Jerry," his heart sang.

Of course Ginger knew the Jerry smell perfectly without having to rely on Jerry's old sweater. But this was to be his first experience at real hard trailing. It could not be compared with the easy following of the fresh trail of a dog, a cat, a chicken, or a chipmunk. Jerry had left some time ago. This meant a real hard trailing job and Ginger did not want to fail.

The first rule in trailing was, get the smell thoroughly inside himself. The next was, nose to ground. He had the smell. So now, nose to ground. He pushed his nose along the floor to the front door and paused, for the moment, stalled.

Fortunately, just then Gracie-the-cat decided to go outdoors herself. She leaped in the air in her own smart fashion, sprung

5

open the latch, and she and Ginger Pye went outside, leaving the door open behind them. And there Ginger Pye was, on his front lawn, surveying the scene.

At this moment, who should be coming home from the grocery store, her arms filled with bags and bundles, her face stern, as stern as her gentle face could get, but Mrs. Pye.

"Ginger," said Mrs. Pye. "Where are you going? You are not to chase Mrs. Carruthers's cat any more. And there has been a complaint that you chased a chicken. Mrs. Finney told me in the grocery store. If you keep up this outrageous behavior, you shall have to stay on the leash!"

Leash! Hated hateful word. Ginger shuddered. The leash was coiled like a snake on the stoop right now. It was an awful thing to have on the neck. Ginger had suspected it was awful, and he was wary of it the first time Jerry fastened it on. But he had not imagined, no dog could possibly imagine, how very awful, how completely horrible a leash was, until he had one on.

When he had the leash on, Ginger would struggle and struggle to get it off, pawing at it, shaking his head wildly, and showing the whites of his eyes. And if, forgetting for a moment he had the dreadful thing on, he made a dash for the Carruthers's cat, wham! The leash would nearly break his neck and down he would fall, gasping and rolling on the sidewalk. Jerry's concern over him would be pleasant, that was all that was pleasant about the leash.

"Aw, Ginger," Jerry would say. "You mustn't tug at the leash so."

Whenever Ginger saw the leash coming he would cower and quiver, hoping Jerry would change his mind and put it, perhaps, on Gracie instead.

But Jerry would say, "Now come on, Ginger. You've got to learn to walk nice on the leash."

Ginger merely strained the harder, and struggled and tugged and chortled and gasped and dragged Jerry along.

"Walk nice, Ginger," pleaded Jerry. And he would point out other dogs that pranced along neatly at the end of their leashes with never a gasp or a choke. The owners of these dogs would walk along in dignity or jauntiness, in an upright position and not in this disgraceful jerking struggling fashion.

"That way, not this way," urged Jerry.

"You must train him," suggested Mama.

"I'm tryin'," said Jerry gloomily. "But he won't walk nice."

Jerry did try to train Ginger. Once he even spanked him. Nothing did any good, not even bribery with candy. Ginger continued to gasp and choke and drag. Sneeze, he would do for Jerry. Shake hands, he would do for Jerry. Beg, walk on his hind feet, and be dead dog. But walk nice on the leash? Never.

At last Jerry gave up trying to train him to walk nice on the leash. He would carry the leash along with him on their excursions, and he would put it on after Ginger had chased a cat or a chicken. *After,* not before.

Soliloquizing in this manner with his nose in the grass, Ginger

7

looked meekly up at Mrs. Pye who still towered over him with her bags and potatoes and things. He was winning, he thought. Mrs. Pye no longer looked so stern; her eyes were laughing in fact. But to assure victory, Ginger cringed. He was not cringing in his heart. But if he presented a humble front, he thought Mrs. Pye would not bother him any more and he could finish that which he had started to do. And what was that? Chase Mrs. Carruthers's cat? Goodness no. He had almost forgotten. Interruptions were so bad for the game of scent trailing. But he remembered now. He was on the trail of Jerry Pye, his master.

Concealing his impatience, since the leash was still handy, Ginger looked up at Mrs. Pye with what, in the past, he had found to be a winning pose, head to side, tongue dangling out. Mrs. Pye gave him a little pat, spilling out all her potatoes as she did so. Of course Ginger had to help gather these up, by making a game of it, nosing them all over the lawn. When finally all the potatoes were recaptured Mrs. Pye said, "There, there. I didn't mean to be cross, Ginger. But you must be a good dog, do you hear?"

And at last she went into the house, leaving Ginger on the front lawn with his nose buried in a patch of thick short grass that was just covered with Jerry scent. Jerry must have flipped his knife here, dropped his books here, or something. Ginger decided he'd better be on the trail before Mrs. Pye again thought of putting the hated leash on him, or of giving him a bath, or a brushing. So. Now. Nose to ground.

Leaving his own yard and going on past Dick Badger's, it was easy enough to follow the Jerry scent, and Ginger pasted his nose to that scent. It led past the Carruthers's house. Actually without sniffing so hard, Ginger knew this was the direction Jerry had taken because he could always see him this far. However, in trailing, a dog has to sniff and snort like the dickens because that is the way it is done. He kept his nose plastered to the ground and he was concentrating so hard his whole face was pushed in and wrinkled up. It looked as though he were pushing his nose up the street in front of him. He kept getting sand up his nose and he had to wheeze it out of himself in long

8

deep exhalings. This was hard work, but it was wonderful work, and it was apparent he was born to be a regular trail hound even though he was mostly fox terrier.

Now Ginger was going past the Carruthers's driveway. He paused for a moment with his nose glued to the pavement. He was still drawing in the Jerry scent, but it had merely crossed his mind to wonder whether or not the old Carruthers's cat was anywhere around.

Keeping his nose plastered to the ground, not moving his head one inch, he turned his eyes way to the corners so that from in front one could have seen only the whites. Then, from out of the corners of his eyes, he spied her, spied the Carruthers's cat sitting under a rosebush, her favorite spot, watching for birds. Her back was to him. She was, perhaps, not aware that brave Ginger was right here?

He could surprise her. He could corner her, that was what he certainly could do, before she had a chance to run up a tree. His eyes turned back to his nose. He snuffed in the Jerry smell. Jerry, Jerry, where are you anyway? His eyes roved back to the cat. She had caught sight of him and all her fur was electric and stiff. But she had not run. She was in exactly the mood in which he loved to engage her in battle.

Still, Ginger did not give chase. Again he sniffed deeply of the Jerry scent. Then, a little sadly, he started shoving his nose up the street again. He had won over temptation. He snuffed on for a few paces when, "Pfsht!" The Gaines's cat, a tremendous gray one, spit insultingly in his direction and turned and fled challengingly into the Gaines's vast backyard.

Ginger couldn't help it. He forgot his quest. After the Gaines's cat he dashed, sneezing the gravel out of his nose as he went. He ran so fast he skidded around the corner to the backyard. From there, presently, his short, sharp yelps and the cat's long venomous hisses and yowls echoed in the quiet of a school morning in Cranbury.

Fifteen minutes later Ginger ran jauntily out from the Gaines's backyard where the old gray cat was now up a huge red mulberry tree. One of Ginger's ears was torn and bleeding, true.

9

And he had clawings on the white fur of his back. But he didn't care, for it had been a glorious bout.

Happy though Ginger felt, all tingling and exhilarated, nevertheless there was something bothering him deep inside himself that kept him from feeling the complete contentment a fight with a cat usually inspired in him. He could not immediately put his paw on this certain something. It was like a bone he knew he had somewhere that he couldn't recall the exact location of.

He lay panting on the soft green grass in his own front yard again. Mrs. Pye came out and said, "Oh, there you are, Ginger. Good dog," and she went back in again.

Ginger wagged his tail self-righteously. He licked his paw and applied it to his wounded ear. He should improve his technique with the Gaines's cat, for he had received too many digs. Ginger felt vaguely dissatisfied with himself and melancholy. He knew his hurting ear, alone, was not the cause of this feeling, for Jerry could fix that. Jerry would put something cool and soothing on it. Jerry . . . Jerry . . . Oh, Jerry! That was what it was! There Ginger had been—on the trail of Jerry, to find out where he went always. And then this! This fight with a cat! He had fallen into temptation after all. What a reflection upon his character!

In his shame Ginger stuck his tail down tight. He felt like a traitor, a deserter. But there was still time. He could still go

10

and find Jerry. He had started out to do one thing and he had ended by doing another. All right. It would not happen again because he was Ginger, the purposeful dog. His tail perked up and he pasted his nose to the ground again.

This time, as Ginger steered his nose past the Carruthers's and the Gaines's tempting houses, all he permitted himself was a slight reminiscent wag of the tail. That was all. Not even a peek from the corners of his eyes. And from his mind he banished thoughts of all the eyes of all the hidden cats that probably were on him. Scrunching up his nose, pushing it on up the street, he lost himself completely in following the trail of Jerry Pye.

At a certain point, going through a small field, the scent led Ginger to a little crabapple tree. He stood on his hind legs and inhaled the scent as far up the tree as he could thrust his nose. Jerry had been up this tree, but he certainly was no longer there for, of course, there would be a much keener scent if he were. The quest was by no means over.

Ginger remained poised there against the tree in contemplation. Jerry's going up the tree might be what was known as a decoy. Decoys were difficult, though not impossible, to outwit. For instance, the person a dog was trailing might leap from treetop to treetop. A dog had to work doubly hard and might have to explore in every direction before finding the trail again. But then, that is all part of tracking.

Ginger wagged his tail in appreciation of his master's cleverness, and he keenly anticipated matching his wits against his. No doubt, Jerry had suspected that Ginger would try to trail him. So, up the tree he had gone to throw Ginger off his tracks.

Thus Ginger analyzed the difficult situation before leaping down. He then began spiritedly to go round and round the tree in ever-widening circles. By the time he was ten dog-lengths away from the tree his nose picked up the scent again. And the decoy was over.

Apparently Jerry had swung out of the tree on a limber branch and had landed way over here on all fours. Here, also, was one of Jerry's pencils with Ginger's tooth marks on it as well as Jerry's own. Jerry had then proceeded in the same direc-

11

tion as before the tree decoy, and this Ginger did likewise, with the pencil in his mouth.

The pencil made trailing considerably more difficult than hitherto, if not well-nigh impossible. In the end, Ginger had to drop the pencil, find the trail, go back for the pencil, and bring it to the farthest point of trailing. Of course he could not abandon the pencil. The going, therefore, was slower now, not only because of the complication of the pencil, but also because suddenly there seemed to be a very great many more smells to weed out before locating Jerry's.

Ginger snorted and blew and carefully cherished the faint but certain scent that was Jerry's. So close to the ground did he keep his nose, he bumped right into the cement stoop of a candy store. He raised his head, sniffing expertly and gently. He allowed the enticing chocolate and peanut smells to mingle with Jerry's.

Was it possible that here was the end of the trail, the end of the long quest? Did Jerry spend all those hours away from him in a candy store? How marvelous, if true. He wagged his tail expectantly. His mouth drooled, for he loved candy, and he trotted into the candy store.

Jerry was not there, Ginger soon found out as he sniffed busily around the floor, eating bits of sweet that had been dropped and giving an excited bark when he found a piece of sticky paper Jerry had thrown down. It had had licorice in it—not one of Ginger's favorites; one of Jerry's though.

Ginger chewed all the sweetness out of the paper and re-luctantly let that go. After all, he had still to push his nose and Jerry's pencil up the street, and that was just about all he could manage. The trail was certainly hot now, what with having found Jerry's pencil and then this piece of sticky paper. Yes, this was what was known as being "hot on the trail."

Sniff, sniff here. Snort and blow there. A great, great many feet had passed this way, and Ginger lost the trail. He just fol-lowed the lead of all those feet and at last he paused to take his bearings. He looked about him. He had come through the wide open gate of a tall brown wooden fence and here he was,

12

in an enormous yard, half pavement and half worn down grass. He lay down on a little patch of this grass close to a big brick building. His nose stung and his neck ached from the long push and hard concentration. The pencil lay safely between his paws. He licked his tongue over his dry nose until it became moist and cool again, and he studied the building before him.

The building was big, hard, and brick. If this was where Jerry came every day and spent his time, Ginger was no longer envious. Why come here, though? Why come here when he and Jerry could tramp up Shingle Hill or tear through the woods around the reservoir picking up acorns and finding frogs? Still, inside might be pleasanter than outside, and Ginger toured the building to find a way in.

All doors were closed. All Ginger could do now was to sit and wait for Jerry to come out. Imagine Jerry's pleasure when he saw his faithful dog waiting here for him, choosing to wait here for him instead of chasing cats, moreover.

Ginger lazily crossed his front paws the way he always did while resting. He felt drowsy. Now and then he twitched his back to get rid of a fly circling around in the warm October sunshine. He listened to the sounds coming from the big building. There was a sound as of many bees droning. A sharp voice gave a command, and this droning stopped. The sharp voice gave another command, and there was a burst of singing. "Hats off, hats off, the flag is passing by." This was pleasant and Ginger was sorry when it stopped. After the singing there was quiet for a time, with only an occasional sharp command from the one in charge of all these goings on.

The long quest, the warm sunshine, the quiet, all contributed to Ginger's sleepiness. With one vigilant eye half open, he began to nod.

Then—was he dreaming? He heard Jerry's voice. Jerry's voice loud and clear and all by itself. Ginger sat up. His tail began uncertainly to wag. Then it wagged uncontrollably, for he was not dreaming. Jerry's voice was coming loud and clear from one of the high windows. Jerry was not using his regular voice that he used with Ginger or with any of the Pyes. He was

13

using a high and loud and clear voice. But it was Jerry's voice, even so.

Ginger listened, in a transport of delight. Then he gave a short bark announcing, if Jerry cared to know, that he, Ginger, was right out here. Not only was he out here, he would manage to get to Jerry somehow, so there would be no more separation.

Ginger no longer felt tired. He tore around the building barking and wagging not only his tail, wagging his whole body. He was looking again for a way in. All entrances were closed. He came back and longingly stared up at the window from which he judged Jerry's voice was coming. Jerry was still talking, though the one in command kept butting in.

There was a perilous-looking iron stairway leading up to the open window through which Jerry's voice was floating. Standing beneath this curious stairway Ginger could see sky through the open work of the steps. Cautiously Ginger put one paw on the bottom step. It was hard to get a grip on but at least it did not wobble. He put his other front paw on the bottom step and carefully pulled his body up onto it.

The main difficulty was that his paws kept sliding through the iron bars. What peculiar stairs. No carpets at all, as at home. Even so, by being extremely cautious, he might be able to drag himself to the next story, pencil and all.

Carefully, step by step, Ginger crawled up the extraordinary stairs. This was not a decoy. This was a dangerous undertaking. He did not dare look down between those iron bars. He had looked down once and nearly dropped Jerry's pencil out of terror. Up, up, up he crept until there at last he was—at the open window. Gasping in relief Ginger climbed onto the window sill and stood there, drooling, pencil in mouth, tail wagging in delighted expectation.

This room happened to be filled with boys and girls all seated at little desks. They looked sleepy and the place did not seem anywhere near as enticing as up at the reservoir. But anyway, there was Jerry, standing by his seat, his voice coming out clear and high and loud again.

The teacher issued a command. "Read it again, Jerry, more distinctly, and pay more attention to your final g's."

"My dog, Ginger," read Jerry Pye, and he cleared his throat.

Well. When Ginger heard Jerry say his name he let out one short yelp of greeting. Ginger! "Yes, here I am, right here, Jerry," was what his bark meant. Of course he dropped Jerry's pencil but fortunately it dropped on the window sill and not down below. Ginger quickly picked it up again and held it triumphantly in his mouth.

The minute Ginger let out that little yelp of greeting, what a hullabaloo came over the place. Some little girls screamed and some laughed. All the boys cheered. The person in command clapped her hands, but no one paid any attention to her. Jerry dropped the paper he was holding and for a moment he stared at Ginger, too stunned for words or action. Then he rushed to the window and patted his dog to make him feel at home.

Ginger jumped into the room, dropped Jerry's pencil at his feet, and looked up at Jerry. He was inviting him to throw it so he could run after it and bring it back, the way they played the rock game at home, or ball, or stick.

Jerry picked up his pencil. "He even found my pencil I lost on the way to school this morning," he said in greater astonishment than ever. "What a smart dog!"

15

"Your dog?" asked Oliver Peacock, a boy with glasses, in admiration.

"Yeh," said Jerry proudly. "My dog. Trailed me here."

"The dog brought a pencil with him because it's school," shrilled one little girl.

"Whew!" whistled Oliver Peacock.

Ginger wagged his tail and looked as though he were laughing, the way he always did when he understood that pleasant things were being spoken of him. He licked Jerry's hand. So. Here he was! It was not much of a place, but if Jerry could put up with it, so could he. He trotted around the room, his toenails making a pitter-patter. He smelled here and sniffed there. In one corner by a cupboard he kept his nose glued for some time. There was the possibility of mice there.

He detoured around the tall person who was still clapping and giving orders that no one was minding any more than he minded anyone when he was off after a cat.

Suddenly the tall one took a long stick and she brought this down on her desk with such a bang it broke in two and went sailing through the air.

"Quiet!" she bellowed.

The hullabaloo stopped short then. This was a welcome relief to Ginger, who did not see how Jerry stood this sort of a noisy life. His ears hurt him.

"Jared Pye!" the tall one said. "Either take your dog home or make him lie down under your desk until dismissal time which is, thank merciful heavens, only a few minutes away. And, Jared," she added. "See that this disgraceful performance is not repeated, or I shall have to report you to Mr. Pennypepper. Even so, you shall stand in the corner all this afternoon."

"Always the same old punishments," groaned Dick Badger wearily to Jerry.

"Come here, Ginger," said Jerry. As though he could help it, he thought, if the dog he owned happened to be so smart he could trail him all the way to school. You would think the teacher could see that, wouldn't you? he asked himself. "Come here, pup," he urged.

16

Ginger recognized the pleading note in Jerry's voice and he pattered over to him, for he wanted nothing to do with the tall one and her sticks and shrill voice.

"Lie down, Ginger," said Jerry. "Dead dog," he begged.

Being awfully tired, Ginger was happy to lie down. He licked his nose with loud smacking noises, and he washed his torn and bleeding ear, and he washed himself all over. He was right under Jerry's desk, and every now and then Jerry gave him a nice pat with his foot.

There was complete silence now except for Ginger's loud paw licking and the occasional loud nose blowing of the tall one. In this quiet Ginger stopped licking himself. With a contented sigh he slipped into a thoughtful doze. He scarcely did more than twitch his ears when, from another room, he heard some more of the droning, as of bees, that he had heard outside. Now he could hear what the droning was saying, though.

R-A-T rat. C-A-T cat. Apparently the boys and girls were being instructed in the best way to manage these creatures. As for Ginger, he was too tired to listen and, besides, he knew the best way to handle them. As though one had to come to a place like this to learn such things.

17

Elizabeth Rhodes Jackson

THE HOLIDAY CUP

ILLUSTRATED BY *Marguerite Davis*

THE very first day we came to Bungay Island in summer, Jack said, "I wish I had a sailboat. I think I'll make one."

He got some boards and started sawing them and began to make a boat.

One day there was a beautiful breeze and Beany said, "Jack, if only your sailboat were finished, this would be just the day to go sailing."

"Well, we'll go sailing anyway," replied Jack. "I'll show you how."

He got a sheet from Mother for a sail, and we took the rowboat and rowed up to Mosquito Point.

It's quite a long way, probably half a mile from the island, and we were rowing against the wind. Jack and I took turns rowing, and my arms became very tired.

When we got there, Jack said, "Now we can sail home."

We held the sheet up against the wind, he on one side and I on the other, while Beany held it at the bottom. The wind blew us straight back to the island, just as it would a sailboat. We came down zipping, and it was all we could do to hold the sheet.

We did that over and over until the wind went down. Every time we rowed back against the wind, it was such hard work that we said, "Well, this will be the last time!" But it was such fun blowing home with the wind that we'd always say, "Let's try it once more."

When Daddy came home to the island that night, we were still excited about our sail, and we talked about it all through

18

supper. "How would you like to have a sail that would go, not only *with* the wind, but *against* it, too?" asked Daddy.

"A *magic* sail?" asked Beany, hopefully.

Beany is always hoping to have fairy stories come true.

Daddy and Mother smiled, and Mother said, "Well, sails *are* a sort of magic, just as radio is."

"I'll bring a sail home, and you can be the magician, Beany," Daddy said.

The next day Daddy came home with a big package.

"May we open it, Daddy?" we all begged.

It was filled with ropes and metal rings and very strong canvas, folded up. We spread the canvas out on the ground and found that it was three-cornered.

"That's your magic sail," Daddy said.

Then Daddy went all over the island, looking at the young pines. He picked out a straight, slender one and cut it down for a mast to hold the sail up, and a smaller one for a boom to go at the bottom of the sail. Then while Jack and Beany planed the mast smooth, Mother and I sewed the metal rings along one side of the sail, and Daddy nailed blocks in the bow of the rowboat, with a hole in them to hold the mast.

The mast went right through the metal rings and held the sail firm. There was a rope through the rings to raise and lower the sail, and another rope at the outside end of the boom to hold it when the wind was blowing. Such ropes are called sheets. We thought the sail was the sheet, of course, but Daddy said, "No. Sheets are what sailors call the ropes."

We thought the port side of a ship was the side toward the harbor, but Daddy said, "No, the port side is the left side, and the right side is called starboard." He told us that "starboard" once meant "steer board," or the steering side of a boat, and that "larboard" once meant the "lade side," or loading side of a boat. But "larboard" sounded too much like "starboard" when shouted from one part of a boat to the other, so in time the word "port" took its place.

The first sail we took was with the wind, which was blowing from the north. We sailed south from the island, blowing down

19

very fast before the wind, with the sail almost straight out from the boat.

When we got beyond Mosquito Point, Daddy said, "Now I'll show you the magic of sailing against the wind."

He pulled the sail in closer to the boat and turned the boat sideways to the wind, heading toward the east shore. The north wind blew on the sail and kept the boat moving, but it couldn't blow the boat south, because the rudder and the keel kept it headed northeast. With the wind blowing against the sail at a slant, the boat moved slowly toward the east shore.

When we had almost reached the shore, Daddy turned the boat about so that it headed the other way, and the north wind against the sail blew it toward the northwest. Now we were quite a little nearer the island, and so we zigzagged back and forth across the lake, blown by the north wind and always getting nearer the island. And that was the way the magic sail took us home against the wind. We called it "zigzagging," but Daddy called it "tacking."

After that we went out in the boat every day, and Daddy taught us all how to tack. It's fun to sail away from the island, flying before the wind, but it's fun, too, to zigzag back against the wind, getting nearer and nearer home on each tack.

As the summer went on and more people came to the lake, there were more and more sailboats out every week, like white birds flying over the blue.

The largest boat on the lake was the *Argo,* but the one we liked best was the *Seagull.*

We learned how to handle our boat when the wind changed suddenly; and we learned where the shallows were, where the boat might get stuck; and which little coves and points of land had unexpected whirlpools and currents of wind.

When the wind blew from the north, there was always a steady breeze straight off the west shore, where the wind struck the top of the dense woods and shot off, back over the water. The water was so shallow along that shore, though, that we could never run up close to get the west breeze.

All the time between sailings, Jack was working on his own

boat. Sometimes Daddy helped him. When it was finished, it had a rather queer shape, but it would float. Jack painted it white with a beautiful bright green trim.

The first time he put it in the water, Beany exclaimed, "Why, it looks just like a pea pod floating!"

"That's a good name for it," said Jack.

He painted the name *Pea Pod* in gold letters on the side. Daddy fixed the sail, and it sailed very nicely, except that it tipped over if you moved around in it. Mother made a rule that we must always wear our bathing suits in the *Pea Pod*.

One day Jack was sailing the *Pea Pod*, and the Trafton boys were out in their *Argo*. They were big boys, fifteen and sixteen.

They called out to Jack, "Hey, what do you call that craft?"

Jack said, feeling proud of his boat, "I call it the *Pea Pod*."

Then the Trafton boys began to laugh very loudly. "It looks it," they said, and one of them added, "I'll bet you made it yourself."

"Yes, I did," Jack answered.

"It looks it!" they said again. "I suppose you'll enter it for the Holiday Cup." Then they sailed off, laughing.

Jack didn't mind very much, because the *Pea Pod* is his own, and he knows it's a good boat. But he began to think about the Holiday Cup.

Old Mr. Holiday has lived on Bungay Lake for ever and ever so long. Everyone likes him, and the children all call him Grandpa Holiday. He loves to sail. He owns the *Seagull*, and there's a beautiful silver cup that he bought for the lake. Each year there's a sailing race, and Grandpa Holiday presents the cup to the winner. The winner has his name and the year engraved on the cup and keeps the cup for his own until the next race.

Now Jack knew that the *Pea Pod* couldn't possibly win the Holiday Cup, but he began to think it would be fun to be in the race anyhow.

The next day we all sailed down to Grandpa Holiday's place —Jack and Beany and our dog Reginald and I.

Grandpa Holiday was on his wharf, getting ready to take a sail in the *Seagull*. When he saw us, he called out, "Hello, youngsters! Fine day for the race!"

We were very much surprised, because we hadn't heard there was to be any race that day.

"What race, Grandpa Holiday?" asked Jack.

"The human race, son," said Grandpa Holiday, and he laughed all over his face. Jack and I laughed too, because we saw that it was a good joke, and Beany, who didn't see the joke, laughed just to be polite.

"I thought at first you meant the cup race," said Jack. "We came down to ask if we can be in the cup race this year."

Grandpa Holiday said, "Well, I don't see why not. The cup

race is open to all the residents on the lake, but only two of you can go, one as captain and one as crew."

"Jack will be captain," I said, "and Beany or I will be crew."

"I'd rather have you, Dee," said Jack. "You can handle it better than Beany."

Beany looked very sad at that, but he knew that Jack was right, and so he didn't say anything. He put his arm over Reginald's neck and hugged him.

"Is that the boat you're going to enter?" asked Grandpa Holiday, looking at the *Pea Pod* with the sail that Father had given us.

We said it was. Grandpa Holiday cleared his throat. "Well, now," he said, "that's a very nice boat to learn in, but it isn't by any means the fastest boat on the lake."

"Oh, no," said Jack. "The *Argo's* the fastest boat on the lake. It belongs to the Trafton boys."

"The *Argo* is built the best for speed," Grandpa Holiday admitted, "but those two young whippersnappers that own her haven't the brains to sail her. The *Seagull* here isn't as fast a boat, but properly handled she could beat the *Argo*, with them in it, any day."

"I believe she could," said Jack.

"I'll tell you what I'll do," said Grandpa Holiday. "I've watched you youngsters and your little craft this summer, and you've got the right feeling for a boat. I'm going to let you sail the *Seagull* in the cup race."

We thought he was joking again, but he wasn't. He really meant it.

"Oh!" said Jack, and "Oh!" said Beany and I.

"Of course, you ought to get used to her," he said. "You tie your boat up here, and we'll take the *Seagull* out, and I'll give you some pointers."

We were so excited we nearly tipped our boat over. To think of sailing the *Seagull*, the finest boat on the lake! The *Argo* might be faster, but the *Seagull* was more beautiful.

We had a wonderful sail in her, and Grandpa Holiday let us take her out for practice every day after that. Sometimes

23

just we three went alone, and sometimes he went, too, to show us the best ways of handling her.

"Keep clear of the *Argo* in the race," he said. "Don't let her get to windward of you, or she'll take your wind from you and get ahead of you. That's a trick the Trafton boys tried last year, and they'd have won by it, too, but they ran into a calm just off the island."

The day before the race was cloudy. We were very anxious about the weather; but Grandpa Holiday looked all around the sky, and then he looked at the pennant on the mast and said, "Don't worry, youngsters. If this wind holds, it'll blow the clouds away. Looks to me as if 'twould be a good day tomorrow."

Sure enough, when we woke, the sky was blue. A light steady breeze was blowing over the lake, and little waves were swishing along the shore of the island.

Jack and I sailed down to Grandpa Holiday's place to board the *Seagull.*

"It's a fine day for the race, Grandpa Holiday," said Jack. "And I mean the *cup* race."

"Yes," said Grandpa Holiday, standing on his wharf with a package in his hands. "It's tricky, though. This wind may change any minute."

"Is that the cup, Grandpa Holiday?" I asked.

"Yes," he said. "Haven't you seen it?" He unwrapped it and showed it to us, all silver-shiny in the sunlight.

"My! I'd like to win that," said Jack.

"I hope you will win, son," said Grandpa Holiday. "I'd like to see your name on there. Remember, next thing to being a good winner is being a good loser. If you don't win, don't forget to shake hands with the winner and congratulate him."

"No, sir," said Jack. "I won't forget."

"There's a little prize here for the winning crew, too," said Grandpa Holiday. "It's a silver medal."

He showed it to us—in a white box lined with satin. It had a little sailboat on one side, and on the other, a place to engrave the winner's name.

"I'm the crew," I said.

The race was to start off our island, and so Grandpa Holiday sailed there in our little boat, while we proudly sailed the *Seagull* down to the starting line.

From all over the lake people were coming in rowboats and motorboats and canoes, and anchoring along the shore of our island to watch the race. The eight sailboats that were to be in the race were bobbing and circling near the start.

The Trafton boys were sailing the *Argo,* of course, and one of them called out to Jack, "Hey, you! What are you doing in the *Seagull?* Where's that fast *Pea Pod* of yours?"

The other one said in a surprised voice, "There's the *Pea Pod* now. Look at her! She's going into the race."

We looked, too. There she was, the little *Pea Pod*, with her gay white paint and her sail blowing out in the wind, and there was Beany in his striped bathing suit at the helm, with Reginald in the bottom of the boat.

"Oh, Beany," I called out, "are you in the race?"

"Yes," he shouted back. "Grandpa Holiday just now said I could be, and Reginald's my crew!"

By this time everybody was looking at the *Pea Pod,* as she drifted up toward the starting line. A wave of laughter rolled along the shore. The *Pea Pod* was so little and had such a comical shape, and Beany was so little, too. And of course everybody thought Reginald was a very unusual crew.

Jack said under his breath, "People needn't laugh. The *Pea Pod's* good."

Beany didn't mind. He laughed, too, and Reginald started barking at the people on shore, and someone shouted out, "Good luck to you, Beany! Hope you win."

That was a kind thing to say, because everyone knew he couldn't win against the bigger boats.

Then Grandpa Holiday stood on the shore and explained the rules of the race through a megaphone.

When Reginald heard the megaphone boom out, he began to bark, and Beany had to hold his muzzle to keep him quiet. The course, Grandpa Holiday said, was to be from our island, half-a-mile south down the lake to a buoy opposite Mosquito Point, around the buoy, and back to the island. The start and the finish were to be in line with our wharf and the big pine on the west shore.

There would be three whistles, half a minute apart. The first two meant to get ready, the third to go. Anyone who sailed across the starting line before the third whistle would be counted out of the race. There would be one long whistle as each boat finished.

Then in a moment we heard the first whistle, and we got ready. At the second whistle, we edged up to the starting line, but not too close, for fear of blowing across too soon. Then at the third whistle, everyone was off. Everyone, that is, except Beany.

The crowd and the megaphone and the whistles had got Reginald so excited that he reared up on the side of the boat to bark. You can't do that in the *Pea Pod*. You have to sit still. The boat tipped, of course, and Reginald lost his balance and went overboard. Beany made a grab at him as he went, and he overbalanced, and the *Pea Pod* capsized.

Beany did manage, as he went over, to seize the sail and hold it out of the water till help came. He was very near shore, and someone rowed out and pulled the boat in, Beany holding the sail dry all the time. Reginald swam to shore and stood there barking at Beany. He thought Beany had pushed him overboard.

Beany bailed out the boat and got in again and tried to get Reginald in. Reginald was very unwilling, but finally Beany persuaded him. Of course, by that time the rest of the race had left Beany far behind, but he started out just the same.

Jack and I were too busy sailing our own boat to know just what had happened to Beany, but we saw that he was still away back at the starting point when we were almost down to the buoy.

I had always thought the boats in a race stayed side by side and you could see which was winning, but the wind was against us, and the boats all had to tack back and forth. It was very confusing to see, and hard to tell which boat was ahead. Our *Seagull* and the *Argo* seemed to be a little ahead of the others. We thought we were ahead of the *Argo*, but the two boats were on opposite tacks, and so we couldn't tell until we reached the buoy.

"If we round the buoy first," said Jack, "I think we can win; but if the *Argo* gets there first, she'll win. Going back, we'll all have the wind at our backs and blow straight home, and the *Argo* is built for speed, provided she goes with the wind."

When we got to the last tack, it was the most exciting thing I've ever seen. There was the *Argo*, heading for the buoy from one shore of the lake, and there were we in the *Seagull*, heading from the other shore. You couldn't tell which was nearer.

I looked around, and there was no other boat near enough to count. They were all back of us, some on one tack and some on the other.

The sail of the little *Pea Pod* was a white spot in the distant rear, and back of it we could see the crowd of people on the island and along the shore. Some of them were watching through spyglasses that glittered when they caught the sunlight.

As we drew nearer and nearer to the buoy, we were more and more sure that we'd get there ahead of the *Argo*. And we did! We made it!

We rounded the buoy and let out our sail, and the south wind

27

that had been in our faces was at our backs now, a nice friendly wind blowing the *Seagull* straight toward the island. We had a good start before the *Argo* rounded the buoy and came after us.

Then one of those queer things happened that are always to be expected on our lake. The wind shifted suddenly. One minute it was from the south, blowing us straight ahead. The next minute Jack had to bring the boat about suddenly to catch a north wind. There we were, with the wind in our faces now, instead of at our backs, and the ripples of the lake all blowing toward us again. Instead of flying easily down to the island, we would have to beat our way back.

"We'll have to tack again!" I shouted.

"So will the *Argo*," Jack shouted.

The other boats that were still on the first lap had the wind with them now, and we met them all, flying like autumn leaves blown across a lawn. Of course, as soon as they rounded the buoy, they all slowed down, because the wind was against them.

Last of all, the little *Pea Pod* raced by us on its way to the buoy. Beany, in his striped bathing suit, had the helm in one hand and the rope in the other and was holding Reginald tight between his knees.

He shouted out, "Good for the *Seagull!*" as he blew by.

Jack called back, "The *Pea Pod* isn't so bad, either!"

We had the start of the *Argo* on the home stretch, and at each tack we hoped we were gaining on her. The wind was blowing more and more gently. Both boats moved rather slowly. I could see that it was going to be a long race.

I looked back at the other boats. Swiftly, one by one, they reached the buoy and began a slow zigzag course on the return trip. I watched the little *Pea Pod* sail down to the buoy, round it safely without spilling, and then head for the west shore on the first tack back to the island.

As we drew near the finish line, we could see plainly that we had gained on the *Argo*.

"Oh, Jack, the *Seagull's* going to win," I called out. "We've surely won now."

But Jack said, "Sit still, Dee, or you'll go overboard. Grandpa Holiday says a sailing race is never won till it's finished."

In a moment I saw what Grandpa Holiday meant. He meant that no matter how good a sailor you are, you can't control the wind. There we were, well ahead of the *Argo* and almost home, when suddenly our wind died down and left us hanging in a calm! We stood absolutely still!

The *Argo*, across the lake, was still moving steadily on her tack in a light breeze that fluttered her pennant.

The wind caught up with us again and we started on, but by that time the *Argo* had gained on us. We were afraid—we were almost sure—they were going to win. The Trafton boys were quite sure. As we passed near them, crossing the lake on opposite tacks, one of them called out, "I guess it's our race, all right! You'd better stick to your *Pea Pod* after this!"

Jack didn't even hear them. He was looking across at the west shore. He said to me, very low, "For goodness' sake, Dee, look at Beany!"

29

I looked. "Oh, oh!" I whispered to myself.

Beany wasn't tacking, like the others. He was sailing the *Pea Pod* close to the west shore—closer than the bigger boats could get in that shallow water—so close that he was blown by the steady breeze that always blows off that shore when the north wind strikes the tall woods!

While the rest of us had been tacking slowly back against the wind, he had been running from Mosquito Point straight along the shore, getting ahead of all the other boats by hugging the shore. At last he was passing even the *Seagull* and the *Argo*, and he had almost reached the big pine that marked the finish of the race!

"Oh, oh!" I said again, and Jack just stared.

The Trafton boys didn't notice Beany. They were still shouting at us and all puffed up because they thought they were winning.

Suddenly came the shrill sound of the judges' whistle.

"First boat across the line!" called Jack.

There was the little *Pea Pod*, just passing the big pine on the west shore.

"Beany, Beany, Beany!" I screeched.

Of course he couldn't hear me. In his striped suit, he was hanging on to Reginald, who started barking again.

It was nearly two minutes later that the whistle sounded for the *Argo*, and ten seconds after that, we crossed the line in the *Seagull*.

Everyone was cheering for Beany, and Reginald was barking his head off when we landed at the island.

Grandpa Holiday patted Jack hard on the back. "Fine sailing!" he said. "Couldn't have done better myself. But oh boy! Did the little *Pea Pod* have it all over the *Argo!*"

Everybody crowded around Beany, and Jack and I could hardly get through to shake hands with him and congratulate him, as good losers should.

The Trafton boys were not very good losers. They didn't shake hands with Beany. They sailed off home across the lake without even landing on the island. All the other racers shook

hands with Beany and said he sailed a fine race, and some of them shook hands with Reginald, too.

Then Grandpa Holiday made a speech and presented the cup to Beany. He presented the crew medal to Reginald, only he handed it to me to keep for Reginald.

Everyone shouted, "Speech! Speech!" and Grandpa Holiday stepped back and left Beany standing there facing the crowd. Beany held the silver cup hugged up against his bathing suit.

"I don't know what to say in a speech," he said, "only, Jack built the *Pea Pod* himself, and it's a good boat. And I thank you for the cup, Grandpa Holiday. And wasn't it a fine day for the race!"

When he heard that, Grandpa Holiday put his head back and laughed, and everybody clapped.

Beany has the cup on his bookshelves. His name is engraved on it, and he can keep it a whole year. Reginald wears his medal on his collar along with his license tag, and Grandpa Holiday says Reginald can keep it as long as he lives.

Helen Diehl Olds

THE BASKETBALL MYSTERY

ILLUSTRATED BY *Sylvia Haggander*

JEAN ducked into the old trunk and clawed at the things in much the same fashion that Mugs, the Boston terrier, dug in the yard. Old sweaters, old hats, bundles, bedclothes were scattered over the attic floor. Then she straightened up, and called, "Mother! Are you *sure* those knee-guards are up here?"

As Mother was two flights down in the kitchen, she did not hear.

"Don't get so excited. Let me look." Winnie touched Jean's arm. "Your mother said they were in this trunk, so they must be. Why, here they are, and good as new."

The dimness hid Jean's shamed look. She dumped the other things back into the trunk and shut the lid, which closed with a puff of dust. "I wish I were calm like you, Winnie. Aren't you thrilled about playing in the big game?"

"Of course I am," Winnie answered, as they went down the stairs. "But you mustn't get so hurried. Take your time!"

Take your time! That was what Mother and Daddy sang at her every minute. But how could she? There were so many things to hurry her. Just this morning, on the day of the big game, she had decided that she simply must have those knee-guards to complete her outfit.

The big game of the year always came on St. Patrick's Day, and this year she and Winnie were to play. They were both forwards and had played together so much that they could signal back and forth to each other without uttering a sound.

32

The girls went down the second flight of stairs and turned into the kitchen. Jean sat down and tried on the knee-guards. Seven-year-old Bets begged to try them on, too. Mugs sniffed at the leather things.

But it was almost schooltime. Jean yanked on her things and grabbed her books, and the two girls started off. Bets and Mugs trailed along behind.

"Let's ask Miss Stevens if we can't have a little extra practice at noon," suggested Jean.

"All right." Winnie nodded.

"Mugs and I'll come and watch you." Bets was looking down cross-eyed at the shamrock she wore pinned to her coat.

It was nice to have her small sister so admiring and interested, but Jean got rather tired of it. Mugs always went to school with Bets every day and waited in the yard until noon when the 2B was dismissed.

Jean and Winnie and several other Seventh-Grade girls were practicing free throws when the door of the gym opened a crack, and there was Bets, with Mugs' brown head thrust between her short legs.

Miss Stevens, the gym teacher, who thought Bets "awfully cute," told her to come in and watch from the side lines.

They couldn't practice long as it was lunchtime. "Just one more," begged Jean.

Miss Stevens was picking up her heavy white sweater. "Well, all right. One more try apiece, and then, Jean, will you put the ball away?"

Jean nodded, as she threw the ball to Mary Toms to take her turn. Mary wasn't a regular player, only a "sub." She had wanted to be on the team, too, but Miss Stevens had decided to take Jean, who was taller, instead. Jean had practiced baskets fifteen minutes every day for weeks.

Jean often felt that Mary was hurt about it all. Her face now was as cross as a thunderstorm. Mary was not very popular with the other girls.

She caught the ball now, and her face brightened a little.

"Of course, I don't wish anybody any bad luck this afternoon,"

she said. "But if anything happens—if a player gets knocked out, or doesn't play well enough—I'll get into the game. Miss Stevens promised."

Jean said nothing. She was as tall as any of the team, but she was not a strong player. "Too flighty," Miss Stevens said. "Always in too much of a hurry to play your best." Well, she would be calm this afternoon—she must, she told herself.

"You go on—I'll catch up," she told Winnie and Bets, while she started over towards the locker-room to put the ball away. The ball was just a new one, and they were all so proud of it. The other two went on out of the school building, and Mugs followed Jean's skips and jumps.

"I guess you know this ball is made out of the same, nice, smelly leather as those knee-guards." Jean laughed at him.

She dashed over the cement floor of the locker-room, opened Miss Stevens' locker with one hand, tossed the ball in with the other, and shut it with her foot as she turned around. In almost no time, she was panting alongside Winnie and Bets on the sidewalk.

"You surely are fast," said Winnie admiringly. "Miss Stevens says you're the fastest player on the team."

"But you're the *surest*," returned Jean.

"I guess Mugs just decided to go home by himself a different way," piped up Bets. "He's nowhere about."

At lunchtime, Bets begged, "Mother, can't I go to the game?"

"I wish you wouldn't bring her, Mother. I'm afraid I'll get stage fright with so many of the family watching."

"She wouldn't understand the game, anyway," pointed out brother Bill.

"I would, too!" Bets protested. "You just throw the ball through the basket."

"You might not like it anyway, dear," Mother answered soothingly. "You stay with Grandma, and she'll let you help her make doughnuts."

Bets looked as though doughnuts were nothing to be compared to seeing big sister play basketball. Finally, she promised to go to Grandma's, if Jean would tell her every single thing about the game that evening.

The game was to begin at three o'clock. The mothers of most of the girls on the team attended, and they sat on folding chairs around the side of the room. The school pupils came in then— the girls with bright scarfs, the boys in shapeless sweaters. The basketball team came in, all the members dressed alike in gay scarlet gym suits and flaring green neckerchiefs, in honor of the day. Several had the ridiculous knee-guards, like Jean's.

Miss Stevens hurried up, a worried frown between her eyes. "Jean, didn't you put the basketball away this noon?"

"Why, of course I did!"

"It's gone!" said Miss Stevens.

Gone! The new basketball that the girls themselves had bought with the bazaar money. Gone. Did that mean—deliberately taken? And who could have done it? Perhaps it was Chick Waite, that big boy in their grade, who was always up to something. But no, Chick would have no reason.

35

Jean glanced at the side lines. There was Mary Toms, sulky as ever.

"There's no time to try to solve this mystery," said Miss Stevens.

At the word mystery, Jean and Winnie edged toward each other. They had been playing detectives for months now, and they were always looking for mysteries. It was funny that Miss Stevens should use that very word. Well, it was a mystery!

"We must decide what to do," she went on. "I've asked the janitor and we've searched everywhere, and the ball has not been found. And it's time for the game to start."

"But the Valley Team—"

"No, they didn't bring a ball," Miss Stevens answered Jean's half-question. "It was agreed that the home team should furnish the ball. And there isn't another in the whole village. We'll have to use our old one."

The old one! That awful ball whose seams had burst during a game last year. The tear had been mended, but the ball had acquired a lopsided bounce if it landed on the patched place. The girls were almost ready to cry at the thought of playing the big game with the old ball.

"It's an equal handicap for both sides," Miss Stevens decided, as she brought out the old ball. "There's no help for it. Here, take a bit of practice."

Then the opposing team came in. What big girls they were!

Soon, the shriek of the whistle pierced the room, and the game began. There was wild scrambling and falling, twisting, and hurrying about the floor. And that crazy ball was always bouncing just the way you didn't expect it to. Jean glanced at the side lines again. Could Mary have taken the ball in hopes that one of the players would do so badly with the old ball that *she* would get into the game herself? It seemed a rather far-fetched notion, but Jean was so wrought up about the game, now, she could not think clearly.

River Dale had a free throw. A foul had been made. Miss Stevens ran across the room, her whistle in her mouth. She took the ball from the two girls who were struggling over it, and

36

motioned to Nora, the best forward on the River Dale team.

"River Dale! River Dale!" shouted the lines, and Lank Henderson led the school in a bit of song:

> "Let it go,
> Let it go.
> Basket made
> With every throw!"

Nora pressed the heels of her sneakers against the mark, took aim, and let the ball go. It went to the basket, scooped around it tantalizingly, tipped over the edge and dropped in a player's hands. The game was on again, white middies flashing.

One quarter was over—the Valley girls were ahead. It almost seemed as if the Valley girls did not mind the bewitched ball. At least, they managed to make baskets with it, which was more than River Dale team could do. The players draped their sweaters around their necks and sat with the subs, panting and chatting, the perspiration standing out on their cheeks like tears.

Basket after basket was made by the other side. Jean choked back tears of disappointment. She had never worked so hard. She darted here and there, losing her guard, eyes always on the ball. She would manage to catch the ball, hurting her fingers, only to lose it again as her opponent batted at it. Bang! It knocked her in the face that time, and the whole hall was blotted out of sight for a moment. Now the ball was up at the other end, and she could take a few easy breaths and wonder about the mystery.

It wasn't fair! All of them were trying so hard, and they couldn't do a thing. She could see Mother's blurred face across the room. Oh, why had she ever told anyone she was going to play in the St. Patrick's Day game? She wasn't doing a thing— and all on account of that old ball. The ball looked all right, and they'd never believe how hard playing with it really was.

"Take your time," cautioned Miss Stevens when Jean had a free throw, but Jean's habit of hurrying was too strong. The ball leaped from her hands and missed the basket.

It was that way every time she got a chance. But Winnie, aiming cautiously, made a basket, even with the lopsided ball, and tied the score just at the end of the last quarter.

Miss Stevens was standing between the two center players, who, with right hands upraised, awaited the toot of her whistle and the toss of the ball, when—

"Stamp! Stamp!" sounded at the big middle doors and there seemed to be a vigorous tugging on the other side. The doors opened and Bets, followed by Mugs on pattering paws, came in. Oh, how could she come in like that, her sturdy shoes squeaking on the slick floor, right in the midst of the game? Miss Stevens turned her head and waited, the ball ready.

"Jeannie!" came the piping voice, and Jean reddened.

"Jean," she raised her voice. "Jean, look! I found the basketball in Gran'ma's backyard and I brought it to you!"

Jean and the others looked. Bets hugged to her fat stomach the school ball, the new, smelly, leathery one that had disappeared and whose disappearance had made the big game harder than ever. The two teams crowded around Bets.

"Mugs had it," she explained, simply. "But don't you always keep it locked up tight?"

Miss Stevens looked at Jean.

38

She flung the ball at the basket—so that the guard could not interfere.

"Oh, Miss Stevens," she wailed, "I put it in the locker, but I was in such a hurry—I always am—I—maybe I didn't shut it. And Mugs was right with me, I remember."

"Well, it doesn't seem any the worse for wear." Miss Stevens was examining the lacings of the ball. "But, Jean, we would have won the game, I believe, if we hadn't had this trouble. You see, it never pays to hurry. You always lose out when you do."

Hot tears rushed to Jean's eyes and she had to blink fast. She had lost the game! Oh, why was she such a hurrying person? Even in basketball, where speed counted so much, it didn't pay to hurry an aim. Well, she was cured. She'd never do things fast again. It was too dangerous. Why, just think what awful things she had been thinking about Mary Toms.

Miss Stevens blew the whistle. The girls took their places, and the game went on with the new ball. How silently and swiftly the girls jumped about! There was a hard struggle lasting over ten minutes, and neither side had scored. The Valley girls had the ball now. Would they make a throw? Just then Nora's strong arm hurled the ball in Jean's direction. She jumped for it, caught it, lost it, caught it again, twirled herself around and was about to fling it recklessly towards the basket when she saw Winnie's brown eyes signalling, *"Take your time!"*

Well, she *would,* she'd take time to take a good aim, even though she risked losing the ball. Steady, steady, now her guard was upon her, anticipating and blocking her moves, but she wouldn't throw until— There, that was just the right kind of an aim. She flung the ball at the basket, a sure aim and yet so planned that the guard could not interfere. The whistle, signifying the end of the game, blew at the exact minute that the brown ball dropped through the hoop. She had made a basket! Above the shrieks and cheers, Jean could hear Bets squealing, "Jean throwed it through!"

Nora and Winnie were beside Jean, and the team put their heads together, arms about each other's shoulders, to give a cheer for the losing side. "Valley Team! Valley Team!"

"You won the game." Winnie was whispering in her ear.

39

Ruth Gipson Plowhead

JOSIE'S HOME RUN

ILLUSTRATED BY *Janet Smalley*

TEN-YEAR-OLD Josie and Joe Dawn were twins. And from their sturdy little bodies up to their smiling red mouths, freckled noses, and wavy red hair, they were as alike as two peas in a pod.

Josie had one deep trouble—she was not a boy.

"Why, oh, why, Mother, couldn't I have been a boy like Joe?" she would ask. "I can run faster than he can and climb higher, and I know I'd be a better ball player if I had a chance."

Josie was never so happy as when tagging after Joe, dressed as nearly like him as possible in overalls, sport shirt, and tight cap.

One day when she came home with her brother, she was almost in tears.

"Mother," she cried, "Joe won't let me play with the ball team when they are practicing."

"Aw, Mother," said Joe, who was very fond of his sister, "I like to play with Josie, and the boys like her. But when there's a whole crowd of boys and only one girl, it makes a fellow feel funny if the girl's his sister."

"Joe is right, Josie," said her mother. "You must come home if the whole team is playing, but when there are only two or three of Joe's friends, you may play with them if they want you."

"I'll have a ball team of my own," said Josie.

Alas, for Josie! Most of her friends preferred girls' games. However, she managed to find many chances to play ball. She found two or three girls who would play occasionally if she

40

gave them candy or peanuts. She even persuaded her parents to pitch for her. And many an evening she and Joe's friends spent playing in the vacant lot across the street. She became a fair pitcher and a good batter.

"Watch out for Josie when she bats," the boys said. "If she hits the ball, you may have to run all the way to China to find it."

Josie did not mind their joking. And when the different school teams began playing each other in the spring, she was more excited than Joe.

Finally the Lowell fifth-grade team, of which Joe was a member, had only to beat the Whittier fifth-graders to become champions. Besides, the winning team was to go to Allentown, six miles away, and play a game there.

Again and again Josie clenched her hands over the thought that she couldn't play on the team. No one wanted to play as much as she did.

If she could only play, how she would work! How she would run! How she would bat that ball, so that it would fly *beyond* China if necessary! Every evening she worked with Joe, and occasionally he grew cross when she insisted that he practice.

"You might let me alone a minute," he growled one night. "A fellow has to do something in this world besides play ball."

"I won't let you alone until the game is over," Josie said firmly. "If I can't play, you'll have to play well enough to make up for it."

And in spite of Joe's protests Josie kept her word. She made him practice.

The Friday before the great game came at last. The game was set for nine-thirty on the following morning. The team had their last practice after school, and Joe didn't come in until dinnertime. Then he sat hunched up in a big chair close to the fireplace.

"I don't want any dinner," he said, when his mother called him to the table. "I'm not hungry."

"Why, what's the matter?" asked Josie in alarm.

"Nothing. I'm just cold and tired," replied Joe crossly. "Can't

41

a fellow rest a minute without everyone thinking something's the matter?"

Although Joe kept insisting that he was all right, his mother noticed that he was shivering. He went to bed very early.

By morning Joe admitted that he was too sick to play ball that day. "Oh, Mother," he said, "the team needs me. What shall I do?"

Josie was almost crying. "I'm sorry, Joe," she said. "What can I do for you? Shall I go and watch the game, or shall I stay with you?"

"Go and cheer for the boys just as loud as you can," answered Joe. "You know they always say that your cheering helps as much as my playing. And remember all the plays, so that you can tell me about them."

"Yes, Josie, you had better go," agreed Mother. "But you must hurry to the barber's before the game. Remember, you cannot go to Judy Ann's party this afternoon unless you have your hair trimmed. Tony knows the way I like it cut."

"All right, Mother," answered Josie. "And I'll go straight to the game from the shop. Oh, I wish you could play, Joe. But I'll remember everything and tell you all about it."

Joe groaned. "Go by and tell the fellows, will you?" he said.

A block from the house Josie met Roy Vane.

"Say, Josie," he roared, "have you heard about our bad luck? Bill hurt his knee last night. He and Joe are our stars, and we need them both to win. Good thing we still have Joe, but even with him we may not win, now that Bill is hurt."

Josie opened her mouth to tell about Joe. Then something stopped her. She had an idea. "You needn't go by for Joe," she said. "He can't come now. I'll be at the field to cheer for you at nine-thirty sharp." Then Josie ran like the wind, fearing she would be questioned about Joe.

All the way to the barber-shop Josie debated a problem in her mind. But once in the chair, her mind was made up.

"Tony," she said, "cut my hair like Joe's. For once I'm going to have it cut the way *I* like it."

"I like it very short myself, Miss Josie, but your mother al-

42

ways seems to want your curls to show," said Tony doubtfully.

"Mother will like it short this time, I'm sure," said Josie. And she meant it. Her mother had never failed her and Joe when it came to a question of helping one another.

"If Mother knew I was doing this for Joe and the school, she wouldn't care," Josie argued to herself.

When Tony had finished, she looked in the glass with great satisfaction. "Oh, I look more than ever like Joe," she thought.

"I look so much like him that no one will know me." Then she jumped out of the chair and sped home like lightning.

It was easy for Josie to creep unseen into the basement, where the twins' bicycles, balls, bats, and play clothes were kept. It was also easy to slip into her brother's baseball suit.

When she had the red cap pulled down over her eyes, no one would have dreamed that it was not Joe himself who stepped gaily onto the ball field just before the game was called. Least of all did the team suspect.

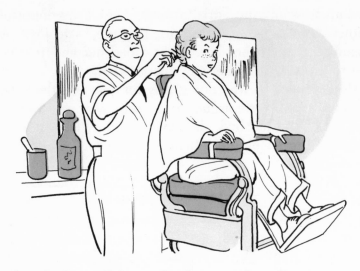

They had a yell for each player. When they saw Josie, they stamped their feet and chanted:

"Here's Joe—Joe—Joe!
Now we'll go—go—go!"

Thrills ran up and down Josie's spine. "I have to make it go!" she thought. "If I don't, and the boys find out who it is, they'll tease me forever."

Finally the game started. But poor Josie was so excited that when her turn came to bat, she quickly fanned.

"What's got into you, Joe? Have you forgotten how to bat?" called the boys.

After that Josie settled down and played better. She got two hits, but it was not until the end of the last inning that her real chance came. The game had been evenly balanced—the score went up and down like a seesaw. First Lowell was ahead, then Whittier, next Lowell, and then Whittier again—on through the whole game.

The score now stood 15 to 14 in favor of the Whittier team. It was the last inning, two of the Lowell batters were out, there were three boys on base, and Josie was at bat. Her heart was thumping furiously, and her hands shook as she picked up the bat. Never before had she felt so strongly the need to win. Not for her own sake, but for the honor of the team and for Joe.

"They think that Joe has not played his best, and I mustn't go back on him," she said to herself. "I must not lose this game!"

The little freckles stood out all over her face, like crowded blossoms on a pansy bed, as she gripped the bat. The ball was coming.

Josie swung furiously and missed. The umpire called, "Strike one."

Again the ball came, and again and again and again. Ball one. Ball two. Strike two. Ball three. Only one more chance!

Then Josie's courage came. She swung the bat, there was a loud crack, and away the ball soared! As the baseball flew, Josie flew, too. Her feet skimmed along, barely touching the ground.

First base!

From the corner of her eye Josie saw a boy run home. The score was even, 15 to 15. On she sped. The ball had landed in a patch of weeds, and the Whittier fielders were frantically hunting it.

Second base!

The second runner had gone home—now the game was won.

Third base! She reached it just as the third runner touched the home plate. Then Josie saw the fielder pick up the ball and throw it. "Go it, Joe!" cried the spectators. "Beat the ball! Run!"

Josie flew—the ball flew, too, straight into the hands of the Whittier catcher. He fumbled, and down it rolled. Josie made a slide, just as she had seen the boys do many times. She reached out her hands, touched base, and lay there panting. The score was 18 to 15 in favor of Lowell.

> "Hurrah for Joe!   Hurrah for Joe!
> He made things go!   He made things go!"

yelled the boys in a frenzy of joy.

A tall man who was passing had paused to see what was going on. He was greeted by a dozen eager voices.

45

"Oh, Mr. Dawn," cried the excited captain, "you ought to have seen Joe! He won the game for us. Just made a home run!"

"Joe made a home run?" cried the amazed man. "What do you mean? Joe's at home in bed."

Hurriedly Mr. Dawn pushed his way through the crowd, until his eye lighted on his red-faced and panting little daughter just getting up from where she had been lying. He could always tell her from her brother by her sheepish little grin and the funny dimple that appeared in one cheek when she was embarrassed.

"Josie," he gasped, "what does this mean?"

Josie had recovered enough breath to pant, "I wanted the team to win. I can play as well as Joe, even if he is one of their best players. When he couldn't come, I thought I would take his place and not let anybody know. I was going to tell Joe, of course."

"Oh, Josie, Josie," said her father, "what will you do next? Do you think your brother would be willing to take credit for something you did?"

But Josie looked up at him with a comical, half-guilty grin, and he could not help laughing. The team yelled and cheered. Even the Whittier boys joined in the chorus.

"Josie! Josie! Josie!
Ring around a rosy!"

And that was the way the Lowell fifth-graders became champions. When the game at Allentown was played, Josie cheered so loudly for Joe's team that she helped win another Lowell victory.

JENNIFER lived in the early nineteen hundreds. Here is one of the amusing episodes in a book about her.

Eunice Young Smith

THE PRIZE

ILLUSTRATED BY THE AUTHOR

THE sound of sleigh bells tinkled in the clear, cold night air. The moon was high and unclouded. The Hill family was on its way to the schoolhouse.

From away down the Butternut Road came a steady tinkle, tinkle. Straight ahead on the Portage Road they could hear a chorus of bells, "Jingle, jangle, jingle."

"Jingle, jangle, jingle," chimed their own loud bells as Dobbin cantered over the snowy road. "Jingle, jangle, jingle," sang the bells behind them.

"That's the Barneses up ahead," Kevin said. "I know their big sled. And I can see Miss Rhul."

"Is Benjy there? Can you see him, Kevin?" Holly asked from her place in the back seat between Mother and Jennifer.

"I think Sam and Molly Bingham are right behind us," Mother said.

"Everybody will be here tonight," Jennifer told them for the hundredth time. "Mamie says this is the biggest doings of

48

the whole year. Even people who don't have kids come to hear the program and find out who wins the prize."

"I know my piece," Holly confided softly.

"I know mine too," Jennifer said. "Only I hope I don't forget when the time comes to say it."

She felt tight with excitement. She sat up straight when Father drove into the schoolyard. Not one sight or sound of tonight must she miss.

All week long at school the children had rehearsed their acts for tonight's program. Over and over at home, parents had listened to lines and gestures and songs as each child strove to become letter-perfect in his part. Now the time for practice was over. Tonight they would perform.

The schoolyard already was full of horses and sleighs and closed-in buggies. Several rigs lined the road. The Binghams drove in right after the Hills. Sam turned his horses around and pulled them up facing Dobbin, across the yard. He lifted the big weights out of his sleigh and anchored his geldings. He threw blankets over them. Father did the same for Dobbin.

People were alighting from rigs and greeting one another. Voices were gay and excited. Everyone appeared to be arriving at once. Bells jingled; sharp yells directed nervous horses; children squealed; men called. Nobody wanted to be late.

"That's Mr. Bins driving in now." Mrs. Barnes pointed him out to Mother and Emma as they all walked together toward the schoolhouse. Jennifer stared.

"He's the school superintendent, you know," Miss Rhul informed them. Then she hurried on ahead, surrounded by chattering children.

Mother and Emma and Mrs. Barnes waited for Molly Bingham. Sam and Father hailed each other.

Father poked Sam. "Who have you performing tonight?"

"Whole danged-blasted caboodle." Sam snorted. "Wouldn't miss this for a hundred dollars."

"Big crowd tonight," Hiram Barnes observed. He waved a greeting to the Lempkes and the Crumpets. Little Mabel broke loose from her mother's hand and skipped up to the school

49

porch. Her tight corkscrew curls bobbed. Her skirts stuck out stiffly under her coat. All the children left their parents as soon as they arrived and ran on ahead into the school.

Never were children so scrubbed and brushed and starched and curled. Behind the screens that made an offstage room they milled and fumed and worried. They kept Miss Rhul in a dither.

"Benjy, stop shoving. You'll have Elijah's clothes all mussed up. And don't look so cross. You're supposed to be a cheerful duck. There, Mabel, your sash is tied. No, your curls aren't out in back. Zealous, please don't do that in here. You'll knock the screens down. All you big boys and girls go out and sit down now. Double up in those seats in front. But stay in order so when you are called there won't be any scramble. Sadie, I've heard that part five times. I'm sure you know it. And if you forget I'll prompt you. Don't worry. Holly, please stop counting Annie's petticoats. You'll have her costume all awry. And if you'll stop patting Benjy's head it will look neater. All you fifth graders line up back there against the wall. Kevin, don't forget the gestures that go with a poor shepherd. You get so lordly in that last stanza. Shush now. Everyone calm down."

Jennifer wished mightily that she could calm down. Her stomach felt as though she had just eaten too many green apples.

Miss Rhul peeped nervously through the crack in the screen. "The place is jam-packed," she said. "I think they must all be here now. It's seven-thirty. Mr. Amos is in his seat. So is Mr. Bins, and Mr. Lloyd. Mrs. Tuttle is opening the organ."

Jennifer's hands were tightly clenched. She watched Miss Rhul ease out from behind the screens and flutter across the room. She whispered something in Mrs. Tuttle's ear. Mrs. Tuttle nodded. Miss Rhul fluttered back.

Jennifer peered around the edge of one screen. The schoolroom looked as though it would overflow. Every seat was filled. Gam had made benches of planks resting on oak stumps. These had been placed along the walls on either side of the room, and there were several along the back. All were filled. The latecomers were standing. Men rose to give their seats to women holding babies. There was a great deal of shuffling of feet.

Gam had made a big fire in the stove. The crowded school-room was hot. People removed their coats, and mothers un-swathed babies. Jennifer felt perspiration prick along the back of her neck.

Now Mrs. Tuttle sounded the first chords of "The Star-Spangled Banner." The notes wheezed and gurgled from the ancient organ. Everyone stood up. Every voice was raised heartily. Then they all sat down.

Miss Rhul appeared on the platform. Her striped green silk dress looked very festive. She bowed to the judges of the contest who were seated on the platform facing the audience. The performers would necessarily have their backs to the judges most of the time, but this could not be helped.

"I hope you will enjoy our program this evening," Miss Rhul was saying in her special-occasion voice. "And after the children have finished we will hear from Mr. Hugo Bins, our esteemed superintendent."

Everybody clapped. Jennifer gazed through the crack in the screen at the esteemed Mr. Bins. She put first one eye and then the other to the crack, trying to see the whole man. Mr. Bins was exceedingly plump, with a round bald head and short arms and legs. His eyes, staring through very thick glasses, had a fish-like pale roundness.

Jennifer stood by Mamie. "If he is one of the contest judges," she whispered, "I bet turtle chowder wins again this year." But she fervently hoped it wouldn't.

Mamie snickered.

Miss Rhul had finished speaking. Now she was pushing the first performers onto the platform. Holly and Mabel Crumpet were to give their dialogue, "The Gossips."

Holly knew her lines frontward and backward and inside out. She rattled them off lickety-split in the kind of voice she believed a squirrel would have. At each point where a "Caw" was due she would nod at Mabel. With this cue Mabel could hardly miss. But once toward the end Mabel's "Caw" was slow in coming, so Holly said "Caw-caw" in a deep voice herself, and then went right on with her own lines.

51

When they had bowed and retreated the applause was deafening.

Jennifer grabbed Holly backstage and hugged her. "You did just fine, honey," she whispered. "Now go out and sit down and wait for me."

Miss Rhul had announced that the next selection was "The Hunter and the Duck," a pantomime.

Benjy Barnes was pushed out onto the platform with Elijah McIlwethy. Benjy glared at the sea of faces before him. His carefully learned gestures evaporated. He could not seem to move a muscle. A loud whisper directed him. His arm shot out straight and stayed there. He looked like a stationary road sign pointing the way. Miss Rhul hissed more directions. Mamie added her urging. Jennifer, watching, croaked frantically, "Flap your wings, Benjy. Flap 'em!"

But Benjy was deaf to all help. Elijah went right ahead with his part regardless of Benjy.

Jennifer wrung her hands. At the end Benjy was dragged off, still stiff-armed and expressionless. But the applause was as appreciative as though nothing had been wrong.

Jennifer smoothed her dress. She wondered with a sinking feeling if she would remember all the lines of *her* long poem.

Miss Rhul announced each selection and named the performers. Most of the pieces were given without any major dramatic calamity.

When Zealous and Kevin and Jan recited "King John and the Abbot of Canterbury" the audience seemed spellbound. The story was about King John, who coveted the possessions of his abbot. He sought by a ruse to confiscate all the abbot's lands. The king told the abbot he must answer three questions or lose his head. The abbot couldn't answer the questions, but he finally persuaded a poor shepherd to dress in his clothes and come to court to answer for him.

Kevin was the poor shepherd, and answering those questions was a pleasure for him. Jan was the king. He was asking:

> "And first, when thou seest me here in this stead,
> With my crown of gold so fair on my head,
> Among all my liege-men so noble of birth,
> Tell me to one penny what I am worth."

A murmur of approval simmered through the house. Jennifer felt stirred by the words as she had every time she had heard them before, when the boys had been learning their parts. She felt a glowing pride in her brothers. She thought Kevin's acting was wonderful.

Kevin was now answering the second question: How long would it take to ride around the earth? He said:

> "You must rise with the sun, and ride with the same
> Until the next morning he riseth againe;
> And then your grace need not make any doubt
> But in twenty-four hours you'll ride it about."

Then the king said:

> "Now from the third question thou must not shrink,
> But tell me here truly what I do think."

Kevin's effort to keep his tones humble and not victorious was evident when he answered:

"Yea, that shall I do, and make your grace merry;
You think I'm the Abbot of Canterbury;
But I'm his poor shepherd as plain you may see,
That am come to beg pardon for him and for me."

And with a flourish Kevin took off his hat and revealed himself. The king was highly amused by this cleverness and forgave them both. All ended happily, especially for Zealous and Kevin and Jan who stood there grinning like chessy cats at the tumultuous clapping.

Jennifer forgot she was backstage and not one of the audience. She clapped wildly until Mamie nudged her and said "Shush!"

The excitement behind the screens grew with each performance. The three youngest Wentzels tripped onto the stage and gave their poem, "Pop, Pop, Bang." At the end of each stanza were the words "Pop, pop, bang!" and each was said by a different Wentzel. This piece proved very popular with the small fry in the audience. They continued to "Pop, pop, bang!" long after the piece was finished and the actors had retired.

Annie Zarka then gave a folk dance. The Binghams had lent their gramophone, and she danced to a Hungarian rhapsody. She wore a native costume which was elaborately embroidered and trimmed.

"Isn't it just bee-utiful?" Jennifer breathed to Mamie.

As fast as the children finished each performance they sat down in the audience, edging in beside proud parents or little brothers and sisters.

Then came the older boys' and girls' selections. Gussie Craven sang "When You Were Sweet Sixteen." Gam read the poem "Woodman, Spare That Tree." Mamie gave "The Man in the Moon" and Jennifer recited "Columbus."

By the time her turn arrived Jennifer was at a pitch of excitement. The emphasis and expression she injected into that poem were such that no one there would ever be likely to forget the lines:

"Brave Admiral, say but one good word:
   What shall we do when hope is gone?"
The words leapt like a leaping sword:
   "Sail on! Sail on! Sail on! and on!"

She had been afraid she might forget some of the words. But once started, she found them coming quite naturally. She forgot the audience and her voice rang. She felt like Columbus. Her gestures were full of spirit and fire.

When she finished and had made her bow the clapping and stamping were a din. Jennifer went out and sat down beside Mamie. She could see Sam Bingham nudge Molly and nod his head and wink as though Jennifer belonged to him. She saw Mother and Father and Emma smiling broadly, but trying to look modest. She guessed she had done all right.

One after another the perspiring children performed. The room was unbearably hot. Miss Rhul was limp. "Couldn't we have some air in here?" she gasped. "Gam, tiptoe back and open the door, will you? And leave the cloakroom doors open. We'll suffocate if we don't have some air."

Gam obediently moved through the crowd to do her bidding. The lamps flickered with the sudden draft.

Mr. Amos was saying how pleased the school board was with the fine program of the children. He gave a little speech. Then Mr. Lloyd gave a speech. He said practically the same things. All during the speeches Mr. Bins looked uncomfortable. He kept mopping his bald head and around his tight collar.

Mr. Lloyd finished, and then it was Mr. Bins's turn. Jennifer was surprised to see him get up as though it were no effort at all and float up onto the platform. He was very hot. She could see that. He mopped his face with a big white handkerchief. He glared at the stove. He wiped the top of his shiny bald head and ruffled the fringe of hair. Then he adjusted his glasses.

The audience shuffled.

Holly had squeezed into a seat with Mother. She had her hands clasped before her on the desk and she wore a happy, self-satisfied expression. Anyone would think *she* has an essay in the contest, Jennifer thought, and smiled. She wished Mr. Bins would hurry.

At last he was speaking. His voice was thin and rather piping. "My dear friends, I am happy to be here tonight and to welcome you all on this happy occasion."

He went on at some length about the fine performance, and the gifted teacher, and the promising young citizens, and the hopes of all for continued scholastic achievement.

Everyone listened politely. Jennifer rolled her handkerchief into a tight ball. I wish he would hurry. I wish he would hurry, she thought. I'll die if he doesn't hurry and say who won the prize.

56

Finally he paused and cleared his throat. "Ahem. Tonight it is my privilege to announce the winner of the annual essay contest. Mr. Clancy Yoder is the donor of this year's prize. He is presenting the winning contestant with a fine yearling heifer."

The audience gasped. A murmur of astonishment swept through the room. Glances of amazement were exchanged. Mr. Yoder! A yearling heifer! Never before had anyone given so valuable a prize. And Clancy Yoder had contributed it! It was incredible! It was wonderful! Every person in the schoolroom prickled with anticipation. Backs straightened. Necks craned. Ears were cocked for Mr. Bins's next words.

He mopped his face again. He took a folded sheaf of papers from Mr. Lloyd and opened it. His lips twitched as though he were about to smile, but he straightened them out.

"I have here the winning essay, carefully chosen from the many fine papers which were submitted. The judges feel this essay is a distinguished account of historical significance and rightly should be preserved."

Jennifer stiffened. Could it be on the American flag? Or Bunker Hill? Or George Washington?

Mr. Bins paused so long to adjust his glasses that Jennifer felt she was sprouting all over with thistles. Then he continued, "I will now read the winning essay." He cleared his throat. "The title of this story is 'The Redskins' Retreat, or, A True Account of the Trials of Our Early Settlers,' by Jennifer Hill."

There was a gasp and a long "Ooooooh." Every head turned and every eye searched out and fastened on the white-faced, gaping Jennifer. She sat stunned while Mr. Bins read from the paper: "This is a true story. I heard it from an authentic person who was never known to tell a lie. It is about a boy named Johnny Whistler, and some of the old settlers hereabouts can prove it because Johnny was one of their ancestors."

Jennifer could hear Father "Ahem" loudly. From the corner of her eye she could see Mother and Emma and Holly glance at her proudly and then back at Mr. Bins. She caught the rustle among the children. She saw Sam Bingham lean forward to stare at her. Mamie gripped her arm tightly.

When Mr. Bins read the description of the Indians, Gib Rettis and the rest, a ripple ran through the listeners, but Jennifer did not notice. She still had to pinch herself to be sure she was not dreaming.

Mr. Bins was reading: "And those Indians were going to steal old Tipper Magargle's elixir and his pig Rosamond, and Mr. Magargle was desperate. Because if they took his pig he wouldn't have any bacon for the winter. And if they took his elixir he wouldn't have anything to rub on his wooden leg when it hurt."

Sam Bingham started to shake with laughter. Jennifer looked at him crossly. He should pay attention, she said to herself.

The story went on. When Mr. Bins came to the part describing Johnny in the corn shock waiting for the Indians to come, Jennifer shivered. That's even better than I'd have expected, she told herself.

The story progressed rapidly to the point where the guns were going off and Johnny emerged from the corn shock. " 'Put out the fire!' he yelled to Magargle, as he sped after the Indians, loading his gun as he ran."

How exciting that sounded now with somebody reading the words she had written! Jennifer sat motionless. Her hands were

hard little fists on the desk before her. She was following Johnny now, hanging on Mr. Bins's words as though she had never heard them before.

But something had begun to happen to the audience.

The men standing near the door had vanished through it like shadows. Then people sitting in the back seats gradually evaporated. Not a sound was made. No one hurried. Along the benches on both sides, one after another, men, women, and children got up and quietly slid toward the door.

Mr. Bins looked up for a moment, a frown on his face, before he went back to his reading.

The exodus continued. Seats were emptying silently, gently, surely. People moved with the slow, yet urgent motions of a nightmare. One after another they disappeared.

Mr. Bins looked pleadingly after them. Jennifer saw what was happening. She wanted to cry out, "Wait! Wait! It isn't finished. Don't go yet!"

Then she saw Father and Mother and all her family drifting silently out through the cloakroom door. Jan flung a curious look back at her and pointed to something. He held his nose and vanished.

Mr. Bins said, "My dear people, this is unseemly——" Then he ceased speaking. His eyes were riveted on the floor.

Jennifer heard Mamie gasp. "What is it? What's the matter?" she whispered hoarsely. She leaned past Mamie who was trying to shove her the other way. Then she saw.

There, walking down the center aisle with great self-assurance, was a little black and white animal.

A skunk!

Mamie pushed Jennifer out of the seat. She pulled her along toward the door. Miss Rhul and most of the other children were close at her heels.

The schoolhouse had emptied—except for the three school officials trapped up on the platform.

Outside, buggies and sleighs and rigs were pulling away in frantic haste. No one waited even to bid his neighbor good night.

Olive Burns Kirby

THE ICEBOAT RACE

ILLUSTRATED BY *Keith Ward*

Pierre Coulard ran down the snowy path leading to the lake and slid across the ice to meet his older brother.

"Raoul!" he called excitedly. "Will you take me with you tomorrow? I'll promise not to be any bother."

Tall, good-looking Raoul shook his head. "Not this time, *mon petit*. I'll need all my wits about me to win the race. I'm trying her out this morning, though, and I'll take you then."

Pierre turned away, his lower lip quivering with disappointment. "I told Jean I'd go skiing after breakfast," he said slowly.

"Too bad! Never mind, in another year or so you'll be sending the *Shooting Star* across the ice all by yourself. Then we'll see what you can do."

The iceboat races were scheduled for the following afternoon. It was the annual week of winter sports in the little French-Canadian village of St. Etienne. For five days the snow-capped Laurentian Mountains had echoed to the shouts of eager competitors and onlookers, and tomorrow was the final day of the series. The iceboat race was the main event of the week, and there were five boats competing for the cup.

After dinner Pierre stole down to the tiny harbor where the *Shooting Star,* her sails furled, rode at anchor on the glistening sheet of ice. He had learned to drive the boat the previous winter and he knew almost as much as Raoul about tacking and steering. Behind the village towered the snowy hills and, to the northeast, Pierre could see the ski jump. Jumping was to take place that afternoon, and the slope of the mountain was dotted with moving figures, but the boy had no interest in anything but the wedge-shaped boat that was to figure in the next day's race. He had helped Raoul build her and he had held the rope, while Monsieur Reaume, the village schoolmaster, had christened her the *Shooting Star.*

A roll of homespun blankets lay at the end of the boat. Pierre stared at it resentfully. His mother had woven the blankets on her loom, and they were used whenever she or Marie were on board. Or, maybe, when Raoul took the silly, giggling Anne Philabert for a breath-taking ride over the lake, bluish white in the moonlight.

"Raoul'd take *her* if she asked him," muttered the boy, unhappily. "And she wouldn't keep quiet, either.''

That night Pierre did not sleep well. He dreamed he was driving the iceboat over a glassy lake bordered by towering snow-capped mountains. The wind had carried him across the ice, over the treetops, and had landed him on the peak of the tallest elevation. There he was, teetering perilously in a sudden squall, expecting every minute to be dashed to earth, when he awoke to find his mother bending over him.

"Pierre, wake up! Breakfast is already over. Have you forgotten what day it is?"

As if he could forget! He rubbed his eyes, tumbled out of bed, and pulled on his clothing. The sun was shining brightly and the air was crispy cold, with a brisk wind blowing from the north. It was an ideal day for the races.

Pierre bolted his porridge, drank a glass of milk, and hurried

61

down the street leading to Lake Cecebe. Dorien, his younger brother, begged to go, too, but the older boy slipped away before his mother came downstairs. Like as not, she would insist upon his taking him. And Pierre wanted to be alone.

Raoul was examining the sails on the *Shooting Star* when Pierre reached the lake. He did not see the boy dodge behind the boathouse that housed the iceboat during the summer. Two little furrows had appeared on the dark brow underneath the knitted toque, and Raoul paused in his task to rub his jaw tenderly. Then he picked up the roll of blankets and trudged up the hill.

Madame Coulard had dinner ready at twelve o'clock. Neither Raoul nor Pierre had arrived, but Dorien was in his chair, clamoring for potatoes and pork. She had taken M. Coulard's dinner to him at the little store, where he sold everything from butter to blankets and hooked rugs. Ordinarily, Gabriel Coulard would have locked his shop door for an hour at noon, but it would have been poor business to be away when St. Etienne was teeming with countryfolk come to see the races. So his wife packed him a box and filled it with slabs of cold pork, thick slices of bread smeared with golden butter and a generous segment of apple pie.

"I wonder what is keeping Raoul?" she murmured, giving Dorien a piece of bread sprinkled with brown sugar. "There is very little time—and Pierre! The child is usually here before dinner is ready."

"Here's Raoul!" shouted Dorien, pointing to the window. "He's got a red face."

Raoul stamped the snow from his boots, threw his cap and blanket coat on the sofa, and slumped into a chair. His right jaw was badly swollen.

"Raoul, is it that tooth again?" inquired his mother anxiously, placing a plate of meat and vegetables before him.

He nodded, took two or three mouthfuls and pushed away the plate. "I can't eat, Mother. It's driving me crazy. I've a notion to take Pierre with me this afternoon. I'll be glad of company. Where is he?"

62

"I don't know. He left the house after breakfast and he hasn't been back. Wasn't he at the lake?"

"Didn't see him. Maybe he is with Jean Laurent. They are probably looking for grandstand seats. Is Father going to see the race?"

"Why not? There will be nobody in the shops. And," proudly, "he will want to see the *Shooting Star* beat the *Chat Noir*. And that, after all François Laurent's bragging!"

"She can do it, if—ouch! My jaw is jumping like a shuttle." And Raoul threw himself on the sofa and buried his aching face in the pillow. His mother brought him a bag of hot salt, and the application gave him temporary relief.

His thoughts wandered to the forthcoming race. It was scheduled for two o'clock. Jacques Laurent was doubtless there already, maneuvering his *Chat Noir* into favorable position. It was the *Shooting Star's* most dangerous rival. Raoul would never have named his ship "the Black Cat." He didn't like cats, least of all black ones. They never brought anyone luck.

"It's time to go, Raoul," called his mother from the kitchen. "You'll have to hurry."

But when he hurried, the aching tooth seemed to stab his nerves with sharp thrusts. There was no use, he couldn't race the old boat; he'd never be able to hold to the course with his head jumping like this. He'd withdraw from the race. That would mean that Jacques Laurent would keep the cup for another year. None of the other entrants had the *Chat Noir's* speed.

It was a bitter blow to his hopes. He knew he owned the better boat and he knew that Jacques knew it. Had there been a dentist or a doctor in St. Etienne, he would have had the tooth pulled, but the nearest dentist was fifty miles away and there was no doctor in the village.

He reached the lake as the boats were jockeying into position, trim-looking craft that suggested sea gulls, poised for flight. The shore was lined with people, and inside the buoys a fleet of sleighs, each filled to overflowing with a French-Canadian family, formed an array of grandstand seats.

The wind whistled across the glistening ice and the shadowed

63

snow, high up on the slopes of the Laurentian hills, was softly
blue. A day to be skimming swiftly over the frozen water, a day
to be crossing the finishing line well ahead of one's rival!

For a moment Raoul repented his decision not to race. "I
could have beaten him, hands down," he muttered. "The *Shooting Star* is worth—ouch!" The jumping agony that shot upward
through his jaw left him weak and wordless. He stumbled forward, all ambition gone, his one desire to get home as quickly
as possible.

"Raoul! What kept you? You'll be late for the race. Hurry,
I'll help you get her out."

It was Pierre. The boy's face was tense. It was ten minutes
to two, and there was no time to lose. The judges had been asking where the fifth boat was and whether it had withdrawn from
the race.

"I'm not racing," mumbled Raoul, burying his chin in his
scarf. "My tooth is pulling my head to pieces."

"Not racing?" repeated the younger boy incredulously. "But you've got to. They're waiting for you."

"Let them wait!" muttered Raoul. "I'm not going to, I tell you." He was off, through a drift of snow, toward the judges' stand. Pierre followed him, his young mind playing with a daring thought. Why not? If the *Shooting Star* was to lose the race anyway, one way was as good as another.

"Raoul!" He held his brother back. "I'll drive the *Shooting Star* for you. Stay in the race."

"You?" Raoul laughed, in spite of his aching jaw. "Say, kid, you wouldn't have a chance against the *Black Cat*. You've never raced a boat."

"Yes, I have," began Pierre, then checked himself fearfully. He had borrowed the *Shooting Star* several times when Raoul was away, and he and Jean Laurent, in the *Black Cat*, had raced the boats up and down Lake Cecebe. But it was better that Raoul should not know that.

"Please, Raoul!" he begged, his eyes imploring. "I won't hurt the ship."

"It's a crazy idea," said the other, his words almost lost in the woolen scarf. "You couldn't do it."

"Yes, I could!" Pierre caught him by the arm. "You know I can drive her. You taught me how. Say I can go, Raoul."

"All right," agreed Raoul, reluctantly. Maybe it was better than withdrawing from the race. There were few enough entries as it was. "But don't get in a jam. Steer clear of Jacques around the buoys. He's apt to be dirty. Beat it, kid, and good luck!"

It was one minute to two when the *Shooting Star*, her sails billowing smartly in the wind, drew into fourth place beside the *Chat Noir*. The starter was getting ready to send the first boat over the line. Jacques Laurent, snugly ensconced on the little deck, looked up as his rival's ship nosed into position.

"Thought you'd dropped out—Pierre!"

Crack! A blank cartridge awakened echoes in the nearer hills, and the leading boat crossed the starting line like a winging bird. Pierre, lying full length against the rail, his body propped on one elbow, felt the steel runners gliding smoothly beneath

65

him. The shore of the lake was black with onlookers, and there was a tumultuous shout as the people recognized the driver of the last boat. Pierre was a favorite with the villagers. He was always willing to run an errand or do an odd job.

The triangular course was charted well down the lake, and there were to be three laps, a distance of fifteen miles. Past the whitewashed houses in the villages, across the little cove at the foot of Louis Corriveau's farm, out over the open ice sailed the five boats. Pierre kept on the outside of the *Chat Noir* and did not give the *Shooting Star* too much sail. They were overhauling the other boats, which were holding the same positions as when they started. He bore sharply to the right to avoid a collision with the *Black Cat*, the latter swerving sharply to escape hitting the third iceboat, a trimly built craft with a medium-sized sail.

"I'll have to watch Jacques," muttered Pierre. "That may have been an accident, but I know he's tricky."

The wind stung his cheeks and brought the blood to the surface. His mittened hands were stiff, but the boy did not feel the cold. He passed the buoy and tacked across the ice, well abreast of Jacques' ship. Then the wind caught the sails and the *Shooting Star* sped swiftly down the steely blue stretch of ice. Pierre laughed aloud as he pulled ahead of the other boat. Who said he couldn't race? He hoped Raoul was watching from the shore. They were nearing the end of the first lap, and he could hear the cheering shouts of the spectators, but he did not know whether they were for him or for Jacques.

The second lap brought them almost neck and neck to the finishing line, Jacques' boat lagging behind by a few inches. Pierre's feet were numb and he could scarcely move his fingers, but he was not conscious of the cold. He was not aware that his ear, oddly pale below the woolen toque, was badly frost-bitten. All he knew was that the wind was driving his boat across the glittering ice to the final sprint on the road to victory.

Around the buoy, up the triangular stretch on a wide tack and around the second buoy sailed the two boats, the *Shooting Star* still in the lead. Pierre's delight knew no bounds. Never

66

again could Raoul exhibit a brotherly superiority about sailing the iceboat. If he could maintain the lead, the trophy would be his, and Jacques Laurent, the village braggart, would be put in his place.

Suddenly Pierre's joy was choked by a spasm of terror. The *Black Cat*, slightly to the right of him, was bearing down swiftly upon a dark object sticking out of the ice. The boy remembered it, a water-soaked log that had been a menace to canoes the previous summer. They must be off the course. He screamed a warning but Jacques paid no heed to the shrill cry.

Seconds passed and Pierre forgot the coveted prize, forgot that Jacques had tried to crowd him off the course earlier in the race, forgot everything but the need for swift action. With a quick intake of breath, he pulled sharply across the path of the *Chat Noir*, forcing the older boy toward land. He could hear the latter's angry shouts and felt rather than saw the threatening gestures, then—crash! The runner of his own ship struck the log, and Pierre was catapulted over the deck, through a ripping sail, onto the ice. There was a sickening thud, a moment of blackness, then a hammering on the top of his head and a sharp pain shooting up his left arm. Someone was bending over him. It was Jacques Laurent.

"Pierre, you saved my life." His voice was husky. "I'm sorry I tried to jam you a while ago. You're a plucky kid and you know how to sail a boat. I hope you're not hurt."

The pain from the broken arm was draining the blood from the boy's face, but he smiled proudly. It was something to be told by Jacques Laurent that you could sail an iceboat. Hurrying toward them across the ice came a group of men. Pierre recognized the foremost figure. It was his brother.

"Say that again, Jacques," he pleaded, when the men were within earshot, "about my knowing how to sail a boat."

Jacques grinned. The tall youth, with a woolen scarf wrapped high about his chin came closer. Pierre's eyes gleamed with excitement.

"You're one grand, little iceboat sailor, Pierre." Jacques spoke loudly and his words could be heard distinctly by the approaching men. "If you can beat Jacques Laurent, you can beat anyone else on this lake. Say, Raoul," wheeling swiftly to meet the keen gaze of Raoul Coulard, "why didn't you tell me I was going to be up against a tough proposition like Pierre. He's the best little sailor in these hills. He deserves the trophy."

"No! No!" cried Pierre, from the security of Raoul's arms. They had brought a sleigh and were taking him home. "I didn't win the race. But I'll race you next year—if Raoul'll let me."

Raoul placed him on the sleigh. Jean Laurent had gone for the doctor, but it would be hours before he arrived. The older boy's face softened. Plucky little kid—Pierre! And Jacques was right. The youngster knew how to race a boat.

"Next year? Sure you can, Pierre. And, Jacques," straightening proudly, "you'll have to be on your tiptoes when he races you next year!"

Georgene Faulkner and John Becker

THE MOST WONDERFUL THING
IN THE WORLD

ILLUSTRATED BY *Helen Prickett*

ON THE Monday after the Sunday on which Melindy's grandmother told Melindy's father's story, Melindy came home from school very late. She was all out of breath and very excited, and her eyes kind of popped out of her head like saucers and she said, "Guess what happened?"

"I guess," said Melindy's father, "that you saw a red-breasted grosbeak dance a jig on a pink elephant's back."

"No," said Melindy, "seriously . . ."

"Seriously," said her grandmother, "I guess that you had a double chocolate frosted malted milk."

"No," said Melindy, "it was something even better than that. Do you give up?"

"I gave up a long time ago," said Melindy's grandmother.

"Well," said Melindy, "I told a story."

"Where?" said Melindy's father.

"In assembly," said Melindy.

"And how come?" said Melindy's grandmother.

"Well," said Melindy, "it was all on account of geography."

"Whose geography?" said Melindy's father.

"France's geography," said Melindy. "We were reciting our geography-economics lesson . . ."

"What," said Melindy's grandmother, who did not know how to listen to a story, "is economics?"

"Economics," said Melindy, "is the reason why and what and where people eat."

69

"I know the reason why and what and where people eat, and it's *not* called economics," said Melindy's grandmother.

"No," said Melindy, "economics is the really true reason."

"The really true reason," said Melindy's grandmother, "is that people are hungry."

"Yes," said Melindy, "but when people are hungry what people eat has to do with importing and exporting."

"I do not understand it," said Melindy's grandmother.

"Well, if you'll listen," said Melindy, "I'll explain it to you. You see we were talking about France, and Miss Johnson said, 'Does anybody know the most important thing imported to France?' And I said, 'Of course, I know—mules.' "

"People do not eat mules," said Melindy's grandmother, who did not know how to listen to a story at all.

"No," said Melindy, "but in the First World War our people could not have eaten anything if they hadn't imported mules to pull around those little rolling kitchens."

"That is right," said Melindy's grandmother.

"Of course, it's right," said Melindy, "but when I said 'mules,' everybody laughed, and Miss Johnson said, 'Melindy Eloise Miller, I knew you were poor in arithmetic, but since when are you poor in geography too?' And then I got mad."

"So?" said Melindy's grandmother, who was beginning to catch on to how to listen to a story.

"So," said Melindy, "I stood up and I said, 'Nothing is more important than importing mules.'

"Then even Miss Johnson laughed and said, 'Where did you get that idea?'

"So I stood up again and I told my father's story, starting at the beginning and ending at the end, just the way you told me.

"When I got through, everybody stopped laughing altogether and then Miss Johnson said, 'Why, you told that story wonderfully, Melindy.'

"And I said, 'Yes'm, I did.'

" 'And your father was a real hero, Melindy,' Miss Johnson said.

"And I said, 'Yes'm, he sure is.' And I told Miss Johnson that

70

"*Then when I finished that big room was so still and quiet . . .*"

everybody in our family was a hero, except me, because I'm a girl, and I invited Miss Johnson up to see our medals."

"And?" said Melindy's grandmother.

"And," said Melindy, "Miss Johnson said she'd like very much to come up some day and see our medals, but what she'd like even better was to have me tell my father's story in assembly. Because we have talks about national heroes."

"Am I a national hero?" said Melindy's father.

"You are now," said Melindy. "Because in assembly, after everybody was seated, Mr. Timberlake stood up and said, 'Now I want you all to listen very attentively because Melindy Miller has a story to tell.'

"So," said Melindy, "I stood up and walked up to Mr. Timberlake's platform . . ."

"Were you scared?" said Melindy's grandmother.

"Yes," said Melindy, "but then I thought how my father gets up on the Black Diamond Troupe platform every night and he isn't scared, and he wasn't even scared in the whole of the First World War. So I just started in.

"And when I started in I could see Billy Gumpers and Buddy Williams and Frank the Crank and all the great big boys kind of laughing at me and Priscilla Marie Leroy, who's always fidgeting and fussing with her pretty dresses and looking at the big boys and doing what they do—she was laughing, too.

"But pretty soon, after I'd told how my father landed at St. Nazaire and built over the big docks and was called to the front by the French Red Hand, they stopped laughing. And then I told how they'd given my father a little rolling kitchen and a mule called Fanny and how he took care of Fanny and loved her. Then I told how he was riding in the Argonne Forest, and his Captain had seen all those Germans, and how his company went down and hid in that little French street, and how my father drove Fanny down into the town. And when I came to the part about Fanny lying down and dying in that little French street, I could see that everybody was kind of crying and even Frank the Crank was wiping his eyes. When I finished, that big room was so still and quiet that you can't imagine."

71

"Yes," said Melindy's father, who had been very still and quiet too, "I can imagine."

"And then," said Melindy, "nobody said anything for it seemed like a whole minute. Then, all of a sudden, somebody started to clap and then everybody clapped, and Miss Krumm smiled at me, and Miss Johnson came up and said, 'You told that story better than ever, Melindy.' Then Mr. Timberlake, *Mr. Timberlake right in front of everybody*, stood up and shook my hand."

"And then?" said Melindy's grandmother.

"And then," said Melindy, "that's all."

"I wonder," said Melindy's father, "from whom you ever could have learned to tell a story?"

"Yes, I wonder too," said Melindy's grandmother, and she went off into the kitchen, laughing, to get the breakfast-equals-dinner ready.

After the Monday on which Melindy stood up in assembly and told her father's story, nothing really extra-special happened for a whole month. Melindy went to school, of course, and she did get a little better in her numbers, and Miss Krumm gave her a new classical piece to learn, and in assembly she played the TRAMP TRAMP TRAMP fire-drill music twice and she played FROM THE HALLS OF MONTEZUMA TO THE SHORES OF TRIPOLI once. And one day, when Elly and Nelly were having a fight in the coatroom, they saw a red-breasted grosbeak from the coatroom window. They stopped fighting, and everybody went and looked out and saw the red-breasted grosbeak in the schoolyard and everybody was very excited—that is, everybody except Melindy, because she had kind of expected to see a pink elephant, too.

Then, one Sunday, after Melindy and her father and her grandmother and General Shaw had had their Sunday-afternoon-at-home jam session, Melindy said she had a head-ache, and she went to bed. The next morning, which was a Monday, when Melindy was ready to go to school, she sneezed four times straight without stopping.

"Come here, Melindy," said Melindy's grandmother, and she

put her hand on Melindy's head. "I don't think you ought to go to school today."

"Oh *please*, Gran," said Melindy.

Now, except for that one day long ago when Melindy and her father and her grandmother and General Shaw had celebrated about moving to the Bethune Building, Melindy had never missed a single day of school. And Melindy—maybe because she didn't have a war record for bravery in the field of honor—was extra proud of her school record. Her grandmother knew how proud Melindy was of her school record and she knew, too, that Monday was the day for Melindy's music lesson with Miss Krumm.

"You know, I really shouldn't let you," her grandmother said.

Now, as soon as Melindy heard her grandmother's "I - really - shouldn't - let - you," of course, Melindy knew that her grandmother really would. So Melindy put on her hat and coat, and then came back and kissed her grandmother on the nose and went off to school.

But when Melindy got to school, she felt funny. Somehow she couldn't pay attention to *anything* Miss Johnson said, and she mixed up her numbers worse than ever and she thought, once, that Miss Johnson was looking at her kind of peculiar and after that, in the afternoon, her head began to hurt like anything.

Then, just as the children got up to march out to the assembly room, Miss Johnson said, "Come here, Melindy." She put her hand on Melindy's head and said, "I think you're sick, Melindy, and I want you to go right home."

Then, even before Melindy could get out her "Oh-please-Miss-Johnson," Miss Johnson said, "Now, don't argue with me. Just go along, Melindy." And Miss Johnson and the class marched off to assembly.

Melindy was left all alone in the schoolroom, and she felt even sorrier for herself than on the day when the most terrible thing happened. Because, of course, Melindy couldn't help thinking that it would have been bad enough to have to stay home altogether. But to go to school and to get almost next to the assembly hour and to get right up near to playing her new piece for Miss Krumm was just about the end of everything. So, when Melindy walked slowly up to her desk and started to take up her books, the first book dropped down on the floor, and she just left it lying there. Because then Melindy knew that she was going to cry. And because she came from brave people and couldn't let anyone see her cry, she crossed over the empty hall into the coatroom and she put her head in a coat—she didn't know or care if it was her coat or Elly's coat or Nelly's coat—and there she started to cry good and proper.

Melindy was really feeling terrible, crying there in the coatroom. She'd just come to the *boo-hoo* place, and she'd gotten out her first *boo*, and she'd taken a deep breath to get the *hoo* out, when all of a sudden, she stopped crying. She stopped crying because she thought she smelled smoke. She took another breath and she sniffed again. Sure enough, she smelled something burning. She looked around and there, from the crack in the coatroom floor, there was a little trickle of smoke trickling out.

For one whole minute, Melindy didn't know what to do. She thought maybe that she should yell and she wanted to, but then, because she'd been crying, it was hard to yell and, besides, as everybody was in assembly, there was no one to yell to. Then, somehow, in that one minute, Melindy thought how once her father, without thinking twice, had acted without orders. So, she ran out of the coatroom, down the corridor, and up the stairs into the assembly hall. She ran down the side of the hall and up to the piano. She opened it and started to play the TRAMP TRAMP TRAMP fire music.

Now, just when Melindy started to play the TRAMP TRAMP TRAMP fire music, Mr. Timberlake was making his principal speech. If Melindy could have seen Mr. Timberlake's face she would have seen that he first looked surprised and then he looked annoyed and then he looked just plain angry. But all Melindy could see was Billy Gumpers and Buddy Williams and Frank the Crank in the front row and how they started to

74

laugh, but this time Melindy didn't care if they laughed or
not. All Melindy cared about was that Billy Gumpers and
Buddy Williams and Frank the Crank were standing up. And,
although they were still laughing, they were swinging their
arms and throwing out their legs and marching out right in time
with the TRAMP TRAMP TRAMP. Maybe they thought it
was just a joke or maybe they just didn't want to hear any
more of Mr. Timberlake's speech. But the important thing was
that they *were marching out*. And when the big boys started
to march out Priscilla Marie Leroy naturally got up and
marched out, too. So, of course, all the big girls did just what
Priscilla Marie Leroy did.

Melindy played the TRAMP TRAMP TRAMP fire music as
it had never been played before. She played it loud and clear
and sure—and still there was something scary under it. Melindy
kept on playing it even though Miss Krumm came over and

said, "Why, Melindy!" She didn't stop when Miss Johnson came over and said, "That child's sick!" She didn't even stop when Mr. Timberlake came over and shouted at her.

And all the time the assembly room was getting emptier and emptier, because the rule was that when the TRAMP TRAMP TRAMP music started and the fire bell sounded, everybody was to march out no matter what. Now, of course, when Melindy started playing, the fire bell hadn't sounded. It didn't sound until after Melindy had finished playing the TRAMP TRAMP TRAMP twice and started on it for the third time. But when the fire bell sounded, it didn't ring on and off the way it rings for drills. It rang without stopping. And when it started to ring like that Mr. Timberlake rushed right out ahead of the fourth grade without even waiting for Melindy and Miss Krumm the way he was supposed to. And all the time it was ringing, Melindy went on playing until the room was empty altogether. Then she and Miss Krumm walked out last.

When Melindy got outside, there was a terrible commotion. People were running, and the fire engines were coming down the street. Melindy could see that the old building was blazing up almost as much as a bonfire that Melindy and her grandmother had once seen on Halloween. But Melindy wasn't paying much attention to the fire or the fire engines or anybody because this time Melindy was crying, just as if her heart would break, right out in front of everybody. And Melindy had her head hid in Miss Krumm's skirt, and Miss Krumm was petting her.

Melindy didn't even pay attention when Mr. Timberlake came up and said, "The child has saved the whole school," nor even when Frank the Crank came up and said, "You done fine, Melindy."

Then Miss Johnson came up with the keys to Mr. Timberlake's *own* car, and Miss Johnson and Miss Krumm drove Melindy and carried her upstairs to 3B. But when they got Melindy up to 3B and started to tell Melindy's grandmother about what she had done, Melindy's grandmother didn't seem to pay attention. She was busy getting Melindy's bed ready and getting it warm and undressing Melindy and putting her in it. Then,

76

after Melindy's grandmother put Melindy in her bed, Melindy was sick for a long time.

While Melindy was sick she didn't know anything. She didn't know that Mr. Timberlake came to see her every day and that every day he brought his own doctor. All Melindy could remember was that whenever she woke up her grandmother was always sitting there holding a cool cloth next to her head. And one time, when she woke up, Miss Krumm was sitting there holding that same cool cloth. And another time when she woke up, she could see her father standing in the doorway, and her father looked as if he'd been crying, and he had General Shaw's cage in his hand, and the General looked as if he'd been crying, too.

Then, another time, Melindy thought she heard some men talking in the parlor. She thought she heard Mr. Timberlake's voice and she thought they were talking about medals and that she heard Mr. Timberlake say, "The Carnegie Medal." But

77

Melindy wasn't sure about it because everything she heard kept getting mixed up with the old dream that she kept dreaming over and over again about the ruby red and the navy blue flag with the stars shining out like diamonds from its field of honor as someone carried it on, up and over the hill.

Then one day Melindy went to sleep, and she slept all night through and didn't dream at all. In the morning, when she woke up, her fever was gone, and she felt very tired and sad and happy, too.

The next day her father and her grandmother came in her room, and her father was carrying General Shaw's cage in his hand, and in her grandmother's hand there was a brand-new medal. And her grandmother said, "This is your medal."

"Is it for bravery in the field of honor?" said Melindy.

"Shucks, no," said Melindy's grandmother. "Any old man in our family can win a medal for bravery in the field of honor any old day in the week. It takes a girl to win a medal for *just pure bravery*. This here medal's worth more than all the medals than *even we've* got in our family."

And Melindy and Melindy's father and Melindy's grandmother and General Shaw looked at Melindy's medal, and they thought it was the most wonderful thing in the world.

Ruth H. Colby

HORSE MACKEREL

ILLUSTRATED BY *Keith Ward*

ERON ISLAND has just one road. Over this walked Ben Loomis, his whole sturdy figure expressing decided discouragement. As he reached the top of a hill, he saw a small figure flying along the road toward him. It was Jimmy, whom Ben considered his brother, but who was really a little orphan cousin. Now he greeted him breathlessly. Jimmy was nearly always breathless or talking at top speed.

"Ben! Ben! Ollie Simpson is down at the wharf with a horse mackerel. He's a whopper—five hundred pounds at least. Come along and look at him. Hurry!"

"Where did Ollie get him?" Ben quickened his steps. The capture of a horse mackerel, that enormous fish often called tuna, was a great event on the island.

"Right here, south of Fuller's Point," said Jimmy. "He thinks there will be more around here."

For a moment Ben forgot his discouragement; forgot that his father had been ill all winter and spring, and that even now he could only sit in the sun by the doorway; forgot his own hard work doing odd jobs for the summerfolk; forgot how slowly the money came, and how great was the need. He even forgot—for the moment—the new boat that Mr. Loomis must have before he could hope to earn a living again for his family by fishing, and that this meant one hundred dollars. All the afternoon, at his work, that refrain had haunted Ben. "One hundred dollars! One hundred dollars!"

They were approaching the wharf and could see the crowd gathered there. They were weighing the huge fish.

"Three hundred and ninety pounds," drawled Asa Smith, who

79

was doing the weighing. "Ain't sech a big one, after all, Ollie."

"Well, I'm takin' it to Portland jest the same. Last I heard, horse mackerel was fetchin' ten cents a pound. Thirty dollars ain't to be sneezed at, Asa." Ollie's tone was pleased.

Ben and Jimmy looked hard at each other. With the reserve typical of island-bred boys, they said nothing until they were well away from the crowd.

"Ben! Ben! Can't we go horse mackerelin'?" Jimmy fairly pranced along. "Ollie told me once they sometimes weigh as much as seven hundred pounds. Just think, one of those would pretty nearly buy a new boat."

"Seven-hundred-pounders ain't so very common, Jimmy," was Ben's slow-spoken comment, "but I wouldn't throw away a three-hundred-pound feller, would you?" He grinned at the eager Jimmy.

"Then you *will* go, Ben?"

Ben nodded.

"You'll take me?" Jimmy held his breath.

"I figger this way," said Ben slowly. "Young Asa or Sam Field would be glad to go. But then I'd feel as though they ought to have half of all we caught. So I guess the two of us had better handle it alone. Ollie will lend us their motorboat, the *Mary L.*"

That afternoon Ben busied himself putting up the harpoon stand on the borrowed boat.

Ollie Simpson strolled down to the wharf. "Good idea. I'll help you nail her up."

The stand was simply a fifteen-foot plank, railed in on three sides, nailed on the bow of the boat like a huge and clumsy bowsprit. At the end of the plank, thrust well out over the water, the watcher stands, harpoon in hand, looking for the first glimpse of the huge fish, swimming close to the surface of the water.

"Got your spear?" asked Ollie.

Ben nodded toward the great eight-foot pole, thick as a man's arm, with the big iron barb on the end. While Ollie made a stout rope fast to the harpoon, Ben coiled the rest around a small

keg, taking care that it should unwind easily when need came. A snarl might mean the breaking of the rope and the loss of the fish.

Early the following morning Ben and Jimmy left the cove in their borrowed motorboat. The sun was bright and hot. It promised to be an ideal day for horse mackerel. The big fish only appears on hot, calm days. Perhaps he likes the feel of the sun on his back. Back and forth cruised the *Mary L.* but never a glimpse of a big fish rewarded her eager crew. By ten o'clock Ben turned the bow homewards.

Jimmy was so disappointed he could hardly keep from crying.

"I thought sure we'd find a big one this morning. Nobody needs a horse mackerel right now more than we do." His tone was so mournful that Ben, equally disappointed, under his indifferent appearance, had to smile.

"Maybe they'll come in tomorrow, Jimmy." And Jimmy felt comforted.

The weather favored them again the next morning. Once out of the cove, Ben took his place in the stand, his eyes anxiously scanning the water for the dark shadow that would betray the big fish, his harpoon ready to his hand. Jimmy, at the tiller, handled the *Mary L.* surprisingly well.

A little motion of Ben's hand southward caused Jimmy, tense with excitement, to swing the boat in the direction indicated.

Dead ahead was a big dark shadow on the water. Jimmy

81

caught his breath. The shadow looked enormous! If only they could steal up on him without startling him before the huge fish became frightened and sank!

Sluggishly he moved along. They were getting close now. Still the huge finny thing swam, undisturbed.

Splash! The harpoon, hurled with all the strength of Ben's sturdy arm, found its mark.

The huge bulk stiffened, then fairly tore through the water, all sluggishness changed to lightning speed.

Sizz-zz! The rope almost burned its way out of its coil.

Ben, white with excitement, all but tumbled out of the stand, seized the keg and hurled it overboard. The two boys watched it bobbing and spinning, as the enormous monster tried to rid himself of the harpoon.

"Jimmy, I'll bet he *is* a seven-hundred-pounder after all. Look out! He's going up the bay."

Even before Ben got the words out of his mouth Jimmy had swung th*e Mary L.* up the bay. There was no chance of the sturdy motorboat keeping pace with the express-train speed of the fish. All they could do was to keep the keg, serving as a marker, in sight, and wait until their huge prey weakened. Then his struggles would become more feeble, his lungs would fill with water, and they could safely approach the huge, drowned carcass.

Jimmy was on tiptoe with the thrill of the chase. "Ben, quick! Speed her up. He's going out through Cedar Ledges! Oh, we mustn't lose him."

The bobbing keg was tearing through the deep, narrow channel of Cedar Ledges.

"I kinder thought he'd head out to sea." Ben speeded up the engine.

For a long time the boys drifted around on the quiet ocean. Once the keg was so far away it seemed about to slip out of sight.

Ben stopped the engine, and Jimmy saw the new boat disappearing with the keg. "Shouldn't we start, Ben? Suppose we lose him?"

Ben, on the tip of the stand, watching no less anxiously, turned round with a grin. "He's comin' back. We're savin' gas."

An hour passed this way. Then suddenly the wildly bobbing keg ceased to whirl and rested quietly on the gentle waves.

"Guess he's done for, Jimmy. Let's go over and pick him up."

Expertly Jimmy swung the *Mary L.* up to the keg, while Ben, equally expert, caught its rope with a boat hook, drew the keg in, making the rope fast as he did so. He began to haul, slowly and easily.

"Jimmy, he's a whopper!"

"Didn't I say we'd get one? Didn't I? We'll sell him, we'll get—"

Crash! The *Mary L.* shivered from stem to stern. The rope slid through Ben's hands, blistering them before he could drop it. Jimmy, flung against the side of the boat, automatically reached for the tiller as he fell. The monster had come to life. The *Mary L.* boiled along in his wake as he once more tore seaward.

The two children recovered themselves. Ben switched off the engine.

"Might as well save gas again." He managed a grin at Jimmy but made sure of a big knife to cut the rope if need be.

"Suppose the harpoon comes out?" Jimmy's voice shook.

"We'll lose him. I can't get the keg overboard again. Rope's too taut. Guess we're in for a free ride, Jimmy."

There was silence for a while. Straight out to sea went the fish, and straight out to sea went the *Mary L.* with him.

"How—how far will he take us?" Jimmy asked.

"Can't tell." Ben was remembering a tale Ollie told of a four-hour ride back of a horse mackerel. To be sure that was in a dory. The *Mary L.*'s solid weight ought to help. Four hours out to sea would take them a long ways from land.

"He's running with the tide, too. Want me to cut him loose, Jimmy?"

Jimmy, true to his fisher breed, scanned sea and sky and the receding islands before answering.

"Well, I figger—" His tone was a funny, unconscious echo of Ben's. "—it's a calm day, and we've got plenty of gas. Let's go."

They were going, without question. Green Point Light, marking the wickedest shoals on the coast, had dropped astern. Ahead were the white rips where the swift-flowing Kennebec entered the ocean. Jimmy scanned Ben's face. The rips were a bad place. But to lose that seven-hundred-pounder! To lose the boat that would help Father and all of them so much!

Were they slowing down? Jimmy tried to gage their speed by the distant land. The rope slackened, then drew taut again. The *Mary L.* swung round sharply. There was a sudden commotion

84

in the water. The huge fish's last struggle had begun. There was no mistake about it this time. Ben, with strained face, stood ready to cut the rope if the boat were endangered.

The struggle took some time. Jimmy, white and awed, found speech difficult.

"Ben, I'm sort of sorry for him."

Ben, with a flash of understanding rare in a lad brought up to consider all the creatures of the deep man's lawful prey, nodded gravely.

"Yes, but think what that big feller will mean to Pa, Jimmy. I guess Pa is really more important."

Jimmy kept his head turned away and thought hard of the boat which would make Ben's father independent and able to earn a living again when he was well. Ben's steady haul on the rope recalled him, as he drew the great carcass close to the boat, made it fast to the stern, started the engine, and headed for home.

As they rounded the wooded end of the island and entered the cove, little Reddy Soames caught sight of the boat and the dark mass towed behind. His shrill voice quickly emptied the post office and general store. When Ben brought his boat alongside the wharf there was a joyous crowd to welcome and praise him. Many hands helped prepare the fish for the weighing scales.

The crowd pressed forward. A little hush fell as Asa Smith leaned forward to read the scales.

"Gosh! Seven hundred and twenty pounds!"

A little cheer went up.

Jimmy seized Ben by the arm.

"Let's go quick and tell Pa and Ma. I want to be the first. If that Reddy Soames has dared to go—" He looked around anxiously.

"Aw, go on yourself, I'm here." A very red head bobbed indignantly.

So, amid the friendly laughter of their neighbors, Ben and Jimmy trudged over the hill toward home, conquerors in every line of their plain little figures.

Helen Gregutt
JAM SESSION AT ABBY'S

ILLUSTRATED BY *Sylvia Haggander*

ABBY TIGHE pinched herself. Five whole weeks at the academy hadn't convinced her that all this could be real and actually happening to her. The hard pinch left a red wheal on her arm, but nothing changed. Kay Torrence and Shirley Graff were very much alive on the big sofa. *Orange Juice* still blared from the radio, and in the cleared space before the couch, Alice and Jane continued practicing the samba energetically.

Abby drank in the scene. The Exchange didn't look like school, at least like any school she had ever been to before she was admitted to the academy. The Exchange was a bright room with deep armchairs, draperies, and a gaily decorated snackbar along one wall. Abby blessed the half scholarship that had made it possible for her to become part of this fine music school which had seemed so inaccessible.

"I don't really belong here," she thought, looking at Shirley admiringly. Among the eight girls who were second-year students, Shirley stood out. She was pretty, smooth, and an outstanding musician in a school that headlined musical talent. "Maybe they'll never know that I don't belong," Abby thought with awakening confidence.

"What started you, Abby?" Shirley asked, jerking Abby out of her thoughts.

"A toy piano." Abby laughed, realizing that the talk had turned inevitably to music. "Mother gave it to me when I was little, and she noticed how I loved it and picked out tunes by myself, so the family acquired a real piano and I started lessons." What she didn't tell Shirley was that the piano was a secondhand upright.

"It's a shame your mother's not alive to hear you play now," Kay said.

Abby flushed with pleasure at the implied praise, but an old ache started up inside her. Even when Mother was ill she had stubbornly insisted that Abby continue with her lessons. The expense of her mother's long illness and death had put Dad in debt, but Abby's music lessons never stopped. Only Dad had become a quiet, unsmiling man who never talked much to Abby about anything except her music, and now home was no more than a place to eat, sleep, and practice. Abby shook off the depressing thoughts, conscious that the talk had shifted.

"When do we start our jam sessions again?"

Abby looked at them inquiringly. The jam sessions were something she hadn't heard about.

"We all live in such scattered parts of the city," Shirley explained, "that last year we had weekly jam sessions, to give us a chance to get together outside of school one evening a week."

"Friday night was best," Kay picked it up, "because we could stay out later, and no studying. Each week we held the session at a different girl's house. That means you play hostess once in eight weeks."

Abby sat very still. It had to happen. She might have known. Things couldn't go on being perfect. She tried to imagine Kay and Shirley and the others in the tiny two-and-a-half-room walk-up she shared with Dad.

Kay had a paper and pencil. "Friday at my house," she said as she wrote. "Who's next?"

"Shirley!" Alice and Jane said together. "Her jam sessions were always best."

"I'll have to be third," Shirley laughed. "We're being painted."

Kay wrote swiftly. "Alice second. Shirley third. Jane fourth." She paused. "Can we make you fifth, Abby, and then fill in the rest when we see the other girls?"

Suddenly Abby was conscious of their eyes on her. There was no way out. She nodded dumbly. Five weeks was a long time, she consoled herself. But it wasn't really. Look how quickly these past five weeks had flown. Five weeks to build up in, and five weeks to be let down in. Why had she ever hoped these girls wouldn't find out she really didn't belong?

Mechanically she gathered up her books and followed the others out to the locker-room. She slid into the jacket of the glen-plaid suit Dad had bought for her, along with the other clothes that made her look in place at the academy.

"Can you stop at my house for a while, Abby?" Kay Torrence asked.

"Sorry, have to be home early," Abby answered quickly, unable to face the thought of Kay's house.

Now they were out on the street, saying good-bye. Abby struck out alone for the subway that would carry her to Brooklyn. The other girls lived in Manhattan, in homes that were probably all like Kay's. Last week Abby had visited Kay, and the memory of it was vivid. The Torrences lived in a modern apartment building overlooking Central Park. There was a doorman, a carpeted, mirrored entrance hall, an elevator man.

Abby lifted her head to the breeze. Her face felt hot and flushed. She was remembering how hard it had been not to show her amazement at the Torrences' apartment with its living room the size of a skating rink, its fireplace, and the beauty of the grand piano that was the focus of the room.

"You've got plenty to be grateful for, Abby Tighe," she scolded her blurred reflection in a grimy platform mirror. But the scolding didn't cheer her, and she boarded her train and rode glumly to her station.

She left the subway, turned off the boulevard, and walked down streets which grew progressively shabbier. She held her slim figure erect and set her small chin firmly. No use crying over what you didn't have, when you had so much in other ways. Hadn't there been Mr. Alessi, the music teacher in the public school she had attended, who had been quick to spot her talent and to encourage her? He had been the first to tell her about the academy.

"They have high standards, musically and scholastically," Mr. Alessi had told Abby, "but I'm sure you'd qualify."

"They have high tuition, too," Abby had answered. "Dad couldn't possibly afford it."

"They have half scholarships for promising musicians who couldn't afford to attend otherwise," Mr. Alessi had said thoughtfully.

Still Abby had been doubtful, but Mr. Alessi hadn't given up. When Dad had come to the school recital, Mr. Alessi had buttonholed him and told him about Abby, the academy, and the scholarship.

"She should have the chance," Dad had agreed. And the chance had been given her.

Abby walked up the steps of the old brownstone to which she and Dad had moved to make up the rest of the tuition money. She climbed the stairs to the third floor and fitted her key into the door of the apartment. The living room was small and its furnishings tired. At one end of the room a screen half concealed the kitchenette. There was a tiny cubbyhole that was Dad's room, and an old-fashioned bathroom.

Abby threw her books dispiritedly on the couch that served as her bed at night. Kay Torrence had a big bedroom to herself, with built-in shelves that housed her books, her own radio. Tears slid down her face.

Sure, the music was what counted, and she'd been more than lucky that Mother, Mr. Alessi, and Dad had helped her along. But music wasn't everything! She was young, and why couldn't she have some of what the other girls had? What would they think of this dreary hole-in-the-wall?

"Maybe I'll think of something," Abby tried to reassure herself. "I must."

But as the weeks slid by, she wasn't so sure. They were busy weeks, busier even than the first five. Besides the usual high-

89

school studies, there were the extra music classes and the private instruction with teachers who were exacting. Abby worked harder than she had ever imagined she could or would, and she found herself loving it.

The strange part was that the jam sessions were at once high spots and low spots. After the jam session at Kay's, Abby worried more than ever. Kay's house was all that Abby remembered and more, and Kay's mother, a fashionable, charming woman, had been on hand just long enough to welcome them and start the evening off smoothly. Kay had played her latest records, a set of Chopin's *Études* by Alexander Brailowsky.

The second session, at Alice Bowers', was no more consoling. The Bowers had a whole house to themselves, and when a maid appeared to serve refreshments after the girls had worked out their own orchestration of a piece Shirley had composed, Abby gave up.

"I won't go to any more jam sessions," she decided, "and then they won't expect me to have one."

The idea seemed sounder than a dismal try at entertaining, and she determined to have an excuse for next week. Remembering how eager the girls were for this jam session at Shirley's, Abby guessed how perfect her house must be.

It was Thursday before she summoned the courage to speak. She walked into the Exchange quickly, hating to face what she must do, but eager to get it over with. For the first time, she joined the girls without giving her usual quick look about.

"Jane's caught the measles from her little brother," Shirley told Abby ruefully. "She can't come tomorrow night, and she won't be able to have us at her house next week."

Abby's heart beat painfully. Her name was after Jane's on the list! How could she refuse now? Why had she waited so long? She opened her mouth to speak anyway, but Shirley was saying something else.

"Abby, you have such a long trip to Brooklyn. Would you like to come to my house right from school tomorrow? You could have dinner with us."

"I'd love to," Abby heard her own voice say. And she couldn't really be sorry that the words were out. She wanted to go to Shirley's, even if it meant holding the jam session at her house next week.

All the way home, determination hardened in Abby. There must be something she could do, and she would! Up in the apartment, she studied the living room grimly. For the first time she realized fully just how cramped and colorless it was. Mother had been so anxious to give Abby's musical talent full scope that she had never asked her to be domestic. Dad, in his turn, never expected her to do anything that might interfere with her practicing, and he had done all the moving and arranging with no help from her.

Abby's mind raced and ideas, some wild and impossible, rioted. She couldn't wait for dinner to end. When the dishes were put away and the usual conversation with Dad about her music finished, she faced him anxiously.

"Dad, there's something I'd like to do," she began slowly, and then the words rushed out. "That is, if you'll help me, and you've just got to help me. You see, I only have a week, and it means so much and—"

Dad looked puzzled, and Abby smiled at her confused beginning. She backed up and explained again slowly.

"There's no reason," she ended, "why even a small apartment can't be pretty, and without spending much money. I thought—if you approved, and would help me—we could re-

91

arrange the furniture, get rid of some things that just take up space, do some painting, dip the curtains a bright color."

The expression on her father's face stopped her. He didn't look tired any more, and his eyes were bright.

"It sure would look good to me," he said, and all at once it struck Abby that maybe Dad had missed a real home, too.

They made a list of what they would do and what they would need, and sorted out things that just made useless clutter. They kept interrupting each other with ideas and once they burst into laughter because they were talking together. Abby thought with surprise, "Why, I haven't laughed with Dad in years." After that she thought less of the girls and only of what fun it was to be planning with Dad about their home.

It was Dad who suggested cider and doughnuts for refreshments. "They're perfect for fall," he said hesitantly. "Your mother used to serve them at parties, and everybody loved them. No fuss, and inexpensive. Don't you think the girls would like them?"

When she fell into bed at last, Abby was content. She went to sleep immediately, and it seemed no time before morning.

"We take the El to my house," Shirley said when they left school that afternoon. "Will you be able to take the jam session next week?" she asked.

"I can take it all right," Abby answered lightly, "if you can. Dad and I live in a two-by-four, but we'd love to have you." But some of last night's sureness was gone.

"Wait till you see our mansion, and you'll be jealous," Shirley grinned.

Abby looked at her in surprise. It wasn't like Shirley to boast, yet— They were leaving the El. The neighborhood, Abby saw quickly, was as like the one in Brooklyn where she lived, only more so. But you could never tell about the east side of Manhattan. One minute you were in slums, and the next you were in the middle of swank.

But there was no swank about the building into which Shirley turned. "How's your wind?" she asked Abby. "Last year the girls had to take it in sections!"

Abby saw what she meant after the fourth floor. Shirley lived on the fifth floor, and the flights were steep and long. Abby was puffing before she was halfway up.

"This is how I keep my figure," Shirley laughed.

Everything happened so fast, after that, that Abby didn't have time to think. Shirley lived in a railroad flat, six rooms that ran straight through from front to back, each opening into the other. The kitchen was the only big room. Besides Shirley, there were her parents, two brothers, and a sister. Abby had never seen another household like this one. In the crowded, old-fashioned rooms the family talked, laughed, planned, shared, with a jaunty spirit that was infectious. Everybody helped prepare and serve dinner, and they ate with gusto in the midst of general teasing. Cleaning up was fun because they sang and told silly riddles. The girls arrived earlier than usual and stayed later, and Abby at last understood why.

It was still later when she made her way back to Brooklyn. Her feelings and her thoughts were confused, and she knew it would take time to sort them properly, yet one feeling, stronger than the others, emerged from the jumble. She had been right when she had thought music wasn't everything.

"But, I was right for the wrong reason," she found herself saying. Music wasn't everything, and neither was a house.

She fitted her key quietly into the lock and opened the door slowly. A tuneless whistle met her ears. She stood silently on the threshold. Dad was squatting on the floor in front of the old bookcase, whose contents had been spilled on the floor. He was wielding a paintbrush vigorously, and it dripped a Chinese-red paint that made a splash of color in the room, bright as a promise. The bookcase would be lovely, Abby thought fleetingly. But what really held her attention was the whistle. It sounded sweet and tuneful to her ears, because it had been years since she had heard it.

"Hi, Michelangelo!" she called softly.

Dad turned, and the grin made his face almost boyish. "Not bad, is it?" he asked.

"Wonderful!" Abby said, and her heart was in it.

Part II: FOR OLDER READERS

B. J. Chute

ANYBODY CAN SKI

ILLUSTRATED BY *Walter R. Sabel*

TOMMY ANDERSON raised his nose from his stamp album. "Anybody can be taught anything," he said firmly.

"That's ridiculous." Joe Keene, who had been lying with two sofa pillows under his head and his feet in the fireplace, sat up in outrage. "You're blithering."

"Not at all," said Tommy. "I taught myself stamp-collecting, beekeeping, and photography, all out of books. Even allowing for my natural genius—Did you grunt?"

"I did."

"Well, don't do it again. Even allowing for my natural genius, I still say that anybody can be taught anything."

"Some people, maybe," said Joe. "Anybody, no."

"Anybody," said Tommy, now completely sold on his theory. He paused to anchor Switzerland to the page, and then added, "Of course, a person has to *want* to learn."

Joe shook his head. "Wanting's no help. If it was, Dubby Wells would be the world's greatest athlete."

"Nothing's wrong with Dubby that a little applied intellect wouldn't cure."

Joe stifled a sob. "Thomas, how can you say such things? Why, the only time in his life Dubby got into a basketball game, he shot for the wrong basket and scored for the other side."

"He did?" Tommy, having stuck Nicaragua on the end of his nose where he could find it when needed, gave Joe an interested and slightly cross-eyed look. "How come he got into the game in the first place?"

95

"The whole team came down with colds, and Dubby went in as a substitute for a substitute for a substitute. The coach figured he couldn't do much harm, and the coach was wrong."

"Ah, well-a-day," said Tommy sympathetically. "Still a thing like that could happen to anybody."

"But it always happens to Dubby," Joe pointed out. "He means well and he tries hard, but he's just a natural-born calamity. He's probably the only guy in history who not only managed to knock himself out cold in a hurdle race but knocked out the guy next to him too. It took genius."

Tommy looked properly respectful. "A man like that should go far."

"And now," said Joe, "the poor deluded nut wants to join the Skiing Club."

"No soap?"

"None whatever. There's a feeling abroad that a member should be able to go down at least one hill, standing up. I know it's a very revolutionary idea, but that's the way we feel." Joe's sigh mounted from his shoelaces. "I like Dubby and I want him to be happy, but I'd rather have a kangaroo in the Skiing Club."

"You should teach him to ski the right way."

"Athletically speaking, there *is* no right way for Dubby."

"Anybody can be . . ."

". . . taught anything," Joe finished for him. "This is where I came in, and it just ain't so."

"It is too," said Tommy stubbornly, "and to prove it *I'll* teach him."

"To ski?" Joe burst into a merry peal of laughter. "You can't even ski yourself, you poor fish, much less teach Dubby."

"I can read a book," said Tommy coldly, "and that's all that's necessary." He rose and removed Nicaragua formally from his nose. "Good-bye."

"Where you going?"

"To the library. To get a book on skiing so I can teach Dubby."

Joe laid himself down tenderly, folded his hands and closed his eyes. "Now I've heard everything," he said. "Farewell."

"Farewell," said Tommy. He turned back for a moment to

place Nicaragua on Joe's brow and after that he departed.

Tommy surveyed the snowy landscape thoughtfully and then transferred his scholarly attention to Dubby Wells. Dubby, tall and thin and sprouting red earmuffs, reminded his teacher of a carelessly-built but eager afghan, an illusion greatly enhanced when Dubby moved forward on his skis, making progress in a sort of fluttering lope.

"Like that?" said Dubby, peering back over his shoulder.

Tommy looked into his "How to Ski" book, borrowed from the public library and snugly wrapped in a kitchen towel to protect it from drafts and snow. He read three pages, scowling, and shook his head. "Try it again. It says here it should be an easy, rhythmical motion."

Dubby tried it again. It was rhythmical, in the way that a rather dreamy camel is rhythmical. Tommy told himself that the camel was a noble animal and said "Okay" without much conviction. "Now," he went on, "you're supposed to learn to turn around before you learn to go downhill. Can you turn around?"

"Sure," said Dubby, and began to inch one ski sideways and then follow it up with the other. The rate of progress was very stately and rather like a minuet.

"All wrong," Tommy informed him briskly. "You're supposed to kick one ski up front, pivot with it, lay it down, and bring the other ski around. Here, look in the book."

Dubby looked, and a happy smile wreathed his ears. "Why, that's wonderful. It turns you right around."

"You learn to do that," Tommy promised, "and the Skiing Club will be begging you to join." He gave himself a mental pat on the back. All this poor guy needed was a sensible, scholarly approach.

"Now," he said instructively, "when I say One, put your right pole forward and your left pole back. When I say Two, kick your left ski out and up. And when I say Three, pivot it and lay it flat in the snow. Got it?"

"One, poles," Dubby repeated. "Two, left ski up. Three, swing around. I've got it."

"Ready, set . . . ONE!" Tommy gazed upon his pupil with

97

pride, one pole forward and one pole back. There may have been a slight unsteadiness east and west, but north and south he looked perfectly lovely. "Two," he said, "left ski up . . . GADZOOKS!"

He wouldn't have thought it was possible. Dubby's ski, rising alertly from the snow, had contrived to sock its owner square on the nose. This splendid achievement had apparently exhausted him, and he immediately lay down full length in the snow and made exotic noises. "How on earth did you manage to do that?" Tommy demanded.

Dubby said that his legs were too long. He said they always got in his way. "Extraordinary," said Tommy with a kind of reluctant admiration and scooped Dubby out of the snow. "Now, this time, take it slower."

"Yes," said Dubby meekly.

"Are your poles right? Okay, now, bring your ski up—I'll hold you. Steady to port, old man, steady—Ahhhhh." He peered over Dubby's shoulder approvingly; the position arrived at was definitely the number two position in the book. "Do you feel safe?"

"Sort of," said Dubby uncertainly.

"Good. Because I'm leaving you." He backed off cautiously, Dubby stayed upright, and Tommy returned to his book. "All right. You now swing the upright ski around and lay it parallel to the right ski, with its point going in the opposite direction. Swing!"

98

Dubby swung. He swung magnificently; in fact, he swung too far. The left ski landed directly on top of the right ski, effectively nailing its owner to the ground.

"Go back!" said Tommy.

"I can't."

"Go forward?" said Tommy in a small voice. It was, he realized, a foolish question. Dubby had gone all the forward that was possible. "How do you *do* these things?" he asked vainly.

"I don't know. They just happen." There was a pause. "What do I do now, Tommy?" he asked plaintively.

It was a time for frankness. "I can't imagine," said Tommy. "I could take you home and put you in the garden and we could grow vines up you, I suppose." He looked into his book again, but there was nothing in it about first aid to trellises. The next page, however, dealt with something called a herring-bone, a method for skiing uphill. After all, skiing was a downhill sport and, to go downhill, one must learn to go up. Also, it seemed to be a project in which long legs might come in useful.

"I think the thing for you to do is to fall down," he decided. "Later on in the book, there's a whole page about falling down, and you might as well get the experience early.—Oh, very nice! You fall beautifully, Dubby."

Dubby removed his face from the snow and requested politely that Tommy take his right ski out of his left ear. This was not easy, as Dubby seemed to have more legs than a centipede, but nothing was too much trouble for an old friend.

"There, there," said Tommy soothingly, propping him upright once more. "Now, look, Dubby, we're going to abandon the kick turn for the moment and come back to it later. I want to teach you to herring-bone uphill. You'll like that."

"No kick turn?"

"Not just now," said Tommy. "I'm not as young as I was ten minutes ago." He referred in a businesslike manner to his book. "The herring-bone is really very simple. All you do is kick your left ski out, shift your weight, stick your right ski out, shift your weight again, and so onward and upward with the arts."

99

Dubby humped himself around obediently until he was facing the slope. He swung his left ski out and stamped on it, and then turned his attention to the right ski. Steam coming out of his ears, he stamped his way up five steps more and then came to a sudden stop. "Go on," said Tommy, "you're doing fine."

"I can't go on."

"Why on earth not?"

"Something's standing on my tail," said Dubby plaintively. "I can't move."

Tommy lumbered uphill through the snow to investigate. It was quite true; Dubby's right ski was firmly anchored by his left one, a variation on the theme of his kick turn. "Lift the left ski," said Tommy.

"Can't."

"Slide the right one out, then."

"Can't."

It seemed to Tommy that what some people lacked was initiative. "Well, hold on, and I'll hoist the left ski up for you. When I hoist, you get the right ski loose and go on from there."

On paper, it would have been a splendid idea. Unfortunately, when Tommy yanked up the left ski, the right one—over-stimulated by its sudden freedom—galloped backwards, with Dubby still on board. Tommy, caught off-balance, went flat on his face in the snow. Dubby, encountering obstacles, went backwards, his arms flailing wildly. He landed with his feet going uphill and his head downhill, squarely on top of Tommy who was traveling in the opposite direction. Together, they presented a pretty, if confusing, pattern in the snow.

Tommy was the first to speak. His voice had a bitter, snowy, and subterranean sound. "Get offa me," he said.

"How?" asked Dubby, rather in the manner of an upper berth speaking to a lower berth.

"Never mind how," said Tommy, flapping about restlessly below. "Just get off before I smother. Roll sideways, you idiot. Do something!"

Dubby rolled, and after a brief and vigorous quarrel with the hillside Tommy managed to stagger erect. He gazed upon

Dubby glumly. "I don't understand it," he said. "Does this kind of thing always happen to you?"

Dubby nodded. "Generally."

"Well, it's remarkable. Look, we'll try going downhill. After all, that's really what the Skiing Club seems to want." He then added thoughtfully, "Once you get in, it's their worry if you knock all the members out."

"Huh?" said Dubby.

"Nothing," said Tommy hastily. He took a look at the hill. "This isn't too steep. We'll go to the top, and you try coming down."

"Shall I herring-bone up?"

"Uh, no. Go sideways or something. It takes longer, but I'm not insured."

Together, they surged upwards at the rate of about one surge a minute, Tommy filling in the pauses by studying his book. By the time he got to the summit, some of his enthusiasm had revived, and he was back at his "This is really very simple" philosophy.

"All you have to do, Dubby, is assume the correct posture

101

and let nature take its course. Bend the waist, flex the knees, and balance on the balls of the feet. Your knees do flex, don't they? Splendid. Yes, that's right. You look just like the picture." He admired him for a moment, and then said blithely, "Now give yourself a brisk push forward with your poles . . ."

Dubby pushed, shot forward, and went approximately ten feet downhill, arms, legs, poles, and ears waving discordantly. At this point, as Tommy had promised, nature took its course. Dubby's bent waist joined his flexed knees, his knees sank to the balls of his feet and, rolled up like some impassioned hedgehog, Dubby went the next several yards in a state of violent disintegration.

"It's incredible," said Tommy to himself, and went to join him. Dubby rose from the snow in a localized blizzard and gave himself a shake. Tommy went on talking in a mystified manner. "I don't understand it. In the book, it looks perfectly simple."

"It's different on skis," Dubby assured him.

"Yes, I suppose it is, but, even so, there's something about the way *you* do do it . . . Dubby, get out of those skis for a minute and let me try them, huh?" He frowned. "Maybe my theory's wrong. Maybe a person can't be taught skiing out of books, although I must say this one seems perfectly straightforward."

He took the skis from Dubby, strapped them on, and glanced rapidly into his book again. Then he nodded, gripped the poles, edged himself around, and started off.

For a moment, life seemed terribly perilous, until he remembered the instructions about bending forward and balancing on the balls of his feet, and, shouting a proud song in praise of himself, he succeeded in maintaining a perpendicular attitude to the bottom of the hill. "Ha! Quite simple," said Tommy, and took a look at the hill behind him. Truly, it wasn't much of a hill, but still it was his first, and he felt he had acquitted himself in a highly scientific manner.

He waited while Dubby galloped through the snow to his side. "You didn't fall down," said Dubby, obviously incredulous.

"I followed instructions."

Dubby's ski contrived to sock its owner square on the nose.

"*I* followed instructions, Tommy. My feet get in the way."

"They do, don't they?" Tommy scratched his ear. "You know what, Dubby? I think the trouble with you is that you don't have a scholarly mind. I think you need to have everything translated to you in dynamic action."

"Dynamic action?" said Dubby wanly.

Tommy nodded with great wisdom. "Exactly. You need to *see* a thing done, instead of being told about it."

"I don't get it."

Tommy sighed, although this proved his point. "Listen," he said patiently, "*I* learn from the book, you learn from me. I'll borrow some skis somewhere, and tomorrow afternoon we'll come out again. I'll try it on skis first, and then I'll teach you."

"Well . . . it might work."

"It's going to work," said Tommy determinedly. "I'm going to teach you to ski if it's the last thing I ever do."

By the end of the week, Tommy had developed a passionate dislike for everything to do with snow, especially the way it sparkled softly in the sunshine and then turned to solid rock when a person landed on it.

On the other hand, Dubby seemed to be acquiring a slight mastery over his feet, and in fact had arrived upright at the bottom of the hill several times, although on each occasion he had collapsed at his destination, presumably from shock. Tommy's efforts to teach him the rudiments of a snowplow, intended to slow the skier up in time of crisis, finally had to be abandoned. "After all," Tommy decided, "once we get you into the Skiing Club, your fellow-members can teach you all the fancy bits." He suppressed a moment's pity for Dubby's fellow-members and concentrated instead on Joe Keene's astonishment when he should observe the success of Tommy's theories on learning how to ski.

In spite of progress, however, there still seemed to be no visible limit to the ways in which Dubby could get into trouble. If he started with his skis together, they separated and he fell between them. If he started with them safely apart, they crossed and he finished the tour on his nose. If there was a bush or tree

103

within ten miles, some strange internal radar caused Dubby to head for it like a homing pigeon and plunge himself into branches up to the ears.

Because of this, Tommy was obliged to inaugurate a System. The system consisted of his going downhill ahead of Dubby to make a track for his earnest student to follow. This restricted Dubby's rather unusual creative talents somewhat, and the tenth time that Dubby landed upright at the bottom of a hill, in Tommy's tracks, Tommy decided he was ready for a tryout with the Skiing Club.

"Or as ready as you'll ever be," he added. "If we wait much longer, it'll be summer."

Dubby sighed. "You'll come with me, won't you, Tommy?"

"To the tryout? I wouldn't miss it for the world."

Neither, it turned out, would the Skiing Club. Joe Keene had been busy notifying all concerned, and a fascinated audience assembled to observe the fruits of Tommy's intellectual approach to what was considered an insoluble athletic problem.

Joe, as president, welcomed Dubby gravely and presented him with the hill which he was expected to navigate. It was a rather fine hill, steeper than the ones they had been practicing on, but absolutely clear of any kind of foreign entanglements. Not a bush marred its pure expanse. It was impossible to see how Dubby could get into any kind of trouble, if he would only remember what he had learned.

Tommy accompanied him to the top and helped him strap on his skis. "Lean-forward-relax-bend-your-knees-and-balance-on-the-balls-of-your-feet," he said rapidly.

"There's no track to follow," said Dubby.

"Of course there's no track, you idiot. It's a lovely clear hill."

"It's much easier with a track. I don't get mixed up in things."

"Dubby! There's nothing to get mixed up in here." He took a look around and changed his mind. The onlookers had infiltrated and were lining the hill. Tommy was not the man to be caught off guard. "There's your track, right there," he said cheerily. "Just stay between the people."

"I don't think . . ."

"You aren't supposed to think. Just ski."

"You know how I feel?" said Dubby. "I feel just the way I did when I tried out for the swimming team."

"What happened?"

"I sank."

"Dubby, old man," said Tommy earnestly, "will you please kindly stop brooding on your past glories and pay attention to what you're doing? After all, my honor is just as much at stake as yours. Relax. All you have to do is go downhill."

"Standing up," Dubby amended.

"Well, yes, that would help." He gave Dubby's shoulder a bracing pat. "Stick your poles in, and just shove off."

Dubby pushed his chin out about six inches, adopted the look of a Roman gladiator, and jammed his poles firmly into the snow. "Okay, here I go," he said, and pushed. Unfortunately, he had jammed his poles in not wisely but too well. His feet went, and the rest of him stayed behind with the poles. Dubby lay down in the snow.

A cheer arose from the spectators. Tommy wailed. "Dubby! You never did that before!"

Dubby sat up, and Tommy hauled him to his feet and gave him a shake. "You know better than that," he said crossly. "Now, this time do it right."

Dubby gulped audibly, nodded, and pushed off again. He achieved a promising start and then, inscrutably, managed to shift his weight over his right ski. Considering that Tommy had wasted several days trying to teach Dubby to stem-turn by exactly this method, it seemed hard that the talent should blossom forth within him so suddenly and at such a moment. Dubby veered to the right, and spectators scattered. Only one moved too late. That was the one that Dubby hit.

Tommy gave a moan and buried his face in his hands. Someone touched his shoulder, and he turned to find Joe Keene looking at him sympathetically. "Look, Tommy," Joe said kindly, "don't you think you and Dubby better go home and take up some quiet sport like tatting? I hear there's nothing quite so exhilarating as tatting down the homestretch."

"You shuddup," said Tommy. "Anyone can have a couple of spills, and anyhow it's not Dubby's fault that the hill's all cluttered up with people." He stalked off to rescue his unhappy friend. "Dubby," he said earnestly, "pay close attention to me. Do you think you could get down that hill in one piece if I go ahead of you and make a track?" Dubby nodded. "Well, then, that's what I'm going to do. There's no law against it, and anyway this is a very unusual situation." He turned toward the skier who had been the victim of Dubby's gallant charge. "Can I borrow your skis?"

"Oh, sure," said the victim, who was still taking snowballs out of his collar. He sounded rather huffy. "Don't mind me."

"Thank you kindly. Now, look, Dubby, give me time to get out of the way, and then you follow my tracks. Don't look at the audience, don't think about the Skiing Club. JUST FOLLOW MY TRACKS."

"Just follow your tracks," said Dubby wisely.

"That's right." Tommy fastened his skis on, picked up the poles, and led the way.

Joe greeted him inquisitively. "Where you going?"

"I'm making a track for Dubby."

"You?"

"Me." With an air of calm conviction, intended to mobilize Dubby's nervous system, Tommy took his place at the top of the hill with Dubby behind him. "I'm going to make it nice and wide so you can't miss," he said sternly. "If you *do* miss, I'm going to come back and make you into mincemeat pie. Okay?"

"Okay," said Dubby.

Tommy gave himself a gentle push forward, gradually forcing the tails of his skis out and bringing the points together. He had studied the snowplow enough to realize that this would assure a conservative progress through the snow, leaving a boulevard for his student to follow.

It worked splendidly. An elephant could have followed the track he was preparing, even a dignified elephant with a poor sense of balance. Unfortunately, Tommy was not dealing with an elephant; he was dealing with Dubby.

106

Halfway down the hill, stately and controlled, Tommy heard a sudden shout. He looked back over his shoulder.

Dubby had shoved off. With the uncanny sense of timing of a cuckoo clock gone berserk, lured by the splendid trail he had to follow, as confident now as he had been unnerved before, Dubby flew in Tommy's wake.

Tommy screeched, stopped snow-plowing, and gave a frantic push with his poles, trying to race his doom to the finish line. It was hopeless. Dubby overtook him in a matter of seconds, there was a spectacular instant of collision, and then the two skiers, intricately tangled together, rolled, bounced, thumped, and battered their way to the bottom.

Dubby was the first to rise. After a moment, Tommy sat up stiffly, not speaking. He undid his skis and pushed them aside. He reached over, still in a state of terrible calm, and undid Dubby's. He then staggered to his feet and took Dubby by the hand. "Come," said Tommy.

"Where?"

"Away," said Tommy in hollow tones.

"Away where?"

"Anywhere," said Tommy, "so long as it's away from skis."

"I'm awfully sorry," said Dubby. "I started too soon."

"Well, you're finished now," said Tommy. "In a year or two, my bones may knit themselves together, but I very much doubt it." Limping, he led the way off the field of battle.

Dubby started to speak, thought better of it, and followed him. The Skiing Club watched them go.

Several hours later, Joe Keene found them. They were in the living room of Tommy's home, Dubby sitting cross-legged on the floor with Tommy's stamps spread around him, Tommy lying on the sofa with eight cushions located at his more tender points.

They both looked up as Joe walked in, and Tommy said two words. He said, "Go away."

Dubby said, "Where does an Australian stamp go?"

"Under Australia. . . . Joe, go away. I don't like you."

"That's gratitude," Joe said. "I only dropped by to . . ." He broke off, suddenly aware of what was going on. "Dubby! What on earth are you doing?"

Dubby looked up, beaming proudly. "Fixing Tommy's stamps."

"Fixing his stamps? He wouldn't let the Postmaster-General himself do that."

"He's letting *me*," said Dubby happily. "You see, Joe, Tommy's been talking to me, and he's convinced me that I'm not really suited to athletics. He says my type of brains needs a more satisfying outlet, so he's teaching me philately."

Joe said thinly, "He's teaching you what?"

"Philately. Stamp-collecting." Dubby looked at Joe with beatific calm. "You see, you have an athlete's mind—you don't even know what philately means." He got to his feet with tremendous dignity. "I'll be over tomorrow, Tommy, and put some more stamps in for you, and you can explain about perforations." He handed the album graciously to its owner, nodded to Joe with the gravely superior air of one who has come to realize that brains are mightier than brawn, and made a thoroughly well-adjusted exit.

Joe watched him go. "Well, I'll be darned," he said softly.

"Philately." He looked at Tommy, but Tommy was sitting bolt upright, peering into his stamp album and making loud moaning noises. "Oh, no," said Tommy. "Oh, no!"

"Oh, no, what?"

Tommy hit himself distractedly on the brow. "Joe! He's stuck at least half those stamps in upside down."

Joe regarded him with a certain sympathy. "I don't see what else you could expect, you chump. What possessed you to let him loose in your precious stamps?"

Tommy drew a deep breath, calming himself somewhat. "Because the alternative was absolutely unthinkable," he said sternly. "Joe, do you realize that lunatic actually wanted me to go on teaching him to ski? After what happened this afternoon! Me without a single muscle I can call my own. No!" He gave his stamp album a remorseful pat. "This is a terrible sacrifice, Joe, but it's worth it. I never want to see a snowflake again as long as I live."

There was a short but profound silence. Then Joe said, "Tommy, old man, I have some news for you. After you and Dubby left, the Skiing Club met and elected a new member."

"As if I cared," said Tommy callously. "Give me his name and I'll send flowers. I . . ." He broke off. There was something about Joe's expression that caused him to turn pale. "Joe! You don't mean . . ."

"Yes, old man," said Joe. "We elected *you*. Unanimously." He gave his friend a hearty pat on the shoulder. "And I must say, Tommy, that I think you deserved it. With a little coaching, you'll make a very fine skier."

There was a sound of groaning. Tommy collapsed against his pillows, and the stamp album fell from his nerveless fingers. He closed his eyes.

Joe looked at him thoughtfully. If there had been a lily nearby, he would have put it into Tommy's hand. Instead, he carefully removed his Skiing Club badge from the front of his own jacket, pinned it to Tommy's shirt, just under his chin, and then tiptoed softly out of the room.

Tommy opened one eye. "This," said Tommy, "is . . ."

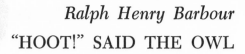

Ralph Henry Barbour

"HOOT!" SAID THE OWL

ILLUSTRATED BY *Seymour Fleishman*

Hᴵˢ name was Ernest Pitts. He came to Potter's School about a month after Fall Term began, and they stuck him over in Avon House. There were eight of us in Avon when school began, and then they dumped Pitts in Room E, which is only large enough for one, and then there were nine. Room E is over the downstairs hall and beastly cold in winter, but Pitts seemed to think it was all right. He seemed to think everything was all right, which was one reason he had such a hard time. Of course we pied his bed the first night, and somebody piled some books on top of his door so that they fell on him when he pushed it open. And the next day Zack McIntosh, who is House Leader, sent him on some fool errand, and the rest of us wrecked his room something scandalous. He took it beautifully. Never said a word. So, seeing that he liked it, we kept on deviling him.

He was seventeen and pretty sturdy looking, but he sure was quiet and sober. You couldn't get him to talk much. He just looked at you, serious-like, through a pair of those tortoise-rimmed spectacles and said "Yes" or "No" or "Thank you." Zack dubbed him "The Owl" and the name stuck. After two or three days we older chaps let up, but the youngsters, Samson, Browne, Jewel, and Stockman, kept right on making his life miserable. Once he flared up—the time Bob Glenn glued some of his photographs together face to face. That was a couple of days after he arrived and the only time he showed fight. Zack, though, stopped the ruckus and gave the Owl a lecture.

110

"We don't pull that sort of stuff here, Pitts," he said severely. "If you must fight you come to me and I'll arrange it for you all nice and orderly. But you mustn't get mad because someone plays a joke on you."

"Was—was what he did—a joke?" gasped the Owl.

"Sure it was."

"And I—don't do anything—about it?"

"You just laugh it off, kid. Always keep your temper. Any fellow who can't take a joke doesn't belong in Avon."

Well, Zack's a big fellow and has an important way with him, and the Owl was impressed. After that, no matter what was done to him—and the kids pulled off some pretty raw stuff, I thought—he never seemed to resent anything. If he did he didn't let anyone know it. He didn't laugh, but he did keep his temper. I was sort of sorry for him, even if he was such a dumbbell, and advised him one day to hand Lige Stockman or one of the others a punch in the nose, but he looked at me like I was talking treason or something. It seemed as if he never would get good sense! But, shucks, you just can't tell about folks.

The day after Thanksgiving, or, rather, the night after, we were sitting around the fire in the parlor. Bob Glenn and Joe Dewar—Joe was my roommate in Room C—were playing parchesi, but the rest of us were just talking and yawning and feeling bored to death. There didn't seem to be a blessed thing to talk about that night. Then, finally, Zack said: "Gosh, fellows, I wish there was something we could do tomorrow!"

Charlie Jewel suggested challenging the Simms House gang to a game of baseball, but we all sat on him. Then I said: "How about hare-and-hounds, Zack?"

"Paper-chase stuff?" Zack yawned. "Too much trouble. We'd have to tear up newspapers for a couple of hours. Maybe it will be warm enough for some tennis."

We knew well enough it wouldn't be, but there wasn't any use saying so. A couple of minutes passed and then the Owl asked in a sort of apologetic voice, "Do you ever play Fox and Hunters?"

He was sitting off at one side, and when we all turned to look at him—on account of that being about the first time he had ever spoken without being asked—he seemed painfully embarrassed.

"What," inquired Zack sarcastically, "is that, young Pitts?"

"It—it's a game the Indians play—the Wampoo Indians."

"Never heard of the Wampoo Indians," said Zack. "Never heard of the game, either. How's it played, Owl?"

So the Owl explained, sort of breathlessly, looking very solemncholy with the firelight reflected on the big round lenses of his specs. You chose one fellow for the Fox, and the rest were the Hunters. The Fox carried a freshly peeled stick which was called the Brush. The Hole was wherever you started from —say the front door. The Fox had a ten-minute start and had to go to a certain place agreed on beforehand and put the Brush there. Then his stunt was to get back to the Hole without being tagged by one of the Hunters. If he did he won and took the Brush. If he didn't the Brush went to the fellow who had caught him, and he had lost.

"I don't get it," said Zack. "What's to prevent the Hunters from sitting on the doorstep and waiting for the Fox to come back?"

"That's against the rules," said the Owl earnestly. "You see,

there's the Lair. The Lair is a half-mile circle around the Hole. That is, it's the ground inside the circle. And the Hunters must go outside that and mustn't return inside it until the Fox does. You see, it's played like this. The Fox starts out first with the Brush. Then the Hunters start. The best runner makes straight for the Scent—"

"The what?" I asked. It sounded to me like the Owl was making it up as he went along. Or it did at first. Afterwards I decided he wasn't.

"The Scent," said the Owl. "That's the place where the Brush is hung. They call it hanging the Brush, you know."

"Oh," said I. "All right. Then what?"

"He goes straight to the Scent and gets the Brush. He has to do that because if he didn't the Hunters wouldn't know whether the Fox had really gone that far, don't you see. The other Hunters don't have to go any further than just outside the Lair if they don't want to. Of course if they stick too close there's the chance the Fox may sneak by and get to the Hole before they can run him down. Generally some of the Hunters scout around about halfway to the Scent, and the others watch the roads nearer the Hole. Of course the Fox can make a wide circle, which is what real foxes generally do, and come back to the Hole from the other side, if you understand what I mean. So the Hunters have to keep spies posted all around. If the Fox is seen the one who sees him shouts 'Yoick!' and that lets the others know what's up."

"Sounds complicated," said Joe.

"Sounds like awful rot," I said. "Say, how far's this Scent place from where you start, Owl?"

"It may be any distance you like, but it's usually about two miles. If it's much longer than that it—it slows the game up. I just mentioned it because you spoke about wanting something to do, and it's a good cold-weather game."

"You've played it, eh?" said Zack. "What were you, a Hunter or a Fox?"

"I've never been a Hunter yet," answered the Owl sort of regretfully. "You see, I'm a pretty fair runner and fellows generally don't want to go so far, so—so they choose to be Hunters. Of course it's easier. Even if you're Head Huntsman—"

"Who's he?" asked Ray Samson.

"He's the one who goes and gets the Brush where the Fox has left—has hung it. Even he doesn't have to do as much running as the Fox because after he's got the Brush he can take his time about coming back."

"You'd make a good Head Huntsman, Bim," said Zack.

"Not with this bum knee of mine," I told him. I'd hurt it playing scrub football a week or so before and it was still on the fritz. So the choice fell on Joe. Charlie Jewel wanted to be the Fox, but Zack told him to dry up, that the Fox would have to be some fellow who knew all about the game. "Young Pitts will be Fox," he said.

"Really," protested the Owl, "I—I—"

"Shut up. You're elected. Maybe you can be a Hunter next time—if there is a next time. Say, you guys, let's try it!"

Well, we sat and made plans, and it didn't look to me as if the Fox would have the ghost of a chance to get back. For one thing, we chaps knew the ground thoroughly, while the Owl had scarcely been out of bounds since he arrived. We set three o'clock the next afternoon as starting time, after Joe had positively refused to run any earlier on account of our always having roly-poly for dessert on Saturdays. And for once the Owl went to sleep without a thing happening to him!

He was late to dinner the next day and got a couple of hard looks from Mrs. Candish, our matron. He explained, when Zack called him to account, that he had been over to the big boulder a mile and three-quarters away, selected as the Scent. "I thought," he said seriously, "that I ought to know how to get to it. That was fair, wasn't it, McIntosh?"

Zack said he supposed so, but he didn't look pleased.

The Owl got away pretty close to the minute, swinging a willow wand he had peeled and running like he meant to be back before the rest of us got started. I wasn't feeling very ambitious myself, partly on account of a bum knee but more especially because Mrs. C's roly-poly was feeling mighty heavy

114

under my sweater. So when it came time for the Hunters to take off I did not hurry any. First thing I knew the others had left me away behind, and I sat down on Magoun's stone wall and thought it over. It seemed to me seven fellows were enough to attend to one Fox, so pretty soon I went back to the house and up to the room. From the south window I could see three or four of the gang spreading out across the landscape about half a mile off. The Owl wasn't in sight—he'd cut around behind Magoun's big barn, across the road from the house, and we never had seen him after. And Joe, who was a pretty good runner, had long since taken to the woods beyond the farmer's cornfield. The sun was shining, but it wasn't doing so well at it, and the afternoon was blamed chilly. So I didn't think I'd made such a rotten decision. I had my feet on top of the radiator and had read about a dozen lines in a book when I heard the front door open and close. Of course I thought it was another Hunter who had got cold feet and sneaked home, and I tiptoed out into the hall to surprise him. But I was the surprised one, for it was the Owl, and he was coming upstairs whistling softly and swinging that Brush. He had his head down and didn't see me, and I beat it back into the room and slipped behind the door.

At first I couldn't make it out. He couldn't have done three and a half miles across rough country in eighteen or twenty minutes, of course. Besides, he still had the willow stick! Then I got it, and I began to laugh so hard that it was a wonder he didn't hear me. He would have, I guess, if he hadn't been making a lot of noise himself. The Owl was having a beautiful joke on the whole bunch of us!

Well, that was a bit of a jolt, but I had a stiffer one a moment later when it dawned on me that the Owl wasn't making all that noise in his own room but in Zack's! I tried to see what was happening, but I was at the back of the house and Room A was at the front, and looking through the crack of the door got me nothing. I listened there three or four minutes, and then curiosity pretty nearly got the better of me, and I was just on the point of finding out, when the Owl came out of A and down the hall to B, right opposite me. He seemed very happy and was whistling a funny little tune. He had got rid of his cap and the willow stick—Brush I mean—and had a piece of paper in his hand. He pushed open the door of Samson's and Browne's room and, since he left it open, I had a fine view of proceedings. And what I saw sure made my eyes stick out. The Owl was methodically wrecking the joint!

He tore the beds to pieces, turned the study table upside down and dumped the contents in a sheet. Then he took a length of rope from a pocket, gathered the corners of the sheet together, tied the rope around them and hung the whole thing out of a window. He changed the drawers in Ray's dresser to Peter's and put Peter's in Ray's. He took down four framed pictures and rubbed soap all over the glasses and then hung them up again facing the walls. He gathered all the loose photographs and such truck from the dressers, climbed on Peter's bed, and tucked them along the molding. He took the bulb from the drop-light and set it afloat in the water pitcher. He made a pyramid of all the shoes in the closet on the over-turned table and then sprinkled a ring around it with a box of talcum powder. Finally he took some squares of cardboard from a pocket, selected one, and leaned it against the drop-light, which was looking silly on the floor. The card had one word on it, printed in big black letters—"HOOT!"

He started across the hall then, and I did the first thing that occurred to me. I dropped to the floor, rolled under my own bed and then under Joe's. Of course the sensible thing would have been to chase him out, but somehow I was enjoying it. You see, here was the downtrodden, much-abused Owl, who had had his own room wrecked half a dozen times and who had had about everything done to him that anyone could think of, getting his innings. It was certainly what they call poetic justice, and I just lay there under Joe's bed and never made a sound. I could see his feet and legs as he moved around and hear his whistling and I could see the furniture assembling strangely in the middle of the room. He didn't work hurriedly, but he sure was thorough!

116

Presently what I'd been expecting right along happened. Mrs. C. called sort of nervously from the foot of the stairs: "Wh—who's that up there?"

"It's only me, ma'am," said the Owl reassuringly. "Pitts."

"My sakes! I thought it was a burglar! What are you doing in that room, Ernest?"

"I'm doing aplenty," answered the Owl cheerfully.

"Doing *what?*" The Owl didn't answer, but went right on whistling and piling things up, and I heard the stairs creak as Mrs. C. decided to see for herself. Then I saw her feet at the doorway, and, "*Sakes alive!*" she exclaimed. "Ernest Pitts, are you *crazy?*"

"No, ma'am."

"Then—then—now, look here, you stop that at once! Why, what do you suppose those fellows will say?"

"How do I know, Mrs. Candish?" the Owl asked reasonably enough. "That's what I'm going to find out."

"Why—why, the *idea!* Stop, I tell you! Do you hear me? Do you want me to telephone to Mr. Potter?"

"I'd rather you didn't." There was an awful crash and a shriek from Mrs. C. "It's all right," said the Owl soothingly. "It looks just as well there. You don't want things too stiff!"

"I'm going to telephone to the Cottage!" Mrs. C. was getting a bit hysterical. "I'm going to have Mr. Potter come *right over* and—"

"No, ma'am, he's gone to Walpole."

"Then—then when he comes *back you will hear* from him, young man! I would not be surprised if you were *expelled* for this, not one *bit* surprised! It's—it's perfectly *criminal!*"

"How come it wasn't criminal when they upset *my* room, ma'am? And broke my water pitcher so I had to buy me a new one? And pasted my photographs together and poured water on my mattress and—"

But Mrs. C. was beating it downstairs, still muttering. I thought it was about time to crawl out then and take a hand, and so I did, and when I looked at what that young villain had done I couldn't help getting a bit peeved. He didn't hear me until I was standing up, and then he didn't look half as surprised as I expected him to. He didn't look scared, either.

"Oh!" he said. "I thought I didn't see you with the rest of the Hunters, Taylor."

"You darn little rat!" I said. "Get out of here before I skin you!"

He was leaning against the door now, but it didn't occur to me that he was up to anything until he said, sort of smiling: "Not a rat, Taylor. An Owl. And this is my day to hoot!" And with that he slipped out quick, closed the door behind him, and turned the key from the outside! I made a run for it, but I was too late, and the door was locked fast. Then something slid into sight underneath it, and the Owl said from outside: "I forgot to leave my card, Taylor. I'm pushing it through." I picked it up, and of course it was another of those "Hoot!" things. Well, it began to strike me funny again by that time, so I put the card against Joe's suitcase, which was the apex, as you might say, of the pile, and got out the window. It was easy enough to walk along the roof to the next room, and fortunately the kids had left their windows open. The Owl was just starting things in Room D, and he looked a bit discomfited when I slid in. He stopped whistling and stared at me doubtfully through his specs, but I said: "Don't let me cramp your style. It's your day, sure enough, and I'm not going to interfere a mite."

"Gee," said the Owl gratefully, "that's mighty decent, Taylor, because I'd hate to show partiality, and if I didn't mess things up in here Charlie and Lige might think I hadn't treated them square."

"Owl," I chuckled, "there's more to you than I thought there was. How'd you happen to think of this magnificent scheme?"

"Well—" The Owl stopped stuffing Jewel's clothes into a pillow slip and sat down on a bed. "You see, Taylor, things couldn't go on like they've been going forever. It—it gets a little wearing after a while. And Zack McIntosh said I mustn't get mad, you know. So I didn't. I thought that perhaps if I gave them all a taste of their own medicine they might take the hint and let me alone."

118

"Fine!" I said. "But have you thought what they're going to do to you when they get back?"

"Do to me?" asked the Owl, sounding surprised. "Why, they won't do anything to me, Taylor. They can't, can they? Didn't McIntosh say the thing to do was laugh it off?"

"Yes, I heard him say that, but—look here! Hadn't you better hurry along?"

"Oh, there's lots of time." He looked at his watch. "They won't be back for an hour yet, I guess."

"They won't, eh? Let me tell you something. Just as soon as Joe gets to the rock and doesn't find the—the whatyoucallit—"

"Brush?"

"Yeah. Well, don't you see that he will know you haven't been there at all and beat it back here as fast as—"

"Oh, but he will find it," said the Owl calmly.

"He *will*? How come?"

"Because I put it there this noon."

"You—for the love of Mike! You mean you had *two* and—"

The Owl nodded. "Yes, I stuck one there about half past twelve. I guess he won't suspect anything. They'll wait around until about dark and then I'll let them know I'm back. Of course they may get tired before that. It's pretty fairly cold today."

"Kid," said I, "you're a marvel! Look here, about that game. Where'd you see it before? Was it really played by the Whatyoucallit Indians?"

"The Wampoos? N-no, not exactly. I had to make up that part. Of course if there were any Wampoos they *might* play it."

"Then you never—you made up the whole business?"

He nodded modestly. "Yes, but really, Taylor, I believe it would be a pretty good game if—if you really played it!"

Well, I had to laugh then, and while I was doing it the Owl got busy again. After I'd wiped my eyes I lent him a hand with Samson's steamer trunk, which he kept under his bed. It was too heavy for the Owl alone. We put it out on the roof, and the Owl draped it with Charlie's pajamas and held the pajamas down with four books and a tooth mug. Finally he took a slip

of paper out of his pocket and looked at it. Then he got three big books, set the door so we could squeeze out, and balanced them on the top of it. "I almost forgot that," he murmured. "Lucky I looked at my list, wasn't it?"

"Mean you made a list of—of things?" I gasped.

"Oh, yes. I wanted everything quite fair, you know. Maybe I've forgotten one or two things. In fact, I'm pretty sure it was Browne who put kerosene on my toothbrush, but I'm not certain; it may have been Stockman. So I'll leave that out. Well, that's about all, I think. Except this." He arranged the last of his "Hoot!" signs against a pair of Charlie's shoes on the radiator and looked around in a pleased, satisfied way. "Looks all right, don't you think?"

"It looks grand," I agreed. "They won't know it, Owl."

The Owl chuckled, which was about the first time I'd ever heard him come so close to laughing. "It does look different, doesn't it? And—and infinitely better?"

"Infinitely," said I.

We went into his room and had quite a talk. He was a heap calmer than I would have been in his place. He told me quite a little about himself and his home and his folks, and we got real thick while the afternoon wore away and twilight gathered. Finally the Owl said: "It's awfully comfortable in here, isn't it? I mean more comfortable than it would be standing around outdoors." I grinned and said: "Zack chose the top of Barnard's

121

Hill for himself. Of course you can see further from there, but it's a chilly place." The Owl nodded soberly, and then after a minute, he said: "I suppose I'll get fired for this, but it's worth it!" I told him I guessed Mrs. C. would listen to reason and that he didn't have to worry nearly so much about what old Potter would do to him as what would happen when the gang got back! And just then we heard them coming up the drive!

"I guess," said the Owl, "I'll just lock the door, so if you want to go—"

I went. When Zack and the rest came in, looking just about frozen, I was in the parlor. Joe had the Brush all right, but he threw it on the table and began to beat his hands together. Of course they were all sore on me, but I had a good alibi. I said: "Well, what happened?" And Zack muttered something and started upstairs, and the others followed, Joe saying stubbornly. "Here? Of course he isn't! Haven't we been watching the place for more than an hour? I tell you—" And then the storm broke!

I piled upstairs and gathered with the rest about the door of Zack's room. At first it didn't look so awfully different, but a second look revealed several changes.

For instance, all Zack's ties were knotted end to end and looped from the transom to the electric fixture. It was very effective in a decorative way, but Zack did not approve. There were other changes, too. Almost everything movable had been laid on the floor, so it would have been very risky to have walked around much. Bob was trying to separate two of his photographs which had somehow got glued together. I guess Zack saw me grinning, for he yelled: "You did this, you big hunk of cheese!"

"Who? Me?" I shook my head. "That isn't *my* visiting card."

I pointed to the square of white cardboard on Zack's chiffonier. Zack turned and stared at it. Everyone else looked, too. " 'Hoot!' " growled Zack. "What's 'Hoot' mean? Wh—"

"Hoot! Hoot! Hoot!"

Everyone jumped. The sound came from Owl's room. They hadn't noticed before that the door was closed, but now Zack and Bob made a rush for it.

122

"Pitts! Are you in there?" howled Zack, rattling the knob.

"*Hoot!*" said Pitts.

"Did you—did you—" But words failed Zack and Bob picked on me.

"He wouldn't have done it if someone hadn't put him up to it," he sputtered. "Bim helped him!"

"Is that so?" I asked. "If you think so go and have a look at my room!"

"*Wha-a-at!*" yelped Joe, and made a dash for C. And all the others went to look at *their* rooms, and oh, boy, what a rumpus there was! Zack was begging the Owl to unlock his door. He said he wanted to speak to him. The Owl said he could understand him perfectly with the door locked.

"Pitts," said Zack with awful calm, talking close to the door so the other could hear him, "you might as well come out right now!"

"*Hoot!*" said the Owl.

"If you don't it'll be the worse for you!" Zack tried to break the door down, but it only bulged. "I'm going to whale the daylights out of you, you fresh kid!"

123

"Why, McIntosh!" said the Owl. "You sound angry! It's only a joke. You can take a joke, can't you?"

"Joke, eh? I'll joke you!" I could almost hear Zack's teeth grating.

"But you mustn't be angry," the Owl protested. "You must laugh it off!"

"Listen," I said, "the whole bunch of you. Come in my room and stop talking a minute. I've got something to say." I finally got them there and induced them to shut up. Then I talked. When Joe learned that the stick he had been lugging around all afternoon was a fake I thought he'd throw a fit, but I got them grinning when I described the Owl talking to Mrs. C., and after a bit even Zack saw that there wasn't anything to do but take it smiling. "You see, you poor goops, he hasn't done a thing to any of us that we didn't do to him first, even to pasting Bob's photos together," I said. "Those things were jokes when we did 'em, and they've just got to be jokes now. Yes, sir, fellows, we've got to laugh it off!"

After a while we all went back to the Owl's door.

"Owl," I said, "it's all right. You can open up now."

"Are you laughing it off?" asked the Owl.

"Sure."

"I don't hear you."

"Ha, ha!" said Zack like it hurt him a little.

Then the key turned, the door opened, and Pitts stood staring at us gravely through those specs of his. "You darn little shrimp!" chuckled Joe.

"Shrimp?" Young Pitts shook his head gravely. "No, Dewar, I'm an Owl, and this is my day to hoot!"

We nodded.

And he hooted.

Owen Johnson

BEAUTY'S SISTER

ILLUSTRATED BY *Hilda Frommholz*

"His hair it is a faded white,
His eye a watery blue;
He had no buttons on his coat,
No shoestrings in his shoe."

B EAUTY" SAWTELLE, or Chesterton V. Sawtelle, as it was pronounced when each Monday the master of the form read the biweekly absences from bath, sat adjusting his skate on the edge of the pond, with a look of ponderous responsibility on the freckled face, crowned by a sheaf of tow hair, like the wisp of a Japanese doll. Presently he drew from his pocket a dance-card, glanced over it for the twentieth time, and replaced it with a sigh.

"Cracky!" he said, in despair. "Sixteen regulars and eight extras; sixteen and eight, twenty-four. Gee!"

Beauty's heart was heavy, and his hope faint, for the sinister finger of the Prom had cast its shadow over the lighthearted democracy of boyhood. Into this free republic, where no thoughts of the outside society should penetrate, the demoralizing swish of coming petticoats had suddenly intruded its ominous significance of a world without, where such tyrannies as money and birth stand ready to divide the unsuspecting hosts.

Now Beauty's woes were manifold: He was only a second former, and the Prom was the property of the lords of the school, the majestic fourth formers, who lived in the Upper House, and governed themselves according to the catalogue and a benevolent tempering of the exact theory of independence.

A few rash under-formers with pretty sisters were admitted on sufferance, and robbed of their partners if the chance arose.

125

Beauty, scrubby boy of fourteen, with a like aversion to girls and stiff collars in his ugly little body, had been horrified to learn that his sister, at the invitation of Rogers, the housemaster, was coming to the Prom. On his shoulders devolved the herculean task of filling a card from the upper class, only a handful of whom he knew, at a moment when the cards had been circulated for weeks. So he stood dejectedly, calculating how to fill the twenty-four spaces that were so blank and interminable. Twenty-four dances to fill, and the Prom only two weeks off!

In the middle of the pond boys were darting and swaying in a furious game of hockey. Beauty lingered, biding his opportunity, searching the crowd for a familiar face, until presently, Wash Simmons, emerging from the melee, darted to his side, grinding his skates and coming to a halt for breath, with a swift: "Hello, Venus! How's the Dickinson these days?" [The Dickinson was a dormitory.]

Beauty, murmuring an inaudible reply, stood turning and twisting, desperately seeking to frame a demand.

"What's the secret sorrow, Beauty?" continued Wash, with a glance of surprise.

"I say, Wash," said Beauty, plunging—"I say, have you got any dances left?"

"I? Oh, Lord, no!" said the pitcher of the school nine, with a quick glance. "Gone long ago."

He drew the strap tight, dug his hands into his gloves again, and with a nod flashed back into the crowd. Beauty, gulping down something that rose in his throat, started aimlessly to skirt the edge of the pond. He had understood the look that Wash had given him in that swift moment.

In this abstracted mood, he suddenly came against something angular and small that accompanied him to the ice with a resounding whack.

"Clumsy beast!" said a sharp voice.

From his position, Beauty recognized the Red Dog.

"Excuse me, Red Dog," he said hastily; "I didn't see you."

"Why, it's Beauty," said the Red Dog, rubbing himself. "Blast you! all the same."

"I say, Red Dog," said Beauty, "have you any dances left?"

"All gone, Beauty," answered Red Dog, stooping suddenly to recover his skate.

"Nothing left?"

"Nope—filled the last extra today," said Red Dog, with the shining face of prevarication. Then he added, "Why Venus, are *you* going to the Prom?"

"No," said Sawtelle; "it's my sister."

"Oh, I'm sorry. I'd like to oblige you, but you see how it is," said Red Dog, lamely.

"I see."

"Ta, ta, Beauty! So long!"

Sawtelle shut his lips, struck a valiant blow at an imaginary puck, and began to whistle.

> " 'Tis a jolly life we lead
> Care and sorrow we defy—"

After piping forth this inspiring chorus with vigorous notes, the will gave way. He began another:

> "To Lawrenceville my father sent me,
> Where for college I should prepare;
> And so I settled down,
> In this queer, forsaken town,
> About five miles away from anywhere."

The bellows gave out. Overcome by the mournfulness of the last verse, he dropped wearily on the bank, continuing doggedly:

> "About five miles from anywhere, my boys,
> Where old Lawrenceville evermore shall stand;
> For has she not stood,
> Since the time of the flood—"

Whether the accuracy of the last statement or the forced rhyme displeased him, he broke off, heaved a sigh, and said viciously: "They lied, both of 'em."

"Well, how's the boy?" said a familiar voice.

Beauty came out of the vale of bitterness to perceive at his side the great form of Turkey Reiter, preparing to adjust his skates.

"Oh, Turkey," said Beauty, clutching at the straw, "I've been looking everywhere—"

"What's the matter?"

"Turkey, I'm in an awful hole."

"Out with it."

"I say, Turkey," said Sawtelle, stumbling and blushing—"I say, you know, my sister's coming to the Prom, and I thought if you'd like—that is, I wanted to know if—you wouldn't take her dance-card and get it filled for me." Then he added abjectly: "I'm awfully sorry."

Turkey looked thoughtful. This was a commission he did not relish. Beauty looked particularly unattractive that afternoon, in a red tobogganing toque that swore at his faded white hair, and the orange freckles that stared out from every point of vantage.

"Why, Beauty," he began hesitatingly, "the way it is, you see, my card's already filled, and I'm afraid, honestly, that's about the case with all the others."

"She's an awfully nice girl," said Sawtelle, looking down in a desperate endeavor to control his voice.

"Nice girl," thought Turkey, "ahem! Yes; must be a good-looker, too, something on Venus's particular line of beauty."

He glanced at his companion, and mentally pictured a lanky girl, with sandy hair, a little upstart nose, and a mass of orange freckles. But between Turkey and Sawtelle relations had been peculiar. There had been many moments in the last year at the Dickinson when the ordinary luxuries of life would have been difficult had it not been for the superior financial standing of Chesterton V. Sawtelle. The account had been a long one, and there was a slight haziness in Turkey's mind as to the exact status of the balance. Also, Turkey was genuinely grateful, with that sense of gratitude which is described as a lively looking forward to favors to come.

"Oh, well, young un," he said with rough good humor, "give us the card. I'll do what I can. But, mind you, I can't take any myself. My card's full, and it wouldn't do for me to cut dances."

Jumping up, he started to escape the effusive thanks of the overjoyed Sawtelle, but suddenly wheeled and came skating back.

"Hello, Beauty!" he called out, "I say, what's your sister's name?"

"Sally—that is, Sarah," came the timid answer.

"Heavens!" said Turkey to himself as he flashed over the ice. "That settles it. Sally—Sally! A nice pickle I'm in! Wonder if she sports spectacles and old-fashioned frocks. A nice pickle—I'll be

129

the laughingstock of the whole school. Guess I won't have much trouble recognizing Beauty's sister. Whew! That comes from having a kind heart!"

With these and similar pleasant reflections he threaded his way among the crowd of skaters until at length he perceived Hickey skimming over the ice, stealing the puck from a bunch of scrambling players, until, his progress checked, and the puck vanishing into a distant melee, he came to a stop for breath. Turkey, profiting by the occasion, descended on his victim.

"Whoa there, Hickey!"

"Who it is!"

"How's your dance-card?"

"A dazzling galaxy of beauty, a symposium of grace, a feast of—"

"Got anything left? I have a wonder for you if you have."

"Sure; twelfth regular and sixth extra—but the duchess will be awfully cut up."

"Twelfth and sixth," said Turkey, with a nod; "that's a go."

"Who's the heart-smasher?" asked Hickey, with an eye on the approaching puck.

"A wonder, Hickey; a screamer. There'll be nothing to it. Ta, ta! Much obliged."

"What's her name?"

"Sawtelle—some distant relative of the Beauty's, I believe. I'm filling out her card. Obliged for the dance. Ta, ta!"

"Hold up!" said Hickey, quickly. "Hold up! Jiminy! I almost forgot—why, I do believe I went and promised those two to Hasbrouck. Isn't that a shame! Sorry. To think of my forgetting that! Try to give you some other. Confound it! I have no luck." With the most mournful look in the world he waved his hand and sped ostentatiously toward the bunch of players.

"Hickey's on to me," thought Turkey as he watched him disengage himself from the crowd and skate off with Sawtelle; "no hope in that quarter."

Finally, after an hour's persistent work, during which he pleaded and argued, commanded and threatened, he succeeded in filling exactly six of the necessary twenty-four dances. Indeed, he would have had no difficulty in completing the card if he could have passed over that fatal name. But each time, just as he was congratulating himself on another conquest, his victim would ask, "By the way, what name shall I put down?"

"Oh—er—Miss Sawtelle," he would answer nonchalantly; "a distant relative of the Beauty—though nothing like him—ha! ha!"

Then each would suddenly remember that the dances in question were already half-promised,—a sort of an understanding; but of course he would have to look it up,—but of course, if he found they were free, why, then of course, he wanted, above all things in the world, to dance with Miss Sawtelle.

"Well, anyhow," said Turkey to himself, recapitulating, "I've got six, provided they don't all back out. Let me see. I can make the Kid take three—that's nine—and Snookers will have to take three—that's twelve,—and, hang it! Butcher and Egghead have got to take two each—that would make sixteen. The other eight I can fill up with some freaks: some will snap at anything."

That night at the supper-table Turkey had to face the music.

"You're a nice one, you are," said Hickey, starting in immediately, "you arch deceiver. You are a fine friend; I have my opinion of you. 'Handsome girl,' 'a wonder,' 'fine talker,' 'a screamer'—that's the sort of game you try on your friends, is it? Who is she? Oh—ah, yes, a *distant* relative of the Beauty."

"What's up now?" said the Kid, editor of the "Lawrence," and partner of Turkey's secrets, joys, and debts.

"Hasn't he tried to deceive you yet?" continued Hickey, with an accusing look at Turkey. "No? That's a wonder! What do you think of a fellow who tries to pass off on his friends such a girl as the Beauty's sister?"

"No!" said Butcher Stevens.

"What!" exclaimed MacNooder, laying down his knife with a thud.

"Beauty's sister," said the Egghead, gaping with astonishment.

"Well, why not?" said Turkey, defiantly.

"Listen to that!" continued Hickey. "The brazenness of it!"

The four graduates of the Dickinson, after a moment of stupefied examination of Hickey and Reiter, suddenly burst into roars of laughter that produced a craning of necks and a storm of inquiries from the adjoining tables.

When the hilarity had been somewhat checked, Hickey returned to the persecution of the blushing Turkey.

"Bet you three to one she's a mass of freckles," he said. "Bet you even she wears glasses; bet you one to three she's cross-eyed; bet you four to one she won't open her mouth."

"Hang you, Hickey!" said Turkey, flushing, "I won't have her talked about so."

"Did you take any dances?" said the Kid to Hickey.

"Me?" exclaimed the latter, in great dudgeon. "Me! Well, I guess not! I wouldn't touch that tribe with a ten-foot pole."

"Look here, you fellows have got to shut up," said Turkey, forced at last into a virtuous attitude by the exigency of the situation. "I promised the Beauty I'd fill his sister's card for him, and I'm going to do it. The girl can't help her looks. You talk like a lot of cads. What you fellows ought to do is to join in and give her a treat. The girl is probably from the backwoods, and this ought to be made the time of her life."

"Turkey," said the malicious Hickey, "how many dances have you eagerly appropriated?"

Turkey stopped point-blank, greeted by derisive jeers.

"Oho!"

"That's it, is it?"

"Fake!"

"Humbug!"

"Not at all," said Turkey, indignantly. "What do you think I am?"

"Pass over your list and let's see the company you're going to introduce her to," said Hickey, stretching out his hand for the dance-card. "Ah, I must congratulate you, my boy; your selection is magnificent; the young lady will be charmed." He flipped the card disdainfully to the Egghead, saying, "A bunch of freaks!"

"Hang it all!" said the Egghead, "that's too hard on any girl. A fine opinion she'll have of Lawrenceville fellows! We can't stand for that."

"Look here," said the Kid, suddenly. "Turkey is at fault, and has got to be punished. Here's what we'll do, though: let's each take a dance on condition that Turkey takes her out to supper."

"Oh, I say!" protested Turkey, who had other plans.

The others acclaimed the plan, gleefully rejoicing in his discomfiture, until Turkey, driven to a corner, was forced to capitulate.

That evening on the esplanade he called Snookers to him, and resting his hand affectionately on the little fellow's shoulder said, "Old man, do you want to do me a favor?"

"Sure."

"I'm filling up a girl's card for the Prom, and I want you to help me out."

"Certainly; give me a couple, if the girl's the real thing."

"Much obliged. I'll put your name down."

"Second and fifth. Say, who is she?"

"Oh, some relative of Sawtelle's—remember you used to go with him a good deal in the Dickinson. It's his sister."

"Whew!" said Snookers, with a long-drawn whistle. "Say, give me three more, will you?"

"Hardly," answered Turkey, with a laugh; "but I'll spare you another."

"I didn't think it quite fair to the girl," he explained later, "to give her too big a dose of Snookers. Queer, though, how eager the little brute was!"

The last week dragged interminably in multiplied preparations for the great event. In the evenings the war of strings resounded across the campus from the "gym," where the Banjo and Mandolin clubs strove desperately to perfect themselves for the concert. The Dramatic Club, in sudden fear, crowded the day with rehearsals, while from the window of Room 65, Upper, the voice of Biddy Hampton, soloist of the Glee Club, was heard chanting "The Pride of the House is Papa's Baby" behind doors stout enough to resist the assaults of his neighbors.

Oil-stoves and flatirons immediately came into demand, cushions were rolled back from window seats, and trousers that were limp and discouraged, grew smooth and well creased under the pressure of the hot iron. Turkey and Doc MacNooder, who from their long experience in the Dickinson had become expert tailors, advertised on the bulletin board:

REITER AND MacNOODER
Bon Ton Tailors
Trousers neatly pressed, at fifteen cents per pair;
all payments strictly cash—IN ADVANCE.

Each night the dining room of the Upper was cleared, and the extraordinary spectacle was seen of boys of all sizes in sweaters and jerseys, clasping each other desperately around the waist, spinning and bumping their way about the reeling room to the chorus of:

"Get off my feet!"

"Reverse, you lubber!"

"Now, *one*, two, three—"

"A fine lady you are!"

"Do you expect me to carry you around the room?"

"Darn you, fatty!"

"Hold tight!"

"Let 'er rip now!"

From the end of the room the cynics and misogynists, roosting

134

on the piled-up tables and chairs, croaked forth their contempt:

"Oh, you fussers!"

"You lady-killers!"

"Dance, my darling, dance!"

"Squeeze her tight, Bill!"

"That's the way!"

"Look at Skinny!"

"Keep a-hoppin', Skinny!"

"Look at him spin!"

"For heaven's sake, someone stop Skinny!"

Of evenings certain of the boys would wander in pairs to the edge of the woods and confide to each other the secret attachments and dark, forlorn hopes that were wasting them away. Turkey and the Kid, who were going as stags, opened their hearts to each other and spoke of the girl, the one distant girl, whose image not all the fair faces that would come could for a moment dim.

"Kid," said Turkey, in solemn conclusion, speaking from the experience of eighteen years, "I am going to make that little girl—my wife."

"Turkey, old man, God bless you!" answered the confidant, with nice regard for old precedents. Then he added, a little choked, "Turkey, I, too—I—"

"I understand, Kid," said Turkey, gravely clapping his shoulder; "I've known it all along."

"Dear old boy!"

They walked in silence.

"What's her name?" asked Turkey, slowly.

"Lucille. And hers?"

"Marie Louise."

Another silence.

"Kid, is it all right?"

The romanticist considered a moment, and then shook his head.

"No, Turk."

"Dear old boy, you'll win out."

"I must. And you, does she care?"

135

A heavy sigh was the answer. They walked back arm in arm, each fully believing in the other's sorrow, and almost convinced of his own. At the esplanade of the Upper they stopped and listened to the thumping of the piano and the systematic beat from the dancers.

"I wish it were all over," said Turkey, gloomily. "This can mean nothing to me."

"Nor to me," said the Kid, staring at the melancholy moon.

On the fateful day the school arose, so to speak, as one boy, shaved, and put on a clean collar. Every boot was blacked, every pair of trousers creased to a cutting edge. The array of neckties that suddenly appeared in gigantic puffs or fluttering wings was like the turn of autumn in a single night.

Chapel and the first two recitations over, the esplanade of the Upper was crowded with fourth formers, circulating critically in the dandified throng, chattering excitedly of the coming event. Perish the memory of the fashion there displayed! It seemed magnificent then: let that be the epitaph.

The bell called, and the group slowly departed to the last recitation. From each house a stream of boys came pouring out and made their lagging way around the campus toward Memorial. Slower and slower rang the bell, and faster came the unwilling slaves—those in front with dignity; those behind with despatch, and so on down the line to the last scattered stragglers, who came racing over the lawns. The last peal sounded, the last laggard tore up Memorial steps and vanished within. A moment later the gong in the hall clanged, and the next recitation was on. The circle, a moment before alive with figures, was quiet and deserted. A group of seven or eight lounging on the esplanade were chatting indolently, tossing a ball back and forth with the occupant of a third-story window.

At this moment Turkey emerged from the doorway in shining russets, a Gladstone collar, a tie of robin's-egg-blue, and a suit of red and green plaids, such as the innocent curiosity of a boy on his allowance goes to with the thirst of possession.

"Hurrah for Turkey!" cried the Kid. "He looks like a regular fashion-plate."

136

In an instant he was surrounded, punched, examined, and complimented.

"Well, fellows, it's time to give ourselves them finishing touches," said the Egghead, with a glance of envy. "Turkey is trying to steal a march on us. The girls are coming."

"Hello!" cried the Kid, suddenly. "Who's this?"

All turned. From behind Foundation House came a carriage. It drove on briskly until nearly opposite the group on the steps, when the driver reined in, and someone within looked out dubiously.

"Turkey, you're in luck," said the Gutter Pup. "You're the only one with rouge on. Go down gracefully and see what the lady wants."

So down went Turkey to his duty. They watched him approach the carriage and speak to someone inside. Then he closed the door and spoke to the driver, evidently pointing out his destination, for the cab continued around the circle.

Then Turkey made a jump for the esplanade, and, deaf to all inquiries, seized upon his roommate and dragged him aside.

"Great guns! Kid," he exclaimed, "I've seen her—Beauty's sister! She isn't like Beauty at all. She's a stunner, a dream! Look here! Get that dance-card. Get it, if you have to lie and steal. He's in recitation now. You've got to catch him when he comes out. For heaven's sake don't let anyone get ahead of you! Tell him two girls have backed out, and I want five more dances. Tell him I'm to take her to the debate tonight, and the Dramatic Club tomorrow. Kid, get that card!"

Releasing his astounded roommate, he went tearing across the campus to meet the carriage.

"What's happened to our staid and dignified president?" cried the Gutter Pup in wonder. "Is he crazy?"

"Oh, say, fellows," exclaimed the Kid, overcome by the humor of the situation, "who do you think that was?"

The carriage had now stopped before the Dickinson, and Turkey, arrived in time, was helping out a tall, slender figure in black. A light flashed over the group.

"Beauty's sister."

"No!"

"Yes."

"Impossible!"

"Beauty's sister it is," cried the Kid; "and the joke is, she's a stunner, a dream!"

"A dream!" piped up the inevitable Snookers. "Well, I guess! She's an all-around A-No. 1. Gee! I just got a glimpse of her at a theater, and I tell you, boys, she's a paralyzer."

But his remark ended on the air, for all, with a common impulse, had disappeared. Snookers, struck with the same thought, hastened to his room.

Ten minutes later they reappeared. Hickey, in a suit of pronounced checks, his trousers carefully turned up *à l'Anglais*, glanced approvingly at the array of manly fashion.

"And now, fellows," he said, pointing to the Chapel, which Turkey was entering with Miss Sawtelle, "that traitor shall be punished. We'll guard every entrance to Memorial, capture our friend, 'Chesterton V. Sawtelle (absent from bath),' relieve him of that little dance-card, and then, Romans, to the victors belong the spoils!"

The Kid having delayed over the choice between a red-and-yellow necktie or one of simple purple, did not appear until Hickey had stationed his forces. Taking in the situation at a glance, he chuckled to himself, and picking up a couple of books, started for the entrance.

"Lucky it's Hungry and the Egghead," he said to himself as he passed them and entered the Lower Hall. "Hickey would have guessed the game."

He called Sawtelle from the second form, and, slipping his arm through his, drew him down the corridor.

"Sawtelle," he said, "I want your sister's dance-card. There's some mistake, and Turkey wants to fix it up. Thanks; that's all. Oh, no, it isn't either. Turkey said he'd be over after supper to take your sister to the debate, and that he had seats for the Dramatic Club tomorrow. Don't forget all that. So long! See you later."

In high feather at the success of this stratagem, he skipped

138

downstairs, and, avoiding Hickey, went to meet Turkey in the Chapel, where he was duly presented.

When Sawtelle emerged at length from the study-room, he was amazed at the spontaneity of his reception. He was no longer "Beauty" or "Apollo" or "Venus."

"Sawtelle, old man," they said to him, "I want to see you a moment."

"Chesterton, where have you been?"

"Old man, have you anything to do?"

Each strove to draw him away from the others, and failing in this, accompanied him to the jiggershop, where he was plied with substantial flattery, until, having disposed of jiggers, soda, and eclairs, he cast one lingering glance at the tempting counters and said with a twinkle in ugly little eyes:

"And now, fellows, I guess my sister must be over at the house. Come around this afternoon, why don't you, and meet her?"—an invitation which was received with enthusiasm and much evident surprise.

When the Prom opened that evening, Beauty's sister made her entree flanked by the smitten Turkey and the languishing Hasbrouck, while the stricken Kid brought up the rear, consoled by the responsibility of her fan. Five stags who had been lingering miserably in the shadow searching for something daring and imaginative to lay at her feet, crowded forward only to be stricken dumb at the splendor of her toilette.

Beauty's sister, fresh from a Continental season, was quite overwhelmed by the subtle adoration of the famous Wash Simmons and of Egghead, that pattern of elegance and *savoir-faire*—overwhelmed, but not at all confused. Gradually under her deft manipulation the power of speech returned to the stricken. Then the rout began. The young ladies from city and country finishing schools, still struggling with their teens, were quite eclipsed by the gorgeous Parisian toilette and the science of movement displayed by the sister of Chesterton V. Sawtelle. The ordinary ethics of fair play were thrown to the winds. Before the eyes of everyone, Turkey held up the worthless dance-card and tore it into shreds. Only the brave should de-

serve the fair. Little Smeed, Poler Fox, and Snorky Green struggled in vain for recognition, and retired crestfallen and defrauded, to watch the scramble for each succeeding dance, which had to be portioned among three and often four clamorers.

In fact, it became epidemic. They fell in love by blocks of five, even as they had sought the privileges of the measles. Each implored a memento to fix imperishably on his wall. The roses she wore consoled a dozen. The Gutter Pup obtained her fan; the Kid her handkerchief, a wonderful scented transparency. Glendenning and Hasbrouck brazenly divided the gloves, while Turkey, trembling at his own blurting audacity, was blown to the stars by permission to express in a letter certain delicate thoughts which stifle in the vulgar scramble of the ballroom.

When the last dance had been fought for, divided, and redivided, and the lights peremptorily suppressed, the stags *en masse* accompanied Beauty's sister to the Dickinson, where each separately pressed her hand and strove to give his "Good night" an accent which would be understood by her alone.

On that next morning that somehow always arises, Turkey and the Kid, envied by all, drove her to the station, listening mutely to her gay chatter, each plunged in melancholy, secretly wondering how she managed to conceal her feeling so well.

They escorted her to the car, and loaded her with magazines and candies and flowers, and each succeeded in whispering in her ear a rapid, daring sentence, which she received from each with just the proper encouragement. Then, imaginary Lucilles and Marie Louises forgot, they drove back, heavy of heart, and uncomprehending, viewing the landscape without joy or hope, suffering stoically as men of eighteen should. Not a word was spoken until from the last hill they caught the first glimmer of the school. Then Turkey hoarsely, flickering the air with the last of the whip, said:

"Kid—"

"What?"

"That *was* a woman."

"A woman of the world, Turkey."

They left the carriage at the stable and strolled up to the jiggershop, joining the group, all intent on the coming baseball season; and gradually the agony eased a bit. Presently a familiar little figure, freckled and tow-headed, sidled into the shop, and stood with fists jammed in empty pockets, sniffing the air for succor.

"Oh, you Beauty! oh, you astonishing Venus!" cried the inevitable persecutor. Then from the crowd MacNooder began to intone the familiar lines:

> "His hair, it is a faded white,
>   His eye a watery blue;
>   He has no buttons on his coat,
>   No shoestrings in his shoe."

"Doc," said the Beauty, blushing sheepishly, "set me up to a jigger, will you? Go on, now!"

Then MacNooder, roaring, shouted back: "Not this year; next year—Sister!"

William Heyliger

HIT OR ERROR?

ILLUSTRATED BY *Walter R. Sabel*

NO ONE would ever have picked Buck Everts to blossom forth as an inspiration. Not that there was anything wrong about him, but he had built up a national reputation as a tough nut, a baiter of umpires, a snarling wrangler when close decisions went against him. You remember Buck, of course. Third baseman for the Panthers when that fast-stepping team won three pennants in a row, and rated by the critics as the greatest man who had ever played the hot corner.

After the third pennant Buck was caught in a streetcar accident, and his right arm was broken in two places. That finished him with baseball. He could still handle anything that came at him, high, low, or on the side, but his throwing arm was gone. A third baseman has a long peg to first, and he must let the ball go on a line. With a fast man streaking it down to first, the throw must be just a white streak. Buck, with that smashed arm, couldn't do it.

He dropped out of baseball and came to Woodbury to take charge of the lumberyard of the Woodbury Coal & Lumber Company, which was owned by old John Everts, a second or third cousin. The Everts home stood next to the home of Horace Hicks, the man who was owner, publisher, and editor of the Woodbury *Herald*. Old John took Buck in to live with him—and there's where Jimmy Hicks comes into the story.

Jimmy was sixteen. Thrown on his own resources, circumstance might have toughened him and turned him to a fighting pitch. He had found life too easy and had grown soft. His

143

pathway had been smoothed, and it came to pass that, in time, he instinctively chose the road of least resistance. His rangy build suggested athletic possibilities; he liked baseball, but for two years at Cromwell Academy he had avoided the fight for place on the school nine. He had musical ability, but had never bothered to cultivate it. He had opinions, but never expressed them. Confronted with a contrary viewpoint, he smiled pleasantly and politely yielded. A disdainful Cromwell boy had once called him a jellyfish. This was not strictly true. It would have been more to the point to dub him a sloth who had never developed a backbone.

The day that ended his sophomore year at Cromwell he came back to Woodbury and the next morning walked down to the office of the *Herald*. The editorial room had an early morning air of desertion. His father, in a little walled-off space, was running his eyes through a stack of out-of-town newspapers. Two men were wading through the overnight copy. The reporters had not yet begun to straggle in from their districts, and all the desks in the center of the room were empty and idle. The door leading to the composing room opened, and the sport editor came through carrying a sheaf of damp galley proofs.

"Hello, Jimmy," he greeted. "Back from school, eh? Remember the time last summer you said Buck Everts was the greatest third baseman in the game? Well, you can tell him all about it now; he's your next-door neighbor."

"Buck?"

"Buck himself. I'm running the story this afternoon. Funny none of us ever knew that John Everts is his cousin. He's come to Woodbury to work in the lumberyard, and he's living right next to you. His baseball days are over, but he certainly was a bearcat in his time. Look him up; he's worth knowing."

Jimmy, for all his polite aloofness, had found time to worship at the shrine of two heroes. One of these was Buck; the other was Arlie Pierce, star pitcher of the Cromwell nine. His worship of Buck had been open; his veneration of Arlie had been secret. Arlie was the campus idol. The biggest fellows in the school

144

flocked in his wake. Jimmy, not used to going out for what he wanted, could not even go out for friendship. He hung on the edge of a crowd of worshipers, a mere shadow, reluctant to push forward and claim his share of attention. At the end of two years Arlie scarcely knew his name.

With Buck things had been different. The Panthers' third baseman had the vague, legendary quality of one who lives far away. Jimmy could speak of him with freedom, as he might speak of the King of Siam, and never expect to meet him. But now Buck was here, and the same shrinking that had held him aloof from Arlie began to work its spell on him again.

At noon, from the safe retreat of his porch, he watched Buck come home to eat—a short, rugged man who cocked his cap to one side and walked with a swagger that was well known to the fans in the big league cities. He saw the man go back to work, and his heart fluttered. An urge that he could not explain sent him that afternoon toward the village field with bat, ball, and glove. Hours later, he came back, with the whistle of the paper mill across the river booming its hoarse notice of quitting time. He dropped on the grass of the lawn, the bat across his knees, and was there when Buck Everts came swaggering up the street.

The big leaguer, almost at the Everts's porch, saw him, hesitated, and then came striding across the grass.

"You the fellow who thinks I was the greatest third baseman in the game?" Buck's grin was wide and friendly. "The sport's ed was telling me about you. Well, I guess I was as good as any of them, if I do say it myself. Play baseball?"

"A—a little." Jimmy's stammer was a confession of his confusion. To hold conversation with the great Buck had never entered the wildest of his dreams.

"What position?"

"I like to play third."

"Now you're talking. What's that school you go to the sport's ed was telling me about?"

"Cromwell."

"That's it. Did you make the nine?"

"No, sir."

"Huh! Somebody beat you out of it?" Buck reached down for the bat. "Use this? Too light. Get one about two ounces heavier. Get down there and let me hit you a few. Maybe they won't beat you out for it next year."

Jimmy scrambled to his feet, caught up his glove, and walked down the lawn. It was plain to be seen that Buck thought he had turned out for the nine, but had lost the position to another man. The boy flushed, and could not understand why the blood should mount to his cheeks. However, even in the intoxication of the moment, he knew that he would not tell Buck the truth because it would rob him of something Buck thought he had.

The man swung the ball upward and moved the bat forward to meet it. To Jimmy's eyes the sphere seemed to skim the grass with bewildering speed. He made a frenzied stab with his bare hand—and missed. Ten minutes later Buck tossed the bat aside.

"That's all for now. I know why you lost out, kid. You haven't got a thing when the ball's hit to your right. Your start is slow. You've got lead in your feet and glue in your arms. You've got no knack of getting them on your right side a-tall. Want to make the nine next year?"

"Yes," Jimmy said very suddenly.

"All right. Tomorrow you hit to me, and I'll show you how it's done. After that you get about half an hour chasing grounders every night. You leave it to me, kid, and you'll play third for Cromwell. See you tomorrow."

"I—I'm not much of a hitter," said Jimmy.

"Leave it to me," said Buck. "I've peeled the curtains away from more than one batting eye."

And so, for the first time in his life, Jimmy Hicks found that he wanted something badly enough to make a fight for it. Day after day Buck slashed the ball at him, and day after day he ran himself ragged to an accompaniment of barking, rasping directions. Before and after the practice Buck was the soul of genial companionship; while the work was on he was a merciless driver. Had Jimmy kept track of the hits he would have known that most of them were on his right side, but he was too much concerned with getting the ball at all to bother his head with keeping track of where it went.

"Kid," said Buck, "you've got a bum pair of hands."

Jimmy surveyed his palms and fingers. "What's the matter with them?"

"Oh, I don't mean it that way. It's a form of speaking we have in the leagues. When we find a baby who's got a knack of getting his paws on the ball and holding it, we say he's got a pair of hands."

"Then—then I won't make it, will I?"

"Who says so?" Buck bristled. "Ain't I showing you how? You're not much of a natural fielder, but you can do a pretty good mechanical job."

"I'd like to make it," Jimmy said after a while. "There's a fellow at school—"

"Think you'd make a hit with him by getting into the batting order?"

147

Jimmy nodded.

"Leave it to me," said Buck. "What's the guy's name?"

"Arlie Pierce."

"Well, you and Arlie are as good as pals."

That was the joyous prospect that Jimmy, six weeks later, took back with him to Cromwell.

Luck seemed to be with him. Comfortably settled in his dormitory room, he learned that Rice, last year's third baseman, was not coming back to school. The same day, leaving the school office, he came face to face with Arlie.

"Hello!" The pitcher gave him a glance in which doubt was mingled with perplexity. "Your name's Hicks, isn't it? I thought so. You look more rugged than you did. What were you doing all summer?"

"Playing ball. I'm coming out for the nine. Third base."

"We'll have to find a new man for third," Arlie said thoughtfully. "What team did you play with?"

"Oh, I didn't play with a team, but Buck Everts coached me."
The pitcher's eyes opened. "Not—"

"Yes," Jimmy said with inward satisfaction; "the Panthers' old third baseman."

Arlie swung him around by the shoulders and pushed him toward the dormitory building. "Come up to my room," he said, "and tell me all about him. Where does he live since he quit the big show?"

"He lives next door to me."

"He does?" The pitcher urged him forward with a hand on his arm. "Hurry. I want to hear it all before supper."

And thus was the seed of friendship sown between Arlie Pierce and Jimmy Hicks.

That first visit was followed by many others. The two boys occupied separate rooms on the same floor, and by and by they formed the habit of dropping in on each other, loaded down with books, for an evening of study. From the shadowy obscurity of being a mere student, one of the hundreds of un-honored and unsung, Jimmy found himself transported to the realms of the mighty. He had trod the earth with a great man, and became a mirror of reflected glory. The whole school heard of his contact with Buck and eagerly snapped up the crumbs of anecdote that fell from his lips. He had come back to Crom-well hoping that Arlie would admit him to the magic of an inner circle. Instead, by a trick of fate, he found himself on equal terms with the school hero.

Yet he never quite lost a certain feeling of inferiority where Arlie was concerned. It was as though, deep within him, he feared that the miracle of the pitcher's friendship would not last. The diffident streak in him began to come to the surface. Bit by bit, as the fall and winter wore on, he fell into the old habit of shifting ground, surrendering opinions, and smiling his smile of conciliation.

"Great Scot!" Arlie cried in exasperation one night. "You don't have to swallow everything I say. Haven't you got any ideas of your own?"

Jimmy flushed a bit. "Can't a fellow be agreeable?"

"Apple sauce!" Arlie said in disgust. "Isn't there anything you'll say and stick to?"

"Yes. I'm going to play third base."

The pitcher stared at him a moment, started to say something, and stopped. Jimmy had the uncomfortable conviction that Arlie had an idea that he might not make it.

Next day there was nothing to denote that their friendship had passed through a flurry of rough water. But in the back of Jimmy's mind lurked the fear that, come spring, he might lose out. Common sense began to point out considerations that he had ignored. He had acquired skill in fielding a ball, but he had had practically no work in throwing to bases, in judging what to do on a fielder's choice, or in dovetailing his movements with those of other men—the thing that is called teamwork. Then, too, there was Dixie Orth. Dixie had tried for third last year, but Rice had beaten him out. Dixie would try again this year. Dixie had the advantage of experience.

Many a man, finding his courage beginning to shake, has sought to talk himself back to confidence. Jimmy tried the same trick. The campus expected him, because of his summer as Buck's pupil, to make the nine. He began to talk as though his selection were as good as accomplished. One February night, with Arlie's room comfortably filled, he steered the same channel—the things that Buck had taught him and Buck's prediction that he would surely win out. It was not until he had finished that he noticed that Dixie was standing near the door.

"You shouldn't have gassed that way," Arlie said when the crowd was gone. "You'll have to cut it out."

"I didn't know Dixie was there," Jimmy defended.

"Of course you didn't. I don't mean that. But if I were you I'd stop speaking about Buck and about what Buck promised you."

"Why?"

"It might prove embarrassing. You know the athletic committee has been looking for a baseball coach. Well, I guess they've found him. I heard just after supper that they had sent a contract to Buck."

The Panthers' old third baseman arrived at Cromwell early in March, his derby hat pulled down a bit above his right eye and his walk a confident, cocky swagger. The school held a meeting in the gym that night and worked up a lot of enthusiasm. Speeches were made by a faculty adviser, by the chairman of the athletic committee, and by Bagby, the captain of the nine. Then a great shout went up for "Coach, coach, coach."

Buck, to whom baseball had been a bread-and-butter business, gave the shortest talk of the night.

"Lots of pep," he said dryly, "but games ain't won from the grandstand. Now, let's get out and play some ball. We start tomorrow, right here, at four o'clock."

At four o'clock Jimmy was there. He had met Buck shortly after his arrival, had shaken hands with him, and then had effaced himself from the picture. From the time that Arlie had told him who the coach was to be, he had decided upon this course. If he had not spoken so freely of Buck, if he had not boasted so loudly of his own sureness of success, things might have been different. As it was, he had sense enough to know that he would have to guard against campus gossip, and give nobody a chance to say that he was too close to the coach. His plan of self-abnegation gave him a feeling of merited virtue.

At the gym, he gave his name and his history. He had had no real experience playing third. No; he had not tried for the nine last year. He caught a flash of surprise in Buck's eyes.

Then Dixie followed him with his two years on a grammar-school team and his year as a substitute at Cromwell. Jimmy bit his lips.

"What wins ball games," Buck told the candidates, "is speed. From today we're building for a team that will have the sparkle. Cap. Bagby, here, will divide you up—half to the handball court, half to the gym track. When the whistle blows, you reverse. Get that? Don't try to commit suicide in a day. You've got about thirty afternoons before you get outdoors. Take it easy."

Jimmy was counted into the track squad. Three times around the track, and the air seemed to be the scarcest commodity in the world. He slowed down to a walk.

"That's right, kid," came Buck's voice. "No need of trying to kill yourself. Walk about a hundred steps and then trot."

Jimmy walked—and Dixie, breathing easily, passed him like a flitting shadow.

For a week his legs, his back, his arms, ached with a wrenching soreness. More than once he was tempted to quit, the old spirit of surrender whispering to him to get out and take his comfort. Had he not spoken so confidently of his prospects, he would probably have swung up that old road of least resistance. Now, pride, the fear of ridicule, held him to his task in spite of outward soreness and inner squirmings. Had he only known it, it was the first time in his life he had really won a victory over himself. For, compared to this, last summer's practice with Buck had been child's play.

In all that first week Buck did not speak to him three times; and though he had agreed with himself on a policy of keeping in the background, the coach's attitude piqued him.

"You'd imagine," he complained to Arlie, "that he had never seen me before."

The pitcher looked at him curiously. "You're not looking for favors, are you?"

Jimmy awoke to his mistake and achieved a sickly smile. "I was only fooling," he said. Arlie frowned impatiently. Afterward Jimmy asked himself bitterly why he had not told the truth—that he had not expected Buck, in view of past events, to treat him so completely as just one of the squad.

And then came a day when the soreness was gone. His muscles responded like oiled springs. Buck brought out baseballs, and the candidates ranged across the gym and began to throw them around. The pitchers and the catchers retired to the track.

"Just to break in the throwing muscles and get your hands used to the feel of the ball," said Buck. "The first fellow who tries any fancy stuff gets the gate."

The squad obeyed, having already learned that the cocky Buck, while short on words and the niceties of grammar, was long on discipline. Jimmy, watching Dixie, decided that there was nothing outstanding about his rival's plays. Dixie took the ball with a negligent flip of his glove and threw it with a lazy movement of his arm. He seemed to be a careless, happy-go-lucky youth who took baseball as a sort of joke.

But once the squad got outdoors and pranced across the turf of Cromwell Field, Dixie's spirit was reborn. There had been a race for places, and he had cornered third. He kicked the bag, straightened it with his toe, spat in his glove, and shook a fist at Buck, who was waiting at the plate to hit.

"Come on, old timer," he yelled. "Hit one down here with some big league stuff behind it."

Buck sent a smoking grounder almost along the foul line. Dixie made a stab, and the ball struck his glove and rolled away. Headlong he dove for it and, from one knee, threw fast and true to first.

"Not so rotten," said Buck, and hammered the ball at the second baseman.

153

At the end of the afternoon Jimmy walked back slowly to the gym. His throws to first had been uncertain. Four times the ball had been hit to his right—twice to go bounding past him and once to be fumbled. And in front of them all Buck had called: "Same old weakness, kid. Hop to it with more speed."

He survived the first cut, and the second. He was trying now with a desperate effort; but the plays that he made only by giving every last ounce of himself, Dixie seemed to make with ease. One day, on the bench, Arlie suddenly put a hand on his shoulder.

"You're certainly fighting for it," he said in a whisper. "Good luck."

A warmth, such as he had never known before, ran through his veins. Then and there was born the thought of him and Arlie rooming together next year. It grew on him. That night he mentioned it to Arlie.

The pitcher grinned. "That wouldn't be half bad, would it?" Jimmy took it as a tacit acceptance.

Three days before the first game, the squad was cut for the last time, and Jimmy found himself out. His eyes sought Arlie's as Buck called his name, but Arlie was apparently absorbed in examining a bruised finger. In twos and threes the discards walked back to the gym, and presently, alone, he followed them, confronted with the melancholy necessity of clearing out his locker.

"Wait a minute, kid," came Buck's voice. Jimmy waited, and they fell into step. The boy's face was black—his thoughts were blacker. Oh, the coach would talk to him now. He had been cast aside. He wasn't wanted.

"Kid," Buck said feelingly, "you certainly threw some high and fast ones before I came down. In I walk, and find you swinging some wicked conversation about how good you were and how I said you'd make the nine. Fine for me, wasn't it? Half the school was watching to see how I'd handle you. Mind, I'm not panning you. You couldn't guess that they were going to offer me a job here. If you'd had the stuff, I'd have stuck you in. I'm after a winner, and the best player is the chocolate drop

155

with me. I'm trying to fix it so that you can stick around. Wear a uniform and all that. What killed you off this year was lack of experience. Next year you ought to be all set for glory. Do you know how to box-score a game?"

"Yes; I've done it for my father's paper."

"All right: here's the play. I name you official scorer. You keep your locker. You wear a uniform. Afternoons you get some of the practice. On the bench, during a game, you use your eyes and your head. Watch how things are done, and then, during next day's practice, try to do them a little better. I want to hold you with this baseball crowd. I've got a two-year contract, and next year I'm figuring you're going to be ripe. How about it?"

"You said I'd make the nine this year."

"Kid," Buck said frankly, "I did the craziest thing a man can do. I called you safe without seeing the play. I didn't know this outfit. I thought it was just a kid team. Well, I've made you the offer. Take it or leave it."

"I'll take it," said Jimmy.

He took the berth, not because he thought it an honor, but because it held him in the squad and kept him closer to Arlie. After Buck had left him, he retraced his steps and came back to the diamond. Dixie, standing on the third-base bag, spoke to him as he passed, but he did not answer. Arlie, sitting on the bench, was looking his way and seemed to be frowning. He waved a summons, and the pitcher came out to meet him, a strange look of gravity on his face.

Jimmy told of Buck's offer. There was something quiet—too quiet—in the way Arlie accepted the news. A sudden fear gripped at Jimmy's heart.

"It's all right about next year, Arlie—rooming together—isn't it?"

"We don't have to decide that until June, do we?" the pitcher asked. Then Buck called him and he walked out toward the hurling mound. With a sinking heart, Jimmy decided that Arlie was cutting away from him because he had not made the nine. Before the day was out, he had to revise this judgment, for that night Arlie came to his room to study and was as friendly

156

and companionable as he had been before. After the pitcher had gone, long after he himself should have been in bed, Jimmy sat at a window, in the dark, and tried to puzzle things out. What had he done that Arlie should view him as no longer desirable? And if he was not desirable, why should Arlie continue to bother with him at all? Something mysterious and obscure had come between them. What it was he did not know, but he did know this—that he would not give up hope until he and Arlie went home in June. The fighting spirit was growing upon him.

The day of the first game Buck presented him with a new score book.

"Kid," said the coach, "make no mistake, you've got a man's-size job. Every fielding average rests on your judgment. Even the number of hits a pitcher allows depends on how you score them. Hits or errors? You're the baby who has the say-so. A lot of people think you can throw a score book at anybody. That's a laugh. You might as well say you can let players slide into bases, feet first and all stiffened out, and break their legs. A bird who doesn't know what's what can do some goofy scoring and get a good team scrapping among themselves. The better the player, the more anxious he is to have his record straight. Get that, kid?"

Jimmy nodded.

"Hop to it. You're the boss. Whatever you put down in that book goes."

Jimmy scored that game with more seriousness than he had ever brought to a similar undertaking for the sport editor of the Woodbury *Herald*. Only in a secondary way did he pay attention to the score. He knew that Arlie was pitching good ball and that Cromwell was winning. He knew it in the same sort of unconscious way that he appreciated the warmth of the April sun on his knees. Practically his entire attention was given to watching the ball.

In the seventh inning, with Captain Bagby on second, his fountain pen slipped from his fingers and rolled behind his feet. As he stooped to recover it, his eyes off the field, a sudden cry from the crowd told him that something out of the ordinary had happened. His hand felt for the pen; his eyes sought the field. Bagby had been caught napping off second, and was prancing between second and third in an attempt to avoid being run down and tagged. Enemy players were closing in on him. The pen kept eluding Jimmy's hand, and he had to look for it. When he raised his eyes again Bagby, brushing the dust from his uniform, was walking back toward the bench, and the enemy players were jubilantly scurrying back to their positions.

"I saw the players who were in the run-up," said Jimmy, "but I missed the finish. Who made the put-out?"

"Catcher," said Dixie. "He got Bagby sliding into third."

Jimmy ignored the third baseman and looked at Arlie. "Who gets the put-out? Catcher?"

"Didn't Dixie tell you?" Arlie asked sharply.

158

Jimmy flushed and bent down over the score book to mark the play. Ever since his failure to make the nine, a soreness had been growing in him against Dixie. He had adopted a childish attitude of silent scorn, as though by this means he might wither the other boy's victory. That Dixie had done him no wrong had had no effect upon his resentment. Up to the time Arlie had rebuked him, he had taken a grim pleasure in snubbing the player who had beaten him out. Now, all at once, he was conscious that he had acted like a fool.

A Cromwell boy popped to the shortstop for the second out, and Dixie walked up to the plate. Jimmy slid along the bench to Arlie.

"I shouldn't have done that," he said in an undertone. "It won't happen again."

Arlie smiled. "I thought you weren't that kind of loser."

"I didn't think of it in that way until you spoke."

Arlie shook his head in a way that bespoke mingled despair and exasperation. "Jimmy," he said, "why is it somebody always has to make you see things? Why don't you get some first-hand viewpoints?" Dixie hit to the box and was thrown out, and Arlie strode away from the bench to pitch the beginning of the eighth.

Jimmy knew that he had disappointed Arlie again—that the roommate idea had been thrust just a little farther away. He resolved to win back to a friendly footing with Dixie, not because of the effect it might have on Arlie, but because it was the only decent thing to do.

And yet he found it hard to make friendly advances, or even to speak with casual ease. A shy reticence paralyzed his tongue, strangled his vocal cords, and stopped his lips. And so, so far as Dixie was concerned, he sat mute upon the bench—and Arlie watched him with frowning, misunderstanding eyes.

The season ran on. Game followed game. Sometimes Cromwell won, sometimes she lost. Jimmy found himself writing the baseball page for the school magazine and contributing stories of Cromwell's games to the local newspaper at two dollars a column. Even though he had not made the nine, this gave him

159

standing, and the crowd continued to drop in on him after supper in the school dining hall. If, in those days, he now and then looked at Arlie with an unspoken appeal, the pitcher pretended not to see it. And so came, at last, the big game of the year against Brockton.

That morning Jimmy received a note from an old friend, the sport editor of his father's paper.

"Good luck, but, prepared for the worst, I've checked up on a dozen sport pages, and the opinion is that Cromwell will lose. Brockton carries six murderous hitters in its line-up."

Jimmy, thinking this might be news to Buck, took the letter to the coach.

"Shown this to anybody?" Buck demanded.

"No."

"Good!" The coach struck a match and burned the letter. "Told anybody about it?"

"No."

"Wise kid. If you do, I'll chase you out of town with a bat. Baseball is like a lot of other things in life—a closed mouth bites into no trouble."

Jimmy took away from the interview the conviction that the truth was in the newspaper reports, and that Buck knew it. Heretofore, he had been a scoring machine, marking the plays with cold-blooded precision. That afternoon, with two thousand rooters singing and cheering and stamping in the stands, the importance of the contest worked its spell upon him, and his heart did queer things in his breast. The hand that had been steady all season trembled as it wrote the batting orders.

It was Arlie's game. Tall and graceful, the pitcher warmed up in front of the Cromwell stand. By newspaper prediction he was due today to fail, to have his curves slaughtered, to be devastated and buried under a withering volley of drives. Jimmy looked at the crowd that would see his friend's downfall and felt a lump tighten in his throat.

Arlie came back to the bench, ran his pitching arm into his sweater, and leaned back at ease waiting for the game to start.

"How was your control out there?" Buck asked.

"I was putting the ball where I wanted it to go."

"That's shooting. No playing around today; pitch to them. Make every shot count. Keep the batters in the hole and you'll be walking on the top of the world."

The Brockton coach came over.

"Got a first-class scorer?" he asked Buck.

"First class."

"O. K., then. His score goes for us, too."

Ten minutes later, Arlie was on the mound, the first Brockton boy was at the plate, and the game was on. Buck, his hat pulled down low, chewed on a blade of grass and watched the field through narrowed eyes.

Arlie pitched the first ball.

"Strike one!" ruled the umpire.

The next pitch was hit to Dixie, and the batter was out at first. His teammate fouled out on the first ball. The third boy took a called strike, and then hoisted a fly to the right fielder.

"What did I tell you?" Buck demanded. "You pitched only five balls that inning. Keep the batter in the hole, and you'll be sitting pretty."

Bagby walked out to the plate, hitched his trousers, dug his right foot into the dirt, grew tense as the Brockton pitcher wound up—and then drove the first ball into deep center for a home run.

Jimmy found himself on his feet banging his score book against Dixie's arm and cheering. The nine, in a frenzy of chatter, was calling for more action and half a dozen more runs. It looked at that moment as though the final verdict might be written before the game was five minutes old. But the Brockton pitcher was not the type to be broken by one unexpected blow. Slowly and methodically he worked, and three Cromwell batters went out in order. Dixie, the last man to be retired, struck out on three pitched balls and threw the bat from him in disgust.

At the end of the fifth inning the score was still 1 to 0. The stands had cheered themselves out and had reached a stage of breathless hush. Every moment that one run loomed bigger.

The strain was beginning to tell upon the players. Arlie, between the inning halves, sat with his eyes half closed, the
muscles of his mouth twitching.

"Good work," Jimmy whispered in his ear.

He smiled absently, but answered not a word.

An inning later, the score was still unchanged. Jimmy suddenly sat bolt upright as though an electric current had touched
his spine.

"Arlie hasn't given them a hit yet," he cried.

In the excitement of the game nobody had noticed this save
Buck. The coach favored the scorekeeper with a murderous
glance, with no thought in his mind of box-score records.

"That Brockton guy's only given us two hits," he said. But
an inning later the fact was plain and could no longer be denied.
Arlie was on his way to a no-hit game.

"Any other Cromwell pitcher ever do it?" Jimmy asked. "No? Gosh, Arlie, if you can only turn the trick!"

"Only six more men to get," cried Dixie.

"Get 'em," came from Bagby. "Oh, boy! A no-hit game. Wouldn't that look like something in the papers tomorrow. It will go on the sport pages all over the country. Put it over, Arlie, and they'll all know about Cromwell tomorrow."

Buck sighed under his breath. There was no sense in going against such a tide.

"How's the arm?" he asked. "Strong?"

The pitcher nodded.

"Go ahead; shoot for it."

Arlie's face went white. Jimmy's heart missed half a dozen beats.

The stand had awakened to how close Cromwell's pitcher was to baseball's Hall of Fame. A cheer greeted him as he went out to pitch the eighth, and grew in volume as the first batter fouled to Bagby. The next Brockton boy hit long and far, and an audible groan turned to a shriek as Cromwell's right fielder raced under the ball and pulled it down. And the next batter popped to Arlie himself.

Cromwell's song of triumph burst from the stands. The cheer leaders did not call for it. It was spontaneous, impulsive, clarion.

Jimmy sprang from the bench. "Only three more, Arlie; only three more."

The pitcher was trembling. Sitting next to him, Jimmy could feel the twitching of his arm, of his leg. The color that had gone from his face had not come back. Cromwell hitters went up to the plate and came back discomfited. Arlie paid no attention. His mind now was on only one thing.

Bagby shook his shoulder. "Time to do it again. Last crack. We're with you. They won't get a ball past us."

"Feed them that drop," Dixie pleaded. "They can't touch it."

"Easy," said Buck. "Take your time and it's all yours."

Arlie stood up to shed his sweater. As he stooped to throw the garment on the bench, his head came close to Jimmy's.

"Root for me," he said. His voice was hoarse.

163

The pitcher got off to a bad start and served two wide balls to the first batter. The next pitch was over, and the batter drove a savage liner past Bagby.

"Oh!" Jimmy moaned.

But the hit was foul by inches. Then the batter hit weakly to the box and was thrown out.

Jimmy's spirits soared. "Only two more, Arlie," he cried. His voice was drowned in the bedlam of the stands. The cheering had lost all order, all rhythm. It had become a frenzy of hope and expectation.

Arlie was wiping his hands on his uniform as though they were sweating. A Brockton boy, crouched at the plate, moved a nervous bat and waited. The pitcher delivered the ball.

The stands roared as wood met leather. The grounder went straight toward the second baseman. He dug it from the dirt, set himself, and threw the runner out.

"Only one more!" It was Jimmy's voice, lifted in a shriek.

The roaring of the stands was as the roaring of the sea. After the out, the infielders threw the ball around. Arlie walked half-way toward his catcher and then walked back to the mound.

"Can't stand still," Buck muttered. "Keyed up too high."

Bagby threw the pitcher the ball. The cheering tapered off and died. A quiet, startling in its contrast to the tumult, settled over the field. Arlie, the ball against his breast, waited for his catcher's sign.

Buck was muttering again. "Kid, pitch right to him. You're too nervous to try the corners. It's your only chance."

Arlie seemed to have come to the same conclusion. One moment, stretched far back, he was poised; the next, the ball shot forward. The batter swung.

Crack!

"Right on the nose," Buck sighed. He knew the sound. Something like a united sob came from the stands. The score book fell from Jimmy's hand.

The ball, on a line, had shot toward third. Afterward there were those who said it went so fast they did not see it. Dixie made a desperate sidelong plunge. The ball struck the frantic,

164

outstretched fingers of his glove and then caromed off his hands and rolled into left field. The batter raced all the way to second.

Half the stands were crying, "It's a hit," the other half were shouting, "It's an error." Jimmy's eyes were blinded with a stinging mist. He rubbed the tears from his eyes, reached down for the score book, and stole a glance out at the field. Arlie stood there motionless now, looking over at the bench.

"It's an error," Jimmy said fiercely, and poised his pen to charge not a hit to the credit of the batter but an error to the discredit of Dixie.

But something stopped the pen. He knew the rule observed by scorers everywhere—a ball, batted too hard to be handled cleanly, had to be charged as a hit, even though a fielder managed to get his hands upon it.

But after all, it was entirely a matter of the scorekeeper's judgment. If he believed that Dixie should have held the ball, or at least have knocked it down and have thrown the runner out at first, then the third baseman should be charged with an error and Arlie given credit for a no-hit game. Just one little mark in the book and Arlie would have his honor.

"It's an error," Jimmy told himself again.

But still the pen did not move to write it so. The stands were still in turmoil.

"Arlie'd never forgive me," Jimmy told himself miserably.

"Root for me," the pitcher had pleaded. Hit or error? The pen shook in Jimmy's grasp. So easy to mark it as his longings dictated, and yet— He had been trusted. Buck had told him that he held the records in his hands. But an error meant so little to Dixie, and a no-hit game meant so much to Arlie. He had asked Arlie to be his roommate. Perhaps, if he gave the pitcher the benefit of the doubt— But the scoring rules laid down the law that, in case of doubt, the batter was always to be credited with a hit.

"They—they trusted me to do it right," Jimmy said in a choking voice.

A yelp from the stands brought his eyes back to the field. The Cromwell nine was running in; the game was over. He heard someone say Arlie had made a quick throw to second and had caught the runner napping off the bag. Then the nine was clamoring around the bench.

"What was it?" Arlie demanded.

"I—" Jimmy wet his lips— "I had to score it as a hit. It was too hard a ball for Dixie to handle."

"Shucks!" Dixie said in disgust; "I was hoping I had mussed it up for an error."

They did not question his judgment. Jimmy's heart swelled. Yet he was afraid to look at Arlie. Now, at last, he marked the hit, and the out that had followed it, and remained bent over the score book for a long time. When he looked up, the pitcher was on his way to the gym, surrounded by a crowd of admirers who had come tumbling out of the stands.

"Tough on Arlie," said Buck.

"Tough?" Jimmy demanded bitterly. "How tough do you think it was on me?"

"Kid," said the coach who understood, "a square guy always marks 'em as he sees 'em."

Jimmy closed the book and left the bench. For the first time that season he regretted he had worn a uniform; it would have been so much easier to have slipped away to his dormitory room. But he had to change his clothes. He opened the gym door and went in.

The players seemed to have forgotten that they had won the game. They were still talking of how close Arlie had come to what no other Cromwell pitcher had ever accomplished. Every word stabbed him. He noticed that, in all the buzz of talk, Arlie was silent and thoughtful. That stabbed him even harder. He hurried out of his uniform and into his street clothes and moved toward the door.

"Wait for me, Jimmy," Arlie called.

He waited outside because he could not bear to linger in the dressing-room. What Arlie would say to him he did not know. The decision had rested with him—hit or error—and he had decided against his friend. What a fine turn for friendship to take!

"What was it?" Arlie demanded.

Five minutes later Arlie came out. There was a peculiarly dreamy expression on his face.

"You spoke to me about rooming together next year," he said. "Still feel that way? Then let's hustle over to the office and put in a claim for that big corner room on the second floor before somebody beats us to it. That room would be peachy."

Jimmy was bewildered. "You mean you'll room with me after—after—"

"Just for that reason," Arlie said softly. "I was afraid to take a chance on you, Jimmy. If I had to go through a year of studying, living, getting up and going to bed in the same room with a fellow who did nothing but 'yes' me, and agree with me, and salve me, I'd want to murder him. I want a friend I can depend on to stand by me when I'm right and tell me bluntly when I'm wrong. After today, Jimmy, I haven't any doubts. You'll mark them as you see them, as Buck would say. You're there. You'll do. Let's hustle and get that room."

Franklin M. Reck

THE GAWK

ILLUSTRATED BY *Rod Ruth*

R ED GARDNER, dash man on the State College swimming team, came into the locker-room laughing.

"You've heard of dumb freshmen," he said. "Well, listen to this. There's a big gawk named Buck Weaver on the campus, enrolled in forestry. He came up to me after chem class this morning and asked me how to join a fraternity. I told him all you had to do was go up to a house, knock on the door, and ask to see the rooms. If you liked the place and the rates were okay, you just moved in. He asked me to recommend a good house, and I told him the Gams—" He turned to Jack Bartley, acting captain and distance man—"Your house, Jack."

"The heck you did. Did he go there?"

"He did. I met him this afternoon and asked him about it. He said he'd called on the Gams but they were full. They promised to let him know when they had a vacancy. He left his name and address with 'em."

Speed Herbert, breast-stroker and water polo star, scratched his blond hair and grinned. "Does this guy Weaver wear a big mackinaw, square-toed shoes, and a cap with ear flaps?"

"That's the boy."

"I've seen him around the campus." Speed turned toward Jack. "I can't understand why the fellows didn't grab him up."

The husky, black-haired acting captain, busy stuffing his shoes into his locker, didn't seem to hear.

"Imagine," Red said sadly to Speed. "I put an outstanding prep on the Gamma doorstep, and still they don't get him."

168

Jack Bartley slammed shut his locker and mounted a bench. "All right, you comedians, pipe down a minute." He glanced over the assembled freshman and varsity swimmers to get their attention, his brown eyes purposeful.

"Papa's going to make a speech," Red complained.

"You're blamed right I am," Jack said. "When Coach Allen left for the East, he told me to see that you guys worked. All you've done for three weeks is risk your neck sliding around the tile, playing tag."

"Tag's work! It's good for your wind."

Jack snorted impatiently. "You fellows know as well as I do that we're being initiated into the big time this winter. This is the first real squad State's had, and before we're through we'll see the bright lights of Los Angeles and San Francisco. And you fellows seem to think the way to get ready is to horse around."

"For the luvva Mike, Jack," Speed said humorously. "Give us time. It's only the middle of November!"

"You know the coach's idea," Jack said in level tones. "He believes in work. Swimming's an all-year-round proposition. You're supposed to start early in the fall, build up your condition, and stay that way. A mile a day, brother, no less."

"But it's so ha-a-ard," Red pleaded. "Honest, Jack, I hate to see you standing up there, getting all steamed up over nothing."

"Over nothing?" Jack's eyes burned at Red. Always, it seemed, Red met serious talk with chatter. "What am I going to show the coach when he returns in January? A gang of porpoises who swim one length of the pool and come up puffing?"

"Now, now." Red came over and patted Jack's knee. "People who make speeches without any clothes on sometimes get pneumonia. Then where would we be?"

"Applesauce," Jack said disgustedly, and stepped down off the bench.

At that moment, the rawboned freshman, Buck Weaver, was walking eagerly toward the gym. He moved with a swinging stride, like a woodsman used to covering long distances. So deeply tanned was his angular, good-humored face that the whites of his eyes were startling in their contrast. His bony

169

wrists stuck out from the sleeves of his checked mackinaw, and his unpressed pants failed by inches to meet his shoe tops. His neck was thrust forward, chin out, and in his blue eyes there was a questing look that sparkled with sheer delight.

He remembered what his father had said two short months ago, up there in the cabin beside Lake Martin, high in the Rockies. "You're going down into the world, son, and I think you'll like it better than I did. Anyhow, you're going to get your chance, and I know you'll make the most of it. Good-bye, and good luck."

At first, something in Buck had protested against leaving his father alone, facing a long winter of work along the trap lines. The protest had deepened to misery when he had said good-bye to Ned and Jane, their trail horses, and his eyes had grown wet when he had taken his last look at the emerald surface of Lake Martin, cradled beneath great peaks. Then he had waved good-bye to it all and gone down the mountain to his first train, his first large city, and his first campus, with his father's laconic words singing in his mind: "Make the most of it."

From the first he had eagerly sought for some way in which to join the busy activity of the campus, but for two months the battle of books and classes had caught him in its toils, and he hadn't looked up to breathe. He hadn't even read the fresh-man handbook—he had arrived on the campus too late for Prep Week, when new students were initiated into the mysteries of college etiquette and custom.

Only that afternoon had he dared lift his head and look around him with an appraising eye. He had scanned the *Student Daily* and his eyes had fixed on a swimming story. "Jack Bartley, acting captain and coach," the story went, "says that the squad will go to work in earnest this week in preparation for the stiffest schedule in State's history."

"Swimming!" Buck Weaver murmured between parted lips. "That's something I can do!"

It was a great discovery to learn that there was competitive swimming at State. Why, swimming was his meat! What could these town-bred people know about swimming? The feel of a damp granite ledge on bare feet, the icy shock of a snow-fed lake at six in the morning, the surging joy of a half-mile splash before breakfast?

He arrived at the locker-room just as Red Gardner and Jack Bartley, naked and wet from a cold shower, were starting for the pool. Buck's eyes opened with pleased surprise as he recognized his adviser on fraternity matters.

"Hello, Gardner!" he said joyously. "You on the swimming team?"

Red admitted that he was and nodded with a twinkle in his eye toward Jack. "Meet Mr. Bartley," he said. "He's our backstroker and distance man. Bartley lives in the Gamma House and can tell you when there's a vacancy up there."

Buck turned eagerly toward the black-haired captain. "Say, that'll be swell if you will. By golly, you know I'd like to locate there because it's close to the forestry building."

Jack looked at the freshman in amazement. A few minutes before he had listened to Red's story with a grin of disbelief, but here was Buck Weaver in the flesh, outlandish clothes and all.

"Sure," he laughed good-naturedly, and when an expectant pause followed, he added politely: "Are you a swimmer, by any chance?"

"Am I!" Buck thought of the day he had splashed over to Elk Point and back, a total of four miles, without working up a blow. "I read in the *Student Daily* where you go around swimming against other schools, and I thought I'd help out."

Red's eyes sparkled mischief. "That's mighty nice," he said. "Only you're a freshman, aren't you?"

Buck nodded.

"Then you'll have to wait a year before you can swim with the varsity, much as we'd like to have you."

Buck missed the sarcastic note. "You mean a fellow can't swim for *a year!* No matter how good he is?"

"You can work out with the freshmen if you're good enough," Red pursued smoothly. "But you've got to win your spurs first."

Buck smiled confidently. "What do I have to do?"

"Race Jackie Mann," Red said. He was enjoying the moment

171

immensely. "If you can beat him you're plenty good."

Jack laughed. "Don't let him kid you, Weaver. Mann was interscholastic champ last year."

Buck rubbed his hands together in anticipation. "That's all right with me. I don't care what he's champion of. The tougher the better."

Speed Herbert came up grinning. "If you want something tough, take on Red Gardner, here. He's the fastest man on the varsity."

Buck smiled in the knowledge of his own strength. These fellows thought they were putting him on the spot. He almost laughed. "Where do I hang my clothes?" he asked grimly.

"Stick 'em in with mine," Jack said reluctantly. The team would have a good time with this greenhorn, and another afternoon of work would be shot.

"Okay, and thanks!" Grateful and pleased, Buck reached Jack's locker in one long stride and began ripping off his mackinaw. "And don't you fellows go betting any money on Red!" he added as he tugged at a stringy tie.

A laugh followed his remark, but Buck merely smiled to himself, remembering the time he had swum circles around a frantic moose. And those mad, invigorating dashes out to the rock island. Gosh—these fellows had an eye-opener coming! They did, for fair.

At the pool's edge a minute later Buck turned expectantly around to Red. A score of eagerly watching swimmers lined the edge of the tank.

"Shall we start in the water or off the edge?" Buck asked innocently.

There was a ripple of laughter.

"What stroke do you swim?" Red countered, winking at Speed.

"Double trudgen."

The laughter rose to a roar, and the freshman looked around bewildered. Were they laughing at *him?* The smile disappeared from his face. He lifted his head defiantly and swept the pool with a cool, scornful gaze. How many of these fellows had

172

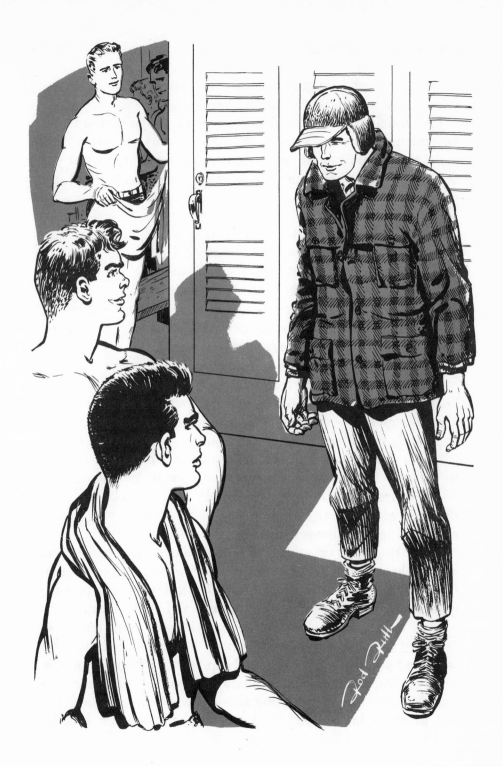

battled the swift current of Timber River and made headway against it?

"Go ahead and laugh," he said. "I'll do my grinning in the water. How far do you want to swim?"

Jack touched his arm. "You dive off the edge of the pool," he explained quietly. "I'll give the signal: 'Mark—set—go!' We'll make the distance eight laps. But you don't have to race if you don't want to. There's no reason why you should give these guys a good time. You come back in a month, and we'll see what you can do."

"If you don't mind," Buck said stiffly, "I'm racing now."

"Let him race," Red yelled. "He asked for it."

"You bet I asked for it," Buck said grimly.

"We're with you, Buck!" somebody called out.

A mock cheer arose as the two contestants stepped to the edge of the tile, Red Gardner beautifully muscled and ivory-skinned, Buck Weaver rangy and browned from the edges of his corn-colored hair to the soles of his large feet.

The word "Go!" left Buck flat-footed. His dive, when he finally made it, was clean and straight, but much too deep for a racing dive. The pool hushed expectantly as his body disappeared, but when it emerged again a wave of incredulous laughter shattered the momentary silence. This was too good to be true! Buck was plowing up the pool in irregular spurts resulting from the drive of his double scissors kick. His arms flailed in great overarm sweeps, and his head swung vigorously right and left with every stroke.

When Buck was two-thirds of the way down, Red passed him coming back. In three great lunges that were amazing in their power, the freshman reached the end of the pool, grasped the gutter with both hands, swung around, and shoved away with a force that sent sheets of water spraying out from his chest.

Seeing Red halfway down the pool, the freshman buried his head and swam the entire second lap without taking a breath.

When Buck was battling valiantly down the stretch on his sixth lap, Red Gardner, gliding along in an effortless crawl, was just finishing his eighth. He looked up and winked broadly

174

at Jack and Speed, then waited until Buck made his turn.

Pacing himself carefully, Red followed the splashing freshman down and back so that they finished in a dead heat. Buck snorted the water from his nostrils and looked with admiration at his rival. The exertion had wiped all trace of anger from his countenance.

"Say!" he said warmly. "You're not so bad! You tied me, didn't you?"

"Don't kid yourself, Buck!" a fellow freshman called down. "He lapped you!"

"He what?" Buck asked, bewildered.

"He swam ten laps while you were swimming eight. He could have done twelve if he'd wanted to."

Buck colored red under his deep tan. Slowly he drew himself out of the pool and stood up, his head bent forward.

"I guess I don't know much," he murmured. He looked around at the ring of faces and saw men biting their lips to hold back the smiles. "Go ahead and laugh," he said huskily. "You don't need to hold back on my account," and strode out of the pool to the locker-room.

The pool burst into prolonged and uproarious laughter, but Jack looked after Buck with a speculative, appraising look in his eye.

An hour later, as the captain emerged from the side door of the gym, his overcoat buttoned closely under his chin, a rawboned figure waited for him in the darkness outside, hands thrust deep in the pockets of his mackinaw.

"Bartley," Buck Weaver said hesitantly.

"Oh, hello, Buck," Jack said cordially.

"I wonder," Buck said slowly. "There's a few questions—"

Jack felt a wave of sympathy. Buck's shoulders were drooping and his face, beneath that rough cap with its fuzzy earflaps, seemed utterly crushed. Buck looked so *blamed* forlorn. The captain remembered how he had felt just two years ago at this time, before companionships were formed and the swing of activities had caught him up in its exhilarating current. He acted on a sudden hunch.

175

"Listen, Buck," he said casually. "I don't feel like going up to the house to eat. Let's go down to the Grabbit and Growl and eat together."

"Oh, you don't want to do that—"

"Why not? Come on."

In a sheltered booth at the restaurant, Buck looked humbly at the handsome, dark-haired junior.

"Bartley," he said earnestly, "I want to know how anybody could beat me two laps like Gardner did."

Jack sensed the bewilderment lying underneath the freshman's controlled exterior. He told him about the fine points of swimming—the crawl thrash and disciplined arm stroke, the breathing, the turns. Buck's jaw dropped lower and lower.

"I see," he said hopelessly. He shrugged his shoulders. "Well, I won't forget this afternoon for a lo-ong time."

"How did it happen, anyhow?" Jack asked curiously. "You should have known better than to go in there and offer to lick the best swimmer in school."

Buck flushed. "You may not believe it, Bartley," he said, "but until I came down here I'd never been in a town bigger than Rock Ledge."

"Never heard of it," Jack confessed.

"It's a great big city of a hundred people plastered on a mountain forty miles from a railroad."

Jack began to see. "Well, you don't want to let our gang of comedians get you down. As a matter of fact, they're always looking for a goat, and if it isn't you, it's me."

Buck looked up with intense interest, and Jack went on to explain.

"You probably saved me from a riding this afternoon," he said. "When the coach left town he put me in charge, and the gang thought it was a swell joke. Ever since, they've been having one long party."

He could have said more. He could have added that Red Gardner resented Jack's being put in charge. That four others of the team belonged to Red's fraternity and all of them were as irresponsible as Red.

"Well," Buck said forlornly, "they're too good for me. I'm going to sign up for gym next quarter and learn something about swimming."

All through dinner an idea had been buzzing vainly around in Jack's head, and now it settled into place. He had noticed certain points about Buck that the squad in its hilarity may have missed. A great chest capacity. Long, loose muscles and a supple grace born in a mountain lake. Another thing he had noticed, too—a direct way of looking at you, and a purposeful set to the mouth.

A fire began to course through the captain's veins. His fingers began to itch to take this material in hand. He shot questions at Buck about his life at home, his swims in Lake Martin. As he listened his eyes grew wider.

"Listen, Buck," he said hotly. "I'm going to teach you to

177

swim. At six-thirty that pool is deserted. Everybody on this campus eats at six-thirty. You meet me there tomorrow night."

The freshman was stunned. "Why d'you want to do that?"

"I'll tell you—later."

Jack left a dazed freshman at the corner and walked slowly homeward through the darkness. He could have gone to the athletic director and told him of the state of the squad, but that would have been confessing defeat. This was his job, and his alone.

And the fates had handed him Buck Weaver, raw, unsophisticated, and crude. Crude, yes, but with a great power to be harnessed. Power! Jack thought of those three unbelievable lunges that had carried Buck a third of a length down the pool.

The next evening in the deserted pool Jack began directing that power into Buck's long legs.

"Swing from the hips," he called to a brown body below him in the water. "Not too stiffly. Pigeon-toed—that's it. That's it!"

Three days later he directed power into the lanky arms and shoulders, woven with flat spring steel.

"Not too far!" he barked. "Don't reach too far. Here, let me show you," and he dived in and swam patiently up and down while Buck watched intently from the pool's edge.

Details came next. The sudden flip of the head and quick intake that lets a swimmer breathe without disturbing the line of his body. The arch that carries him over the water, not through it. The above-water turn that lets him take a breath and a quick glance over the pool.

And as Jack worked his amazement grew. "The son-of-a-gun won't get tired," he breathed.

At four o'clock, ten days after Jack had begun his secret campaign, Red Gardner came into the locker-room waving the latest copy of the *Student Daily*.

"Did you see this?" he yelped. "The Board of Commerce is giving me a trip to the Château Leeds Skiing Carnival, Christmas week."

"What do you mean, giving *you* a trip?" Herbert asked.

"It's the same thing," Red said blandly. "They're holding an

178

invitational 440 between the fastest varsity man, the fastest freshman, and the fastest unattached entrant at the December Water Show. That means Jackie Mann, yours truly, and one other. The winner is sent to Château Leeds."

"You'd better begin training, hadn't you?" Jack suggested. "You wouldn't want Jackie to win."

"There you go," Red complained. "Acting solemn again." He turned to the freshman star. "Jackie, you wouldn't go beating Papa Gardner, would you?"

The December Water Show, to be held this year on the 10th, was an annual carnival to interest the campus in the swimming team. Diving, clown acts, over-water acrobatics, and exhibition races comprised the program, but this was the first year that a Château Leeds trip had been offered. An all-expense three-day trip to the American St. Moritz!

The result seemed a foregone conclusion. Red Gardner had no opposition at 440 yards. Jackie Mann, possibly. But Jackie, a comer, was still five seconds away from Red's time. Give Jackie another year, and you'd see a race.

The campus buzzed, and in the gossip there was some speculation as to who the third entrant would be. "A town swimmer," someone hazarded. "Somebody from the inter-fraternity league," another guessed.

Meanwhile, at 6:30, while the school was eating dinner, Jack was crouched at the pool's edge, stopwatch in hand, intently watching a tanned form boiling a white streak down the center lane. The rough edges were gone—the head swinging, the flailing arms, and the drawn-up knees of the outmoded trudgen.

Jack knew that the form wasn't perfect, but there was no time to do more. It was just two days before the Water Show, and this time-trial would tell whether Jack's work had borne fruit. As the lank swimmer coasted into the finish line Jack snapped the watch and sat on his heels studying the results.

Breathing normally, Buck hung to the side of the pool, his eyebrows raised. "What does the stopwatch say?" he asked.

"That you're seven seconds slower than Red and two seconds slower than Jackie." The captain's brows creased in thought. Then, softly: "You've never been in a competitive race before, Buck. People will be looking on—the same people who laughed at you three weeks ago."

But Buck was thinking what he could do on Timber River now, with the polished tools of motion Jack Bartley had given him. His face was unafraid.

"Gosh, Jack," he burst out. "I hope I don't disgrace you!"

The tenseness flowed out of Jack's limbs. He took the freshman by the arm. "Let's go eat," he said.

Fifteen minutes before the swimmers in their purple suits were due to march out for the grand parade of the Water Show, Jack slipped over on the bench toward Red Gardner.

"Bet you a steak at the Grabbit you don't win tonight."

Red clanged shut his locker. "Say, I've been wondering," he said with a puzzled frown. "Do you suppose they're importing outside talent for that 'unattached entrant'?"

"I doubt if they'd go to all that trouble."

The frown left Red's face. "Then it's in the bag," he said with a cocky flip of his head.

Jack wondered. He was betting on the vast endurance and simple courage of a rawboned freshman against the oil-smooth form and competitive experience of Red Gardner.

One event before the special 440, Jack sent a freshman up to Coach Allen's office where Buck Weaver was waiting. When the feature race was announced, however, no third entrant had as yet appeared, and Jackie Mann and Red Gardner, stepping to the edge of the pool, looked around expectantly. Eyes swung toward the locker-room hallway, wondering.

In that moment of hush, Buck Weaver walked out into the brilliantly lit pool, over to a position alongside the other two swimmers. He wore a black suit. He nodded briefly to Jackie and Red and stood with his eyes on the rippling lane of water ahead of him.

The hall broke into a buzz of chatter. A member of the swimming team laughed aloud. The story had spread, and to scores of minds sprang the vision of a trudgen expert wallowing up and down the pool. In the confusion of glee and craning necks, Red ran over to Jack.

"Not bad, brother!" he said admiringly. "I didn't think you had it in you!"

"What do you mean?" Jack asked innocently.

"A comedy stunt to end the Show! It's swell! Good going, Jack!" As he started back to the pool's edge he turned. "Listen —I don't mind swimming in the same race with that clown, but tell him not to get over into my lane. I don't want to be fouled out of a trip."

"Listen yourself," Jack replied bluntly, "you may not buy me a steak tonight, but you're going to come so close to it your hair'll curl."

They lined up with Jackie Mann in the left lane, Red Gardner in the middle, and Buck Weaver at the right. The command "Get set!" found Buck Weaver properly flat-footed. With the bark of the gun he was in the air, his body straight, his arms straining out, ready to stroke.

"Good boy," Jack breathed. "That's keeping your head."

Down the first stretch three frothy wakes of white widened and lapped against each other in little clashing waves. Red Gardner, breathing under his left arm, could see only Jackie, and as they came toward the end of the pool the varsity man surged ahead to make the turn a full stroke in front of the freshman star.

On the backstretch Red could see the other side of the pool, and his eyes beheld a miracle that sent a queer chill down his spine. The miracle was a pair of brown, flashing arms just a stroke ahead of him.

At first he didn't believe it. Then came the fantastic idea that Jack had somewhere found a big-time swimmer who was the exact double of the clumsy and ludicrous Buck Weaver.

Finally his panic-stricken mind came back to normal, and he knew this must be Buck. Red decided to put the awkward freshman in his place without delay. If Buck was even with him, then the pace was too slow!

In the next two laps he surged ahead three full lengths and felt more contented in his mind. He knew now that Jack had been coaching the big prep. And done a good job, too! But not good enough! Buck's stroke was crude.

And for a moment he had been actually worried! The fastest man on the varsity, worried! Red laughed and churned exultantly down lap seven.

His eyes swept the pool at the end of the lap, and a prickly feeling assailed the back of his neck. What was this guy Weaver doing, barely two strokes away from the turn?

There was something about the untiring regularity of those brown arms that gave Red the silly illusion that he had been tossed to the lions. He put on more speed down laps eight and nine in order to get away from the tanned pursuer.

It was like a nightmare, he thought, in which the dreamer was trying to run from an ogre but could run only so fast and no faster.

On lap ten he tramped on the accelerator and gained back his three lengths, but on laps eleven and twelve he regretted his rashness exceedingly. On each breath his chest overexpanded convulsively. There were tight bands around it, choking off his wind.

He was sorry now that he had set such a stiff pace so early in the race. But had it been a stiff pace? How could it be stiff when a trudgen expert stayed on your heels?

He made the turn for lap fifteen and couldn't see Buck Weaver at all until a sudden swirl of water beside him told him that Buck, too, was making the turn. Buck was even with him!

Red groaned aloud and lifted arms that suddenly began to ache unbearably. I'm done . . . done . . . done. I've swum a lousy race. . . . Should have saved something. What lap is it?

He turned for lap seventeen a body length behind Buck Weaver and frantically dug into his depleted reserve for the final sprint.

"Only down to the end," he panted. "Down to the end and fifteen yards back!" That was all!

On this lap Buck was on Red's blind side, but he saw with renewed hope that he was two lengths ahead of Jackie. The gun would tell the story. When the first swimmer reached the end of the pool, the gun would sound to send the contestants away on the final fifteen yards.

"If it goes off when I get there, I'll know I'm even with Buck," he thought. "I'll have a chance!"

But he was still three strokes from the end of the pool when the gun barked, and the starch flowed out of him like water from a broken barrel. For an instant, Red Gardner felt like coasting down to the bottom of the pool and staying there until June.

As he flailed past the finish mark, he lifted his strained, gasping face and beheld the utterly unbelievable sight of Buck Weaver, up ahead, rolling over on his back to breathe. He was dimly conscious that the people were cheering.

"Winner of the four-forty," called the announcer, "Buck Weaver, freshman, unattached! Time: 5:09, four seconds slower than the school record set last year by Red Gardner!"

In the locker-room an abashed varsity squad dressed in silence. On a bench in the corner Jack put a hand on Buck's leg.

"Red did just what I thought he would do," he whispered. "The first time he saw you staying up with him, he turned on the juice and burned himself out. By the time he reached lap ten he was all washed up, and he drew Jackie Mann along with him. Maybe he'll get down to business now. Maybe the whole team will get down to business."

Then his eyes twinkled. "Buck, do you remember three weeks ago, I promised to let you know when there was a vacancy at the Gamma house?"

Buck blushed to the roots of his hair. "Aw, heck, Jack!" he protested.

Elizabeth Janet Gray

BIG MOMENT

ILLUSTRATED BY *Sylvia Haggander*

ON A warm evening in early June, Serena Page, the youngest of the five young MacNeils, dressed for the most important event of her life—so far. The house was quiet, so quiet that Page could hear Zoe humming in the kitchen as she washed up the supper dishes, hear a mockingbird in the grape arbor pretending to be a cardinal. Nobody was at home but Zoe and Page and Granny. It was horrid. This was not the way she had planned her big moment.

Page was sixteen. She was slender and sturdy both, and pretty too, with light brown hair that had red glints in it, very blue eyes set wide apart, high cheek bones, a short, straight nose, a wide mouth with a long upper lip, and a chin at once delicate and square. She looked, her father often said, like his MacNeil grandmother, with whom he used to spend his vacations when he was a boy, in a mist-wrapped stone house on one of the western isles of Scotland. She had thin, sensitive hands with long, spatulate, artistic fingers, which at the moment were busy removing metal curlers from her freshly shampooed hair. Her graduation dress lay waiting on the bed, crisp, fragile, airy —white organdy living out its potentialities to the utmost.

Cautiously she combed out the little sausages bobbing around her face and tickling her neck. Close to her head her hair was straight and shining like a cap; around the edges it flared out in a halo of light brown curls touched with red by the late sunlight slanting through the windows. If only it could look like this always! " 'If what my soul doth feel sometimes' "—she

185

muttered the bit from George Herbert that she was going to quote in her valedictory—" 'my soul might ever feel.' "

A pang smote her, a cramped feeling around her heart. How did it go on from there? "And now, classmates . . ." That came later. Her hands went cold and clammy. "To make . . . No, to take the moment . . . No, to take *what* the moment on the mountain top has given us of inspiration and courage down into the more level paths of our daily lives. . . ."

She breathed again. The rest was easy. If only her mother were there to hear her say it through one final time and to give her that last brisk word of reassurance that she—that any girl with her responsibilities—needed. But her mother was in New York, meeting Alison's boat. Page's married sister Alison was coming home from Panama with her three children, and of course her ship would have to choose this particular time to land. Mrs. MacNeil and Robin, who was Page's favorite brother, had driven to New York to meet Alison and bring her home. Obviously she had to have help, with three small children, one of them a baby, and piles of luggage. If only her ship had got in a little sooner!

The essay wouldn't be so bad. She could hold the manuscript and read, but the valedictory she had to speak from memory— and what was she to do with her hands? Miss Abbott said to let them hang naturally at her sides, but they didn't feel natural that way; they felt like weights, and enormous. But the dress would help. The skirt would billow out around them and hide them.

She powdered her short, straight nose, and then removed most of the powder. No lipstick. Daddy hated it, and besides, her mouth was too big to draw attention to it. Daddy at any rate would be there—if the bus wasn't late. It was due at 8:17, and the "Exercises" were to begin at half-past eight.

"We have come this evening to a milestone in our lives . . ." Humph. We are having this evening our first really big moment, and there won't be anybody there to see us do it. The youngest of a family of five children graduates with honors, and nobody is on hand for the occasion. Daddy will be there anyhow. I'd

186

rather have him than anyone but Mother, if I had to choose one. And Granny, of course.

She stepped gingerly into her slip and wriggled it up. It was intended to go on over her head, but it seemed more natural to step in.

After all, she reminded herself briskly, she wasn't the only one. Jean too had had a commencement this afternoon. She was at this moment a full-fledged trained nurse. Page dutifully devoted a little thought to Jean's graduation, but she could not make it seem as important as her own. For one thing Jean was going to be married soon to a young doctor. For another she had had her real graduation, her school graduation, four years ago.

Now that, thought Page, teetering on white kid slippers with high heels for which she had fought and bled and of which she now began to doubt the wisdom, was a real graduation. It had seemed to Page ever since a very pattern for graduations. No dressing in dreary silence for Jean. The house had heaved and seethed with MacNeils like a kettle on the boil. They had all been there, all talking and dressing at once and getting in one another's way, telling Jean how beautiful she looked, giving her no chance to get scared. Not that she had anything to be scared about; she had had nothing to do but sit on the platform and look sweet and beautiful, which she did with such success that Page, who had been twelve at the time, nearly swooned with love and pride.

There was a knock at the door, and lanky, freckle-faced Zoe came in.

Zoe Sparrow was the MacNeils' maid of all work, a white girl from the mountains in the western part of the state. She had come to Little Athens to work in the cotton mill, and when that closed down she took a temporary job in the MacNeils' kitchen—and liked it so well that she had been there ever since. That was eight years ago. She was quick and deft and not one bit thorough. She made things look nice without dusting behind anything or polishing the side of anything that did not show. She was a good cook on the whole; her pies and biscuits were delicious, but her cakes were terrible. Alison and then Jean and finally Page had learned to make good cookies and cakes in self-defense. Mrs. MacNeil herself removed the dust that Zoe overlooked; the boys when they were home hosed the porch and waxed the floors. Managing things this way, they all thought Zoe was perfect, because she adored the ground they walked on, would go to any amount of trouble to do anything for them that they wanted, took the most unselfish delight in their joys and triumphs, and mourned over the least of their troubles.

"Oh," said Zoe now, reverently, as if she had met an angel fresh from the upmeads of eternity, "oh, Miss Page, you look so *purty.*"

She forgot the telegram she held in her hand. Page reached for it, so encouraged by Zoe's admiration that it did not even enter her mind that there might be bad news in that yellow envelope. Mother, she thought in a vague, happy way, must be going to fly home for Commencement, or Jean had decided to come with Dad instead of going home with Bill to visit his family.

She mangled the envelope opening it with her forefinger, and read: "DEAR CHILD I HAVE MISSED THE ONLY BUS HUNTING TAXI DAD."

"Ow!" Page uttered a howl of anguish. "Zoe! Daddy can't come! He missed the bus!"

"Oh, now, ain't that too bad!" Zoe's slow tongue and her falling inflection gave full weight to every word. "Ain't that just too bad!" Her good plain face was full of love and sympathy. "Maybe he'll git yere some other way."

Page shook her head, dismissing the taxi idea without comment. A taxi all the way from Exeter? He might as well buy a car. She wanted to fling herself down on the bed and cry and kick, but instead she stood stiff and forlorn, looking at the telegram with eyes that made splinters and darts around the nasty blue typewritten words. Presently something splashed on the word "bus" and blotted it out.

The door opened again, this time without a knock, and Page's grandmother, in a stately dressing-gown, sailed in. Mrs. Richard

Page never knocked on the children's doors, and they never thought of minding. Granny was subject to none of the laws that bound ordinary folk.

"I saw the telegraph boy from my window. What's happened? Who's broken a leg?"

Page sniffled and handed her the telegram. She fumbled at her chest for the little gold arrangement that held her glasses and then, not finding it, stretched the message out at arm's length and read it slowly aloud.

"Dear me," she commented, folding it. "What a pity. Poor Jamie, it will break his heart not to see his baby graduate."

The thought of her father's disappointment had up to that moment not occurred to Page. The situation at once became blacker. In despair she returned to the taxi idea. "He's trying to find a taxi," she said.

"Nonsense. Nothing in that. It will be much too expensive— and your father was born in Scotland. I notice that for all the stress of emotion he got his telegram into ten words."

Page's mind wanted to laugh, but her heart was too woeful.

"Now," said Granny with the briskness that she and Mother both had, "no doubt you're disappointed too."

"Too!" thought Page. "*Too?*"

"But you've got me—and Zoe. Zoe, you go straight away and dress yourself in your very best. No, not your best, that's too short. Put on the dark blue silk I gave you. That's suitable— and the suitable is the beautiful. Come, Page, I need you to help me dress."

Granny's room was at the front of the house on the southwest corner. It contained an enormous, high-topped carved walnut bed that had been brought by her colonizing ancestors up the James River in a boat, and according to tradition had almost caused the boat to capsize. There was a marble-topped bureau of the type fashionable in Granny's youth, a low slipper-chair that every grandchild in turn claimed for his or her own, a mahogany desk bulging at every pigeonhole, and a cherry sewing-table with a green shot-silk bag at the bottom of it. The walls were covered with the pale yellow satin-striped paper that

190

had been immensely stylish when the house was built, but scarcely a segment of stripe, now faded white, was to be seen between the jigsaw-puzzle appliqué of photographs and pictures that showed Granny's taste in art and her loyalty to her children, grandchildren, and great-grandchildren, her friends, and their descendants, and her forebears back through daguerreotypes to silhouettes, American primitive oil-paintings, and exquisite miniatures. The dominant, because the largest, picture in the room was a huge steel engraving of a reindeer on a rock.

Granny's graduation costume, like Page's, was spread out on the bed. The basic dress was made of soft cream-colored Chinese damask, which a friend had brought her from a trip around the world. The dressmaker had made it up so that it was easy to get into, with only one fastening at the neck and another at the side, but Granny had effected some complicated alterations of her own. In addition, she had fashioned a little cape of the left-over material, which had to be pinned just so at the shoulders. An old and fragile lace collar had also to be pinned on, and then came a string of Venetian beads which promptly got tangled in her hair. Page carefully separated the fine white strands, thinking that she wished she had inherited Granny's naturally curly hair, and that it was getting late and she wasn't dressed herself, and whose graduation was this anyhow?

"There!" said Granny. "How do I look?"

At eighty Granny was still the family beauty. Only Jean had inherited her delicate, regular features and deep-set brown eyes, but even Jean had not got anything of Granny's presence. Even at twenty Granny must have been statuesque. The tributes that her admirers wrote in the autograph album still in her desk all compared her to regal lilies and goddesses.

"You look beautiful," said Page sincerely, but hurriedly.

"Wait a minute. I have something to say to you."

"But it's getting late, Granny, and I'm not dressed. Can't you tell me afterwards?"

"These affairs never begin on time. I must have spent five years of my life altogether going to commencements, and I've never been late to one. I have a present for you. It was my

191

dearest treasure when I was a young girl, and I have kept it for you because you are my namesake—and a very dear child."

She took from the desk a little box and laid it on Page's palm. Inside was a gold ring with a little cameo set in seed pearls. Page gasped with pleasure.

"It's lovely, Granny. It's the loveliest thing I ever saw." She put it on her right hand and spread out her fingers, tilting her hand from side to side.

"*My* hand was as white as the little figure in the cameo. I worked as hard to keep it white as you young people do to get yourselves brown. Sunburned? Charred, I call it. Now, Serena Page, a piece of advice goes with it. You are undoubtedly a bright child, but don't let your brains go to your head. Remember, men like women to have intelligence, but they don't like it to show. What are you laughing at?"

"You," said Page, kissing her.

Three long toots of a motor horn sounded outside.

"That's Emily and her father come for us—and I'm not ready."

"I'll go down and distract them, and you come as soon as you can. Don't worry. Mr. Bynum is a nervous train-catcher—always gets to places half an hour before anything happens. My lavender scarf, Page—not in that drawer, the other one. No, the other."

By the time Granny had gone down the stairs and trailed her draperies along the gravel path that led between the spirea hedges to the gate, Page was fastening her organdy belt around her slim waist. The sun was gone, and the room was dim. She switched on the overhead light, and even in that glare, even in the midst of brass bedsteads, and shabby furniture strewn with discarded garments, she thought she did look nice. If only Daddy were going to be there!

She turned off the light and skimmed down the dim stairs and out the front door, letting the screen door slam behind her. Nobody ever locked up in Little Athens.

Mr. Bynum and Granny were in the front seat of the car, Emily in the far corner of the back.

"We have come tonight to a milestone in our lives," said

Emily. "Don't come any nearer to me than you have to—I'm crushable. You look lovely. Are you scared? I'm so glad I don't have to do anything but grab my diploma when Theodore shoves it at me. We took Mother over first because there isn't room for three dressed-up fimmales in this back seat, and I expect she's biting her fingernails—though we told her you'd be late."

Emily nodded significantly toward Granny's back, and they both grinned. Emily had been Page's best friend ever since they were both seven and Mr. Bynum had come to Little Athens to head the Mathematics Department in Middleton College. Emily was small and dark and vivacious, with piquantly irregular features. She was known for talking continually and occasionally saying something amusing enough to be widely quoted. She and Page had gone through dolls and skates and stamps together, but Emily was a little ahead of Page on clothes and boys.

They drove slowly along East Main Street under the great oaks and turned at the stoplight into Buchanan Avenue. The fraternity houses were all alight; shining cars and battered stripped-down Fords were parked in rows; boys on porch railings shouted across bits of lawn to boys on porch steps. Middleton College would be having its commencement soon. Page wondered if Granny really had spent five years of her life going to commencements. Daddy taught Latin and Greek at Middleton, and Granny went to most of the college commencements; she had, furthermore, seen fully half of those whose photographs peppered her walls graduate from one learned institution or another, and some from more than one. What could one more high-school commencement be to her? And yet, she was acting as if she wouldn't miss this one for the world.

Page stretched out her hand with the ring on it. "Granny gave me this for being named Serena Page MacNeil." She would make the name famous. Valedictorian tonight? Pooh. That was nothing. She would win her scholarship to Van Welmar, of course, and after that—some day—she would paint wonderful pictures. Yes, that's a genuine Page MacNeil. We got it when she was young and unknown. We couldn't possibly afford to buy one now.

The High School loomed behind its columns and shed light out into the soft Southern night. Through the tall open windows of the auditorium they could see potted palms and heads of people and hear a shrill bumble of talk. Below, cars crept up the driveway and dark figures and foamy white ones milled about on the porch. A great many boys in white trousers and dark blue coats appeared to be dashing about on errands of the utmost importance. Page and Emily sat tense while the car in front of them, containing part of the orchestra, unloaded.

"To take—no. To make—no. To take *what* the moment on the mountain top," muttered Page.

"Johnnie Doak has got his hair so wet it's dripping in his eyes and still his cowlick won't stay down," said Emily. "Hi, Johnnie, how're you? Oh, I'm scared till my teeth chatter and I haven't got anything to—Page, *where's your essay?*"

Page's heart gave a leap and ceased beating. Part of her seemed to have fallen off a precipice. "I left it home," she said faintly. "It's in Mother's desk."

The front seat now revealed that it was palpitatingly aware of the back seat. Granny turned to look at Page over her shoulder as if she had never seen her before.

"Dear me, Page, why didn't you tell me you had to bring an essay? I thought of course your teacher was taking care of that. It seems to me the teachers should take charge of all important documents at a time like this. They know how fly-up-the-creek girls are—or they ought to. Now you tell me exactly where it is, and *I* will go get it."

Mr. Bynum sat still and looked annoyed without moving a muscle.

Page was paralyzed. The whole Commencement seemed to be tumbling about her ears. At that instant there seemed to be nothing that anybody could do to restore the devastation she had wrought.

"Come on, Granny," said Emily cheerfully, "you and I'll get out and go find Mother and hold a place for Dad, and he and Page can go back for the essay. It won't take a minute—and they haven't even got the cello in yet." She leaned over and patted Page's arm with a firm light little hand. "Don't worry, honey," she said. "It won't matter one bit."

At such moments Page loved Emily from the bottom of her heart and freely forgave her hours of talk about boys and what boys liked in girls. She pulled herself together. "I'm so sorry, Mr. Bynum," she said sanely. "It was a stupid thing to do. But I know exactly where it is, and it won't take me a minute to get it."

Mr. Bynum helped Granny out and then skillfully extricated the car from the line and started back past the fraternity houses. His annoyance vanished, and his kindness came back.

"Too bad your father couldn't get here," he said, "and your mother too. Here we are. Now take your time. Don't tear your dress or lose any of the pages out of that essay."

"I won't be a minute."

Anyhow, Commencement couldn't begin before she got there; she was Valedictorian! Suddenly the tenseness was gone. She felt detached and grown-up and wonderfully calm. She

knew she had been too well drilled to make any mistakes in
her part in the ceremony, and that nobody would notice it if
she did. They would all be concentrating on their own darlings.
True, her family would not be there, except Granny and Zoe,
but what of that? It was only one milestone after all. She had
bigger and more important ones ahead of her.

The orchestra crashed into "Pomp and Circumstance." To its
ponderous strains the girls entered from one side door, the boys
from the opposite one; they met in the center aisle and marched
slowly toward the stage. The audience rose respectfully to its
feet amid a creaking of chairs and a rustling and scraping of
shoes. Page was aware of the indrawn breath of countless admiring fathers and mothers, uncles, cousins, grandparents—and
siblings, she added, using a word she had recently acquired.
She was aware of Marshall Wood at her side, high-school football star and Emily's present most attentive boy-friend. Then
she was aware of the steps mounting to the platform, con-
structed, and apparently none too stoutly, for the occasion. The
two ahead of her swayed, and for a moment she thought they
were going to sit on her head. Marshall seized her by the elbow
and masterfully propelled her upward.

In the center of the stage stood a table piled with long white
cylinders tied with bows of blue and gold; in front of this the

196

lines parted, the girls going to the right and filing into the first row of seats, the boys going left and passing behind the girls into the second row.

Mr. Elliott, the principal, whom traditionally the Senior girls always called Theodore behind his back, the Reverend Alfred Higgins, whose turn it was to give the Invocation, and Dr. Howard Henry of State University, who was to make the Address, came last and sat down in the three carved chairs of state behind the table with the diplomas just as the orchestra achieved its final chord. The audience, after a moment's uncertainty, also sat. Then Mr. Elliott rose and stepped forward.

Page gripped her essay and searched the upturned faces for Granny and Zoe. Granny was sitting between Mr. Bynum and Mrs. Wood; Zoe was far at the back under the gallery, beaming. The big room was full; only one empty seat could Page see, near the front, and she felt a moment's idle pity for the late-comer who should get ushered conspicuously into that.

After the Invocation the prizes were given. Almost everybody got one. Emily's was for Posture. The two most important were the Perry cup, which went to the one who had "done most" for the school (usually interpreted as the captain of the football team), and the Arden medal for the highest scholastic standing. Marshall Wood was summoned, blushing, to the front of the platform to receive the cup, and Serena Page MacNeil followed, pale, for the medal. Everybody clapped heartily. Nobody was surprised, not even Marshall and Page.

Page sat down again, not certain how to manage both her essay and the medal, which, though small, occupied a sizable blue velvet case. She was glad they had voted not to carry flowers. She herself had held out for that in the class meeting because of what Zoe had told her. "The girls that come in from the country—*you* know, Miss Page—from the tinnant farms, they feel so bad because they cain't carry hothouse flowers like the faculty girls do." Page had not said why in the meeting, of course. "Flowers are a nuisance," she had insisted, "and they cost a lot, and they're no good next day after we've toted them for a whole evening. Besides, they spoil our dresses."

Annie Belle Fuller, sitting next to her in a stiff, skimpy white frock from the cheap little store near the garage, came from an unpainted frame house that sat up on stilts high enough for the chickens and the hound dog to run underneath; except for a chinaberry tree there was no green around the house at all, no flowers; the rows of cotton plants ran up to the very door. Thinking of that gaunt house and the struggle that it meant for Annie Belle to come to high school at all, Page felt a twinge of discomfort: why should she have so much and Annie Belle so little—and thousands of others, no doubt, even less than Annie Belle?

Annie Belle nudged her. "I'll hold your medal," she whispered.

Page realized that her moment had come. She clutched her essay.

"The first of the Senior essays," announced Mr. Elliott, "entitled 'William Blake, Artist,' will be read by—" He paused.

There was a flurry in the audience. Page could see heads turning, and she raised herself up a little to look around Mr. Elliott. An usher, very red in the face, stalked solemnly down the center aisle. Behind him, tall and imperturbable, came a gray-haired man with keen blue eyes and a long upper lip. He sat in the one vacant seat near the front and folded his arms.

"—by Serena Page MacNeil," finished Theodore, half turning toward her.

Page came to the front of the stage, all her joy shining in her face, and sent a rapturous smile down to the fifth row, where her father nodded back at her. The audience, who to a man understood exactly what was happening, exchanged satisfied glances and settled down to listen to J. D.'s youngest daughter's essay.

Page, with some surprise, heard her own voice going on like a phonograph while she pursued her independent thoughts. He had missed only a little bit, "Pomp and Circumstance," and the prizes, and Mr. Higgins. There's still the Address and the Valedictory and the diplomas.

Why, then he *must* have hired a car!

So it was a big moment after all.

Page came to the front of the stage, all her joy shining in her face.

Owen Johnson

THE THIRD ROUND

ILLUSTRATED BY *James Ponter*

HELLO, there, Stover!"
"Stover, over here!"
"Oh, Dink Stover, this way!"
Over the bared heads of the bobbing, shifting crowd he saw
Hunter and McCarthy waving to him. He made his way through
the strange assorted mass of freshmen to his friends, where
already, instinctively, a certain picked element had coalesced.
A dozen fellows, clean-cut, steady of head and eye, carrying a
certain unmistakable, quiet assurance, came about him, gripping him warmly, welcoming him into the little knot with cordial
acknowledgment. He felt the tribute, and he liked it. They were
of his own kind, his friends to be, now and in the long reaches
of life.

"Fall in, fall in!"
Ahead of them, the upper classes were already in rank. Be-
hind, the freshmen, unorganized, distrustful, were being driven
into lines of eight and ten by seniors, pipe in mouth, authorita-
tive, quiet, fearfully enveloped in dignity. Cheers began to
sound ahead, the familiar *brek-e-kek-kex* with the class numeral
at the end. A cry went up:
"Here, we must have a cheer."
"Give us a cheer."
"Start her up."
"Lead a cheer, someone."
"Lead a cheer, Hunter."
"Lead a cheer, Gimbel."

199

"Lead the cheer, Stover."

"Come on, Stover!"

A dozen voices took up his name. He caught the infection. Without hesitating, he stepped by Hunter, who was hesitating, and cried:

"Now, fellows, all together—the first cheer for the class! Are you ready? Let her rip!"

The cheer, gathering momentum, went crashing above the noises of the street. The college burst into a mighty shout of acclaim—another class was born!

Suddenly ahead the dancing lights of the senior torches began to undulate. Through the mass a hoarse roar went rushing, and a sudden muscular tension.

"Grab hold of me."

"Catch my arm."

"Grip tight."

"Get in line."

"Move up."

"Get the swing."

Stover found himself, arms locked over one another's shoulders, between Schley, who had somehow kept persistently near him, and a powerful, smiling, blond-haired fellow who shouted to him:

"My name's Hungerford—Joe Hungerford. Glad to know you. Down from Groton."

It was a name known across the world for power in finance, and the arm about Stover's shoulder was taut with the same sentimental rush of emotion.

Down the moving line suddenly came surging the chant:

"Chi Rho Omega Lambda Chi!
We meet tonight to celebrate
The Omega Lambda Chi!"

Grotesquely, lumberingly, tripping, and confused, they tried to imitate the forward classes, who were surging in the billowy rhythm of the elusive serpentine dance.

"How the deuce do they do it?"

"Get a skip to it, you ice-wagons."

"All to the left, now."

"No, to the right."

Gradually they found themselves; hoarse, laughing, struggling, sweeping inconsequentially on behind the singing, cheering college.

Before Dink knew it, the line had broken with a rush, and he was carried, struggling and pushing, into a vacant lot, where all at once, out of the tumult and the riot, a circle opened and spread under his eyes.

Seniors in varsity sweaters, with brief authoritative gestures, forced back the crowds, stationed the fretful lights, commanding and directing:

"First row, sit down."

"Down in front, there."

"Kneel behind."

"Freshmen over here."

"Get a move on!"

"Stop that shoving."

"How's the space, Cap?"

In the center, Captain Dana waited with an appraising eye.

"All right. Call out the lightweights."

Almost immediately, from the opposite sophomores, came a unanimous shout:

"Farquahar! Dick Farquahar!"

"Come on, Dick!"

"Get in the ring!"

Out into the ring stepped an agile, nervous figure, acclaimed by all his class.

"A cheer for Farquahar, fellows!"

"One, two, three!"

"*Farquahar!*"

"Candidate from the freshman class!"

"Candidate!"

"Robinson!"

"Teddy Robinson!"

"Harris!"

"No, Robinson—Robinson!"

Gimbel's voice dominated the outcry. There was a surging, and then a splitting of the crowd, and Robinson was slung into the ring.

In the midst of contending cheers, the antagonists stripped to the belt and stood forth to shake hands, their bared torsos shining in high lights against the mingled shadows of the audience.

The two, equally matched in skill, went tumbling and whirling over the matted sod, twisting and flopping, until by a sudden hold Robinson caught his adversary in a half nelson and for the brief part of a second had the two shoulders touching the ground. The second round likewise went to the freshman, who was triumphant after a struggle of twenty minutes.

"Middleweights!"

"Candidate from the sophomore class!"

"Candidate from the freshmen!"

"Fisher!"

"Denny Fisher!"

The sophomore stepped forth, tall, angular, well knit. Among the freshmen a division of opinion arose:

"Say, Andover, who've you got?"

"Anyone from Hotchkiss?"

"What's the matter with French?"

"He doesn't know a thing about wrestling."

"How about Doc White?"

"Not heavy enough."

The seniors began to be impatient.

"Hurry up, now, freshmen, hurry up!"

"Produce something!"

Still a hopeless indecision prevailed.

"I don't know anyone."

"Jack's too heavy."

"Say, you Hill School fellows, haven't you got someone?"

"Someone's got to go out."

The sophomores began to gibe at them:

202

"Don't be afraid, freshmen!"

"We won't hurt you."

"We'll let you down easy."

"Take it by default."

"Call time on them."

"I don't know a thing about it," said Stover, between his teeth, to Hungerford, his hands twitching impatiently, his glance fixed hungrily on the provokingly amused face of the sophomore champion.

"I'm too heavy or I'd go."

"I've a mind to go, all the same."

McCarthy, who knew his impulses of old, seized him by the arm.

"Don't get excited, Dink, old boy; you don't know anything about wrestling."

"No, but I can *scrap!*"

The outcry became an uproar:

"Quitters!"

" 'Fraid cats!"

"Poor little freshmen!"

"They're in a funk."

"By George, I can't stand that," said Stover, setting his teeth, the old love of combat sweeping over him. "I'm going to have a chance at that duck myself!"

He thrust his way forward, shaking off McCarthy's hold, stepped over the reclining front ranks, and, springing into the ring, faced Dana.

"I'm no wrestler, sir, but if there's no one else I'll have a try at it."

There was a sudden hush, and then a chorus:

"Who is it?"

"Who's that fellow?"

"What's his name?"

"Oh, freshmen, who's your candidate?"

"Stover!"

"Stover, a football man!"

"Fellow from Lawrenceville!"

203

The seniors had him over in a corner, stripping him, talking excitedly.

"Say, Stover, what do you know about it?"

"Not a thing."

"Then go in and attack."

"All right."

"Don't wait for him."

"No."

"He's a clever wrestler, but you can get his nerve."

"His nerve?"

"Keep off the ground."

"Off the ground, yes."

"Go right in; right at him; tackle him hard; shake him up."

"All right," he said, for the tenth time. He had heard nothing that had been said. He was standing erect, looking in a dazed way at the hundreds of eyes that were dancing about him in the living, breathing pit in which he stood. He heard a jumble of roars and cheers, and one clear cry, McCarthy crying:

"Good old Dink!"

Someone was rolling up his trousers to the knee; someone

was flinging a sweater over his bared back; someone was whispering in his ear:

"Get right to him. Go for him—don't wait!"

"All ready, there," said Captain Dana's quiet, matter-of-fact voice.

"All ready, here."

"Shake hands!"

The night air swept over him with a sudden chill as the sweaters were pulled away. He went forth while Dana ran over the rules and regulations, which he did not understand at all. He stood then about five feet ten, in perfect condition, every muscle clearly outlined against the wiry, spare Yankee frame, shoulders and the sinews of his arms extraordinarily developed. From the moment he had stepped out, his eyes had never left Fisher's. Combat transformed his features, sending all the color from his face, narrowing the eyes, and drawing tense the lips. Combat was with him always an overmastering rage in the leash of a cold, nervous, pulsating logic, which by the very force of its passion gave to his expression an almost dispassionate cruelty —a look not easy to meet, that somehow, on the instant, impressed itself on the crowd with the terrific seriousness of the will behind.

"Wiry devil."

"Good shoulders."

"Great fighting face, eh?"

"Scrapper, all right."

"I'll bet he is."

"Shake hands!"

Stover caught the other's hand, looked into his eyes, read something there that told him, science aside, that he was the other's master; and suddenly, rushing forward, he caught him about the knees and, lifting him bodily in the air, hurled him through the circle in a terrific tackle.

The onslaught was so sudden that Fisher, unable to guard himself, went down with a crash, the fall broken by the bodies of the spectators.

A roar, half laughter, half hysteria, went up.

205

"Go for him!"

"Good boy, Stover!"

"Chew him up!"

"Is he a scrapper!"

"Say, this *is* a fight!"

"Wow!"

Dana, clapping them on the shoulders, brought them back to the center of the ring and restored them to the position in which they had fallen. Fisher, plainly shaken up, immediately worked himself into a defensive position, recovering his breath, while Stover frantically sought some instinctive hold with which to turn him over.

Suddenly an arm shot out, caught his head in chancery, and before he knew it he was underneath and the weight of Fisher's body was above, pressing him down. He staggered to his feet in a fury, maddened, unreasoning, and went down again, always with the dead weight above him.

"Here, that won't do," he said to himself savagely, recovering his clarity of vision; "I mustn't lose strength."

All at once, before he knew how it had been done, Fisher's arm was under his, cutting over his neck, and slowly but irresistibly his shoulders were turning toward the fatal touch. Everyone was up, shouting:

"Turn him over!"

"Finish him up!"

"Hold out, freshman!"

"Hold out!"

"Flop over!"

"Don't give in!"

"Stick it out!"

With a sudden expenditure of strength, he checked the turning movement, desperately striving against the cruel hold.

"Good boy, Stover!"

"That's the stuff!"

"Show your grit!"

"Hold out!"

"Show your nerve!"

In a second he had reasoned it out. He was caught—he knew it. He could resist three minutes, five minutes, slowly sinking against his ebbing strength, frantically cheered for a spectacular resistance—and then what? If he had a chance, it was in preserving every ounce of his strength for the coming rounds.

"All right; you've got me this time," he said coldly, and, relaxing, let his shoulders drop.

Dana's hand fell stingingly on him, announcing the fall. He rose amid an angry chorus:

"What the deuce!"

"Say, I don't stand for that!"

"Thought he was game."

"Game nothing!"

"Lost his nerve."

"Sure he did."

"Well, I'll be ———."

"A quitter—a rank quitter!"

He walked to his seconds, angry at the misunderstanding.

"Here, I know what I'm doing," he said in short, quick breaths, forgetting that he, a freshman, was addressing the lords of creation. He was a captain again, his own captain, conducting his own battle. "I'll get him yet. Rub up this shoulder, quick."

"Keep off the ground," said one mentor.

"You bet I will."

"Why the deuce did you give in so easily?"

"Because there are two more rounds, and I'm going to use my head—hang it!"

"He's right, too," said the first senior, rubbing him fiercely with the towel. "Now, sport, don't monkey with him until you've jarred him up a couple of times!"

"That's what I'm going to do!"

"Time!" cried the voice of Dana.

This time he retreated slowly, drawing Fisher unwarily toward his edge of the ring, and then suddenly, as the sophomore lunged at him, shot forward again, in a tackle just below the waist, raised him clear off the ground, spun him around, and, putting all his force into his back as a woodchopper swings an ax, brought him down crashing, clear across the ring. It was a fearful tackle, executed with every savage ounce of rage within him, the force of which momentarily stunned him. Fisher, groggy under the bruising impact, barely had time to turn on his stomach before Stover was upon him.

Dink immediately sprang up and back, waiting in the center of the ring. The sophomore, too dazed to reason clearly, yielding only to his anger at the sudden reversal, foolishly struggled to his feet and came staggering toward him. A second time Stover threw all his dynamic strength into another crashing tackle. This time Fisher went over on his back with a thump, and, though he turned instinctively, both shoulders had landed squarely on the turf, and, despite his frantic protests, a roar went up as Dana allotted the fall to Stover.

This time, as he went to his corner, it was amid pandemonium:

"You're a corker, freshman!"

"Oh, you bulldog!"

"Tear him up!"

"You're the stuff!"

"Good head, freshman!"

"Good brainwork!"

Several upper classmen came hurriedly over to his corner, slapping him on the back, volunteering advice.

"Clear out," said his mentor proudly. "This rooster can take care of himself."

Fisher came up for the third round, visibly groggy and shaken by the force of the tackles he had received, but game. Twice Stover, watching his chance, dove under the groping hands and flung him savagely to the ground. Once Fisher caught him, as they lay on the ground, in a hold that might have been decisive earlier in the match. As it was, Stover felt with a swift horror the arm slipping under his arm, half gripping his neck. The wet heat of the antagonistic body over his inflamed all the brute in him. The strength was now his. He tore himself free, scrambled to his feet, and hurled Fisher a last time clean through into the scattering crowd, where he lay stunned, too weak to resist the viselike hands that forced his shoulders to the ground.

Dana hauled Stover to his feet, a little groggy.

"Some tackling, freshman! Bout's yours! Call out the heavy-weights!"

Scarcely realizing that it was his captain who had spoken, Dink stood staring down at Fisher, white and conquered, struggling to his feet in the grip of friends.

"I say, Fisher," he said impulsively, "I hope I didn't shake you up too much. I saw red; I didn't know what I was doing."

"You did me all right," said the sophomore, giving his hand. "That tackle of yours would break a horse in two. Shake!"

"Thank you," said Stover, flustered and almost ashamed before the other's perfect sportsmanship. "Thank you very much, sir!"

He went to his corner, smothered under frantic slaps and embraces, hearing his name resounding again and again on the thunders of his classmates. The bout had been spectacular; everyone was asking who he was.

"Stover, eh, of Lawrenceville!"

"Gee, what a fierce tackler!"

"Ridiculous for Fisher to be beaten!"

"Oh, is it? How'd you like to get a fall like that?"

"Played end."

"Captain at Lawrenceville."

"He ought to be a wonder."

"Say, did you see the face he got on him?"

"Enough to scare you to death."

"It got Fisher, all right."

While he was being rubbed down and having his clothes thrust upon him, shivering in every tense muscle, which, now the issue was decided, seemed to have broken from his control, suddenly a hand gripped his, and, looking up, he saw the face of Tompkins, ablaze with the fire of the professional spectator.

"I'm not shaking hands on your brutal old tackling," he said, with a look that belied his words. "It's the other thing—the losing the first fall. Good brainwork, boy; that's what'll count in football."

The grip of the veteran cut into his hand; in Tompkins's face also was a reminiscent flash of the fighting face that somehow, in any test, wins half the battle.

The third bout went to the sophomores, Regan, the choice of the class, being nowhere to be found. But the victory was with the freshmen, who, knit suddenly together by the consciousness of a power to rise to emergencies, carried home the candidates in triumph.

McCarthy, with his arms around Stover as he had done in the old school days after a grueling football contest, bore Dink up to their rooms with joyful, bearlike hugs. Other hands were on him, wafting him up the stairs as though riding a gale.

"Here, let me down, will you, you galoots!" he cried vainly from time to time.

Hilariously they carried him into the room and dumped him down. Other freshmen, following, came to him, shaking his hand, pounding him on the back.

"Good boy, Stover!"

"What's the use of wrestling, anyhow?"

"You're it!"

"We're all for you!"

"The old sophomores thought they had it cinched."

210

"Three cheers for Dink Stover!"

"One more!"

"And again!"

"Yippi!"

McCarthy, doubled up with laughter, stood in front of him, gazing hilariously, proudly down.

"You old Dink, you, what right had you to go out for it?"

"None at all."

"How the deuce did you have the nerve?"

"How?" For the first time the question impressed itself on him. He scratched his head and said simply, unconscious of the wide application of what he said: "Gee! Guess I didn't stop to think how rotten I was."

He went to bed, gorgeously happy with the first throbbing, satisfying intoxication of success. The whole world must be concerned with him now. He was no longer unknown; he had emerged, freed himself from the thralling oblivion of the mass.

211

Ernie Rydberg

CARICATURE

ILLUSTRATED BY *Matilda Breuer*

FOR years I had been reading in the papers about people being held up and houses being ransacked. But did anything as exciting as that ever happen to me, or to anyone I knew? No. Never once had I seen a thug or a stick-up man and known he was one. I had come to the conclusion that either my friends and I led a charmed life, or we were not normal. And then, right out of the blue, I was involved in a bank robbery.

Kitty Monahan and I were in the little branch bank just off the campus at State. It was closing time, and there were only three or four other customers at the windows. The porter had pulled down the front shades and was standing by the door, ready to lock it.

I'm not sure just what happened. The first thing I knew, the porter was walking backward with his hands in the air, and another man, with a gun in his hand, was locking the door from the inside.

"O.K.," he snapped. "This is a stick-up. Get your hands in the air. Keep 'em there and nobody'll get hurt."

Did I say "involved"? Well, that is exactly what I meant, but it requires a bit of explaining.

Something about Kitty Monahan had bothered me the first time I saw her, one day in the library. It wasn't her clothes. They were a little on the plain side, but not outstandingly so.

It wasn't her hairdo. She had naturally wavy black hair. Later I noticed that she seemed friendly enough, and that her voice was soft and nice. But that afternoon, as she sat scribbling furiously, as if final exams were coming up next day, she sure had me bothered.

I had seen her around the campus any number of times after that. We would say "hello" when we passed, but I never really talked to her until one afternoon, about six weeks ago, when we tried out for positions on the freshman-girls' basketball team.

I arrived early, for once. When I came into the locker-room I saw Miss Humbolt, our physical-ed teacher busy at the blackboard and thought she was the only one there. Then I saw Kitty sitting on a bench in front of the lockers.

Whenever there is something about a person which bothers me, I feel uncomfortable around them. That was the way I felt about Kitty Monahan, and my first reaction was to avoid her. Then, suddenly, I decided to go over and talk to her. She did not hear me coming because of my sneakers. She had a paper towel spread out on the bench beside her, and with quick strokes she was sketching a picture with a lipstick. I only caught a glimpse of it, but there was no mistaking Miss Humbolt.

Miss Humbolt is nice, but I understand on good authority that she tips the scales at slightly over two hundred—and she isn't fat. Her biceps ripple like a lumberjack's, and her shoulders are broader than State's All-American football center's.

Kitty glanced up and, as quick as a flash, crumpled the paper. There was a scared look in her big black eyes.

"So you're the one!" I gasped.

"Shhh!" hissed Kitty. "You won't tell, will you?" she whispered pleadingly.

"Of course I won't tell!" I answered indignantly. "And that is a promise. Here, let me see."

As I straightened out the paper, I could feel a grin creeping over my face. It was Miss Humbolt, all right. Just a bunch of scraggly lines that did not seem to go anywhere, but there she

213

was—all mixed up in tremendous shoulders and muscles twice as big as life.

Just then some more girls came in, and the teacher called to us, so I folded up the paper and gave it back to Kitty. I was so excited that I could not pay attention to anything Miss Humbolt was saying. Kitty—State's mystery artist! I could hardly believe it.

It had started in February with the Freshman Hi-Jinks in the gym. The most hilarious thing about the party was the decorations—life-sized pictures of school celebs tacked all over the walls. Prexy. Dean of Men. Dean of Women. Professors. Glamour gals. Big-shot athletes. All of them done in scraggly lines, but you couldn't miss who they were. Weak chins were twice as weak. Flat chests were concave. Big noses put Durante to shame. We howled until we were almost sick.

Nobody knew who had done them. Nobody could find out— not even Prexy. Word got out that he had confiscated every one of them after the party—for evidence.

Our Prexy is a tall, gaunt man—very brilliant and very stern. His Adam's apple has a way of driving up and down his throat like a piston whenever he gets up to make a speech. You can imagine what his picture looked like!

Well, he was hot on the trail. He found that the pictures had been blown up by an art studio downtown from small sketches which had been brought in by Joe Thomas, chairman of the decorations committee for the Hi-Jinks. Joe swore up and down that he did not know who drew them—that he had found them on a bench in front of the library. He stuck to his story and got off with a lecture in Prexy's office. The trail seemed to have come to a dead end, and the culprit was still at large.

I came to as Miss Humbolt was reading off the list of players she had selected. Kitty was a forward on the first team, and I was to be a substitute guard. Then we scrimmaged a little. I was guarding Kitty, and I found her fast and slippery. As she caught the ball in scoring position, I blocked her. But to my amazement, the ball flew through the air and swished into the basket, while I stood there flat-footed!

214

All of a sudden, light dawned! Kitty was a southpaw. That was what had been bothering me—the way she had sat all hunched over in the library, scribbling her notes with her left hand. Of all the ridiculous things, I thought, to take a dislike to a person because she is left-handed. About as logical as a lot of opinions you form so blithely about people.

I dressed quickly and waited to walk home with Kitty. She did not live in the dorm but with an aunt in town. Her bedroom and her studio, complete with big window and all, were actually in the attic—but a charming one. Her pictures—water colors; oils, and charcoal sketches—were all wonderful, as far as I could judge. From then on we were inseparable.

"I started drawing when I was three," she told me one day. "A picture of my father. I guess it looked a little like him, for my folks were enthused and, as I grew up, they gave me all the art I could get in our home town. They wanted to send me east this year, to Arts and Crafts College, but couldn't afford it."

"What I can't understand," I said, "is why someone in the art department here hasn't spotted you as the one who did those sketches. You would think they must know your work by now."

"Those silly sketches!" She chuckled. "I've never done anything like that in class. They're just a habit of mine. For years I've carried a pad and pencil around with me, and the first thing I know—in the park, on the streetcar, anywhere—I'm sketching someone who interests me. But I'm certainly going to be careful about what I do with them from now on."

You see, the excitement over her pictures had flared up again. The sketch of Miss Humbolt, done in lipstick on a paper towel, had been found in a trash receptacle, stuck to a wad of chewing gum, by Freddie Davis who is working his way through school in "maintenance." The search was on again.

"Gee," moaned Kitty, "why wasn't I more careful?"

The basketball tournament moved on rapidly, and the freshmen beat the sophomores in the semifinals. I was thrilled, because I got into the game and won my freshman sweater.

It was a proud moment when Kitty and I, along with the

others, marched up to get the gay-colored sweaters with our class numerals stitched on the left pocket. It was as hot as blazes when we came out of the aud, but we put the sweaters on anyway.

"Jiminy!" exclaimed Kitty in dismay. "What time is it?"

"Quarter to three," I told her. "Why?"

"I have to get a cashier's check at the bank. Come on, perhaps we can make it."

Well, that is what we were doing in the bank that afternoon of the robbery. Kitty was about to fill out one of the bank forms, and I was standing at her elbow, trying to figure out how she managed to write upside down, when the man snapped, "O.K.! This is a stick-up."

Up flew my hands. I was scared stiff. The teller began sliding currency under the grille, and the man scooped it into a bag. Then I noticed something. Kitty was pressed close against me. She had her right hand in the air, but not her left. And with the pen in her left hand she was making swift strokes on the bank form she had started to fill out. The robber evidently did not notice that only three arms were in the air—he was too busy scooping up the money.

It was all over in a couple of minutes. The robber slipped out the front door, and we heard a car drive away. Somebody set off the alarm, and a bell began to clang. Everyone was talking at once. Sirens began to scream, and then the police rushed in.

They asked for a description of the robber so that headquarters could broadcast a general alarm. The responses were amazing. The man was tall. He was short. He was thin. He was husky. He had on a brown coat. He was in his shirt sleeves. Everybody, it seemed, had a different idea. The police did not pay much attention to two frightened girls. They listened mostly to the bank teller and the other customers.

Finally they allowed us to leave, and we went over to Kitty's. We ripped off those smothering sweaters and sank into chairs. Then I remembered something. "Let's see that drawing," I demanded.

Kitty was very sober as I studied the sketch. It looked exactly like the robber. I knew there was something odd about him, but I had not realized what it was until I saw the way the left-hand corner of his mouth drooped in Kitty's drawing.

"The prowl cars will surely pick him up," she said nervously, biting her lower lip.

I knew what she was thinking. "You ought to give this to the police," I advised, handing the telltale sketch back to her.

"But I can't!" she wailed. "Everybody would know who made those sketches. Prexy would find out, and I can't be kicked out of school now."

We sat in her studio, feeling pretty glum. Kitty filled in her sketch with color. Brown trousers. Dark blue coat. A gray slouch hat. Auburn hair. It was the robber to the life.

"I'm sure they will pick him up," I reassured her. "Like as not they've caught him already."

But they didn't catch him. For two days Kitty and I glued our ears to the radio at every news broadcast. We bought the newspapers the instant they hit the stands. There was plenty of space devoted to the holdup, but never a clue as to who had done it. Kitty and I were fit to be tied.

On the third day Kitty said, "I can't stand it any longer. I feel like an accessory after the fact—or whatever they call withholding evidence. I'm going to the police, no matter what comes of it."

We were pretty scared when we walked into the police station. Kitty insisted on seeing the chief himself, but the chief was in no mood to be bothered, for the newspapers had been riding him. But we waited, and finally he stomped angrily out of his office.

"Well?" he snapped. "What is it? What do you kids want?"

"We were in the bank when it was held up," Kitty blurted out nervously. "I—we saw the robbery. I drew this picture of the thief."

The chief looked at it, and his mouth fell open. "Lippy McConnell!" he gasped.

You should have seen the excitement. Everybody crowded

around. A light flashed, and a man with a camera darted out the door. Reporters began shouting questions at us. Kitty had intended to ask a pledge of secrecy from the police, but she saw there was no use now trying to hold anything back.

It was dark when we were allowed to leave, and we stopped at a drugstore for a sandwich. A man came in with a bundle of papers, and we fell over each other to buy one. Right in the middle of the front page was a big picture of Kitty, with the chief holding up her sketch, which was as plain as all get out in the photograph.

"I guess it is all over but the shouting," Kitty moaned as we trudged miserably home.

At two the next afternoon Kitty was in Prexy's office, and I paced up and down the corridor outside for almost an hour.

"What happened?" I cried, when she finally came out. "Are you expelled?"

"No. But Prexy gave me fits. Said I was misusing my talent. He was nice, though, when he said I did the right thing in going to the police, regardless of what it meant to my own future, and—say! Did you know Prexy's brother is head of the Arts and Crafts College?"

"He is!" I exclaimed. "Isn't that the one you wanted to go to so badly?"

Kitty burst into tears. "I've got a scholarship," she sobbed happily. "Prexy sent some of those crazy sketches to his brother. And just look at this!" She handed me a check from the bank for five hundred dollars. The police had caught Lippy Mc-Connell less than twelve hours after the description based on Kitty's sketch had been sent out over the teletype.

I'm going to miss Kitty next year. But I'm tickled pink for her. That gal's going places!

B. J. *Chute*

MASTER MIND

ILLUSTRATED BY *Bob Fink*

IF IT had happened to anyone but Irish Mehaffey, maybe it wouldn't have been so crazy.

Irish is the fullback of the Kent High School football team, and he is a nice guy and a great back but very, very dumb. He weighs close to two hundred pounds and has bright yellow hair that stands up like a starched cornfield. We like him fine, but, as I say, he is not the intellectual type.

Now, I don't consider a knowledge of Greek or calculus essential to a fullback, but there is one thing that is essential and, as captain and quarterback of the team, I got pretty worried about it.

Irish couldn't learn signals. You could work out a foolproof system, and then along would come Irish and the backfield would knit itself up like an antimacassar, the ball would travel west and Irish would set off east into the rising sun. It wasn't good.

Finally, one afternoon in practice, he really distinguished himself and crashed into his own center. A second-string player picked up the resulting fumble and ran for a touchdown. In a regular game, it would have been simple murder.

That was when I called Chippy Martin into consultation. Chippy is editor of the *Kent Weekly*, and he is fascinated by psychology. He looked at Irish thoughtfully and then said, "The trouble with you, Irish, is you don't concentrate."

"I don't?" said Irish.

"He doesn't even think," I said gloomily.

"Quiet, please.—Now, Irish, listen. The human mind is capable of practically anything. All of us vastly underestimate our capacities. The subconscious, for instance, is a controlling force which we seldom use. Do you ever use your subconscious, Irish?"

Irish said cautiously that he wasn't sure he had one. Chippy laid his face in his hands for a moment, but came up swinging. "Exactly. You *don't* use it, and it is a great imponderable force." He stopped off to translate "imponderable," and then went on, reeling off a lot of lovely textbook words. I left them alone, certain it would do no good but willing to try anything once, if it would help the Mehaffey subconscious.

The next day, in practice, a miracle happened. Irish ran through signal drills like a veteran. I was stunned but as happy as a bookworm in a one-volume encyclopedia, and I patted Irish on the back exuberantly. He looked at me rather oddly. "It seems to work, doesn't it?" he said.

I said that, whatever it was, it worked fine and to keep it up.

"I don't understand it, Jerry," Irish said, "but Chippy says it's a matter of concentration. It's kind of peculiar."

"You just go on being peculiar that way."

He shook his head and said he hoped it was all right. All right? It was wonderful.

Then came Peabody High. I knew in the first ten minutes that Peabody was going to give us a fight. A pint-sized halfback named Jimmy Alfeo ran forty yards, winding up nice and cozy in our end zone. They converted, and it was seven points for Peabody. We settled down to respecting Alfeo and put a cork in that gentleman's activities, so they started smacking us from end to end. This fine offensive frenzy was rough on their center who was blocking his ears off, and when we got the ball I threw Irish right at him. It was payday for Mehaffey, and he picked up enough yardage to squat us in enemy territory. A pass did the rest, and we scored, tying the game up, 7-7, when the ball sailed over the crossbar. This irked Peabody, and they started tossing the book at us, but we got cagey and play bogged down.

Then, with six minutes to go in the game, Peabody's full bucked almost to midfield again. Two long passes got their ears pinned back, and on fourth down they were on their own forty-six with no future. We spread to receive the inevitable kick.

I went back to safety, and I happened to glance at Irish. He had a most peculiar expression, sort of faraway and baffled as if he was listening to voices, but there wasn't anything to hear. I shrugged and waited for the kick.

All of a sudden, Irish started waving his arms around and yelling for time out. I said to myself, "He's sat on a bee," which was silly because he wasn't sitting and autumn isn't beetime. But I figured, insects or no insects, desperation had set in, so I signaled the referee.

Irish came racing over like a trumpeting elephant and grabbed me with both hands. "Jerry!" he yelped. "They're going to try a pass!"

I said, "Are you crazy?" Risking a pass, with the score tied and Peabody in its own home state, would be just the kind of thing that sets the squirrels looking for nuts. I said again, good and exasperated, "Irish, are you crazy?"

He shook his head. He looked kind of solemn. "No. They're planning a Statue of Liberty."

For a moment, I thought he'd played too much ball in too much sun. Then he suddenly shook his head as if he was getting gnats out of his ears. "Gee, I'm sorry, Jerry," he said. "I just had a sort of—hunch, or something. I guess I'm screwy."

I guessed so too, but I whacked him on the shoulder and told him everything was all right, and he went back into position. The whistle shrilled. I got all set to catch the punt and figured that with good blocking I might be able to put us in shooting distance for a field goal. I waited.

It was a pass.

It was the Statue of Liberty, that gray-bearded, second-cousin-to-Methuselah, old Liberty play. Alfeo sparked it. We were caught as flat as a pancake under a steamroller.

The scoreboard said Peabody 13, Kent 7. And we never got it back.

I walked home very slowly. If I had played Irish's crazy
hunch, we'd have ended with at least a tie. But what quarterback in his senses was going to look for a pass out of a set-up
like that? I took a deep breath but it didn't do any good, and
then I heard footsteps behind me. It was Irish and Chippy.

Chippy said, "Irish told me, Jerry. About the pass."

I said, "Oh."

Chippy poked Irish. "Tell him what happened, Irish."

"I don't know what happened." Irish looked bewildered. "I
was just standing there, Jerry, waiting for the kick, and I didn't
have to concentrate on you because there weren't going to be
any signals, and so I just happened to concentrate on the Peabody quarterback, and—"

"And?" Chippy prompted.

"And all of a sudden," Irish said unhappily, "it was just like being tuned in on a radio set, and I knew he was going to call the pass."

I gulped. Chippy looked at me and nodded very slowly. "That's it, Jerry," he said in an awed voice. "Irish is telepathic."

I said, "That's nonsense!" I think I shouted it.

Chippy reached out a hand and made me stop walking. "Irish," he said, "what's Jerry thinking about now?"

Irish looked at me, and you could see wheels going around in his head. "He's thinking that maybe he's got sunstroke and he'd better go somewhere and have a coke."

I leapt like a porcupine that's sat on one of its own quills. It was perfectly true. I stared at Irish, and I think my teeth were chattering.

Chippy stared at me. "See what I mean?"

I saw. There was no question about it. Kent High School had a telepathic fullback.

Well, of course, in a way it was wonderful. After all, we knew every play before it came, and the sports-writers called us "the team with the sixth sense." But there was one thing that wasn't wonderful, and that was the way it affected Irish. Every day he got sadder and sadder and his piledriver line plunges lost a lot of their power. But it didn't matter. We won anyway. The miracle team. The year's sensation. We couldn't go wrong.

Then, the day before the big game of the season against Pike High, the bottom fell out.

Pike is tradition. If we beat Pike, it doesn't matter what happens the rest of the year, and the corridors at Kent were plastered with signs reading, "Take a poke at Pike," "Make Pikers out of Pike," and "Pike's Peak or Bust."

I was not prepared for what happened.

It was ten o'clock at night and I had just crawled into bed when the doorbell rang. Pop yelled upstairs at me, "Hey, Jerry! Irish wants to see you," and I battled my way into my bathrobe and went down. Irish was sitting on the living-room couch.

"What are you doing here?" I asked. "You're supposed to be in bed."

He put his head in his hands. "I know.—Jerry, I'm resigning from the team."

I felt as if someone had pulled the room out from under me. "You're *what?*"

"Resigning from the team." He looked like one of those hound dogs that practically burst into tears if you speak to them. "I can't possibly go on playing for Kent with things like this. It isn't—it isn't— What's the word for it?"

All of a sudden, I knew what the word was that he wanted. Maybe it had been kicking around at the back of my mind too. It wasn't ethical to use a telepathic fullback.

"That's the word," said Irish. "Ethical."

I hadn't said it. He'd heard it crashing around in my head. It was unsettling. It was more than unsettling, because, now that I honestly thought of it, it certainly wasn't ethical, and what were we going to do? Play Pike without a fullback?

I needed reinforcements, and I walked over to the phone and called Chippy Martin. When I finally got him awake enough to tell him what had happened, there was a short stunned silence. Then he said, "I'll come right over. Just be calm, Jerry. Be perfectly calm."

He was a fine one to go around telling people to be calm. When he came in, he was wearing two unmatched shoes, his kid brother's raincoat, and his father's hat. The raincoat sleeves came to his elbows, and the hat came to his chin.

"Irish," said Chippy, even before he got through the door, "you can't *do* this to us. It isn't ethical."

It wasn't a very good choice of words, and, after a minute, Chippy could see it for himself. Irish was perfectly right. We couldn't argue with him. I went out into the kitchen and got some bananas and cookies, and we just sat, moody as three black crows, and chewed.

After a while, Chippy said, "There's some way out of this. We can't possibly replace you, Irish.—Look, can you play without being telepathic?"

"Huh?" said Irish, rather thickly. He had just peeled his third banana.

Chippy elaborated. "I mean, you only get the other team's plays when you concentrate on the quarterback, don't you? Suppose you concentrated on someone else, like me on the sidelines, then what do you think would happen?"

"I'd know what you were thinking. Like now. You're thinking I'm eating too many bananas and that I'm an awful nuisance and you wish you were home in bed."

Chippy winced. "I don't think you're a nuisance, Irish," he said hastily, "and you can have all the bananas you want. They can pop out at your ears, for all I care. Please stop concentrating on me."

After this outburst, he sat still for a moment. "Well, if you thought about me during the game, you'd be all right, wouldn't you?"

226

Irish said cautiously, "I don't know. I might just accidentally start thinking about the quarterback, and then—"

"Then you'd know the play," I said.

Irish nodded miserably and reached for another banana. I put a cookie in his hand instead, before he started climbing trees and asking for coconuts.

"Well, in that case," said Chippy, "keep it to yourself."

Irish looked at him. "You mean, even if I know what's going to happen, I just stand there and don't tell Jerry?"

"Exactly. When our team's got the ball, you concentrate on Jerry. And, when Pike's got the ball, concentrate on me."

Irish gulped. I gulped. After a moment, Chippy gulped, but that was his banana. He wasn't a football player and he didn't see all the difficulties ahead. Still, it was worth trying. I stood up. "You go home to bed, Irish, and forget about this. All you have to do tomorrow is lug that ball. See?"

"I see," said Irish. He sounded as happy and buoyant as a sick clam.

Chippy got up and put on his father's hat. His ears disappeared. "Look," said Chippy, his worst suspicions confirmed. "I've lost weight."

I pushed them both out the door, and then I staggered back to bed.

It didn't rain for the Pike game. The sun came out and the sky was blue and life was one grand sweet song. Or ought to have been. The way I felt, it could just as well have been raining Maltese kittens and St. Bernards.

We had scouted Pike pretty thoroughly. They had a fine team, powerful and fast. Their quarterback, Joe Nesbitt, had quite a reputation, and their ends were flypaper on passes. I knew we'd need Irish to tighten the line and pull them in. I wanted to be able to mix the plays and use everything we had. This was *the* game. I looked at Irish. He was buckling his helmet and talking to himself. I had never seen Irish talking to himself before, and it made me nervous. I went over and touched his arm, and he jumped like I'd hit him with a cactus.

227

"Oh, hello, Jerry," he said wanly.

"What were you talking about, Irish?"

"Me?" said Irish. "Peter Piper picked a peck of pickled peppers, a peck of pickled peppers—"

I clutched him. "Irish!"

"Huh?"

"Don't *do* that!"

He looked at me reproachfully. "But I have to concentrate on something, Jerry, and Peter Piper helps me keep my mind off Joe Nesbitt and what he's thinking."

"I thought you were concentrating on Chippy."

He shook his head. "I tried that. He thinks too fast. First it's the weather, and then it's the game, and then he starts writing an article in his head, and I get all confused. I thought Peter Piper would clear things up."

I shook my head—it was a fine day for head-shaking—and went back into position with my knees playing reveille. We won the toss and elected to receive. It was a beautiful boot, end-over-end, and I pulled it in on the fifteen and started uptown behind good crisp blocking. Irish took his man out cleanly—him and Peter Piper. I began to feel better, and I hit the thirty-eight before I was stopped.

An end run picked up eight yards, and we were knocking at the midfield door. I called Irish on an off-tackle play and he made the down. I gave him the nod again, and he blasted the Pike line for another first. The Kent stands began to shriek. We pulled a reverse, and it was like taking candy from a baby. First again, on the Pike thirteen.

"We want a touchdown," yelled the stands. We couldn't miss.

We didn't. In three plays, Irish whammed the ball straight through and, on the last one, he went over the line. Six points for Kent, and the game barely started. I felt colossal. We converted, and Pike was seven in the hole. It was Christmas, and Santa was stuffing our stocking.

Joe Nesbit returned our kick to the thirty-eight. Two line plunges netted about seven yards. I took another look at Irish, and suddenly I saw him straighten up and look wildly around

him. He knows the play, I thought.

Well, so did I. We covered for a pass.

We covered, but the pass was good anyhow. Pike had a first down on our forty-seven, and I could see Irish's lips moving. Pike's next pass was incomplete and nearly intercepted; they tried once more and kicked into the end zone.

That threat had failed. We took the ball on our twenty and got ready to roll. But Pike was steadying, and what was more they had an eye on Irish. He made about two inches, and then we were set back five yards for an offside. I kicked, and it was first and ten for Pike on their forty-four. They came up over the ball very fast and hit a stone wall. Then the left half found a hole and scuttled through for twelve. A pass was complete on our thirty, and the receiver added seven yards before he was stopped.

Irish's face was all screwed up. He'd known it was coming. I winced all the way through, from helmet to cleats. Joe Nesbitt passed laterally. The half fumbled, and Irish pounced, re-covering.

Happy days! I thought. Irish couldn't have known the guy would fumble, so it was heads-up playing that did that one for us, not telepathy. I saw Irish beaming for a change.

But they slapped our wrists again, and we made five yards in three tries and kicked out of trouble. At least, we thought we were out of trouble. Joe Nesbitt had his own notions and hiked to the forty-seven. First and ten. They pulled a cute play, a fake pass and a run to our weak side. Irish did a funny thing on that one. He started to drive in, suddenly stopped and just stood, looking helpless, with his hands spread wide.

It was almost a twenty-five yard run. I called for time out and went over to Irish. It was like I thought; he'd known the play, blew in to break it up, realized suddenly he wasn't sup-posed to know it and stopped practically in mid-air.

This was going to be lovely. I told him to pick out a clover or something on the field and concentrate on that. He said, "Yes, Gerry," very meekly, and then added, "Which clover?" I hit my forehead with my hand and told him to go back to concentrat-ing on Chippy. However confused Chippy's thoughts were, they couldn't be any worse than what was happening.

Pike was rolling. It took them two shots to reach out ten. We stiffened and threw them for a two-yard loss, and then their right half wrecked everything with an end run. He downed the ball back of our goal posts, and it was 7-6.

They tied it up in a bowknot on the kick. The quarter ended 7-7.

230

In three plays, Irish whammed the ball straight through.

In the second quarter, we played on the seesaws. Irish was lousy, a word which my English teacher says he deplores, but if he will find me another word for what Irish was I'll be happy to use it. You could see what was happening to the poor guy. He was always concentrating on the wrong thing at the wrong time, and it must have been like chasing ants at a picnic. You scoop them out of the hot dogs, and they turn up in the thermos bottle. I started longing for the good old days when nothing had been wrong with Irish except a genius for mixing signals.

Then, in trouble again on our own twenty-two, we quick-kicked. Joe Nesbitt fielded and, like a little gentleman, he fumbled. We recovered by a miracle and were set up in scoring territory once more. I dropped back for a long pass, it settled like a homing pigeon, and the end stepped over the line without a finger laid on him.

The try for goal was short, but the score was 13-7 in our favor.

In the third quarter, Pike took to the air and camped twice in scoring territory but we kicked out of danger. Then an awful thing happened.

With about five seconds to go in the quarter, Nesbitt squirmed and fought his way into the secondary. The play had exploded out of a lateral and caught all of us off balance, including Irish who had undoubtedly been concentrating perfectly legally on a clover. I saw a startled look spread across Irish's face, and then I saw him spin and start after Nesbitt. Now, Nesbitt is fast, but Irish was coming in on an angle and, by all the laws of mathematics, physics, and luck, he had a good chance to cut Nesbitt off his feet.

But Irish slowed down. I actually saw him doing it. His feet stopped hitting the turf and his hands stopped reaching. When he made the tackle, he was wide out, and his shoulder struck air. Joe Nesbitt didn't even have to shrug to clear him; Joe Nesbitt just kept on running.

Kent 13, Pike 13. I called time out, stalked over to Irish and shook him. "You crazy loon," I sputtered, "what happened to you?"

Irish stared at me. I gave him another shake, like a malted milk. "He's faster than I am," said Irish.

"Who's faster than you?" I yelled.

"Nesbitt."

"Who says he's faster?"

"*He* said so," said Irish, as if that explained everything.

"What do you mean, *he* said so? He didn't say anything—he was running, which was what you should have been doing too."

Irish looked at me forlornly, and then he looked at the ground. "He was thinking about it," Irish muttered. "He was running hard and he was thinking he was faster than I was, and I heard him thinking it and I knew he was right, and so I guess I—I just—Jerry, I'm resigning from the team right now!"

All I knew for certain was that there was nobody to replace him. "Look, Irish," I said firmly, "you've got to stay in. There's only one quarter left in the game." I shut my eyes tight and prayed for strength. "Now, listen," I said, "this sounds crazy, but do it anyway. When we've got the ball, concentrate on me. When we haven't got the ball, just don't think at all. See?"

"But—" said Irish.

"Don't think at all," I repeated. "And don't try to do anything. Just get out of the way. Don't try to make a tackle, don't back up the line. *Just get out of the way.*"

He looked at me. I guess he thought I was crazy. I knew I was, but I couldn't see any other answer. He'd be all right on offense if he concentrated on me, because I'd know what he should be doing. But I couldn't nurse him along on defense, never knowing what to expect, and I figured the only safe thing was for him to keep his paws off the whole business. I said, "Don't argue, Irish. Do what I tell you."

He said, "Yes." He didn't have the slightest intention of arguing.

Time-out ended, and we lined up for the kick. The stands stopped breathing. Then the whistle shrilled, and Nesbitt booted the pigskin. It lifted in the air, hung for a second over the crossbar and dropped, safe—14 to 13 for Pike as the quarter ended.

The fourth quarter was most peculiar. Irish did just what I'd told him to; he concentrated on me so hard when we had the ball that his ears must have been stiff, and he never missed a signal. The only trouble was that Pike, with its one-point lead, had no intention of giving ground.

Time ticked its way out. The clock showed two minutes to go. A sequence of running plays found us near midfield. I thought of a fake center buck and lateral that we had been successful with a few times. It was worth trying. If it flopped, we still had time for a couple of passes that might click.

I called signals. I could almost feel Irish concentrating on me, and I had the consolation of knowing that, anyway, he would get the signals right. The ball was snapped.

And, too late, something clicked in my mind, and I saw the play I should have called, the play I would have called if my brain hadn't been all wound up with Irish's. There was a hole big enough to drive a truck through between defensive right tackle and guard. If I had shot a double spinner at that hole, Irish would be on his way.

And then I saw, too late again, what I had done by thinking about the spinner play. Half of me had directed the fake center buck; half of me was mourning over a double spinner that could have been. And, poor Irish, concentrating on both halves, was a split personality.

Completely lost, he tucked the ball under his arm and ran toward me.

I fled. He chased me. The whole Pike team chased him. I raced for the sidelines. I wanted to tunnel my way under the nearest bench and disappear forever, but some reasonable instinct turned me downfield. One lone thought wavered in my shattered brain. I knew I mustn't run toward our own goalposts. "The other goal," I thought. "The other goal!" And then I simply rolled up like an embattled hedgehog and removed myself from the scene.

Irish didn't follow me, because I'd rolled without thinking about it. He was following my mind, not my legs, and my mind was fixed on Pike's goal line.

It wasn't football; that much I'm sure of. It may have been baseball or water polo. Tiddleywinks, perhaps. It looked like Waterloo. Irish beat a path down the sidelines. Pike pounded after him. I never did know what became of our boys; I guess they just decided to faint in their tracks.

With the Kent stands screaming, Irish stampeded over the Pike forty-yard line, the thirty, the twenty— A Pike runner came up out of nowhere. On the ten, he drew level with Irish. On the three, he hit him. The bleachers rocked with the concussion; I think a couple of clouds fell out of the sky.

Irish fell face down with a mighty thud, stretching for the last precious inch. He wasn't over the goal line.

But the ball was. Kent 19, Pike 14.

He was dazed when he finally sat up, and he was rubbing his head. He said, "What happened?"

I told him. My own head was singing a victory chant, and the sun was as bright as firecrackers. I told him what had happened, how first I'd signalled one play and then thought of another and how he'd mixed them together and gone mad. I told him that he'd won the game for Kent.

Irish looked at me crossly and shook his head hard. "What's the trouble with you, Jerry? You're talking through your hat. How could I possibly know what you were thinking?"

I looked at him, and I tried to be calm. It must have been the crack on his head, I thought, and no doubt Chippy would have eighty-two fancy names to explain it. But, whatever it was, Irish Mehaffey, our telepathic fullback, was telepathic no more.

So that's the story. Chippy said that if I wrote it all out on paper it might clear my mind and I'd stop having nightmares.

In the meantime, if anyone can suggest some way to make a fullback learn how to memorize signals, they may write me a letter, outlining their theories. The address is Kent High School.

Jackson V. Scholz

HOOP HOKUM

ILLUSTRATED BY *Clarence Biers*

THE big moment was approaching, and Sandy Parker hoped he was prepared to meet it. He sat tautly on the side line, watching his team, the Titans, wage a bitter, uphill battle.

The muscles of his legs, beneath the woolen sweat suit, tingled with an apprehension he had never known before. He fought against its weakening effect, telling himself grimly that he'd have to pull himself together for the job ahead of him.

The Titans were discovering in the Baker College Colts an unexpected bundle of co-ordinated power. The visitors' attack was sharp and deadly, their defense was strong. Sandy cracked the knuckles of his tremendous hands, squirming in an agony of suspense. It was vital in his scheme of things that the Titans take the lead before the first half ended.

They almost did. Their brilliant center, Larry Peel, dropped a long set-shot to tie the score 28-28. String Hoffer, towering right forward of the Titans, scored another field goal to put the Titans out ahead. The Shelton College fans went wild. Sandy Parker's breath came easier—but not for long.

The Colts unleashed a blistering pin-point attack which riddled the Titan defense in the closing seconds of the half. The net beneath the Colts' basket jerked convulsively—three times —as Colt sharpshooters found the target. The Titans were trailing 32-28 when the period ended. They were gloomy.

This was the big moment Sandy Parker had awaited. He was supposed to entertain these sour-faced fans, make them laugh. He had hoped the Titan team would leave them in a more responsive frame of mind. He felt that the team had let him down. This was going to be tough.

However, like all true artists, Sandy pulled himself together to face a chilly audience. He even derived a certain satisfaction from the challenge it presented to his talent. He'd make 'em laugh, so help him.

When the two squads left the floor for their fifteen minutes' rest, Sandy peeled off his sweat suit. He was wearing basketball togs with a huge 13 upon them. At first glance he looked tall and stringy, a deception, because his muscles were wiry, flexible and well distributed. His face was long, large-featured, and extremely mobile, a quality which accounted for his gift of pantomime. He could register a gamut of emotions without uttering a word. He took a deep breath, dribbled a basketball toward the center of the floor, and went into the act which his admirers called "Hoop Hokum."

The fans, most of whom had seen the act a dozen times before, were unresponsive at the start. They were brooding about the Titans' trailing score, and about the possibility the Colts might win. They were hard to crack, and Sandy, fighting down his early panic, settled to the job in earnest.

He was good. He had to be to put his act across. All by himself he played the positions of both teams as well as that of the referee. He would dribble down the floor, stop, then guard himself violently with one long arm while he tried to shoot for the basket with the other. He would struggle determinedly with a "held ball," then wrestle his opponent to the floor where the battle for the ball continued.

Tentative titters came from the crowd. Sandy worked harder. Pretty soon the crowd was laughing, and Sandy knew he had achieved an impressive victory. He threw himself into the work with all his skill.

In the role of referee he called fouls on himself, then stared at the official with an outraged who-me? expression on his face. He argued wordlessly with the referee and always lost the argument.

In moments of great confusion he got his feet tangled and

237

fell down. In other moments of high strategy he would spin the ball on the tip of his finger. He had another trick which invariably confused the opposition. In making a bounce-pass he would bounce the ball between his legs with his left hand while his right hand retrieved it in the rear. His finger-spread was such that he could hold the ball as an average man might hold a grapefruit.

His buffoonery almost covered up the fact that he was clever with the ball, clever with the mastery of an experienced player. His bank shots were impressive, his set shots deadly. He moved with a shifty, limber speed.

He finally had the fans rolling in the aisles. Their laughter rocked the gym. It was a great tribute to his genius, the greatest tribute he could ask. Creating laughter was the breath of life to Sandy Parker. He was a natural born comedian and gloried in it. No flattery he could imagine could compare to laughter. It was tops. It was exhilarating.

He was smart enough to end the act while his audience was still convulsed. He went back to his seat breathing heavily, and very happy. Once more he had enjoyed a splendid triumph.

His breathing soon returned to normal, because he was in topnotch shape. He should have been, due to his daily workouts with the Titans for the purpose of learning enough fundamental basketball to perfect his act. Coach Carter had permitted this despite Sandy's stubborn refusal to join the squad. He didn't want to be an athlete, he wanted to be a clown.

There had been considerable resentment among the other members of the team at first, and the fact that they now accepted him was a high compliment to Sandy's personality and his ability to sidetrack all further show of resentment with his timely gags.

He was happy and complacent now as he enjoyed his latest conquest. When the game got under way again he was still wrapped in his own agreeable thoughts. His dream was interrupted by a swift, shocked silence in the crowd. He focused his eyes upon the court, seeing promptly that the crowd's concern was justified.

String Hoffer, jumping for a rebound off the backboard, had landed on the floor unbalanced. He had turned his ankle. He was sitting down now, holding it, an expression of angry annoyance on his face. Coach Carter took him from the game. He was a valuable man to lose.

Brick Brady came in to take his place, a fine player, but a hot-head. Brady lasted for five minutes before losing his temper. He roughed the Colt right guard on a held ball. The referee tossed him from the game, and the Titan fans were plunged into the depths of misery.

As well they might be, because this two-game series with

239

the Colts would decide the Conference championship. The Colts needed both games to win the title, while the Titans could achieve the crown by winning only one. Small wonder that the fans were shocked by the sudden disastrous turn of events. They knew the weakness of the Titan reserves. The only other forward of any class at all was temporarily ineligible because of low scholastic standing.

The fans' shock, however, was minor as compared with the one in store for Sandy. He looked up to find Coach Carter standing before him. Carter said, "I've got to send you in at right forward. There's no one else. Report to the scorer."

Sandy merely gawked at him.

"Snap out of it. I gave your name and number to the scorer before the game. You're an official member of the squad. I didn't think I'd ever have to use you, but I had to cover all the angles. Get moving!"

The sharp authority of Carter's voice lifted Sandy from his chair. He was dazed, dumbfounded at this thing that had befallen him. He started toward the scorer on wabbly knees, which stiffened gradually as his sense of the dramatic took control. This was a role he had never played before. Maybe he could save the game. Why not? What an act!

So when the referee motioned Sandy to the floor, Sandy was his former jaunty self, full of confidence in his own ability. His appearance, it is true, brought worried mutterings from the fans, which he ignored. He had brought them to heel once tonight, and he could do it again. He glanced at the score board, 51-49 in favor of the Colts. The big electric clock told him there were six minutes left to play. Sandy Parker to the rescue!

He entered the game when the ball was out of bounds in possession of the Colts. The ball was passed, and Sandy found himself in the center of swift action. He had practiced enough with the Titans to know his way around the court. He began flattering himself that he looked like the real McCoy. Why not? He was an actor.

The Titans, who had shown no pleasure at Sandy's appearance in the game, were forced, nevertheless, to let him handle the ball a few times, and, as Sandy handled the ball well, they showed more confidence in him.

Fighting desperately, the Titans got some breaks. Larry Peel, with all receivers guarded, sank a long set-shot to make the score 51-51. The Colts bagged another, 53-51. A Colt guard pulled a personal foul on Dave Jeffer, Titan left forward. Jeffer dropped the free throw in the hoop to make it 53-52. The crowd was going crazy.

Larry Peel, finding no receivers, sank another long one to put the Titans ahead 54-53. Peel got a tremendous hand which Sandy resented. He didn't like to hear another man applauded.

So Sandy tried a long shot of his own, despite the fact that Dave Jeffer had shaken his defenders and was waving frantically for the ball beneath the basket. Sandy missed the throw. An angry growl came from the crowd, a troublesome thing for Sandy to hear. Its weight upon his mind was probably accountable for his next colossal blunder.

The game was in its final seconds when Herb Casser, Titan right guard, broke up a Colt attack. He snapped the ball to the nearest Titan, who happened to be Sandy. Sandy, looking for a receiver, made an automatic gesture. He did it by instinct, without thinking. He twirled the ball on the tip of his forefinger, a fine piece of juggling, also a great break for a Colt forward who flashed in behind Sandy, snatched the ball from his fingertip, and whipped it to an alert teammate who was breaking for the basket. The pass made connections just short of the hoop. The Colt sailed into the air and dropped the ball neatly through the net.

The play was followed by an explosion like a clap of thunder, an angry roar from Titan fans. Their rage was aimed point blank at Sandy Parker, and it hit him like a withering blast of heat.

It left him mildly paralyzed with shock. He was accustomed to loud laughter, not to bitter fury of this sort. There was no bulwark in his nature to withstand it. He wanted to crawl away and hide and, following this blind urge, he started dazedly from the floor, another involuntary blunder. Larry Peel grabbed Sandy then and said savagely, "You got us in this mess, you jerk, now show some guts and stick around to help us out of it!"

Sandy stared at Larry blankly, then said dully, "Yeah. Yeah, sure."

The score was 54-53, the Colts ahead. It remained that way when, seconds later, the gun went off to end the game. The grim Titans left the floor without a glance at Sandy Parker, whose only thought was to get out of sight as quickly as he could, away from the pointed comments of the fans. He was grateful that he didn't have to join the others in the Varsity room. He sat before his locker a long time, trembling from the reaction of the terrible experience he had had. He waited until the showers were empty before he took his bath.

He slept fitfully that night. In the morning he had to force himself to go to classes. His entire world, in the space of a few brief moments, had been turned upside down, and he knew no way to bring it back to level keel.

However, when he appeared upon the campus his thoughts began to form into a pattern that made sense, a progressive step for which the attitude of the student body was responsible.

He had been prepared for almost anything, anger, contempt, or open hostility. Instead, he encountered something against which he had erected no defenses, and the revelation shocked him to the marrow of his bones. He was treated with a gentle, rather sorrowful understanding. The implication was that he was not to blame for what had happened. He had been a victim of circumstances, a weakling who had been called upon to do a job too big for him. He was a fine comedian, sure, but beyond that he was a washout.

His palms went clammy with an apprehension he could not control. Maybe they were right. Maybe he possessed nothing, after all, but a gift for clowning. Maybe he *was* the sort of guy who would fold up in the clutch. Had he ever done anything to prove the contrary? He didn't know. He only knew he had failed when thrown into a challenging spot, and he would probably never have a chance to try again.

He was wrong in this respect. When he returned to his room that afternoon he found Coach Carter waiting for him. Carter said abruptly, "Have an early dinner, Sandy. I may have to use you in the game tonight."

A huge lump formed in Sandy's throat. He tried to speak and couldn't. The coach went on.

"Tough luck's hitting us on all sides. Two more of our reserves are out. Jake Miller came down with a strep throat. Harry Lister mashed his thumb in a car door. I'll need every man who has ever shot a basket. Get an early dinner and report at seven."

The coach was out the door before Sandy could get his voice or thoughts in working order. He eased himself weakly in a chair, and before long his weakness disappeared. A tight line formed along his jaw.

"You wanted another chance," he reminded himself aloud. "And now you're going to get it."

The act of putting it in words caused him another sinking spell. He remembered his reception, that day, upon the campus. He didn't want to go through that ordeal again. Thinking of it made him a little peeved and gave him another prop to lean on. If he managed to make a creditable showing in the game tonight, he could tell 'em all to go jump in a lake. Clinging to this sustaining thought, he went out to an early dinner.

When the game got under way, Sandy Parker, for the first time was sitting on the players' bench. He felt strange there and out of place, ignored by the other subs whose attention was riveted upon the game.

String Hoffer, his ankle taped heavily, started the game in his usual right forward spot. It was evident from the beginning, however, that the ankle gave him trouble. He had to favor it, as a result of which the Titan scoring machine was handicapped.

The Colts, with a possible championship within their grasp, were hot as firecrackers. They started off with an inspired rush, hitting on all cylinders. They tallied four goals before the Titans broke into the scoring column, and it began to look as if the Titans were headed for a fine shellacking.

The Titans themselves, however, refused to accept this as a possibility. Instead of going down under the Colts' first broadside, the Titans manned their guns and settled down to a grim uphill battle, and it was uphill all the way. They fought with a desperation which halted the Colts' scoring spree, forcing the visitors to earn their following goals the hard way, which they did, maintaining a dangerous margin as the game progressed.

String Hoffer's ankle gave out midway of the first period. Coach Carter replaced him with the able, but hot-headed, Brick Brady. Brady played with his customary all-out violence and began, as usual, to acquire his collection of personal fouls. At the end of the first half he had been charged with three, each of which had contributed a free-throw point to the Colts' score. They led 34-25. It was a sober, worried squad of Titans who made their way to the dressing room for the fifteen-minute rest.

Sandy, although he joined them, was not particularly concerned with their plight. He was concerned primarily with his own immediate problem—that of getting in the game. It was a pretty safe bet, he reasoned, that if Brady fouled himself out of the game, Sandy would get his chance. If he did he would try his best to make the fans feel cheap for the way they'd treated him. Slow excitement found its way into his nerves.

Brady chalked up his fourth personal in the early minutes of the final half. His fifth personal came but seconds later, and the referee automatically tossed him from the game. The fans groaned. Coach Carter, his face taut with strain, said, "All right, Sandy, get in there."

Sandy thought his heart was going to stop, but it didn't— not quite. It was hammering solidly against his ribs when he took his place along the free-throw lane. He was acutely aware of the fans' solid, disapproving silence occasioned by his entry in the game. The muscles of his jaw went tight. He'd show 'em.

The free throw was successful, bringing the score to 38-30 with the Colts still on the long end. The Colt left guard tossed the ball in from the out-of-bounds line behind the basket. He flipped it to a teammate who started a fast drive for the Colt basket. The Titans scrambled to break up the threat. Sandy raced up-floor with the others, surrounded by players of both teams, yet feeling strangely alone upon the court. The feeling

244

irritated him because he knew its source. His teammates didn't want him there. They felt he was a liability. The Colts, on the other hand, considered him a minor threat at best. His feeling of loneliness was weird. It scared him just a little.

A Colt forward looped the ball on a long pass toward the basket. It was a poor throw, too hard, too flat. The ball struck solidly against the outer rim of the basket, rebounding crazily toward the center of the court. Sandy found the ball in his hands, scarcely knowing how it got there. He saw instantly that the ball had sailed across the heads of almost all the other players presenting him with the sort of break he'd prayed for.

He whirled like a cat and started a rattling dribble toward his basket, his long legs carrying him swiftly across the polished boards. He could hear the pounding of feet behind him. He tossed on more coal. A Colt guard who had held back for just this sort of an emergency, came out to meet him, waving his arms like windmills.

Sandy, without checking his forward speed, slammed the ball over the Colt's outstretched arms, aiming for the backboard. The Colt whirled toward the basket, but Sandy had the jump on him. Sandy got there first. Judging the rebound neatly, he went high into the air to meet it. He fielded the ball like a first baseman fielding a high throw. He grabbed it with his huge right hand and, with his feet still off the ground, he flipped it toward the hoop. He saw it settle in the net before his feet got back upon the floor.

An explosive blast of sound came from the Titan fans. It was impulsive, unpremeditated. It threw Sandy's logic slightly out of gear. He had intended to regard them with a fishy eye as if to say, "Smoke *that* one in your pipe!" He experienced, instead, a swift moment of confusion, as if some force had tampered with his well-laid plans. The yell died promptly, suggesting that the fans regretted the demonstration. This registered upon Sandy too. It peeved him some, but not enough to make him carry out his previous intention of giving them a dirty look. His bewilderment increased. He couldn't understand what was disturbing him.

His teammates showed reserved approval, their attitude implying they were scared to hope that Sandy could repeat his spectacular performance. It was obvious enough they believed he had been lucky, and that they intended to keep their fingers crossed until the proof was more convincing.

The Colts put the ball in play once more from behind the Titan basket, advancing toward their own basket with a series of accurate, sharp passes. The Titans tried to break it up before the danger zone was reached, failing dismally. The Colt center received a pass almost beneath the net. He had an easy shot, so easy that he took a fraction of a second too much time. A long arm snaked out of nowhere. A big hand cuffed the ball as it was rising toward the hoop. The arm and hand belonged to Sandy Parker.

There was a scramble for the ball. Herb Casser, Titan right guard, snared it. The Titans spread out for a fast excursion toward their basket. The play was ragged, yet they managed to retain the ball. Sandy was in a position several times to receive a pass, but the Titans showed distrust by keeping it away from him.

The Colts had time to set up their defense. It was air-tight. The Titans couldn't crack it. Dave Jeffer finally uncorked a long desperation heave which hit against the backboard, bounding back into the court. Sandy judged the rebound neatly, sailed high, and brought the ball down with him. He took two fast dribbles toward the side line, then whirled swiftly toward the basket. A Colt guard reached him in a couple of long strides. Sandy faked a set-pass. The Colt went high to block it. Sandy held his shot until the Colt was on the floor again, unbalanced. Then Sandy took deliberate aim and dropped it through the net.

Once more a violent burst of sound came from the Titan fans. This time they didn't cut it short. It rolled across the court, engulfing Sandy Parker like a wave. He experienced, for the second time that night, a surge of brief confusion. Some great truth was struggling to release itself from the welter of his thoughts. The struggling increased until the thought broke through.

He had been trying to balance the sound of sincere cheering against the sound of laughter, and he had learned now that cheering was equally satisfactory. It didn't surprise him much, because both were tributes to a man's ability. The important thing just now was that the yells were proof he had the stuff to come through when the chips were down. He had proved it to himself and to the fans.

Best of all, he had proved it to the other four Titans on the floor. They finally accepted him as a member of the squad, assured that he wasn't just a dope who could do nothing without clowning. He felt the change at once and found it good. It came upon him swiftly that basketball was a terrific game, even without clowning.

The Titans, possessed of an unexpected scoring threat in Sandy Parker, came to life with a violence which set the Colts back upon their heels, taking them completely by surprise.

The Titans closed the gap to 38-36 before the Colts were able to pull themselves together. The Colts dug in to hold their lead. They began to battle with the savagery of wildcats. The game blazed to new heights of fury while the fans screamed themselves into hysterics and the players fought with all the strength and skill they had for every precious point.

The Titans surged into the lead in the closing moments of the game. They went ahead for the first time, 56-54. The fans went wild. The Titans, however, were tiring fast, worn down by fresh and talented reserves from the Colt bench. The Colts had a strong edge in that department, an advantage which displayed itself as the seconds ticked away.

They tied the score, then went out in the lead again, 58-56. The Titan fans were taut with worry. Sandy, swerving like a flying bat, broke clear from his defenders, took a beautiful pass from Larry Peel, leaped high, and dropped the ball into the net to tie the score. The Titan fans took on new life.

The time, now, was desperately brief. The Titans, forcing themselves beyond their paralyzing weariness, broke up a Colt attack, gained possession of the ball, and started a final, valiant scoring effort of their own.

The Colts threw up a defensive wall. Larry Peel snapped the ball to Sandy. The basket was a long way off, but Larry yelled. "Shoot, Sandy, Shoot!"

It was a last-ditch, hundred-to-one chance, but Sandy set himself. A Colt guard lost his head and came at Sandy hard, barging solidly against him. The referee's whistle and the final gun went off at the same time. The playing time was over. Sandy's spirits hit the skids, until he realized what had happened. The referee took the ball, handed it to Sandy, and motioned toward the free-throw circle. Sandy's breath jammed in his throat as he realized the significance of the referee's decision. He could win the game by sinking his free throw. If he missed, the game would go into a five-minute extra period, and the Titans, he was certain, did not possess the stamina to tackle it successfully.

He walked slowly toward the free-throw lane, trying to control his jumping nerves, trying to ignore the deathly silence

which had settled on the court. Sandy had not practiced free throws very much. He was not an expert. Yet the game depended, now, upon his skill.

He set himself, realizing that he had to hurry, that he dared not give the matter any thought. To weigh the consequences now might be disastrous.

He went into a slight crouch, straightened, and let the ball rise from his fingers. There was a horrifying, frozen instant when he believed it wouldn't reach its target. It seemed to hang suspended in the air before it touched the basket's rim. It bounced, and Sandy died a thousand deaths. It bounced into the air. It nudged the backboard gently, then dropped into the net.

A great roar came from the Titan fans. It sounded good to Sandy. His legs were weak, so weak, indeed, that he obeyed his first involuntary impulse. He sank to the floor, then started for the sideline on his hands and knees, an exaggerated cartoon of an exhausted player.

The cheering stopped abruptly. There was an amazed silence, after which the fans began to laugh. This also sounded good to Sandy. It was evidence that they could still enjoy his nonsense, having learned that he had more than comedy to offer.

William Heyliger

CLUTCH MAN

ILLUSTRATED BY *Lloyd Rognan*

JOE MORTON fed cartridges into the revolver and was haunted by the story in the *Evening Telegram*. The fresh target, tacked to the range butt, seemed to be scored with a flaming, taunting headline:

KEN BOLES A CANDIDATE
Captain of Storm King High Target Team
Yearns for Labrador

Joe snapped the gun shut. Why, he asked himself, had Ken Boles waited so long to ask for a place with the Ethan Scott expedition? His own application had been put in weeks ago and life, somehow, had seemed to date from that hour. In the Scott library, hung with trophies and specimens, the explorer had talked to him of the far corners of the earth, of hard trails and cold camps, of danger and daring and, breathless, he had drunk it all in. That was when he had begun to dream, to dream passionately. If he had known then that Ken Boles wanted to go—

At the left end of the firing line a revolver barked. With the second report he knew that this was rapid fire—five shots in ten seconds and then repeat. The spacing of the explosions was uncanny, almost like the measured beat of music. Nobody but Ken, Joe knew, had that gift of machine-like, deadly, unhurried regularity. Peril might lie in those Labrador wastes, and skill with firearms would count. Count heavily. And with only one boy to be taken along— He rubbed the barrel of the revolver along his sleeve.

251

Behind him Bill Hager spoke: "How, Joe?"

"All set."

Hager's voice became a familiar drone: "All ready on the right? All ready on the left? All ready on the firing line?"

Joe's arm had come up. Ten shots in twenty seconds. Rapid fire had always been his weakness—bad timing and worry strain. Either shooting too fast and losing points through inaccuracy or else shooting too slowly and losing points on overtime. That's where Ken had him. Labrador might produce emergencies where a man had to be able to shoot unerringly and fast.

Hager's whistle piped the command to fire.

The sights had wavered below the back, center bull. They came back. Joe squeezed, and the recoil threw the barrel high. He cocked and came down upon the target and fired again. His nerves began to clamor. Was he shooting too slowly? Time seemed rushing away, and his ears were strained against the feared, expected shrill of the time-up whistle. He'd have to get the shots away faster— He knew instinctively that the third shot was bad, that he had jerked, that the sights had not been centered.

Miraculously the first burst of five was finished. He reloaded, and his eyes ached. His right hand was clammy with sweat; he tried to rub it dry. He knew what happened to a score if a gun-barrel began to slip around in a moist grip. Behind him a car lurched up the rutted mountain road to the range; a motor died and popped. Mr. Scott's car always gave that pop when the ignition was shut off. His eyes ached.

He began to shoot. Four, and still no whistle. He fired again and dropped the revolver to his side.

"Under nine seconds," Hager shouted in his ear.

Joe glanced slowly at his friend and grinned. The grin was stiff. Momentarily he felt all in, gone. It would pass, of course; but this ordeal of rapid fire always left him sunk. Nerve-strain! How, he wondered, could Ken shoot so casually against the second-hand of a watch.

The bitter tang of burnt powder hung in the air. As he walked toward the butt Hager strode on one side of him and Mr. Scott walked on the other. He ripped the target away from the frame. Ragged holes gaped in the black bull, some of them running together. He counted the punctures—seven. In the first white ring he had three nines. Far from the black core another yawning hole gave him a six. That was the hurried shot on which he knew he had been off.

"How?" Hager asked eagerly.

"Seven bulls," said Joe. If he hadn't been so far off on that one shot— But he was always ragged on at least one. Usually two or three.

Ken Boles, recording the practice scores, came along the firing line. "How many, Joe?"

"All."

"Two completed bursts? Who held the watch?"

"I did," said Hager.

Ken said nothing.

Hager flushed hotly. "Look here, Ken—"

The captain ignored him. "What was your rapid-fire score, Joe?"

"Ninety-three," said Joe.

Ken entered the record. "I had a ninety-seven."

"Ninety-three isn't what you'd call bad shooting," Mr. Scott observed.

Ken swung around genially. "Hello, Mr. Scott. Was that your car just rolled in? N-no; ninety-three isn't bad; not if you can turn it in regularly. Too bad Joe can't hit the nineties in the team matches, isn't it?"

A breeze rustled through the trees on the sheer, high ground that made a natural backstop for the butts. Ken closed the scorebook and put a pen away. More cars crawled up the hill and into the clearing as the men of the Storm King Gun Club gathered for practice. Mr. Scott drawled a question:

"All your boys through, Ken?"

Ken's hand made a gesture. "Didn't I promise I'd always have them out of the way when the men came up? Least I could do considering the club lets us use the range."

"Commendable," Mr. Scott murmured.

Was there something in his voice? Joe wasn't sure. And if there was something—what? Men were talking, loading guns, spreading out along the firing line. He left the range clearing with Bill Hager, and together they trudged the sandy, rutted road that wound down through the New Jersey hills to the town. The echo of pistol shots reached them on the wind.

Sand pits, strewn with rocks and boulders, yawned at the sides of the road. The early June sun was hot, and the air was spiced with the fragrance of sweet fern. A lone buzzard circled in a dome of blue, and the firing momentarily died away.

"Well," Bill Hager said out of the silence, "he did it again, didn't he?"

Joe Morton shifted his cartridge belt and said nothing.

Hager made a vicious kick at a stone and sent it hurtling into one of the pits. "Always there with the little dig. Always ready to tell somebody what a great man Ken is and what a small dot somebody else is. 'Too bad Joe can't hit the nineties in the team matches, isn't it, Mr. Scott?' Where does he get that stuff?"

"I don't do it in the matches," Joe said.

But Hager saw that the corners of Joe's mouth had tightened.

254

"Suppose you don't? Does that give Ken any license— Heard the latest?"

Joe waited.

"You're out of it. Labrador, I mean. Ken has it sewed up."

"Who said that?" Joe asked after a moment.

"Ken. Who else? He's already promised caribou horns to one fellow."

Resentment began to burn in Joe's veins.

"If the team had its own range," Hager burst out, "and its own coach—"

"Skip it," said Joe. He had his resentment under control. "That's old stuff."

It was old stuff, but it was nevertheless true. And talking, Joe thought with an ache in his throat, only made it worse. If the high-school team did have its own range and a coach— But a range ran into money—big money. Money to buy land that could be used for only one sport. Money to grade, and to build butts, and to dig out or else throw up a backstop. Storm King High didn't have the money. Not that the range itself made any difference. The team was lucky to have the use of the gun-club property. But if there was a school range there would naturally be a coach. And if there was a coach he would be a team coach and not a one-man look-at-me.

Not that Ken Boles wasn't a good man with a revolver. Joe wanted to be fair. A swell man—by far the best the team had. Confident and graceful and nonchalant. A cool head, a steady hand, a sharp eye, and a sense of rhythm almost as precise as a stop watch. The sort of fellow who filled the eye. And yet— There was the rub—the "and yet." When a fellow had so many gifts why did he make it a point to broadcast himself and stick a belittling knife into everybody else?

The feet of Joe and Hager left sand-ruts and came out upon macadam. They paused at a corner of the town. Hager spoke:

"He hasn't it sewed up, has he?"

"What do you think, Bill?"

"Why—" Hager's eyes were bleak with a loyal distress.

"That's the answer," said Joe. He turned down the street

255

toward a brown house, a lawn, and an encircling hedge. So even
Bill Hager thought— The hedge across the front of the house
needed trimming. He brought clippers from the barn and began to snip. His mind was full of heart-wrenching pictures.
The mounted head of a wild boar in Mr. Scott's library, the
snarling mouth wicked even in death; elephant tusks, chilled
ivory, eternally motionless and yet suggestive of chilled death
in the jungle; an alligator on a high shelf, its yawning jaws still
capable of sending a shudder through a living spine. Hard trails,
cold camps, daring and danger!

Joe sighed. The hedge was finished. He dried the clippers as
his father came along the street.

"Seen the *Telegram*, Joe?"

"Yes, sir."

"Ken's a better shot than you, isn't he?"

"Much better."

Mr. Morton gave him a quick, keen glance. "How is this
going to affect your chances?"

"Well—" Joe spoke the word vaguely. What was the use of
talking about it? His father wouldn't understand the ache that
throbbed deep in him. His father hadn't seen maps on a living-
room wall, rifles and spears, the head of a wild boar—

After supper, in the twilight, he crossed the yard to the old
barn transformed into a garage. Climbing the ladder to the loft
he snapped on a light. A target was tacked to a beam—his prize
score. One hundred at rapid fire. Practice, of course. His lips
twitched. Ken was right, as he had never been able consistently
to hit the nineties in team matches. And Labrador called only

to men who would be there when they were needed, when life and death, perhaps, hung by a thread.

There was a workbench between two windows, and the tools of a pistol enthusiast. A small pot for melting lead, a bullet mold, a scale for weighing powder, caps, empty shells, a small machine that poured the powder into the shell and then crimped the brass around the bullet. He was working at the machine when somebody whistled downstairs and feet mounted the ladder.

"Listen!" said Bill Hager. "This match with Taft High next Saturday is the last."

Joe loaded another shell. He had thought of all that. His last chance to make a showing.

"Ken will probably call two practices this week," Hager went on. "You can get in more than that. Half a mile this side of the bridge the railroad embankment makes a swell backstop. I'll hold the watch."

Joe said slowly: "It will take a lot of your time."

"Heck!" Hager jeered. "Don't you worry about my time. I'll get paid for it. I have a mortgage on the first caribou horns."

Joe Morton's eyes filled with a light.

Caribou horns were, he told himself, practically a dream. Swell of Bill Hager, but still a dream. A friend could hold a watch on you and yet be unable to make you a pistol shark. Nevertheless, the light continued to flame in his eyes. Tuesday afternoon they went to the embankment, and he worked on four targets. Forty shots, rapid fire. He went overtime on the first burst of five; after that he was always inside the whistle. His last three targets gave him a 91, and 93, and a 92.

"Didn't I tell you?" Hager clamored. "You'll be right on everybody's heels."

The gun was hot. Joe waited for it to cool and stared at the targets. This seemed the weirdest dream of all. Three times over 90. Suddenly it was no longer a dream. He exulted:

"I may show them something, Bill."

"May? You're going to. No question. By this time Saturday with the match over—" The words stopped abruptly. "The wind's blowing something in on us," Hager said in a flat voice.

Joe saw Ken Boles coming toward the embankment.

Ken walked lightly, easily, almost negligently. He glanced at the targets in Hager's hands and then at the still hot gun.

"Rapid fire, Joe? That's not a bad idea. You need it. A lot of fellows get sore when you tell them a thing like that, but— Well, it's the truth, isn't it? How were the scores?"

"Fair," said Hager. He folded the paper targets and placed them in his pocket.

Ken gave him a thin smile. "Mr. Guardian Angel Hager," he murmured. Then: "Practice tomorrow, Joe. No more straggling up to the range in twos and threes. We'll meet outside the school at 3:15 and go up in a body."

"What's that for?" Hager demanded.

"You a member of this team?" Ken asked blandly. "As a matter of fact it's a new rule I've made. As captain I'm responsible to Mr. Scott, who got us the use of the range, and I'm not going to have fellows fooling around up there and getting into mischief."

"Sweet potatoes!" Hager fanned himself. "You're getting round-shouldered, Ken. Must be the weight of your responsibilities."

Ken gave him another thin smile. "Tomorrow," he said pointedly, "I'll hold the watch on Joe."

The glory of those three "90" targets was gone. Joe taunted himself. Why was he such a weak sister? Why did he let Ken's manner, Ken's maddeningly superior sort of criticism, get under his skin and goad him?

Hager said: "How do you do it, Joe? Me, I'd be up and down that lad's neck. I'd make him pretty sick of his high hat. You take it without a word. You're not afraid of him?"

"I'm more afraid of myself," Joe said after a silence. Inside he was shaking with a white-hot storm. If he once let himself go— And anyway, what was the use of talk?

"Got time for one more, Bill?"

Hager yelped. "That'a boy. The old fight. Don't let him get you down." He tacked a target to the improvised butt.

258

The storm took its toll. Joe found himself jerking the trigger instead of squeezing. He couldn't stop it, and his arm trembled badly. Hager held the watch and squirmed and wanted to shout "Too fast, Joe, too fast." The last shot was fired, and Hager went to the target.

"Eighty-two," he called back.

"Good as that?" Joe's voice was tight.

"Well—" The loyal Hager tried to find words. "That's out of your system, anyway."

But Joe knew nothing was out of his system. That was the way Ken Boles rubbed him—and might always rub him.

Next day the team, escorted by a sprinkling of students, trailed up the rutted mountain road toward the range. Joe found Ken beside him purring instructions and advice. The trick, the captain explained, was merely a matter of timing. Of course, some fellows didn't have it and never would get it—they didn't have the knack. Not exactly dumb, but— Well, they didn't get the knack. Bland eyes slanted a sidelong glance and Joe, silent, began to stew up inside.

Abruptly Hager pushed through the straggling line and

walked on the outside of the captain. "Sounding off, Ken?" he asked pleasantly.

He might have been one of the mountain trees. Ken said, coolly aloof: "It's this way, Joe—"

"What way?" Hager interrupted unabashed. "Rapid fire?"

The captain flushed.

"Boy, what a guesser I am. You've been talking a lot about rapid fire lately, haven't you, Ken? Bad psychology. A captain ought to understand psychology, don't you think? Suppose Joe gets thinking too much about a stop watch and not enough about his target? That might mean a bad score against Taft. And then, of course, there's Labrador."

Ken's self-sufficient calm was dented. "If you don't get out of here—" he began in a blaze of anger.

"Going," Hager said mildly. "Had a thought on my chest I wanted to get rid of for a long time. Funny about thoughts, isn't it?" He took a dozen steps forward, walking close to the edge of the road, close to the edge of the yawning, rock-strewn sand-pits. He looked back and spoke with mock deference, and Joe saw the dancing mischief in his eyes. "This far enough away from you, Ken?"

Ken seemed to choke. Joe marveled. Ken rubbed him along the raw, and Bill Hager rubbed Ken.

Still looking back, Hager went on. His right foot tickled the edge of a pit.

"Careful," Joe called sharply.

Hager jerked his head around to watch his footing. At that moment the sand crumbled. For an instant he clutched at air, trying to regain his balance. Then his body seemed to slither and to fold up, and he tumbled down into the bottom of the pit.

Somebody called a hilarious "Yea, Hager!" The crowd milled about the pit. Hager, lying prone on his back, did not move.

Joe leaned over the edge. "Are you hurt, Bill?"

Hager did not answer. All at once he seemed frozen, petrified. The dancing mischief was gone from his eyes. They had rolled to the side, and the whites bulged. It was as though he stared in a sort of horror at something—

"Rattler!" a voice shrilled.

And then Joe saw the snake. Evidently it had been sunning in the pit. Now it lay, coiled and deadly, between Hager and a harsh bulk of rock very, very close to Hager's shoulders. Its head was poised, steel-springed, ready to strike.

What Joe did then was done instinctively, without conscious thought. His right hand moved; the gun leaped from its holster. Perhaps he sighted—afterwards he could not tell. Flame roared in a red burst from the barrel.

The snake leaped as though some invisible force had lifted it from the ground. It struck the rock, writhing madly, and then stretched out slowly and twitched.

Joe threw a foot over the edge and slid down into the pit; boys slid after him spraying sand before their heels. Hands reached for Hager and hauled him to his feet. He sat upon a boulder and was deathly sick.

"How was that for rapid fire?" he gulped weakly.

Ken bustled and fluttered. "If you had kept out of my way, Joe— Are we going to stay here all day because a rattlesnake was killed?"

"Maybe it should have been a caribou," said Hager angrily. He crawled up to the incline of the pit.

Walking along the road again, Joe Morton could see the rattler and Hager's rolling, bulging eyes. And his memory was hot with the echoes of a taunting drawl and a sudden, angry outburst. Ken—team scores—Labrador. He had never put them together before—not Hager's way. Was Ken really trying to smear him, break him down and run him out? But Ken, even before there had been any thought or talk of Labrador, had been the same rasping, irritating glory-seeker.

Joe's shooting that day was dismal and ragged. Only 90 at slow fire where they gave a man all the time in the world. Time firing—ten shots in forty seconds—brought him a low 82.

Hager said, "Reaction, Joe. Forget it."

Ken came along the line to hold the watch for rapid fire. "A man can't shrug off bad shooting," he remonstrated; "not unless he's satisfied to do bad shooting always."

261

The captain's voice had been clamorous. Letting the whole world know about it, Joe reflected. He fired, cocked, and fired once more.

"Too bad," said Ken, and clucked sympathetically. Joe bit his lips and went on shooting. When the last shot was out of the gun Ken slipped the watch into a pocket. "Let me know how bad it is," he said, and walked away.

Joe counted the target. A 72. Bad! Impassive he gave the score to Ken.

"You'll do better tomorrow, Joe," Hager insisted.

"Let us hope so," the captain murmured, and closed the book.

Next day the *Evening Telegram* carried headlines:

HIGH SCHOOL BOY'S
QUICK SHOOTING SAVES
CHUM FROM RATTLER

Students bought newspapers and gathered in knots outside the school. Joe melted away. A protestingly insistent voice, not at all bland now, followed him: "If Joe hadn't been in my way—" At 4 o'clock he went to the embankment and waited for Hager. He was still waiting at 5:30. Half an hour later he gave up his vigil and started for home. He was halfway there when Hager appeared, walking rapidly.

"Couldn't make it, Joe. Mr. Scott sent for me. Wanted to know all about what happened yesterday."

Joe couldn't keep the eagerness out of his voice. "What did Mr. Scott say?"

"Nothing; he only asked. How long after I fell in the pit before you shot? How close to me was the snake? He had me draw a diagram showing where everybody stood. Where were you and where was Ken? Asked over and over."

"What question?"

"Where was the snake?"

Joe said a slow "O-o-h!" The last hope of Labrador went out of him. He saw what Mr. Scott had been driving at. A snake only a foot from a man's head and somebody with a gun throw-

Nothing mattered but his gun and the round, black ball of the bull.

ing fast lead. Throwing lead with a chance of putting a bullet through that head. Labrador wouldn't want a cadet who took chances and chanced circus shots.

But if the snake was given time to strike, he asked himself desperately, what then? Punctures in Bill's neck or face and venom in his blood stream. A rotten place to be hit; no chance to use a tourniquet. It was either a case of shoot fast or— Or what? Who knew? Sometimes, if you stayed motionless, a snake did not strike.

"I guess Ken was right about the antlers," he said.

Time nibbled at the remaining hours of the week. It didn't hurt so much now. Once you accepted the sentence that your chance was gone, the sharp ache was over. The worst of it, anyway. Joe continued to practice at the embankment and on Friday shot again at the range. His score was good.

Ken said: "Well, if you can do that tomorrow—"

"I'm going to do it tomorrow," said Joe. Not that accomplishment tomorrow would mean anything, but he wasn't walking out on the job.

The morning of the match brought in a clear, cool day with only a touch of wind. A grand day for shooting! After breakfast Joe went out to the front porch and, sitting on the top step, cleaned and oiled his gun. The screened door opened and closed, and his father stood looking down at him.

"I wish I could be up there today, Joe. I tried to switch a ten o'clock appointment at the office, but it was no go. Got to run along. How do things look?"

"Not so hot," said Joe. Somehow, he found he could open up to his father this morning.

"There's always a last minute," said Mr. Morton.

"I'm not folding up," said Joe.

Strangely, at that moment they grinned at each other as though they held something in common. Joe's father held out his hand. "Great! And no matter how they break—"

"Yes, sir," said Joe. He was glad he had broken the shackles of silence. There was something in his father's eyes that warmed him.

263

The grip on his hand tightened. "I've sat in Scott's library; Joe, it starts the mind painting pictures. It's something worth hanging on for, right up to that last minute. Good luck."

Joe watched his father's tall figure disappear down the street and wiped the pistol. So his father *had* understood! Something happened to his lips. After all, there was a last minute. And when somebody understood about your dream and knew all about that last minute—

The sun crept across the sky. Joe had on the team's match uniform—blue coat with gold braid, blue trousers with a gold stripe down the leg, a gold tie and a brown sombrero to keep the sun out of his eyes. Cars appeared as the men of the Storm King Gun Club gathered to drive the team up to the range. Ken climbed into Mr. Scott's car and sat beside the explorer. Joe moved toward one of the other cars.

"This way, Joe?" Mr. Scott called.

The cushions of the rear seat were soft, luxurious. Ken looked around at him.

"Not nervous now, are you?"

Joe wanted to laugh. Today Ken could not rub him along the raw. When you'd made up your mind about that last minute nothing rubbed you.

The Taft men were already there garbed in forest green. Range officers marked out the firing line with fresh lime; scorers tacked up immaculate targets. Ken gave last-minute orders.

"Take your time. Go slow at the start and warm up to it. Don't let your eyes stray to any other target."

An official called positions. Joe heard "Morton, No. 5 target," and looked toward his lane. Figures began to move up to the firing line—figures in forest green and figures in blue and gold.

"Steady shooting does it," Mr. Scott called from his car.

Joe concentrated on a target and tried to shut out all the rest of the world. The tremor that usually rose in him was absent. He was ice, controlled and disciplined. The last minute:

"All ready on the right, all ready on the left—"

To right and left of him he could sense figures shifting position, straining— He did not move.

264

The whistle shrilled.

Today the gun seemed molded to his hand, a part of him. He brought his arm up almost languidly. Explosions split the mountain quiet; blue smoke drifted on the air. There had been days when gun bursts so close to his ears had caused his taut nerves to twitch. Now the sights merely wavered gently. He fired.

Gunfire rolled along the line, falling into sudden silences, breaking out into quick, ragged volleys. But now he scarcely heard the flaming din. The universe had dwindled to a tunnel with his revolver at one end and black bull's eye at the other. He aimed and fired, aimed and fired.

A sense that was not part of him—a superior sense that seemed to stand aloof and to look on critically—told him that this was shooting. Exaltation crept into his blood, and still he remained icily controlled. The last minute might bring the fulfillment of a dream.

A final shot sounded from some place along the line. The slow-fire event was over. Ken, the captain of the Taft team and the range officers went at the butts. Presently an official was calling the standing:

"Boles, 100; Morton, 97—"

Joe looked down at his gun. Good shooting, but not quite good enough. Not in that event, anyway. An old story—always not quite good enough where Ken was concerned. But if he kept up good shooting, steady good shooting—

The range officers called them back to competition.

Time firing now. Flame and smoke and roar and a haze of

acid tang. The haze blurred the target; wind blew across his cheek, and the target was clear. The man on his right coughed. He chained his mind to concentration. Nothing mattered but his gun and the round, black ball of the bull. The ball seemed to have grown smaller.

The tempo of speed was beginning to take its toll. Eye-strain, nerve-strain, muscle-strain! Men began to crack under the pressure. Not only the pressure of gluing to their own targets, but the combined competitive pressure of every other man shooting to best their scores. But some part of Joe grew slowly tense, hard, tight. That same sense of critical appraisal told him he was still scoring high.

A lull! After the rolling blasts of gunfire the quiet seemed unnatural. This, Joe thought, was where the rank powder reek got you, when you should let down and relax. His nose smarted, and he sneezed. Had he been good enough that time?

Ken was in violent argument at Target No. 1. Joe saw the scorers bring out calipers and magnifying glass. And presently the captain came back in triumph to the line.

"Tried to gyp me out of a bull," he chortled. "I told them. Wanted to call it a nine."

Somebody asked: "What did you get, Ken?"

"Ninety-eight on that one."

Joe stood as though carved. Ninety-eight. He waited for the announcement:

"Morton, 92—"

Storm King was running away with the match.

A breath fluttered in Joe's throat. He had done his best today—the best he had ever done in competition. But his best was still not quite good enough. He had lost. Labrador was gone.

And yet, when the teams faced their targets again, there was no despair, no breaking of the spirit. For once rapid fire had lost its hazard. No haste, no hurry, no tremulous agitation! A man finding himself in adversity and doing his job. Not a good enough job, but doing it, anyway.

Flame leaped in flashes and powder detonated in a crescendo of sound. All that had gone before culminated in a ceaseless roll of red flares and roaring bursts. And in all that welter of explosion the gun trained on No. 5 target, flared in a constant, tenacious, unwavering rhythm. The first ten-second round ended; the second began. And again mysterious holes appeared in No. 5 target as though some unseen hand ripped a hot finger through the paper at picked intervals.

Time-up whistles blew, and the match was over. Without haste Joe emptied out the spent shells. Even lost Labrador could not take from him a certain inner satisfaction. When you went down to defeat with your gun steady you still had something left. He watched the megaphone go up to the announcer's lips:

"Rapid-fire score: Morton, 95; Boles, 94—"

Joe said in a whisper: "That will be something to tell Dad."

A steady gun to the last—the steadiest gun of all at the finish. The big thing was gone, but this was a story in itself. The crowd milled around the team, and Bill Hager pounded his back. Then he was shaking hands with the Taft team and hearing Ken's voice saying something about smoke in his eyes. Joe's nostrils still stung and his head had begun to ache. Things swam a bit. A car slid into his vision, and Mr. Scott leaned out across the wheel.

"Joe." A door swung open.

Joe stared.

"Riding down?"

It was nice of Mr. Scott, of course, but Joe wished the explorer didn't think it necessary to break the bad news gently. The car jolted into the rutted road and took the first drop toward the valley.

"Nice shooting, Joe."

"The best I ever did," said Joe. He wasn't going to hide out. Facts were facts. The best he had ever done hadn't been enough to top Ken Boles.

"Target shooting," Mr. Scott mused. "A grand sport. Builds something into a man—eyes, nerves, co-ordination. But with some men it gets to be something of a parlor trick like making the ace of spades pop dextrously out of a deck of cards. No

267

bone to it, just slight of hand and technique. You come to feel the lack of bone." The man swung a turn and looked across at his companion. "Understand, Joe?"

Joe didn't.

The car eased toward the pit into which Hager had fallen and stopped. Mr. Scott looked down toward the boulder-strewn bottom and whistled so softly that he did not seem to whistle at all. The snake was gone, disposed of probably by carrion birds. And— Joe held his lips steady. And Labrador was gone, and the afterglow of team-match glory was gone, and he wished this ride would come to an end.

"Queer the ideas folks have about exploration," Mr. Scott said casually.

Joe stared straight ahead. Here's where he got it. An easing out. A lot of gab about exploring not being so hot, anyway.

"Danger? Rough! That's mostly story-book stuff, Joe. An intelligently organized expedition looks ahead and guards against danger. That's the reason why, when danger does come, it's the unforeseen. It's at your throat in a flash. Clutch moment. Then is when you need the bone and action of the clutch man. It isn't something you practice on a laid-out range; it isn't a white target twenty-five yards away. It's the world crashing down around your ears; it's coming through in a split second. You never know what the clutch is going to be. That's what makes it a clutch. But you can always depend upon a clutch man, whether the clutch be the surprise charge of a wild animal, an avalanche, the touch and go of unknown rapids, or— a rattlesnake."

Joe Morton's heart gave a throb that hurt. He turned in the seat. His lips were parted, and his eyes were filled with an amazing incredulity.

"Like to read, Joe?"

"Y-yes, sir." The words were almost a whisper.

"That's fine." The car moved away from the pit. A rabbit scurried off the road and disappeared into the brush. "You'd better start reading up on Labrador," Mr. Scott said quietly.

268

Franklin M. Reck

KNIGHTS OF THE RED ROSE

ILLUSTRATED BY *Bob Fink*

NTIL Wally Reade came to State College
for his final year of work at American schools, Bill Crossland
was star of the hockey team. The first time he saw the compact
Wally flash down the ice of Olympia Hall, however, he knew
that his luster was to be dimmed. Not that he resented it—he
was too good a sport for that.

In fact these two—Reade and Crossland—were to blaze a
brilliant trail across the hockey skies. They were to fire State
College with the championship dream—until an unimportant
meeting in the office of the engineering dean proceeded to
wreck the smoothest attack State had ever developed. As the
elephant said when he saw the mouse, it's the little things that
make all the trouble.

There was no hint of trouble to come when Wally first blew
in on the earnest, not-too-hopeful State squad in the locker-
room the first day of practice.

"Will someone show me a locker?" said a pleasant voice.

The squad looked up to see a medium-height boy with well-
set shoulders. They saw flat cheeks glowing with health, a
straight nose, a decisive line of jaw and cheek bone, and blue
eyes filled with the light of hidden anticipation. Bill Crossland
couldn't help but smile in response to those eyes as he pointed
to a row of vacant lockers.

"Help yourself," he said. "Going out for hockey?"

"Right-o," Wally responded. "I play right wing. Need any?"

"We can always use a good man," Bill replied.

"You've found him," Wally replied, but the grin on his lips
belied the egotism of the words.

Bill watched with interest as the newcomer dressed. He had

269

brought his own equipment in a suitcase. Close-fitting shoes of the best kangaroo leather that must have cost at least $25. Specially constructed shin and elbow pads. Brand new tubular skates. Bill glanced at the tailored suit that hung in the locker, the rakish hat, and the English boots. Class and money and a touch that was a bit foreign! Bill wondered if there was as much class to his hockey playing as there was to his equipment.

He had his answer a few minutes later, after they had clumped down the runway to the ice. Not that Wally leaped immediately into the center of the stage. He waited respectfully on the fringes while LeBrun and Oakes and Foster whooped around with the puck like colts let loose in spring pasture. Then, when a wild pass sent the puck scurrying for the sideboards, he skated effortlessly over, intercepted it, and carried it goalward.

The way he did it opened Bill's eyes. It was as though the puck were alive and had found its home at the end of Wally's stick. His stick-handling had the unconscious perfection of long practice. And then Wally passed to Bill, and Bill found the rubber disk coming exactly to the spot where he could take it without altering his speed. There was a cool, sure familiarity about the little incident that thrilled Bill to his toes.

When practice was over, Coach Stewart called to the newcomer. "What's your name?"

"Wallace Reade, sir," Wally replied.

"You're a Canadian, aren't you?" Stewart asked—he was a Canadian himself.

"Yes, sir. Fribourg, Ontario."

Stewart's eyes lighted up appreciatively. "They play a lot of hockey around there. Had much experience?"

"At Fribourg, yes, sir. But the last three years I've been going to college in the States and I haven't had a chance until I transferred here this fall." Wally grinned eagerly. "It's like getting home to have skates on again!"

"You'll have plenty of chance to use 'em around here!" the coach replied.

Bill Crossland felt somebody nudging him and turned to see Dalby, substitute wing, at his side. Red-headed and rough-hewn, Dalby was the crashing type of wingman. His lips were curling now as he looked at Stewart and Reade.

"The fashion plate seems to be getting along well with the coach," he said with a touch of resentfulness.

"You mean Reade?" Bill asked. "That baby's got the goods!"

Then, suddenly, Bill placed a sympathetic hand on Dalby's arm. Up till now, Dalby had been the best bet to fill the vacant spot at right wing. But now, with Wally Reade bursting upon the scene, that chance was wrecked.

"Never mind, Big Boy," Bill said gently. "After all a team needs more than two forwards, you know."

"Sure, I know," Dalby replied gruffly. "But I'm out for the number one spot—and Reade hasn't won the job yet."

But he did. Inside of a week he had the right wing position cinched. Furthermore, his accuracy at shooting for the corners of the cage made him the logical shotmaker for the team, and Bill, who had scored most of the points last year, found himself relegated suddenly to playmaker. Invariably the assaults on the scrub goal ended with Bill passing to Wally and Wally sweeping in for the score.

For an instant, Bill shared Dalby's resentment at being displaced. Then he grinned.

"If a man is better than you are," he said philosophically, "there's just one thing to do, and that's admit it."

As Coach Stewart announced the line-up for the first game of the season, he looked with satisfaction at the three men in his first attacking line. Norm Foster, at center, was fast, heady, and a good passer. Bill Crossland was dogged and courageous— the kind that never gave up. And Wally Reade had the skill and sureness of a born hockey player. Coach Stewart was too sensible to dream yet of the Intercollegiate title—but the fans would be treated to a surprise tonight.

Just before the team left the locker-room for the game, Wally pinned a red rosebud to his jersey. Dick LeBrun, defense man, saw it first.

"Where do you think you're going?" he yelped. "To a tea party?"

271

Wally carefully patted the rose in place. "Milady's color," he said sentimentally. "Deep red."

The team gathered round and gazed in awe at the Canadian. "Do you think he's nutty?" Oakes, left defense, whispered to Bill.

"Maybe we ought to send for Doctor Walsh," Norm Foster said, with a worried frown. "If we let him go out on the ice with us, he might blow kisses to the crowd. We can't have *that!*"

"What's the idea?" asked Greene, the bulky, practical goalie.

"Very simple," Wally replied airily. "Didn't you ever hear of a knight's entering the lists wearing his lady's gage? After all, hockey's a humdrum game. Why not give it a touch of color and romance?"

"What's her name?" Bill asked.

"Lois," Wally replied, instantly and unashamed.

"Is she the drag I saw you with at the Scoreboard last week?" Johnson, substitute wing, asked.

"That?" Wally laughed. "That, my good man, was merely a passing interest. Lois is from the home town. One of the first families of Fribourg. A fair flower of the F.F.F. Yes, sir."

"If you want to know what I think," Dalby interrupted gruffly, "I think it's a lot of boloney."

"What you think in this matter," Wally replied, "is of little moment. Lois is not boloney; she's my everything."

In the roar of the crowd that greeted State's appearance in the rink, Wally skated to the referee. He asked the referee if he might wear the rose, and the referee asked him how it was fastened on. When he showed him the pin the official shook his head and laughed. The rules, he said, prohibited the wearing of any piece of equipment that might injure an opponent, and the pin might so be considered. With evident reluctance Wally skated over to the players' box and entrusted the rose to the care of Trainer Loucks.

After the warm-up, State proceeded to whip Denison by a score of 6 to 0. Last year they had barely managed to nose out the same team 2 to 1 in one overtime period.

Wally Reade made four of the goals, and Bill, teaming with

Wally on those relentless assaults on the Denison cage, felt a thrill he had never known before. What if he wasn't making the shots? It was a greater joy to know that with Wally he could make a play *work*. The game ceased to be the wild, mad scramble it had been last year. It took on sureness and skill and plan. Bill gloried in it, and went off the ice enthusiastically roughing his blond, unruffled teammate.

In the second game, against Worcester, Wally again wore a red rosebud. He skated up to Bill and pointed to it.

"The referee can't complain now," he grinned. "I out-foxed 'im."

Bill glanced more closely. Two strips of tape were sewn to the scarlet jersey, and the stem was twined securely through them.

"I wish she could come down to see me play," Wally said. "But she isn't much interested in hockey. Funny, too, because she's certainly an outdoor girl."

"Doesn't she care for any sports?"

"Strolling and hiking," Wally replied. "Not a day but what she takes a stroll."

The rooters noted the rosebud and yelped. After a hot flurry in which Wally burst through the Worcester defense and scored, they saw him carefully patting his rose to see whether it had been injured, and they howled with glee. When he skated off

273

the rink at the end of the game, his bud still hanging limply to his uniform, they stood and cheered. And in the next morning's paper, the state's leading sports writer dubbed the team, "Knights of the Red Rose."

State won her next two games by comfortable margins, and the meeting places of the campus began to buzz with championship talk. In both games Wally was hounded by the enemy, and twice Bill took advantage of the situation to jam the puck home. Hec Tyler, sports writer for the *Register*, commented on the switch in tactics:

"State's opponents have found out that it doesn't pay to concentrate on one man. Last night Wally Reade demonstrated that he's as good a playmaker as he is a shotmaker. Twice he delivered the puck to Bill Crossland out of a swarm of Lawrence players, and both times his miraculous passes resulted in scores. To the great delight of the fans he emerged from both skirmishes with his red rose intact."

At the Scoreboard, over a malted milk, Dalby scoffed at the paragraph to Bill.

"Why is it that some boys, born with a silver spoon in their mouths, get all the credit?" he asked. "Last night you score two goals, and Hec Tyler merely mentions the fact in connection with Wally's passes!"

Bill looked surprised. He had forgotten how deeply Dal resented being relegated to second string.

"Wally made those goals possible by drawing over the defense," he pointed out.

"Bunk!" Dalby burst out. "I was watching you both every minute, and you handled yourself as well as he ever did! It's just showmanship. I wouldn't mind so much if he wasn't hogging the place that belongs to you. Here you've slaved for three years on the squad. You've had to struggle for everything you've earned. And Wally steps in at the last minute, wears a red rose in honor of some dame that probably doesn't exist, and takes the spotlight!"

Bill was disturbed. "That isn't exactly fair," he said. "Wally's good—"

"Of course he's good! But so are you—and so am I! And what chance do we get with P. T. Barnum in there, fooling the public with theatricals! Nobody else would go into a game wearing a rose! Wally's nobody's fool. He's out after something—maybe a professional hockey contract—and he knows the value of publicity."

Bill laughed. "I doubt it," he said. "I think he's got a sense of humor. He's wearing the red rose for team morale as much as anything."

Dalby glowered and said nothing. After a moment's awkward silence Bill paid for his malted and left, deeply disturbed by Dal's remarks.

But the firm of Crossland and Reade still continued to function, and State continued to win its games. For the first time in history, the school began to talk of a victory over Harland. Harland was the defending champion of the conference. It was a veteran team of hard-driving white demons, but all fandom now began to wonder if she could stand up under the assault of the Knights of the Red Rose. State College, the conference surprise, was riding high.

And then Bill was called to Dean Snyder's office.

"Alfred Smythe is in town," the well-dressed, young-looking dean said.

Bill looked blank.

"He's head of the big Toronto engineering firm bearing his name," Dean Snyder explained, "and he's looking for men. I've picked out three of my best students to interview him, and you're one of them. Smythe, by the way, is a rabid hockey fan. He used to play himself. Naturally, your hockey record won't hurt your chances a bit."

The dean smiled, and Bill went away filled with excitement. Jobs were scarce this year, and to land a position with the firm of Alfred Smythe, Ltd., would be something! At three that afternoon, dressed in his best suit, he walked into the engineering building, feeling more tense than he had ever felt in the final minute before a hockey game. He drew a deep breath and straightened his coat with nervous fingers as he waited in the

275

outer office. His best suit, he noted regretfully, was a bit thread-bare. He hadn't been able to spare much for clothes.

But he forgot his nervousness and his lack of a new suit when he met Smythe. For Smythe was a rawboned Scot who said "aboot" instead of "about," and talked with a rough burr. He took Bill's hand in his big paw, pulled him down to a chair, and assumed at once that they'd known each other for years.

Dean Snyder left them alone, and under the big Scot's friendly glance Bill found himself telling about his home life on the farm, his ambition to become a civil engineer, his struggle to stay in State College, shinny on the pasture pond, and his love of hockey.

"I'm coming back here to see you play Har-rland," Mr. Smythe said at the end of the interview. "They're experienced and tough, but they can be licked. Watch out for their wing-man, Lorimer. He's good."

Bill left the office treading on air. But as he came into the outer office he experienced a tiny shock. Wally Reade was sitting by the secretary's desk.

"Hi, Wally," he said, and received back Wally's " 'Lo, Bill," as the latter walked into the dean's office.

Out in the hall, Bill leaned against the wall, feeling suddenly weak. Evidently Wally was one of the students Dean Snyder had selected to see Smythe. In that case, what chance had Bill Cross-land for the job? Wally had presence—personality—a ready an-swer and a keen wit. Acutely Bill realized how unfavorably he would compare with the pleasant, alert Wally.

And to Smythe, the rabid hockey fan, how would Bill Cross-land, playmaker, look alongside the Knight of the Red Rose? A playmaker was merely an assister—a man who helped the other man drive home the winning punch.

Bill felt a sudden flare of resentment. In one short season, Wally had made himself the most talked-of player on confer-ence rinks. He was good—but other good players had gone through a season without breaking into headlines and picture sections!

With new understanding, Bill visualized Wally emerging

276

from a hot scrimmage and patting his rosebud. Great stuff for
the sports writers and camera men! What was it Dalby had said?
"Wally's no fool! He's out after something!"

Glumly Bill walked to his dormitory room. He found Dalby
there waiting for him.

"What's the matter?" Dal asked curiously. "You look as
though a dog had bitten you."

"It has," Bill growled, and threw himself on the bed. An instant of silence, and then Bill flung himself erect and gazed at
Dalby with burning eyes. "From now on," he said quietly, "I'm
going to play some hockey!"

The bewildered substitute loosed a barrage of questions, but
Bill refused to answer. Why had he allowed Wally to steal his
place? Surely an attack could have been worked out in which
the Canadian didn't hog all the plays! Bill could still shoot goals
—he had shown that against Lawrence.

In a game as fast as hockey, it doesn't take much to wreck
teamwork. A tiny flame of resentment can unsteady the hand as
surely as lack of practice or an unwise diet. A pass that misses
its mark by two feet can cause the receiver to check himself
just long enough to permit the defense to bear down on him.
Eyes blinded by disappointment can fail to see the big chance.

In the Hilltown game, Coach Stewart sat on the side lines and
saw his powerful machine slowly disintegrate before his eyes.
He saw Bill barging blindly into the defense. He saw Wally
hesitating uncertainly in the end zone. He saw Norm Foster
receive a penalty for a high stick. State was lucky to win, 2 to 1.

"They're stale," the coach decided. "They're trying too hard."
And with sympathetic understanding he added to himself:
"After all, they've never been in the running for the champion-
ship before."

During the next week, he gave them Monday off and held
only light practices the rest of the time. But against the weak
Warren team, the last game before Harland, the team if anything was worse. And watching through narrowed eyes, the
coach came to a reluctant conclusion.

"It's Bill," he murmured. "He's the veteran and he feels the

277

responsibility. I'm afraid he s cracked wide open."

The coach didn't know about the meeting in Dean Snyder's anteroom. All he knew was that some obscure trick of fate had transformed his team from a powerful machine into a heap of scattered parts.

In the locker-room before the Harland game, Wally Reade's cheerful whistle cut through the intent gloom. He was threading a red rosebud to his jersey. Norm Foster looked up and attempted a smile.

"Is the fair Lois going to be in the stands tonight?" he asked Wally.

"Nope," Wally replied. "But you'll see her in the rotogravure section next Sunday."

"Society picture?"

"We-ell—social work. Helping undernourished babies to get fat and healthy."

"Tell us what she's like!"

"Big brown eyes and a perfect temperament. Beyond that I shan't describe her. You wouldn't understand—"

Coach Stewart entered with the line-up and gave a ghost of a smile at the tabloid.

"Norman Foster starts at center," he announced. "Reade and Dalby, wings—"

Bill Crossland sat up with a rude shock. The big game of the year, and he wasn't even starting! And Alfred Smythe in the stands! He looked at Wally, who was giving his rose a final pat, and a sudden fury shook him. Theatricals, Dalby had called it. And Dalby was right.

Occupied with his own bitterness, Bill didn't hear the coach's short plea for State to shake off her uncertainty. He was barely conscious of his own teammates as he stamped out to the players' box and sat down between substitutes Devereaux and Johnson.

He leaned forward, chin on fist, only dimly aware of the pelting cheers, the warm-up, and the sudden silence that preceded the referee's whistle. Intently he watched the play.

Harland wasn't overrated. Those white jerseys were fast. . . . Where was this Lorimer, Harland's star wing? Ah-h, there he was, carrying the puck. . . . Watch it, Oakes! You should have checked him harder—you can't treat a man like Lorimer softly! Lorimer's in the clear now, bearing down on the goal. . . . Three white jerseys in front of the goal! Bad!

Bill half rose from his seat as a red light flashed, and Harland went one goal to the good.

Another face-off. Good work, Norm—that's taking it away. . . . Dalby with the puck, now. Take it down, Dal! Feint that defense man! Don't go through. . . . Bad judgment, Dal, trying to barge through those boys!

The play speeded up, and Bill gripped his stick tightly, longingly. Maybe the coach was just keeping him out for a few minutes so that he could watch the play. Hope flared in his breast.

But with the first time out Stewart sent in Devereaux for Dalby and Johnson for Oakes, and Bill continued to sit on the bench. With burning eyes he saw Harland score another goal, and with a groan of despair he hid his head in his hands.

Then a great cry from the stands brought his head up to see Wally whirl around a Harland man, bounce the puck against the sideboard, take it out in the clear, and rifle a 50-foot shot into the corner of the cage. A roar shook the roof.

Coach Stewart sent Dalby and Oakes back in, and Bill clenched his gloved fist impatiently. Why was he being kept out? He sat there and waited and suffered until near the end of the quarter. Then the coach beckoned him, and he leaped from the box—but he had barely started before the gun sounded.

In the second period Bill played less than three minutes. He was conscious that Dalby's play had improved—that the substitute, in fact, was playing over his head. And when Dalby came into the players' box for a short rest, glowing and happy, Bill reflected miserably that he knew just how Dal had felt all season, warming the bench and only getting to play a few minutes per game.

But early in the third period, with the score still 2 to 1, Devereaux came out with a wrenched shoulder, his face twisted in pain. Dalby was still breathing hard. Coach Stewart looked over at Bill and nodded.

Starved for action, Bill fairly leaped out of the box and into battle. From a face-off Lorimer sped away with the puck. With an inspired lunge Bill hooked it from him, pivoted, and started for the Harland goal. Changing direction like a zigzag flash of lightning, he outtricked the defense and carried the rubber over the blue line.

Wally was calling for it, and Bill hesitated. A sudden, overwhelming desire to take the puck in himself shook him. But Wally was in position—he'd better pass. So he swept the puck viciously toward his teammate. Wally slowed up to take it, and two defense men crowded down on him. The next instant one of them had passed to the Harland center.

Wally swirled up past Bill.

"Watch those passes, Bill!" he cried passionately. "Keep 'em out in front!"

"I did!" Bill growled back. "You overskated!"

For an instant, as both men glided into the play, Wally looked blankly at him. Then they were in the center of hot action again. Bill took a pass from Norm and started down. Across the blue line. . . . Pass to Foster. . . . Take it back. . . . And Bill found himself bearing down on the unprotected cage.

Around the rear of the net Wally circled, looking at Bill.

"I'll take this one in myself, Mr. Reade," Bill said to himself grimly. "You missed the last one."

280

He swept a hard shot at the corner. The puck bounced off the goalie's enormous shin pads, and Bill looked at it unbelievingly. He had been sure of that one!

A moment later there was a face-off, and in the short breather Wally skated up to Bill, pounding his stick on the ice.

"Bill!" he cried. "Didn't you see me?"

"Sure," Bill murmured.

"You know I can make those!"

"So can I," Bill replied doggedly.

"Bill!" Wally laid a frantic hand on his teammate's arm. "What's wrong? Why can't we get going—like we used to?"

Bill looked moodily at the ice.

Two minutes later, with half the period gone, Wally took the puck near his own goal and started down the rink. Uncertain of Bill's co-operation he decided on a single-handed march. Leaping outthrust sticks, weaving in and out like a streak of light, feinting and reversing, he took the rubber over the line with the pack on his heels.

With sudden intuition, he saw that he would meet the pack at the goal mouth. Checking himself with scream of steel on ice, he swerved suddenly behind the cage. Alertly the goalie moved over to that side to meet him. Wally was blocked.

Meanwhile, Bill had skated down to a clear spot near the right of the cage.

"Wally'll try it, and muff it—" he thought, but in the middle of his thought he saw the puck gliding accurately to the end of his own stick.

It was easy. A flip of the wrist and the rubber slid into the unprotected half of the net. The score was tied at two-all.

As Bill skated to position he passed a gloved hand over his eyes. In all this yelling it was hard to think. But one fact stood out clear and stark—Wally had passed to him. Wally had made a sensational march on the goal and then had made a perfect pass to Bill.

At that moment Dalby came in for Bill. As Bill took his place in the players' box the coach gripped his arm.

"Just a breather, Bill," he said. "You're getting better."

282

"Yeh," Bill replied mechanically, "but if I'd passed to Wally before that, we'd have been ahead."

He sat down and gazed out on the ice. Old times! He realized all at once that he had lost something in the last two weeks. A feeling of comradeship. The sense of confidence and complete understanding that he and Wally had once possessed, out there on the ice. The knowledge that neither would let the other down.

He remembered their forays together on the enemy goal, each knowing what the other would do, each alert for the big chance. They had been two parts of the same invincible machine.

Why had he lost it? How could he ever have given it up? For an engineering job? Let Wally have the job! Let him wear his rose. That was just Wally's way and couldn't be helped.

And then the coach was calling his name and telling him to go in. Bill reported and skated straight over to Wally.

"From now on, Wally, I'm passing to you," he hissed. "Get it?"

Wally's blue eyes lit up in glad surprise. "Do I get it!" he yelped. "Let's go! For victory—and Lois!"

White and crimson jerseys whirled into the last five minutes of play. For two minutes State grimly stayed on defense, battering off one assault after another. Then Wally checked Lorimer, neatly stole the rubber, and started down. A pass to Norm . . . Norm to Bill . . . Bill to Wally.

And Wally, faced by two men, had no choice but to charge into a white hurricane. He emerged from the melee with his stick broken, but on the ragged end of it he still had the puck. With the stub he flipped it to Bill, yelling:

"Take it in yourself!"

Bill felt a sudden panic. Here was one march he *had* to make good. For two weeks he had wanted to do some scoring of his own. Now he *must* score. He charged down on the cage. A stick came out and tripped him.

He landed on his chest, coasting straight at the goal, his stick out in front of him and the puck just in front of the stick.

Quick to seize the opportunity, the Harland goalie skated out to take possession. Still on his chest, Bill reached out another foot and hooked the puck back to him. The goalie lunged forward, feet wide.

And Bill, coasting slowly ahead, thrust the puck with the end of his stick between the goalie's legs, into the cage.

It was the first goal State rooters had ever seen made by a man skating on his chest, but one old-timer in the stands gave a roar of appreciation. Mr. Smythe had seen that same thing happen once in a Toronto play-off.

He leaned forward with keen interest, for Harland, one goal behind and with a minute to play, refused to concede defeat. She took off her two defense men and put in two forwards. From now on, she would attack!

The entire last minute of play took place in State's end zone, and in that minute Wally proved that he was as great on defense as he was on offense. Not one clear shot did Harland get at the goal. In the midst of every cyclonic scramble was Wally's blond hair, his red rose, and his agile stick.

The last scramble, ending with the gun, laid him sprawling on the scarred ice. Bill leaned over and helped him to his feet. The Canadian's hair was mussed for the first time. There was a cut on his sharply molded right cheek bone. One eye was fast becoming black. Most of the petals were stripped from his rose.

"Look at it," he mourned. "All shot to blazes. What would Lois think—"

"Never mind that," Bill said happily. "I just wanted to tell you that you played a swell game, and I hope you land that job with Smythe."

"Smythe?" Wally said blankly. "You mean Alfred Smythe of Toronto?"

"The same," Bill replied.

"I'm not going to work for him," Wally said, patting the fragment of his rose. "He told me he was going to give the job to you. He's an old friend of the family."

Bill looked so amazed that Wally laughed.

"I'm going to manage my father's dairy farm," he explained.

"What? You, an engineer—"

"Lots of farmers take engineering. Don't they have to handle machinery, build buildings and ditches and even roads? And we're going to build some of those, now that Lois has come across."

"You mean—you mean you're engaged?"

Wally stifled a smile.

"It's this way," he explained. "My dad owns and runs the Red Rose Dairy farms, but this past year he's been afflicted with mortgage trouble. He had it so bad I didn't even know whether I could stay in school. It all depended on Lois. And gosh, she's wonderful, Bill."

"Yes, but—"

"Bill, you ought to see her! She's a vision of perfection—literally one in a million!"

"For cat's sake—"

"And when Dad says to her, 'Lois, my boy wants to stay in school,' she looks at him with those big brown eyes, switches her tail—"

"What on earth—"

"This morning I got a wire from Dad that in the year just completed yesterday, Lois had produced 25,500 pounds of milk, which makes her the most famous Guernsey cow in all Canada. Dad has sold her for ten thousand bucks, which enables us to keep the old homestead. Can you picture her in the barn, slaving over the milk pail, just to keep me in school—"

"Oh—" said Bill, his eyes widening. "So that's why you wore the rose—"

"Sure. What did you think?"

"I thought you were grandstanding to win an engineering job."

"Huh!" Wally carefully removed from his uniform the fragment of rose. "Me, the manager of Canada's greatest cow—Lois Red Rose the Third?"

Irving Crump

THE LITTLE GUY

ILLUSTRATED BY *Hardie Gramatky*

BOB (SUNNY) WARD, clad only in dirty white sneakers and faded and very ragged dungarees, was working diligently on the *Black Dolphin*, the catboat that was his pride and joy. Lying at her mooring in the crowded yacht club basin she was stripped down to bare spars, and Sunny, his compact, sunbrowned torso gleaming with honest sweat and plenty of it, with his black hair dripping and his dark brows puckered in an effort to keep the sweat from running into his eyes, was adjusting a new turnbuckle on the forestay.

It was hot there on the deck of the catboat, in spite of the soft breeze that came in off Gull Haven Sound. Definitely it was no day to be tinkering with any kind of job that needed concentration and effort. Instead, it was the kind of day and quite the proper time for a guy to be over on the bathing beach on the other side of the point with the gang, making the most of what was left of the summer vacation. Sunny guessed all of the fellows were over there, and he was a little surprised when he heard the creaking oarlocks of a dingy. Looking up he saw his two older brothers, Fred and John, and their pal Spike Manton rowing across the basin toward the point, obviously going for a swim.

"Hyah, Sunny!" hailed Spike. "Lay off pampering that boat and come on over for a swim."

"Sure would be good. I'm coming over—later," said Sunny, mopping sweat.

286

"Why don't you knock off, kid? All the messing around you do on that crate won't make it any faster than a mud turtle, and you know it," called Fred with a sympathetic grin.

"Oh yeah? Well, you just let me alone. I'm happy," bridled Sunny with obvious resentment.

"Where's your sail?" queried John curiously.

Sunny looked at him sharply, then sheepishly avoided the eyes of all three of them. "I'm waiting for it," he said. "That's why I can't go for a swim. Got to bend it on as soon as it comes back. Mrs. McGuinness is washing it for me."

"My gosh," exclaimed John. He stared at the others and they all chortled.

"O.K., O.K.," said Sunny uncomfortably. "Look. Like I said, I'm happy. Just leave me alone."

"Sounds like you're slap happy, kid. Whoever heard of laundering sails before the last race of the season?" said Fred, almost derisively. Then, noticing his brother's embarrassment and discomfort, he added: "O.K., Little Guy. I hope the old tub shows us all a clean pair of heels tomorrow."

"Maybe she will. But if she doesn't, it won't be my fault," said Sunny with characteristic earnestness as the dingy got under way. Then he called, "I'll be over for a swim soon's I'm finished here."

But there wasn't any such thing as being finished for Sunny Ward. As soon as he had tightened the new turnbuckle, he adjusted all the others to make the stays properly taut. Then he went ashore and climbed the hill to Mrs. McGuinness's, where he got the bundle of snowy white sail which he bent on with the utmost care. After that he cleaned up the deck and the cockpit, lashed the tiller, and made everything shipshape for the night. And by that time he heard the sound of squeaky oar-locks returning, and Fred and John and Spike were on their way back across the cove. It was too late for the fun of a swim with the gang, and Sunny compromised by diving overboard and swimming back to the yacht club float. But before he turned homeward he paused to look back with evident pride and a certain amount of concern at the *Black Dolphin,* meanwhile

287

checking all the things he had planned to do to make the cat-boat ready for the race next day.

For more than a week, since the last race when his black-hulled boat had come in a bad last, Sunny had been concentrating all his efforts on making *Black Dolphin* ready for the Labor Day regatta. He had careened her on the beach, scraped her bottom, which hardly needed scraping, repainted her in spite of the fact that her paint was immaculate, polished her brass, sanded her deck, and finally, because he liked snowy sails and had a flare for neatness, he had persuaded Mrs. McGuinness to wash and even iron the big Marconi-rig mainsail. All this was a manifestation of Sunny's earnestness and determination to do everything to make it possible for *Black Dolphin* to win that last race of the summer.

Sunny wanted desperately to take that race, not so much because of the little silver cup that went to the winner, but because of the psychological effect it would have around Gull Haven in general and the Ward household in particular. Being low man on the Ward family totem pole—kid brother to two brothers and a sister—hadn't lately contributed much to Bob's peace of mind. And the nurse who called him Sunny as an infant hadn't helped matters very much either.

Sunny had become sonny all too easily, which suggested that he was young and small—just a kid, a little guy. In fact, lately that was exactly what his two older brothers had been calling him—the Little Guy. It had been picked up by the fellows in Gull Haven, too, both in the Scouts and around the yacht club, and the whole thing had commenced to annoy Sunny more than he was willing to admit. He felt definitely put upon. It wasn't his fault that he took after his mother and was short for fourteen, while his brothers were both big enough to play tackle and guard respectively on the high-school football team, though they were only two and three years older. And it irked him plenty when Fred and John adopted a patronizing older-brother attitude toward him, even though their intentions were of the best. And when they dubbed the *Black Dolphin* a mud turtle, that filled the cup of Sunny's indignation.

That Marconi-rigged catboat was the pride of Sunny's many possessions. Interest in Gull Haven, particularly in the summer, centered around the yacht club and its big fleet of pleasure craft that ranged from the catboats of the Fish Class to Bermuda racing yawls like the *Endymion* and the *Lachesis* and the cruising auxiliary schooners like the *Kohinoor* and the *Salmacis*. The Fish Class boats were designed by a man named Fisher for the purpose of giving boys and girls of the families who were members of the yacht club a craft in which to race.

Most boys, and some of the girls who were interested in sailing, began working for and saving money toward their first boat at twelve, and by the time they were fourteen or fifteen they had it. First John, then Fred had bought their catboats, with some slight financial help from the head of the family. Each resolved some day to own one just as trim and as fast. But when Sunny was ready to acquire his catboat there was a lumber shortage and building restrictions. The shipyard had closed temporarily and the only Fish Class boat to be had was an old one named the *Eel* that had been owned by Dave Slater, who had joined the navy.

The *Eel* wasn't much of a boat. It had never won a race. It needed paint and a new sail. And when Sunny announced that he had bought it, Fred and John kidded him about it and made suggestions about renaming it the *Sculpin* or the *Crab*. John suggested calling it the *Mud Turtle*. But the fact that others picked on the boat only made Sunny more earnestly and stubbornly determined to defend it. Heck, they called him a lot of names too, Little Guy, kid, sonny. O.K. He'd show 'em. He'd make them respect him *and* his boat. He'd make it the fastest in the Fish Class and he'd show 'em he was as good a skipper as the rest.

To his credit, he did improve the *Eel* in both speed and appearance. He painted her black, rechristened her *Black Dolphin*, bought a new sail, and worked on her tirelessly until she was the best appearing craft in the fleet of twenty-odd catboats. Scraping and painting improved her speed too, but not enough to win a race with her or even come near it. Fred and John still kidded him about being skipper of a mud turtle. But Sunny stoutly maintained it wasn't the boat's fault and some day he'd surprise them.

He had learned sailing from his father and his two brothers. He knew a great deal about handling a small boat. But what he realized he didn't know as well as the more experienced skippers, like his older brothers, were the vagaries of the tidal currents of Gull Haven harbor and the Sound, where the races were held every Saturday. So with almost desperate earnestness he tried to fathom the secrets of those hidden forces that smart skippers employed to help them win races. He began to get a lot of confidence in himself with each succeeding race, and he fully expected that in a week or two he would be showing the rest of the fleet the way home. But about that time hard luck began to dog him. In one race a stay parted, and he limped home a cripple. In another he got off to a poor start and never did recover, and in still another he and Skip Messner's *Snook* fouled each other, and they were both out of the race. So the summer sped swiftly toward the first week in September and the Labor Day regatta, and Sunny had managed to get exactly nowhere in the races, with Fred and John still kidding him about the mud turtle that thought it was a catboat, and others grinned at him in a way that annoyed him.

He had just one chance left to prove to the rest of the crowd that the *Black Dolphin* was as good as any member of the fleet and that he was just as good a sailor as the next fellow. So for a week he had been working to put the catboat in shape for that final race on Labor Day, while he lay awake nights planning how he would sail the triangular course from Gull Haven harbor out into the Sound and back by way of the Rock Point buoy and the treacherous channel that skirted Rock Point Reef. In fact, he sailed it mentally a dozen times the night before the race, and he was a little groggy for want of sleep when his mother roused him out of bed next morning.

Only twelve of the eighteen boats were entered in the race, but even twelve jockeying to be in position to sweep across the line as soon as possible after the starting gun was fired from the

upper deck of the gaily beflagged clubhouse gave each young skipper plenty to do for a few minutes.

Luck was with Sunny, and he timed everything just right to sweep across the line while the puff of white smoke from the gun muzzle still hung in the air. He was one of the first three across, to windward, under full way and with his big sail drawing well, he headed out for the lighthouse buoy.

It was only with the excitement of the start well behind him and after an inspection of his sail and a careful adjustment of the sheet to get the most out of the *Black Dolphin* that Sunny had a chance to take account of general conditions. It was a fair day with a stiffish breeze almost out of the east. But there were clouds down there on the horizon that suggested weather breeding. In fact, the radio had predicted showers. Sunny decided that they might get some rain, and perhaps quite a capful of wind before the race was over. O.K. That wouldn't worry him. It would have to be stiffish and then some to bother *Black Dolphin.*

He forgot the weather as he looked around at the fleet. There was Jimmy Fitzgerald's *Barracuda* off to port, with brother John's *Tarpon* just beyond and a little astern. Close to John were three other boats, the *Sunfish, Blue Marlin,* and *Amberjack.* Behind them and well behind Sunny were the rest. Sunny felt quite elated. He'd outmaneuvered most of the bunch and got quite a lead on some of the boats that were expected to win this race. If he could only hold it to the first buoy, he felt sure he had a chance to increase it on the second leg of the triangle. They'd be tacking into the wind and they could be taking advantage of all the tidal current to reach the second mark. But Sunny felt he was good at that now. He'd been practicing enough lately until he knew just how the currents ran. The wind and tide were just right for him and the *Black Dolphin.*

He squinted a speculative eye up at the sail, drawing beautifully, and moved the tiller just a little to point her up closer to the wind. But all the time he watched for those telltale wrinkles next to the mast, to be sure she was trimmed correctly. He watched the dark green water slipping past and listened to the gurgle forward. Darned if the old *Black Dolphin* wasn't really footing it. He looked over the *Tarpon* and toward the *Barracuda.* He was holding his own with them—even shoving ahead of them a little, it seemed to him. His eyes swept astern. The fleet was scattering now, but he could see the *Blue Marlin* and the *Seahorse* (his brother Fred's boat), two of the fastest, had drawn up on him a little. In fact, there were now five leaders instead of three, with the rest of the fleet well behind.

"Doggone, those two boats are overhauling me," Sunny muttered.

He studied their position carefully. They were almost directly behind him. He was well in the middle of the channel, where he had discovered this past week the tidal pull was just a bit stronger. He was taking advantage of it. So were Fred and the skipper of the *Blue Marlin,* Sammy Poor. They must know

292

about that current. Sunny grinned. O.K. Who knows the most.

Sunny watched his sail. Then from the snowy white canvas his gaze moved to the sky. Those clouds were closing in. They were darker and heavier. The sun was gone, and the breeze was freshening fast. In fact, as he looked out across the Sound toward the next leg of the triangular course, Sunny saw plenty of whitecaps out there. And the *Black Dolphin* was thumping her way through some fair-sized seas. He had been too darned busy to notice the swift change in the weather. He guessed a blow was coming but he didn't have time to think of that now.

He was fast approaching the first marker, the Lighthouse buoy. He'd have to round close in order not to lose any of his advantage. Turning a buoy required judgment and nice timing. He looked at the craft off to port. Sailing closer to the wind, they had the right of way but he was still out ahead. He was overjoyed to see that both John's *Tarpon* and Jimmy Fitzgerald's *Barracuda* had lost distance. They were behind far enough to give him no trouble at the mark. In fact, he was showing his heels to the whole darned lot of them and he was elated.

In spite of his efforts to remain calm, a sense of excitement gripped him. Maybe he was going to take this race. He was really walking away from the fleet. If he could only hold this lead it would be swell. He was almost at the buoy. He measured the distance with his eye, looked at the sail, then at just the right moment he pulled in his sheet and rounded close—not more than two feet from the mark. No distance lost there! Sunny was pleased with himself. He looked back at the other boats, sort of hoping that they were watching him too. Only a real sailor could turn a mark as neatly as that. But he couldn't look back long. This windward leg to the eastward would take all his concentration. If he came about on the port tack he would have a lee bow tide—a real advantage—but he had decided to stay on the starboard hitch out here in the bay where the tide would not make as much difference as it would closer to Rock Point Reef. After his first stand to the north'ard he planned a long hitch on the port tack where the current would be even more help and the sea should be smoother.

The wind was freshening a lot, and that would help. In fact, it was really blowing now. The *Black Dolphin* was heeling over so that Sunny was sitting well up on the combing. And she was footing along faster than she had ever sailed before. Sunny was delighted.

He glanced quickly over his right shoulder. The *Seahorse* and the *Blue Marlin* were coming along great guns now. They had overhauled John and Jimmy Fitzgerald almost at the buoy and were starting off to the south on the boat tack. They, too, knew about the lee bow tide on the port hitch and were planning to take advantage of it immediately. Sunny still felt he was right, but it took guts to sail the offshore tack alone when the older fellows, who were skippers of the next four boats, did the opposite. He felt he must keep an eye on the other boats but he knew that he could not sail to windward with his eyes astern. The wind was still coming up, and it was cold. Sunny shivered slightly as he turned back to look at his mainsail. Gently he pulled the tiller toward him to straighten out the wrinkles which were appearing close to the mast, and in a second or two he eased the tiller to take advantage of a strong puff. He somehow felt that he was sailing to windward as he had never done before. And how *Black Dolphin* seemed to shoot ahead under his skillful guidance! Again a quick glance over his right shoulder convinced him that now was the time to tack. Instinctively he shouted, "Ready about. Hard alee!" in spite of the fact that there was no crew to hear him. Sunny was like that anyway. He always did the right thing in the right way whether anyone was there or not to see him do it.

Over went the tiller. There was a rattle of gear, the swish and thump of the sail as the boom came over, and Sunny, holding fast to tiller and sheet, scrambled over to the port side as the catboat leaned over and started off on the other tack without losing a single bit of speed. Sunny was pleased. He sort of wished the other skippers could see him.

With critical eye he looked aloft and edged *Black Dolphin's* nose a trifle to windward to be sure he was taking advantage of the increasing breeze and the lee bow tide which was now

With a rush and a roar, a terrific squall of wind hit the catboat.

working to his advantage. He glanced over his shoulder to the eastward and what he saw didn't make him very happy. There was a stinker of a storm bearing down out of that quarter. Far to leeward he saw several boats heading back toward port, their mainsails only half sheeted in, in an effort to spill the wind and stand upright. They weren't willing to take it. Should he give up too? After all, he was a little guy and not much ballast in a wind like this. Far ahead to leeward he saw four boats standing out to sea on the starboard tack. They were too far away to identify with any degree of certainty, but they must be *Seahorse*, *Blue Marlin*, *Barracuda*, and *Tarpon*, two of them obviously ahead of the other pair. No, Sunny would not quit. This was his race, and he would sail it through somehow.

Suddenly everything was wiped from Sunny's mind but the fact that it was too late to do anything but hang grimly fast to sheet and tiller and hope that *Black Dolphin* would stay right side up. With a rush and a roar, a terrific, snarling squall of wind and rain hit the catboat with a frightening impact. The craft heeled so far that Sunny expected any moment she would be going over and he'd find himself scrambling in the dark water. He hooked his toes under the ridge on the centerboard trunk and leaned as far out over backward as he could to balance her. His efforts were successful for, after breath-taking minutes of uncertainty, the catboat righted herself a little. Then, with the wind screaming through his stays and the rain drumming a wild tattoo on a sail that was as tight as a drumhead, the little craft hissed through the water at an amazing speed, as Sunny, high on the combing, became drenched with a mixture of rain and salt spray.

It was a wild storm. The sky was black. The water was dark green and menacing. Waves larger than any Sunny had ever witnessed on the Sound came roaring down to pick the pumpkinseed hull of the catboat up and slam it down soundly. But with all that, the craft was traveling—sailing faster than ever before—and Sunny, though frightened, felt a wild sense of elation.

Cautiously Sunny peered under his boom. There to leeward

were the four boats he had expected to see. In a matter of minutes their paths would cross. Again the older skippers had been right. The tack inshore and the lee bow tide had done the job. Maybe he could just make it across the bow of the *Seahorse* who was in the lead but he was on the port tack and had no—

"Right of way!" bellowed Brother Fred, and automatically Sunny jammed his tiller to leeward just in time to avoid collision.

"Right of way, kid!" yelled Sammy before Sunny even had time to think. But he did think now. If he brought *Black Dolphin* around quickly back onto the boat tack, he could just pass ahead of *Barracuda* and *Tarpon* even without right of way. "Ready about and hard alee," he half whispered to himself as he pushed over the tiller and clambered out onto the port gunwale.

"Right of way!" shouted Jimmy Fitzgerald, but Sunny paid no attention. He could hear the gurgle of the water under *Barracuda's* bow, but she rushed by astern with several feet to spare.

The wind still whistled through the stays; the turmoil kept up. Sonny fully expected the catboat to turn over, the mast to give way, or the shrouds to part. Vaguely he was thankful for the new turnbuckles he had attached to the stays, and all the other little details he had attended to, to make the craft seaworthy. Being fussy was paying off. The *Black Dolphin* was weathering the blow.

Appraisingly, Sunny glanced over his shoulder toward Rock Point buoy. Yes, he could make it. His almost inaudible "Hard alee!" and the movement of pushing his tiller over were simultaneous. He was on the last tack of the windward leg. *Seahorse* and *Blue Marlin* had also come about and were standing for the windward mark, but for once Sunny Ward was right. They couldn't cross his bow again. The stronger tide inshore had done the trick as Sunny had hoped. He was well in the lead. He was elated. He had the race in his pocket. He didn't care how fast their boats were, they couldn't overhaul him before he rounded the last mark nor on the reach home. He'd show 'em now! Maybe he was a little guy, but they'd have to admit that *Black Dolphin*

wasn't any mud turtle. They'd have to admit too that he knew
a thing or two about sailing. Or did he?

Suddenly his elation tapered off as he measured the distance
toward the Rock Point buoy and noticed something. He may
have come about too soon—but the current was with him. It was
stronger than usual. He was getting a lot of side drift. He could
make the buoy and round it on this tack—or would he find, when
he reached it, that he was shy and would have to tack again to
get around it? He pointed the catboat up into the wind as much
as he dared and anxiously watched that buoy as it seemed to
speed toward him. It was going to be touch and go whether he

297

could make it, or whether he would flash by just inside it and have to come back and go around. For a few moments he held his breath. Did he dare take a chance? If he rammed it head on, he would tear a hole in the catboat. Closer it came. Still he held his course. But he was worried.

The buoy, like a big, black, dripping sea monster, heaved heavily up in front of him as if to bar his path. He pushed the tiller a few inches more to leeward. Came an ugly, scraping sound with a hollow, rumbling echo. At the same time the catboat lurched a little, seemed to halt momentarily and then leaped ahead in a renewed burst of speed. Sunny exhaled his pent-up breath with a whoop of joy. He was around. The *Black Dolphin* was headed home on a broad reach, while those guys back there were having plenty of trouble trying to get into position to make the Rock Reef mark. He was in! The race was a cinch now. Nothing to it! They couldn't overhaul him no matter how hard they tried.

With mounting excitement and eagerness, he proceeded to square away and get the *Black Dolphin* all set for a run down the wind into Gull Haven harbor and the finish line. He had made fast time. Maybe he had broken the record for the Fish Boat class. Guess they'd be a little less free with the names they'd pin on him and his catboat hereafter. ·

The blackness was beginning to disperse. The wind was dropping too from a shrieking gale to a steady blow. The whitecaps weren't quite so ugly either, and presently Sunny began to breathe freely again. Then he found time to look around. The storm had really done something to the little fleet of racing craft. Looking back he could see where two or three of them had been blown over. He couldn't make out who they were. Too far off. A cabin cruiser was on the way out to pick up the skippers. The rest of the fleet had been scattered all over the course, that is the rest of the fleet except *Seahorse*, *Blue Marlin*, *Barracuda*, and, oh yes, John's *Tarpon* plenty far behind. They had all weathered the blow, but for once they had misjudged the tide.

Sunny settled down in the stern with his eyes on the club-

house brilliant in all its signal flag decorations, but an un-
pleasant consciousness that something had gone slightly awry
dimmed his jubilation. For a few minutes he was puzzled by a
nagging something he couldn't identify. Then suddenly it
dawned on him. Great hat! He had committed a foul when his
boat touched that Rock Point buoy. Even if his craft was the
first over the line it wouldn't do him any good. He'd be disqualified.

A little angrily he tried to kill the thought. It had been an
accident. And he had only scraped the buoy anyway. And who
was going to know the difference if he didn't say anything. The
other boats had been too far behind to see what had happened.
And it wasn't as if—as if—. Sunny's thoughts bogged down. He'd
have to disqualify himself. It was a point of honor. That's why
they didn't station judges at each buoy. A contestant was expected to report any foul he committed. Sunny just knew he'd
have to do it or he would never be able to look at himself in the
mirror again. *Bang* went the gun!

Being first over the finish line didn't mean a thing to Sunny.
Neither did the booming cannon nor whistles, the cheers and
the waving pennants. Waving back halfheartedly he sailed the
Black Dolphin to her mooring, made things snug, then rowed
back to the clubhouse float in his dingy. His father, a member
of the race committee, sensing something wrong, met him at
the float and Sunny, struggling manfully against tears, blurted
out the fact that he had committed a foul and lost the race. Explaining it as briefly as possible, he beat it for home, deep in the
doldrums of disappointment.

Only the fact that no food was being served at his home that
night made him go back to the clubhouse and the chowder
dinner and ceremonies with which the season was officially
closed that evening. He was still blue and disappointed and he
didn't enjoy having members of the gang and even grownups
commiserate with him over his hard luck. He didn't enjoy seeing other fellows get cups for races they had won during the
summer and listening to the speeches that accompanied the
presentation. And he especially didn't enjoy seeing Sammy

Poor awarded the trophy that would have gone to him if he hadn't sailed too close to that doggone buoy. So he was glad when that part of the evening was all over and there remained the big and handsome Commodore trophy to be awarded before the dancing started and he could sneak away home.

The Commodore's cup usually went to the owner of some one of the big yachts like the *Endymion* or the *Lachesis* for representing the club at Marblehead or in the Bermuda races, and Sunny, his mind busy with other thoughts, was taken completely by surprise when Commodore Robinson called his name and beckoned to him. Never dreaming what was about to happen he advanced to the table on which the huge trophy stood, expecting to be requested to perform some service in connection with the presentation. But to his utter amazement the Commodore began speaking.

"Ladies and gentlemen," he said, "each year the Commodore's trophy is awarded to the boat of the fleet that has reflected the most credit on Gull Haven Yacht Club. For the care he has taken of his craft, for the general appearance of the yacht throughout the summer, and for the fine sportsmanship that has been displayed by its owner, the Commodore's trophy this year is awarded to Robert Ward's catboat, *Black Dolphin*—"

Suddenly the amazed Sunny found himself staggering under the weight of a trophy almost as large as he was, which Mr. Robinson thrust into his arms. At the same time the room resounded with applause and wild cheers and although he could distinctly hear such yells as "O.K., Kid!" "Nice going Little Guy!" and " 'Rah for Sunny!" he didn't resent any of them.

Stephen Meader

THE CUTTER RACE

ILLUSTRATED BY *Lorence Bjorklund*

BUD got up at four-thirty and dressed, in the bleak dark of that Washington's Birthday morning. The cold and the excitement made him shake all over like a leaf as he went stumbling out into the barn. But he climbed the mow and dug into the hay savagely with the fork to pull himself together. And when he came down Tug was there to give his hand a warm, reassuring lick.

The white terrier was all but well now. Only a few healing scars remained from his encounter with the gypsy dogs, and his limp was entirely gone.

Bud hustled through the work in time to give Cedar a last brushing down, then fed and watered him with care and went in to breakfast. For Aunt Sarah's sake he made a valiant effort to eat, but he was keyed too high that morning to enjoy the taste of food. Uncle John came out with him to help harness, and by eight o'clock they were ready to start. Bud waved good-bye to Aunt Sarah and drove the colt out of the dooryard to the musical jingle of bells. Tug went too, sitting erect between their feet.

All down the snowy miles to Riverdale Bud had to check Cedar's pace, soothing him constantly by voice and hand, for the colt felt like skylarking.

"This jog to town is a good thing fer him," Uncle John said. "It'll take some o' the devilment out of him, an' maybe he'll be ready fer business at racetime."

At the outskirts of the town they overtook the Hunters' sleigh, in which Cal and his father were riding, and accompanied them to the speedway. There was still nearly an hour before the first heat was scheduled to begin, and Bud blanketed the colt and walked him slowly up and down while the others were getting their tickets for the grandstand. Uncle John reported his injury to the race committee and made the necessary arrangements for having a substitute drive in his place.

The holiday had brought out a far larger crowd than had been present the afternoon before. Not only had many come afoot, but there were rows of cutters ranged along the side of the track, with an occasional automobile among them. The sky was overcast, and the air sharply cold.

"Looks as if it might snow later," said Uncle John, casting a weatherwise eye aloft. He had come back for a last look at Cedar before the race.

A gong began to clang at the judges' stand. "Ten minutes," said Uncle John. "Warm him up a bit back here, then take him up over the course so it won't be strange to him. Good-bye, lad."

Bud took Cedar's blanket off and let him stretch his legs a trifle on the road back of the stand. When he seemed well limbered up the boy swung his horse to the foot of the speedway and jogged him up past the grandstand. Then along the line of jingling sleighs and pungs he guided Cedar toward the starting-point. There were laughter and a few jeers as they passed—the strong young horse, with his winter coat as smooth as Bud could brush it, but looking a bit rough and uncouth about the legs; the scarred old cutter, its moth-eaten cushions well dusted and its steel runners polished till they gleamed; and sitting very straight under an ancient buffalo robe, the serious-faced boy with his eyes to the front.

Eight horses besides Cedar were moving up to the start. Most of them were local trotters. They had beautiful, clipped legs, and right at their tails—on them, in fact—sat their drivers, in sulky sleighs that were no more than light skeletons of braced steel, with ridiculous little shells of seats above.

As they swung into position Bud looked off down the mile straightaway with a pounding heart. He felt himself in a sort of daze, his arms heavy, helpless. Then almost before he knew it the starting gun had sounded. Ahead of him flew the other eight, close-bunched.

A laugh went up as the boy gritted his teeth and urged the

302

sorrel colt after them. Hot tears of anger filled his eyes. But the swift rhythm of Cedar's haunches under the taut reins brought back his confidence and even a thrill of pride. He steeled himself for the job ahead.

And now from the crowds that lined the snow path came scattering cheers as they went by, for some of the men from the upper end of the county and some of Bud's schoolmates recognized them. Slowly, very slowly, it seemed to the boy, they were coming up—overhauling first one rival and then another, till, as the wire drew close, there were six behind them.

Cedar finished in third place. Bud swung him around to pass the grandstand on the return journey. He could not bring himself to look up. He was red with shame. But there were many good horsemen along the track who had seen the colt's fine spurt and who threw Bud a word of encouragement as he went back for the second heat.

Well, there should be no leaving at the post this time! Bud gathered the reins, and the sorrel picked up speed as he neared the start. Over the line he went like a shot, right abreast of the leaders. Halfway down the track Bud looked sidewise. The winner of the first heat, a game little chestnut gelding named Billy D., was holding even with the boy's sleigh seat, trotting with all that was in him. The rest were trailing behind. Bud thrilled to see the red colt then. As his grip on the reins tightened, Cedar responded, speeding faster and faster, with the wind in his mane, over the hard-packed snow he loved. And he crossed the finish line with a good three lengths to spare.

There was a yell from the crowd as the time went up. Bud looked at the board and nearly choked with surprise. Two-eight, it said. Surely there was a mistake. In a minute they would find it out and change the "0" to a "1." But no, the crowd was still cheering. "Cedar! Cedar!" cried the voices in the stand, hailing a new popular favorite. And flushed this time with pride, Bud grinned up at the throng, trying to find Uncle John and Cal and Tug.

The colt was over his first nervousness now, and Bud let him take plenty of time in going back for the final test. When

they reached the start the boy got out of the sleigh and stooped to rub down Cedar's steaming legs with a dry piece of sacking. A man spoke, so close to his shoulder that it startled him.

"Give 'im the whip, this last heat," he said in a low voice. "They're goin' after yuh. That colt's got better time in 'im yet, an' you'd better use it. Don't look around, but drive like the devil, all the way!" And the man was gone before Bud could open his mouth to reply. The single glimpse he got of him had shown a sallow, thin fellow with a black mustache, wearing a great coonskin coat.

Already the horses were back on the track. Bud was thinking quickly, disturbed by the uncalled-for advice of the stranger. It was true enough that he must do his best to win this last heat, but why had the man been so anxious to tell him so? Was he betting on Cedar? Uncle John's words came back to Bud as distinctly as if he were hearing them spoken: "Don't let any-body tell you how to do. Drive your own race." And the boy resolved that, green as he was in such matters, he would use his own judgment and disregard all outside counsel. Still worrying a little, he swung the big red colt into place above the start.

Down they came, all together, like a cloud before the wind, as the flag dropped.

Cedar was rocking along, smoothly as ever, almost in the center of the group. Suddenly Bud saw two horses moving up, one on each flank, and though less than a quarter of the course was finished their drivers were plying the whip savagely. As the sleighs drew even with Cedar's head both men pulled inward a barely perceptible distance. The colt's flying forefeet were very near to striking their runners.

In another instant he might have broken, for he was disconcerted and tossed back his head. But Bud pulled him far off to the left and spoke to him once or twice as Uncle John would do. The young pacer held his stride and a second later was going again like the wind, outside and nearly abreast of the others.

Beyond the half mile they had passed all but the little chestnut, Billy D. He fought them hard all the way down, but Cedar's mighty strength was too great a handicap. Bud was slacking off on the reins at the finish, and the colt drifted easily under the wire, a length to the good.

The spectators came pouring out of the stand as Bud guided Cedar off the track. A crowd of curious men and boys surrounded them, staring open-mouthed at the young stallion while Bud wiped down his legs and blanketed him. After a moment Uncle John shouldered through the onlookers, followed by Tug and the Hunters. No words were needed to express the farmer's joy. It glowed in his square, brown face.

"That was drivin', boy!" he said, and gripped Bud's hand. Then he looked around at the crowd. "Here, let's git the colt out o' this an' give him a chance to rest," he added.

In the lee of a pine thicket near the upper end of the speedway they found a sheltered place to tie the horses and eat their lunch. When Cedar was cool enough they gave him a light feed and a little drink.

"What was it happened up there near the start in the last heat?" asked Uncle John as they consumed Aunt Sarah's sandwiches and pie.

"Two of the drivers tried to box me," said Bud, and he went on to tell how Cedar had escaped from the trap. "There was another funny thing happened," the boy remarked. "Just before the last heat a man came and warned me to drive for all I was worth and lay into the colt with the whip. Do you suppose he really meant to help me? I didn't like his looks, so I didn't pay much attention to him."

"He might've wanted Cedar to win," said Uncle John, "but it sounds more to me as if he'd been tryin' to use the colt up—kill his speed fer this afternoon. Who was the feller?"

Bud described the stranger, but neither Uncle John nor Myron Hunter could remember having seen him.

The next two hours were hard for the youthful jockey. No one talked much. They all took turns at leading the blanketed pacer up and down to keep his legs from stiffening. Now that the first flush of winning the elimination race had passed, Bud had moments of bitter doubt. He thought of the crudeness of their preparations for the final and compared them mentally with what was going on in the big, steam-heated box stalls at the hotel stable, where grooms and trainers were even then putting the last fine touches on Chocorua and Saco Boy.

He thought of Cedar—a raw young colt, driven down that forenoon over ten miles of country road, raced in three hard heats in the morning, and handled clumsily by an amateur driver. What chance had he to win against those famous pets of the racing-game, fresh from a night's rest and maneuvered by wise and tricky hands?

Then he looked up at the big red horse stepping proudly along at his side, saw the courage that glowed in his eye and the strength of his arched neck—and shame filled the boy's heart. Cedar, at least, had no yellow streak.

Two o'clock came, and the young pacer was put back between the shafts of the cutter. Uncle John pulled the last buckle tight with his left hand and gave the colt's cheek a lingering pat. "I guess it's time to go down to the judges' stand," he said. "They'll make the three hosses parade past 'fore the first heat."

They led Cedar down the track, still in his blanket, as far as the upper end of the grandstand. There the wraps were taken off and Bud took his place once more in the sleigh while the others climbed to their seats in the pavilion.

There was a great throng gathered at the track that cold, gray afternoon. The Governor had come over from Concord, and by his side, in the decorated box, loomed the gigantic figure of a famous New Hampshire Congressman who never missed a good harness race if he could help it.

Driving up past the crowds to the judges' stand, Bud realized with dismay that he and Cedar were a part of the spectacle that these thousands had come to watch. Luckily his stage fright did not pass through the reins into the horse. He was as gay as ever and even danced a little as the band played.

Close by, their blanketed forms the center of deep knots of men, were the colt's two opponents. Bud watched them as their coverings were stripped off. Saco Boy stood forth magnificent— a great black stallion with fire in his eyes and mighty muscles leaping in his neck and shoulders. He was more massive and even taller than Cedar, but, Bud felt, no better proportioned.

Then his glance shifted to Chocorua. Instantly the old hatred he had felt when he first saw her returned. It seemed as if no horse had a right to such slim, long racing shanks. She was built like a grayhound, and the similarity was made more striking by her blue roan color and the clipped smoothness of her chest and legs. Her head was long and narrow and wicked. With her ears back she was like a reptile—venomous.

As Bud looked past her his eye was caught by a coonskin coat and a thin, dark-mustached face above it. It was the stranger of the morning, standing close by the mare's head and engaged in an earnest conversation with two men. One was a hard-faced, smallish man in black furs—Andy Blake, the mare's driver. The other was Sam Felton himself. The fat-jowled magnate's eye met Bud's and flashed with recognition. Was it Cal who had said that the Feltons never forgot a grudge? There was something of vindictive triumph in that glance that the boy did not like. And the mystery that had puzzled him was cleared up at last. Instead of a friend the man who had given him the tip was an enemy—one of Chocorua's backers. No wonder he had urged Bud to drive the colt to a needless whipping finish in the morning race. Perhaps it was he who had engineered the attempt to box Cedar, as well. The boy thanked his stars he had followed Uncle John's advice.

307

From the judges' booth sounded the sharp, impatient banging of the gong. "Ten minutes!" came the call, and Bud gathered the reins once more for action.

Bud took Cedar on a little warm-up spin along the track, then came back with the others to the judges' stand. There was another laugh at the rude racing turnout from Red Horse Hill, for many people in the crowd had not been present that morning. Andy Blake, mounted close behind the tall hindquarters of his mare, grinned spitefully at Bud's reddening face. But old Billy Randall, who held the reins over Saco Boy, gave the lad a friendly nod.

"Sorry 'bout John gittin' hurt," he said, "but you drove a good race this mornin'. That's a great youngster you've got there."

From the judges' stand the horses' and drivers' names were read out and the conditions of the race announced. Three heats were to be driven and the championship decided on points if no horse won twice. As the announcer put down his megaphone a babel of sound rose from the stands—cheers and shouts of encouragement. The three drivers turned their horses' heads and jogged slowly up the track toward the start.

Bud had an entirely different feeling from the one with which he had entered the morning race. He was alert and tense now, determined to fight. They swung around at the head of the snow path and got under way. Nearing the start the big, black trotter flashed out ahead, fiercely impetuous. He left the line a good four lengths beyond the others, and Bud expected to hear the jangling of the recall bell. Instead came the report of the gun, and the starter's flag fell. In spite of an outcry from the crowd and the wild gesticulations of Andy Blake the heat was on.

A great excitement entered Bud's veins. His grip on the reins tightened, and he shouted to Cedar through the whipping wind. The colt was pacing swift and sure as in the forenoon, one pointed ear cocked back for Bud's voice, the other forward. Chocorua's evil head, close by their sleigh-seat at first, dropped back and back till Bud could see her no longer, and the colt drew up little by little on the great trotting stallion.

It was such a finish as horsemen dream of. Scarcely half a
length apart down the last quarter fought the sorrel and the
black. There was so little to choose that many called it a dead
heat. But with the sting of Randall's whip on his shining side,
Saco Boy flung himself under the wire a nose ahead.

"Two-five and a quarter!" bawled the timekeeper. And as
Bud came out of the spell of the race he realized that thousands
of voices had been calling on Cedar to win.

Again the long mile back to the starting-point, and then a
little breathing-spell as they got ready for the second heat.
Blake, sullen and resentful, had saved his mare after the un-
even start. She stood there, poised on her slim legs, hardly
breathing as yet, while the black stallion puffed and pawed and

flung white spume flecks back over his ebony neck. Cedar was quieter, but the exertions of the day had begun to tell on him. His deep sides rose and fell with the effort he had made. Bud soothed him with pet names and rubbed him unceasingly as they stood waiting.

It had begun to snow when the starter called them out—long, slanting darts of white hurled across the track by the keen north wind.

They brought their horses to the right about and came down to the post again. The tall roan mare leaped to the front this time, with Randall and Bud driving close at her heels. Blake was not lagging now. From the start he drove her—drove her with hard hand and hard voice, the whip ever poised above her lean back. And still, as she fled away, came Cedar after her, eager as a hawk, his swift feet thudding on the firm-packed snow. Off to the right the great black horse held the pace for awhile, then burst into a thunderous gallop, and they left him and sped on.

It was a terrific gait the mare was making. And she held it to the end, for Blake began using the whip at the three quarter-post and brought her in under a flying lash. Gallantly Cedar followed, but at the finish there was still a length that his weary legs could not make up.

Bud had to shut his jaw hard, for he wanted to cry as he stood by Cedar's side after that second heat. There was a faint, constant trembling in the steel muscles under the colt's damp hide and his coat was bright no longer, but dark with sweat. Rubbing and working at those beautiful legs as if his life depended on it, the boy talked to him breathlessly, pleading with him, begging forgiveness for the one last trial that Cedar must endure. Twice he had given his best and lost. The race and the purse were gone, of course—utterly beyond their reach, but Bud knew they must keep on and see it through.

When he looked up for a moment men were jumping in the air in excitement, shouting and pointing toward the judges' pavilion. On the board were figures which at first Bud read without believing. They said: "2.04."

310

Then at his elbow he saw Billy Randall standing. The old trainer's voice was queer and husky as he spoke.

"I wanted to look at that colt o' yours, lad," he was saying. "I guess we're through—Saco Boy an' I. Once he breaks in a race he's done for the day. But you've got the greatest snow horse in New England there under that blanket—"

"Ye're durn right!" interrupted a voice behind them, and Bud turned quickly to see Long Bill Amos. "The finest pacer I ever see!" continued the teamster. "An' if you don't beat that roan she-devil—now—" He choked. "Look at her! By gosh, I didn't come all the way from Boston to see this colt get trimmed."

Bud looked at Chocorua. There she stood, ears back and head hung low, her eyes rolling wickedly at the grooms who toiled over her legs. She was fresh no longer.

Randall nodded at Bill in full agreement.

"Now look here, boy," said the veteran driver to Bud. "It would ruin some horses to give 'em the punishment that Cedar's takin' today. But I know him. Know his blood. Know his trainin'. He'll stand it. You beat the mare an' you've *won!*"

"Wh-what?" Bud gasped.

"Sure!" put in Amos. "It'll be decided on points. Take a look at that board, front o' the judges' stand."

Bud's eye followed his pointing finger, and a gust of hope swept through him. The board on the pavilion read:

	First Heat	*Second Heat*	*Third Heat*
SACO BOY	1	3	—
CHOCORUA	3	1	—
CEDAR	2	2	—

To put a figure "1" after Cedar's name in the third heat would give him a first and two seconds, while the best either of the others could make would be a first, a second, and a third.

With Long Bill helping him, Bud bent down and redoubled his efforts on the colt's legs. As he worked he whispered to the brave young horse, over and over, that this time he *must*, and he felt Cedar's soft lips fumbling playfully at his ear.

311

The stand was in an uproar when the red colt and the roan mare went back for the final heat. But through the shouting Bud heard a deep, familiar bark and looked up to see the white terrier between Uncle John and Cal. The farmer was bent forward, his face gray and strained, and Cal was giving vent to shrill yells of encouragement. Bud waved a stiff mitten and went on as if in a dream.

Driven whirls of snow were cutting their faces as the jockeys turned above the start once more. Men along the track were huddled close together for warmth and thrashing their arms to shake off the numbness. It was blowing hard, and Bud knew the temperature must be near zero.

There were only two of them left to race, for Saco Boy had been withdrawn. Bud looked down the track through the white storm that hid the far-off grandstand and the town. The wind had swung to the northeast now, and into it they must go. The boy gathered the reins. Cedar's red haunches quivered into action. For the last time they crossed the starting-line.

How they got down to the half-mile post Bud never knew. The air was full of white, and snow particles bit at his eyelids, half blinding him. He was calling the colt's name again and again and leaning forward, always watching the roan mare's head where she raced alongside.

The smoothness was gone out of Cedar's gait. Every tired muscle of him was in revolt, and he was racked with a mighty effort at every stride. Yet on and on he held and never slackened. Into the final hundred yards they came at last, with the lean gray head still on their flank. And now the sorrel labored hard, his sides all streaked with frozen sweat, his head and neck stretched out. But he paced on with weary legs.

Cut by the whip, the mare came up desperately, inch by inch. Bud knew that no whip could better the valiant fight the red pacer was making. "Cedar—Cedar, boy!" he cried, and to the anguish of his voice some last reserve of the colt's great heart responded, for his nose was still beyond Chocorua's when they lunged under the line of the wire.

Duane Decker

MARSHALL AT BAT

ILLUSTRATED BY *James Ponter*

THE Sox did well against the western clubs in that first home stand, which wasn't too surprising. They'd always been a good at-home club, even in their bad years. Their troubles always developed on the road. Especially in the West.

This time, in the most important series—with the Panthers—they took two out of three. That was important because the Panthers were breathing on their necks, in second place.

Patsy Bates began to hit. Jug jumped him from eighth in the batting order to sixth. It was high praise. Obviously he'd never be a .300 hitter but he could blast a long ball and he had a precious knack of blasting it with men on the bases. Pitchers were showing him more and more respect every day.

He was a fixture by this time—and so was Eddie. As a one-o'clock pitcher.

Jug had been right, as usual. His arm, always accurate, was just what a manager would have ordered for a batting-practice pitcher. He worked on his control, which was naturally good, and pretty soon he could put a ball anywhere a batter asked him to put it. Soft stuff, of course, that they'd gleefully whale all over the park. But that proved you were good at your trade.

Eddie didn't like it, and he liked it less every day. The sportswriters referred to him now strictly as "the Sox' one-o'clock pitcher." He winced every time he picked up a paper and read it.

He kept thinking it over and the more he thought about it, the more he wished Jug would sound out a couple of other

313

clubs on either trading him or selling him. Because there were a couple of clubs with shortstops who did not compare with Patsy Bates. On one of those clubs, he might have a chance. An outside one, but a chance.

Anything, he thought, anything at all to stick in the big leagues and get in a ball game now and then. With the Sox it was never now, it was always then. With the Sox he was fully identified these days as the one-o'clock pitcher.

By the time the Beavers came to town, to wind up the Sox home stand—they'd leave on a long road trip then—he'd about made up his mind to have a talk with Jug and insist upon being sold or traded. Because this was no life for him, he was sick of it, and it was getting him down.

So far down, as a matter of fact, that for the first time since he'd ever played ball he lied, to get out of the day's chore. He told Jug that he had a tooth to be pulled, and Jug gave him the day off. He made a date that night to go to Augie Marshall's house and talk the thing over. Augie was his best friend on the team. He wanted to see what Augie thought.

He wound up, as he knew he would, taking a busman's holiday. He went to the ball game. In the bleachers.

He went with the young son of a friend of his, a twelve-year-old boy named Freddie. He considered Freddie one of the shrewdest baseball fans he'd ever met.

They stopped outside the park while Freddie bought two bags of peanuts. The peanut bags only cost a nickel apiece there and inside the park the price was a dime—for the same size bag. Freddie always said that anyone who bought peanuts inside the park was a dope.

Freddie's mother had given him twenty-five cents more than the cost of the bleacher seat and, the way he explained it to Eddie, he'd figured out some years back that if he ate the peanuts slowly, why they would last almost until the sixth inning and then he would still have enough money left for a bottle of pop or a hot dog. He admitted that he was always in a quandary until the sixth inning as to which it would be—the pop or the dog—but he liked being in that kind of a quandary.

314

Baseball fans under fourteen, Eddie decided, had their own way of looking at these things. They did not throw their money around thoughtlessly. They spent each nickel with a calm and graceful maturity.

Eddie bought his ticket. Freddie bought his ticket. They walked leisurely inside. When they reached the rightfield partition, Freddie selected the seats—about halfway to the top, right behind three men who were sitting in their shirtsleeves, yelling loud encouragement to Augie Marshall, who was very busy catching flies in the pre-game practice.

Eddie settled himself in his seat. Freddie did the same. Immediately, Freddie took one of the bags of peanuts from his vastly over-stuffed pockets.

As he munched slowly, he glanced with amused interest at the trio of men in front of him, still screaming hoarse and frenzied encouragement to Augie Marshall. One of the men was fat. The second was thin. The third had a mustache.

Freddie continued to eye them in the very superior manner of small boys, and penguins.

"Oh you Augie!" the fat man screamed, joyfully. "How many homers today, baby?"

"Whaddaya say, you *Augie!*" the thin man roared.

"How about parking a couple of 'em right here in my lap, Augie!" the man with the mustache bellowed.

Quietly, Freddie leaned forward and tapped the fat man on the shoulder. The fat man jerked his head around.

"Save your breath, mister," Freddie said in a fatherly way. "That Marshall is strictly a big bum."

The fat man glared at Freddie, then snorted.

"The big bum," Freddie added, coolly, "can't hit a balloon."

At this remark, the thin man turned around. The man with the mustache also turned. Three very hostile faces now confronted Freddie. Freddie merely shucked a peanut and smiled pleasantly at them.

"Listen, kiddo," the fat man said, "according to the *official* averages in this morning's paper, Augie Marshall happens to be hitting a cool .338. But maybe you aren't *old enough* to read?"

315

"I read pretty good," Freddie said. He tossed a shelled peanut fairly high into the air, tipped his head back and caught it skillfully as it came down. "But let me ask you fellows—do you happen to remember what Augie Marshall was hitting a *week ago?*"

"Huh?" the thin man said, blinking.

"Well, it's a fair question," Freddie said, "and I just happen to remember. A week ago this Marshall was hitting .370-something. He hasn't made a hit since somebody misjudged a fly ball on him in that Panther series."

Then, abruptly, Freddie cupped his hand to his mouth and hooted in the general direction of Augie Marshall's back: "Yah, Marshall! Ya big bum! Ya can't hit the side of a barn, ya has-been!"

The fat man, the thin man, and the man with the mustache looked at each other with pained, hurt expressions. Then they looked back at Freddie. The thin man cleared his throat.

"Look, kiddo," he said, "we're all willing to admit that Marshall has been in a *little* sort of a slump lately. But even the Babe had those. They all do, now and then."

"Yeah," the fat man snapped, "but it's no reason for calling a great hitter like Marshall a has-been and a bum!"

"Nuts!" Freddie said, contemptuously. "When a ballplayer don't deliver, it's the tip-off he's a bum. And this Marshall has *stopped delivering!*"

"Hold on a minute—" the fat man began.

"Why be soft about it?" Freddie demanded. "Look at yesterday's game, for instance. We lose it, 4 to 3, don't we? And in the ninth, remember, we got the bases loaded, two out, and this bum Marshall comes up. What's he do? He hits one right into the second-baseman's pocket, that's what he does. That big bum just hasn't got it any more. He oughta be in a twilight league somewhere."

The trio growled but they had no adequate reply, apparently, to Freddie's cold facts. Eddie noticed that a big, fierce-looking man in a straw hat, sitting on Freddie's right, was now listening to the argument and nodding his head when Freddie spoke.

316

Now, Straw Hat leaned toward Freddie and the trio. "This kid," he announced in a tone of finality, "is absolutely *right!* Marshall is definitely washed up. A bum. If we want to win another pennant this year, we want to get Marshall out of there. He's been around too long. What we need on this team, we need good, young, fresh blood."

Freddie leered triumphantly at the trio as he silently shucked another peanut.

"Well just the same," the fat man said weakly, "I think we ought to give Marshall a little more time to pull out of his

317

slump before we get drastic, like calling him a big bum and stuff like that."

"You're just soft," Freddie said. "Chicken-hearted. How we gonna win a pennant being chicken-hearted?" He glared sternly out at Augie Marshall who was waiting for a fly ball to come down. "Yah!" he hooted. "Ya big bum!"

"The hitless wonder—Augie Marshall!" Straw Hat screeched, happily.

The trio in front then lowered their heads close together and began to talk rapidly and excitedly among themselves, in low voices that could not be overheard.

When the game began and the Blue Sox took the field, Freddie and Straw Hat cut loose vocally as soon as Augie Marshall reached his fielding position. They both screamed venom and disgust, without let-up. A few others near by joined forces. The trio in front sat in stony silence.

Then, when the Blue Sox went to bat in the first inning, a walk to Johnny Madigan and a single by Vic Valenti put men on first and third with one out, as Augie Marshall advanced to the plate. Freddie and Straw Hat groaned. The crowd was imploring Marshall to get a hit.

"Three outs!" Freddie sneered. "Three outs!"

"Pop-Fly Marshall!" Straw Hat barked.

The fat man turned around with a hurt, harassed look on his face. "Now don't be too sure about that," he said, but with no conviction in his voice.

And, even as he said it, Marshall sent a grounder spinning down to the Beavers' second-baseman who zipped it to the shortstop covering second, then relayed to first for a quick double-play to end the inning.

The whole stadium rocked with groans.

"Yah! What'd I tell you!" Freddie croaked.

"Ya big bum!" Straw Hat shrieked.

The trio in front relapsed into gloomy silence. And then, when Augie Marshall walked out to resume his fielding position, Freddie and Straw Hat screamed their utter disgust in shrill and concerted unison. More fans all around them were picking up the anti-Marshall fever now. A chant sprang up in the right field section:

"Take Marshall out!"

"Take Marshall out!"

Freddie settled back in his seat and listened proudly to the swiftly-mushrooming abuse being heaped upon Marshall's shoulders from everywhere.

In the third inning, Marshall came to bat a second time. He struck out, disgustedly, on three pitches. When he returned to rightfield this time, the entire bleacher section was on him. They released torrents of unbelievable abuse now.

When Marshall came to bat for the third time, in the fifth inning, the entire crowd all through the ball park let out a long groan of disgust. A strike, then a ball were called on him. Suddenly his fury at the crowd crystallized: he got hold of one.

It was a pure Marshallian smash—prodigious. It soared up and up, out and out. It became a mere speck in the sky. It was hit with a majestic kind of authority that few ballplayers ever attained. It dropped, finally, into the rightfield bleachers—not ten yards from the thunderstruck faces of Freddie and Straw Hat.

The trio in front turned around and screamed their supreme joy of fulfillment in hoarse glory.

"Whaddaya got to say *now?*"

"What about *that!*"

"A big bum is he, kiddo?"

Freddie shucked a peanut. But he looked sheepish.

"Lucky!" he said, finally. "The guy simply closed his eyes and swung. Lucky!"

"Longest *lucky* homer I ever saw!" said the thin man, gleefully.

Straw Hat said nothing. He merely watched the field with suddenly-brooding eyes.

The trio in front continued to gloat, in loud voices. They really rubbed it in. Freddie and Straw Hat continued to take it in mortified silence—there was no other way to take it.

And, when Marshall came to bat the next time, and rattled

319

a two-bagger off the leftfield wall, the entire bleacher section screamed their joy with him. He was their Golden Boy once more. Only Freddie and Straw Hat remained sullenly silent.

When the game was finally over, the Blue Sox had won it, 6 to 3, and Marshall had made a third hit in the eighth inning, a single that drove in the final run.

Freddie was silent. Eddie walked out with him and they grabbed a bus—to Freddie's house. When the two of them walked in the front door, Freddie's mother hurried from the kitchen.

"Was it a good game?" she asked.

"We won, Mom," Freddie said.

"And—your father?"

"It worked—again," Freddie said, proudly. "Pop got a homer, a double and a single. I picked out three guys that were good yellers and I went to work on 'em. But they were so loyal to Pop they wouldn't razz him. They were nice fellows all right."

"They must have been," his mother said.

"But," Freddie added, in disgust, "I got hold of one big stiff that helped me. He wore a straw hat. He was a mean one, all right."

His mother smiled. "But remember, Freddie—" She looked at Eddie. "And you too, Eddie, not a word to Augie about this. Don't even let on that you *saw* the game."

"But, Mom!" Freddie protested. "I don't see why we *always* have to keep mum about—"

"Because," she said, firmly, "your father likes to think he cures *himself* of his batting slumps. He wouldn't like it if he knew that we—"

Just then there was the sound of heavy feet coming up the steps. Eddie glanced out the window. It was Augie Marshall, with a big smile on his face.

"Shhhh . . . Mom," Freddie said. "Here comes the big bum now."

John R. Tunis

TWO-MILE RACE

ILLUSTRATED BY *Hilda Frommholz*

DUKE WELLINGTON was watching Gus, the trainer, tape up his tender ankle when the coach came past.

"How you feel, boy?"

"Okay, I guess, Mr. Ellis. Wish the thing was over, that's all. This business of sitting round and waiting!"

"Yes. But that's what makes you a good runner. You feel things. The lads who take it in their stride don't come through in important moments. You'll be right up front there with Painton of Yale in the two-mile race this afternoon. I know your kind."

The Duke shook his head. "Hope you aren't counting on my five points. Remember Painton ran two races against us at Yale, and that was his third mile in one afternoon when he stepped out against me. He'll be fresh today."

"Maybe. Maybe not. We don't know whether he'll run the mile yet. Anyhow, don't go to the start this afternoon beaten. You haven't been licked since you began running, and there's no reason why you should now. You'll find Painton tough if he's fresh. No question about it. If he beats you he beats you, that's all." He leaned over. "Painton'll step out in front, hoping you'll stay back in the ruck the way you did two weeks ago. That was a wonderful sprint you uncorked the last quarter, but he expects to be far ahead of you this afternoon—and maybe fresh, too. Understand? One race takes it out of a man's sprinting stamina."

"Okay, I'll keep right along with Painton. But just the same,

Mr. Ellis, I sure wish you wouldn't count on my five points."

The coach didn't hear. Or refused to hear. He moved off to speak to a hurdler who was just going out for his qualifying semifinal. But the Duke knew the coach had heard, and it gave him a bad feeling in his stomach. They *were* counting on those five points to win the meet. Naturally, why not? It was up to him. Everyone was always putting things up to him. The Yale meet was up to him. Now the Intercollegiates.

"Last call for the semifinals of the one-twenty hurdles," came a shout. "First call for the mile."

The Duke went to the window. He stood watching the men troop out for the mile. When they had all gone over to the track, he leaned out and called to Mike, the doorman, "Did Painton go out for the mile? That Yale runner, Painton?" Mike hadn't seen him. Mike wasn't sure.

A couple of sprinters came in, panting and exhausted. "How's it stand now?" the Duke asked.

They recovered their breath. "We have eighteen. Cornell . . . sixteen . . . Penn twelve. Columbia . . . is up there. Yale's way back. . . . They'll save Painton for the two miles all right. As long as they can't win. You've got to pull it off, Duke."

He dressed slowly and put his track suit on over his running clothes because a cold wind was blowing outside. "Last call for the eight-eighty-yard run. Anyone up there for the eight-eighty-yard finals?"

No, there were no Harvard qualifiers for the eight-eighty. The Duke took a blanket and curled up in a corner, the smell of turpentine and the rubbing solution from the tables across the hall striking his nostrils. This would be his last race, the final time he'd go through all this agony. No next year for him. Made you realize how folks felt before an operation. That's what it was like. If only it were over. He felt cold and found he was shivering. The coach going past noticed it and put another blanket over his legs.

". . . and the bar in the pole is at twelve-six . . ." said a voice underneath the window. "We have a chance all right with Wellington in the two-mile."

Hang it, everyone expected him to win. Then the coach came back with Henry, one of the rubbers. "Start his circulation going a little. Duke, they tell me there's another bad actor in your event. Crouse of Cornell. He placed third to Painton last year, and somebody said he had done nine-twenty this spring. Crouse and Painton; keep up with those two and you'll be all right. Get me?"

The Duke nodded. He had reached the point where he didn't care. Henry was slapping his legs and thighs, kneading the muscles of his back. Finally he felt better.

"Last call for the two-twenty hurdles. First call for the two-milers." The Duke jumped up and tossed off the blankets.

"Take it easy. Take it easy, Mr. Wellington. You can stay here where it's warm for another five minutes yet. They won't start without you," urged the rubber. He had seen many nervous runners before. "You got all the time in the world. Take it easy. You'll get cold if you go out there on the field now."

But it was hard to take things easy when your heart was thump-thumping and you were as cold as ice, when you were so frightened. What was he frightened about? He tried to ask himself. The race? No, the responsibility. The whole meet on his shoulders. For a minute he had the same bewildered feeling he used to have when he went into an examination, that feeling of confusion and helplessness. Then it passed. He regained some slight composure and stood up.

"Feel all right?"

He moved his legs up and down. They felt like lead. "Sure. I'm all right, thanks, Henry."

He went over to his locker and took out his shoes. The spikes had been specially sharpened. His last race. Only his second race, too! Several fellows spoke to him as he went out, wishing him good luck. Well, he'd need it.

On the steps he sat down and put on his shoes. A stream of strange faces in strange jerseys was going in and out. He had a sinking feeling at the sight of this crowd. This meet wasn't the family affair the Yale meet had been. It was a contest of strangers. Painton seemed almost like an old friend compared to these new faces. Duke jogged slowly along the edge of the track.

At the starting line he saw Painton jumping up and down, waiting for his name to be called. So Painton was running the two miles. Of course he wanted revenge. The Yale man saw him, smiled, and held out his hand. Painton's hand was warm, whereas the Duke's was cold. He could see the crowd of starters who were gathered about the Clerk of the Course glancing curiously over at him. He was Wellington, the new Harvard distance man. He didn't enjoy their stares.

The Clerk of the Course began calling out an endless string of names. Seemed as if he never would finish. Gosh, what a gang. Then the Duke saw his roommate, Mickey McGuire, standing by the edge of the track. Mickey beckoned, and the Duke went over.

"Stay with them, old boy. I'll be right down here checking."

"How'd you get on the track, Mickey?" It was strictly against the rules for anyone not an official to be permitted inside the stadium during the meet.

"No. 49. No. 49. No. 49!" bellowed the Clerk of the Course. "No. 49, Wellington of Harvard."

The Duke hurried across the track. "I could disqualify you if I wanted to," growled the official. "Here's your place, fifth in the fourth row. Stay there, will you?"

The crowd tittered. He took the place assigned. This mob of runners was something new to the Duke, and terrifying. In the Yale meet there had been six men; here was a field of twenty-five or more to work through. And he was starting in the fourth row, which meant eighteen men ahead. He realized his inexperience, his lack of knowledge of race tactics. Fighting to the front through that crowd was a real job in itself. Even if there were no Painton of Yale up there in the second row.

"Ready now, you men." The starter stood beside them, his pistol over his head. The gang crouched down, and two or three in front leaned over on their hands the way sprinters do.

Bang! As the pistol went off and he started forward, someone in the row behind him gave him a push which sent him against the man ahead, who to protect himself shoved the Duke viciously with his elbow. For the first five yards he was fighting and struggling to keep from falling under those flashing spikes.

As he reached the first curve, he heard Mickey's steadying voice. "Never mind that one, kid. Stay with them." He forgot his annoyance and set out to fight for his place in the pack. It was a fight, too, and he was in a pack of wolves, all eager for the prey ahead. Already he could distinguish Painton's blond head several yards in front of them round the curve. The Yale man was running easily with that graceful and effortless stride for which he was famous. They turned into the backstretch, and, obeying instructions, the Duke decided to move up.

But it wasn't as easy to move up as all that. He was the center of a shoving, fighting mass, and getting free meant elbow work, and elbow work meant wasted energy needed later on. At last on the next curve he managed to drop back, step outside, and work partly free. By this time he saw Painton and one other man well ahead. Coming down toward the starting line, he heard Mickey and out of the corner of his eye saw his roommate's excited face.

"Get up, Duke, get up!"

The bunch was more extended now and there were several small knots of men ahead: two Yale runners in dark blue; then a couple of scattered men; and then, in front, Painton and another man, matching stride for stride. A white shirt with red on it. That must be Crouse of Cornell. Better catch those birds and soon.

He dug in and moved past a few straggling laggards. It heartened him to hear the roar from the stands when he passed them and reached the curve just behind the two Yale men. Trailing them round the bend, he came into the straightaway, determined to go past. From above they were shouting his name. He increased his pace, but so did the runners ahead. He moved to the outside of the track, and one of the two moved over also. Then he came back near the pole and tried to cut through, but there was no opening. Elbow to elbow the runners in blue kept going at a fast clip ahead.

325

It was a fast pace all right, yet those bluebirds were sticking it pretty well. Have to wait for the next curve and then work past. Painton and Crouse were up ahead; already there was a gap of fifteen yards, and he knew this was just what he had been told not to allow. Pound, pound, pound, went the flying feet ahead. They were coming into the stretch by the start. There was Mickey—shouting something, bellowing at him, but he couldn't make out what it was. Too tired to concentrate on anything but running. Now for a good sprint to leave those devils behind.

But once more, as he moved over on the track, the Yale men moved over, too. That was it. They had him boxed. They were keeping him back until Painton had his lead secure. All the way up the stretch the shouts and yells urging him ahead continued, but as he tried to work his way past, they bunched together to prevent him. Of course he could shove them, but to do this meant a tumble, wrecking his chances, too. He could bring them all down, but they had no chance of winning and didn't care. He became furious as he saw himself hemmed in and unable to move ahead. Teamwork. That was the name for it in sports.

Then without warning the pace told. One of the Yale runners lost a stride, staggered, and fell on the grass beside the track. The pace had cooked him. In the confusion the Duke saw an opening, darted through, and started after the flying figures up front. The stadium rose. The maneuver to keep him back had been plainly apparent from the stands.

Up front were the two leaders, farther ahead than he had realized and going at a tight clip. Already the Duke's legs were aching, and his lungs hurt, but he knew this race was only half over. Could he stick? Would he last? Yes, but this was his final race, this was. Never again.

He came up the stretch to cheers of encouragement from the stands. What had started as a runaway began to show signs of being a real contest. At first he thought the cheering was for one of the men ahead, but words came down and once or twice he distinguished his own name through the coating of fatigue

He was ahead; the thought gave him courage.

that was shutting him in like an anesthetic. The finish line flashed past, and the Clerk of the Course shouted at him, "Three laps to go. Three to go. Three."

Three to go. And Painton twenty yards in the lead. He could see the Yale man looking over his shoulder as he took the turn in long, graceful strides. And Crouse. That boy was a runner. He was all the coach had said. Still up there with Painton. Two of them to catch.

Then a strange thing happened. Slowly at first and then faster, Crouse came back to him. The Duke, seeing this, increased his pace slightly and could soon hear the noise of his rival's feet. As he did so, an answering roar came from the stands. Was he gaining? Yes, he was gaining. That panting, was it his? No, Crouse's. Closer now, closer. He could see the tendons on the back of his neck standing out. Down the stretch they went like that, the other man just ahead, the Duke even, then Crouse a stride in front again, until with an effort the Duke lengthened his stride and stepped out.

If only he hadn't been held back. His whole frame ached, his mouth was dry, and foam was on his lips and drooling down to his chin; but his stride was strong and true as mechanically he forced himself to go out after Painton. More tiring, they all said, to run a front race as the Yale man had been doing. Well, no one could be more tired than he was. Charging up the straightaway, he saw the blue jersey a few yards beyond.

"Go on, Duke, go on. Keep it up. You can. . . ." Mickey by the side of the track. But the Duke didn't feel like going on. His mouth was parched, his legs were iron rods, and every step meant pain. No, not pain, agony. He was suffering so much that the cheering and noise from the stands was confused and nebulous. There couldn't be much more, many more laps to go. There surely . . . couldn't be much more left. Down the stretch they went. Then the cinders from his rival's spikes spattered upon the Duke's bare legs. He could hardly see Painton through the haze of fatigue, but those cinders were a signal. He was gaining.

Clang! Clang! Clang! The bell for the last lap.

Painton lengthened his lead. One more effort. Just one more, to hold him, to stay with him as long as possible. Ridiculous, of course, but he must make that effort. He dug in. He gained slowly, steadily, until he was right back of the Yale man. Then he dropped back and Painton took the curve ahead. They came into the stretch and the Duke made his try, his last, final try. All he had, everything. Elbow to elbow now . . . how long can I stand it? Half a lap. A few hundred yards.

Then he was ahead. He was ahead. The thought gave him courage. Head between shoulders, arms drawn back, he tore down the stretch. Suddenly there was pounding at his heels. Painton's sprint. The famous sprint. He could hear the pounding feet just behind him. Fifty yards, forty yards, thirty. If only he could hold those inches. The breath of the other man was on his back, gaining, coming up, now on his shoulder, now on the side of his face. Then it was back again on his shoulder. That way they fell across the finish.

In an Iowa town the Duke's father and mother listened beside their radio.

The insides of Mrs. Wellington's hands were dripping wet. She felt the handkerchief which for fifteen minutes she had been twisting and rolling up in her palm. It was a wet linen rag. Well, the race was over now. If only he hadn't killed himself. Statistics somewhere proved that athletes—what was it— burned themselves out. They always died young.

". . . had a meteoric career, folks, because, believe it or not, this Iowa boy never ran before in his life until this spring when Coach Slips Ellis urged him to come out for the track team. He won his first race two weeks ago in the Harvard-Yale meet, but Painton had already run one fast mile at four-fifteen earlier the same afternoon, so everyone said it was a fluke, that victory. However . . . well, you all know what happened today, and you heard about the Duke's magnificent battle here on this historic track in the Harvard Stadium . . . believe you me, folks, that was sure some race, hardly a sheet of paper between them at the finish. Now they're going off the field . . . that man beside the Duke is . . . I think it is . . . wait until I get my glasses

328

. . . yes, that's his friend, Mickey McGuire, Harvard's star quarterback, on one side of him there . . . and there goes Painton right behind walking out with a friend and dragging his blue sweater on the ground . . . he looks all beaten . . . in fact both of 'em look beaten after that terrific duel . . . there, listen to the crowd give them a hand. Wait a minute. Here comes the official time, folks."

Mr. Wellington sat straight up in his chair. Then he leaned over and fumbled nervously with the dial of the radio.

"Won by—" It was a voice from the official announcer over the loudspeaker system inside the stadium, but so penetrating that it came through plainly over the air. "Won by . . . James Wellington, Jr., Hahvud . . . second, Harry Painton, Yay-ull, third. . . ." Why on earth did they bother with all that? Who cared about third or fourth places? Had they broken a record? A wave of noise broke through the microphone. Back in Cambridge the crowd in the stadium knew instantly that a record had been approached and that probably it had been broken.

The announcer started again. "Time . . . eight minutes, fifty-six, and ONE-fifth seconds."

Again the cheering broke in. It swelled and grew, louder and louder, wave upon wave. Mr. Wellington adjusted his glasses. He looked over at his wife on the davenport and tried to smile. There was perspiration on his forehead. From where she was sitting she noticed his damp forehead, and realized that not only her boy, but the entire Wellington family, had been running that race in Cambridge.

"It's a record all right, Mother. It's a record. Hear them yell?" He tried to make his voice sound natural, but despite all he could do, it vibrated with emotion. "Yes, sir, a new record, sure enough."

". . . making," continued the announcer, "a new intercollegiate record." The noise increased once more, then suddenly it was cut off as the control switched to the radio booth up top of the stadium.

"You probably heard the official announcer, folks, eight minutes, fifty-six and one-fifth; that breaks Don Lash's record by almost two seconds. Now I'm going to turn you over to George Davis down there on the field, who will try to get both contestants in this thrilling duel to say a word to you. All right, George, take it away."

"Hullo, everybody, we're right down here at the entrance of the stadium waiting for the two men to come across the field on their way to the lockers. And here comes Harry Painton, of Yale, that great runner who was just at Wellington's elbow in this thrilling race. Painton, you know, was about a second inside the record, too. Here he comes now. Mr. Painton, that was certainly a grand race, your last race of all. Would you mind saying a few words to the radio audience?"

There was a pause of a few seconds. It seemed a long while. Then a panting voice, which evinced the struggle its owner had just endured, stammered into the microphone in a tone little above a whisper.

"Yeah . . . ran a great race . . . to finish second . . . what do you . . . have to do . . . to win in this league?"

The announcer laughed. "Mr. Painton, who busted Lash's record and yet finished second, wants to know what you have to do in this league to win. That's pretty good. Thanks lots, Mr. Painton, and all good luck to you. Now here comes the winner, Duke Wellington, who broke the two-mile record held by Don Lash of Indiana, and incidentally gave Harvard her first intercollegiate track meet since 1909. You remember the final score, folks. Harvard, twenty-three and an eighth; Penn, twenty-two; Cornell, nineteen; Yale, sixteen and three-eighths. He seems all in, this boy Wellington; he sure has given everything he's got. They're sort of helping him over to the field-house; so I'll just ask him to say hullo to you." There was a delay. Then some blurring and scratching noises over the air, and finally the buttery voice of the announcer.

"Would you mind saying hullo to the radio audience, please, Mr. Wellington?"

Once again delay. Then a choked and muffled "Hullo." Mrs. Wellington twisted the wet handkerchief in her hands. His father leaned over toward the radio.

"And now, Duke, kindly tell the radio audience how it feels to be the new two-mile record holder." There was no answer. "Why don't they let the boy alone?" demanded Mr. Wellington. "Wish I was there."

The announcer cut in again. "This is Duke Wellington, folks, Harvard's new intercollegiate two-mile champion, who smashed the record held by Don Lash of Indiana this afternoon." He was stalling, and his voice became odiously persuasive.

"One thing more, Duke, then we'll let you go. Please tell the radio audience how it feels to be the two-mile champion."

Instead of the feeble tones of the champion, a strong Irish voice boomed over the air. People heard it in Boston; so did people in Waterloo, Iowa, and in Los Angeles.

"Get out of the way with that thing of yours, big boy, or I'll bust you in the nose. Can't you see he's all in?"

Mr. Wellington roared with laughter. For the first time that afternoon, no, for the first time that day, the tension was lifted and he leaned back, relaxed and amused.

"Wonderful," he said, snapping off the radio. "Wonderful. Mother, that must have been McGuire."

331

B. J. Chute

DENNY PUTS IN HIS OAR

ILLUSTRATED BY *Dorothy Bayley Morse*

E DUCATION," said Denny McCall, "is a wonderful thing."

Kenneth Young considered this statement darkly, said he must try it sometime, and bit savagely at his pencil.

"Take this book," Denny went on. "*Your Mind and What It Is—*"

"*Your* mind?" said Kenneth. "Well, well. They certainly learn more and more about less and less nowadays, don't they?"

Denny ignored him. "It says here that psychology is the key to all human activity, and—"

"It's my opinion," Kenneth remarked, "that if we could accept Bainbridge Prep's challenge and make a halfway decent showing, the trustees might reconsider and let Harford have a regular rowing crew. Boy, just think of it." His eyes became dreamy. "A decent shell, a coach, a—"

"The theory of psycho-physical parallelism," Denny went on patiently, "is one which—"

"—we are not interested in," Ken told him one-sidedly, adding plaintively, "Do you think we should accept the challenge? Since I'm coxswain, the fellows think I'm crew manager too, so it seems to be up to me. If I thought the crew was going to shape up, I'd—"

"Are you interested in the theory of interaction?" Denny inquired wistfully.

"Not unless we could beat Bainbridge with it," Ken said,

332

drawing a picture of a cross-eyed hippopotamus with a forbidding leer and labeling it Bainbridge.

Denny fixed Ken with a glittering eye. "Well, why not?" he demanded. "Your crew's composed of eight minds, isn't it?"

"Not counting the coxswain," said Ken with unconscious humor at his own expense.

"Well, there you are," Denny announced. "All you need is a good psychoanalyst. Just tell *me* your troubles, and I'll solve them for you."

"You and what other professors?" said Ken skeptically, but since telling his troubles was what he had been trying to do anyway, he launched forth gladly. "Take Mike Martins, our Number Seven man. He's got a chip on his shoulder."

Denny looked profound.

"He thinks he knows everything there is to know about rowing," Ken growled. "I can't handle an oar—I'm much too small —but my brother rowed stroke for Yale, and I know plenty about style. But what happens?" He waved his arms indignantly. "I tell Mike he's skying—"

"Whiching?" said Denny.

"Skying," Ken repeated impatiently. "Lofting the blade when it comes back to the catching position."

"Oh. Clear as potato soup."

"And that means he washes out too. And when I—"

"I *beg* your pardon?" said Denny courteously.

"Weak finish at the end of the stroke," Ken interpreted. "Those are both faults he could correct, but he won't pay any attention to me."

"Hmm," said Denny.

"Then there's Bud Sexton," Ken went on mournfully. "Just the opposite of Mike. He's dead sure *everything* he does is wrong, no matter what. He's the poorest oar on the crew, I admit, but he's not that bad. I mean, after all, if he'd just take a brace and—"

Denny held up a hand. "I get it," he said soothingly. "What else is wrong?"

"Well, the other two," Ken meditated, "are Pudge Ewalt

333

and Billy Dean. They've started a grudge fight for themselves. And, since they row three and four," he added, "everything's very cozy. You don't row so well with a guy when you're thinking up ways to crawl down his throat."

Denny nodded his head somberly. "I see what you mean. How did the fight start?"

Ken looked, if possible, sadder. "Well, Pudge had a dog that he wanted to be mascot for the crew. And Billy had Lucius. You know Lucius?"

Denny nodded his head again. Lucius Tarquinius Superbus, Billy Dean's tame raccoon, was a familiar figure around the school. Lucius had once taken a pair of Denny's pajamas and torn them to shreds, strewing the pieces on the library steps.

"I know him well," said Denny, with magnificent understatement.

"Well, the other fellows decided they wanted Lucius as a mascot, and Pudge got sore and said Lucius was a bum pet, and then Billy got sore and— Oh, I don't know. Anyway, now they're mad at each other all the time."

"Just one happy little family," Denny observed, and got to his feet. "My boy, go ahead and accept Bainbridge's challenge. I've decided to take your case."

"You've decided to WHAT?"

"Take your case," said Denny. "I'll apply psychology in the proper places and cheer Harford on to its first great victory. Put yourself in my hands and relax."

"Relax!" Ken exclaimed in a thin croak.

"That's right," said Denny. "And, while I'm on the subject, *your* mind needs a little attention. You have as fine a case of defeatism as I've ever seen. However, just trust Professor McCall, and all will be well."

Ken put his head in his hands and moaned weakly. He felt faint.

The next afternoon, Denny steamed down to the river shore to find the Harford crew pulling a fine stroke upstream, with Ken perched in the stern.

"Get your back into it, Two!" Ken shouted. "Pull harder!"

334

Bud Sexton looked dejected, took a slightly stronger pull on the next stroke, and then outraged Ken and pleased Denny's scientific mind by giving a defeated shrug and shipping his oars.

"What's that for?" said Ken indignantly. "Get going! Wait a minute!" He interrupted the stroke to address Number Seven. "Mike! You're skying again. You crazy idiot, why don't you—"

It was Mike's turn to ship his oars, his expression dangerous and a thundercloud seated on his brow. "Oh, I'm skying, am I?" said Mike, with the sweet restraint of a hurricane going somewhere to blow.

"You sure are," Ken snapped. "I keep telling you not to drop your hands. If you'd pay some attention, instead of—"

"Listen," said Mike, "let me tell you—"

Denny, on shore, interrupted. "Why don't you go on and row?" he yelled. "I'm getting bored."

This suggestion turned the crew's attention to their audience and, after some comments on Denny's character, they actually did start rowing again, the boat running through the water with deceptive ease.

"Hmm," said Denny to himself. "Not bad."

At this moment the blade of the Number Three oar scooped viciously at the water, and missed. From Number Four arose a bitter comment.

"Nitwit," said Number Four.

Number Three took his oar out of the water with deadly deliberation and turned on his critic. "What did you say?" said Billy Dean with cold fury.

"I said nitwit," Pudge Ewalt repeated. "Missing the water on your catch. A cow could row better. Even Lucius could row better."

"You leave Lucius out of this," said Billy gallantly. "*You* threw the boat off-keel at the catch. I couldn't help missing water, you—you—"

"*I* threw the boat off-keel?" Pudge sputtered. "*I*—"

The coxswain raised his voice in a thunderous howl. "Quit fighting," he yelped, "and get going. This isn't Madison Square Garden."

Somewhat sulkily, the Three and Four oars slid into the water. Ken gave them the beat, the men got together on the catch, the bladework was clean and snappy, and hope dawned on the cox's face.

Then suddenly, on the recovery, a blade struck the water and the oar handle jammed against the oarsman. Pudge, his mind and mutterings intent on Billy, gave a hollow grunt as it hit him in the chest, grabbed at the side, and vanished overboard.

The boat spun and rocked like a demented thing, the crew fought for balance, an oar went overboard, and with a happy swoosh the shell tipped up and deposited her cargo in the river.

"Well, well," said the scientific mind, safe on shore. "What interesting things you do see."

He was, however, gentleman enough to lend a helping hand to the dripping arrivals as they stumbled up the bank, and to follow them to the locker room with suitable expressions of sympathy, Ken hissing indignantly in his ear.

"So you still think we could beat Bainbridge, do you?" he sputtered, wringing water out of his clothes.

"Everything's under perfect control," Denny assured him. "Just keep calm. Hello, Lucius."

Lucius got down off a bench and advanced mincingly, wise yellow eyes staring out curiously from the black mask across his pointed face. Denny bent to pat the sooty-gray fur, and Lucius slipped a confiding, fingered paw up Denny's sleeve. Billy, dripping furiously, gave Denny an appreciative look.

"Nice little fellow," said Denny.

Pudge slopped out of a pool of water and reached for a towel. "That thing?" he snorted. "Ha."

"Lucius isn't a thing," Billy snapped untruthfully. "He's an unusually fine animal. Look at his tail."

Everybody, except Lucius, looked at his tail. It was bushy and handsomely ringed, and Lucius was sinfully proud of it. Pudge, however, regarded the appendage with chilly scorn.

Denny left Pudge and Billy to sharp remarks and icy silences and sought out Ken.

Dorothy Bayley Morse—

"This all promises to be very simple," Denny informed him brightly, smiling quite contentedly.

"Simple!" Ken groaned.

"Elementary," said Denny. "Stand by for orders. I'm going into action."

"You can go into a tailspin for all I care," said Ken, his head in his hands. "I'm going to find me a quiet corner and curl up and die."

"All in good time," Denny promised. "I'll come to your case later. It's the last on my list." With this devastating remark, he started gaily toward the door, then paused. "Look. Be sure to accept Bainbridge's challenge, will you?"

Ken looked up. "That," said Ken, in the voice of a disillusioned specter, "is what we experts call the payoff. I *have* accepted it. Pass the arsenic, please."

Denny, with Ken reluctantly in tow, intercepted Bud Sexton the next day and calmly announced that he was undertaking the job of "sort of Ken's assistant."

"Are you?" said Bud glumly. "I've about decided to quit the crew."

Denny succeeded in not hearing him. "We're rather worried about Mike Martins," he said, ignoring Ken's stunned expression. "The kid's getting the most terrific inferiority complex you ever saw."

"Mike?" said Bud. "What're you talking about? Mike's wonderful."

Denny shook his head sadly and glared Ken into silence. "He's got a lot of faults and they worry him. That business of— um—skying, for instance. And—er—washing out." He overrode Bud's feeble protests roughshod. "I think you could help us build up his confidence, Bud. Tell him occasionally that you don't think he does so badly. Tell him his faults aren't so serious. I'd hate to see him quit the crew."

"Gosh," said Bud numbly, "I had no idea."

"Well, make an effort to help the kid along a little, will you?" Denny said persuasively, and departed with a dazed Ken meekly in tow. Ten minutes later they located Mike on the

338

library steps, and Denny commenced to lecture him on the subject of Bud's superiority complex, ignoring the elbow Ken kept digging in his ribs.

"The poor kid," said Denny, "thinks he's so terrific, he won't listen to anyone's advice. You've probably noticed he makes a lot of mistakes—"

"To hear Ken tell it," Mike interrupted blackly, "even *I* make 'em."

"Oh, I wouldn't say that," said Denny soothingly. "Bud—"

Ken, despairing, jerked Denny aside. "You've got 'em mixed," he hissed frenziedly. "It's Mike who has the superiority complex—you—"

"H'st," said Denny, like a villain in a melodrama, "this is Psychology." He then returned to the attack, not leaving it until he had Mike's solemn promise to deflate Bud's ego in the most tactful manner possible.

"Now, let's see," Denny mused, wandering off with Ken. "We still have a grudge fight on our hands. Everything else is practically solved."

"You're stark staring mad," said Ken dispassionately. "What good was all that hocus-pocus with Mike and Bud? You got everything all mixed up, you chuckleheaded flitter-brain."

This scathing character sketch failed to discourage Denny. "I'd better settle the grudge fight at the last moment, I believe," he said thoughtfully. "By that time Bud and Mike will be okay—"

"Ha, ha, ha," said Ken.

"—and then all you have to do is win the race."

"Ho, ho, ho," said the coxswain, and staggered away.

Denny gazed after him sorrowfully. "Defeatist all right," he murmured. "And the cure for defeatism is obviously a victory." He nodded his head with satisfaction. "And what," demanded Denny, "could be simpler?"

Mike put one foot on the bench beside Bud Sexton and began to exercise considerable care in lacing his shoe. Uncertain where to begin on a superiority complex, he sighed, and unintentionally gave Bud the opening he had been waiting for.

339

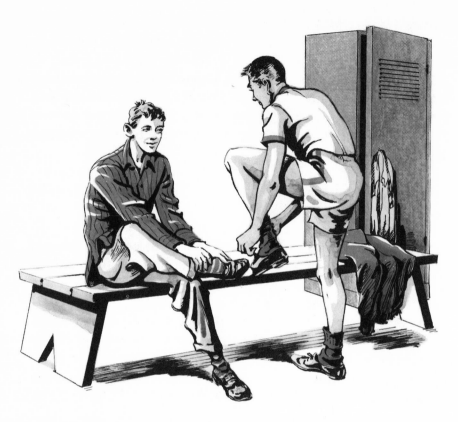

"I wouldn't get discouraged, if I were you," said Bud consolingly. "You're really pretty good."

Balancing on one leg is never altogether satisfactory. When suddenly subjected to shocks, the patient nearly always crashes. Fortunately, this time, the bench got in the way, and Mike merely sat down.

"You wouldn't get *what?*" said Mike, swallowing hard.

"Discouraged," Bud repeated. "Take skying, for instance. Lots of really good rowers do that. It's a fault, I know, but—"

Fortunately Mike had been warned. This, then, was the superiority complex on which he had been lectured. He hung onto his temper with both hands and muttered behind his teeth that he would be tactful at whatever cost. But he would also Deflate the Ego—that was his job.

"You have a couple of faults yourself," Mike began with

340

tender diplomacy. "You'd really be a rather better rower if you got your back into it more, and you have a tendency to knife in on your bladework. You—"

Bud, who could have written a ten-volume encyclopedia on his shortcomings, nearly fainted. The great Mike Martins was accusing him of only two. Maybe, after all, he wasn't so bad. Flooded by gratification, he felt more urgently than ever that Mike must be cheered up.

"Washing out isn't so serious either," he said encouragingly.

Mike's mouth set in a grim line. "Who said anything about washing out?" he demanded.

"Well, *you* do it," Bud said politely.

Mike rejected "Oh, I do, do I?" as undiplomatic. He also rejected the interesting possibility of cramming Bud's teeth down his throat as definitely tactless. "I could give you a few hints on *your* rowing," he growled.

Bud's expression grew beatific. That was what he needed, but Mike had never offered help before.

"And *I'll* watch *your* work too," said Bud eagerly. "You probably don't know when you do it wrong yourself, and anyway it's not so serious. You shouldn't get discouraged."

Mister Bud Sexton had asked for it, and Mister Bud Sexton was going to get it. Tactful, of course, but firm—the iron hand in the velvet glove. Nor would Mister Sexton be able to do any more criticizing. From now on Mike would watch his step and not give this conceited young whippersnapper a chance to tell *him* what to do.

The young whippersnapper was congratulating himself. Mike Martins, top man on the crew, had found only two faults to complain of. Mike had offered to help him. And, best of all, he had been able to cheer Mike up a little.

At least, that was how Bud interpreted the smirk on Mike's face, which was rather like a cat eyeing a bowl of cream. If Denny had been present, his own smirk would have outshone the morning sun, but fortunately neither of his victims could have known that.

The day of the unofficial but titanic race between Harford

and Bainbridge dawned, windy but bright. By afternoon Ken was having a nervous breakdown and blaming the absent Denny for ever letting him get into this mess.

The one bright spot in his life was the considerable improvement of both Mike and Bud but, on the other hand, the Dean-Ewalt feud was getting worse every day, having reached a high point the preceding afternoon when Pudge had accidentally stepped on Lucius' precious tail. Billy had declined to believe it was an accident, and only the intervention of the entire crew prevented a fist fight.

Also a scout had clocked Bainbridge's practice time and it was too fast for Ken's peace of mind.

The arrival of Denny, full of sweetness and light, did him no good. In fact, it did him definite harm—there was something so cheery about the self-appointed psychologist. Denny brightly ignored Ken's grumblings and immediately crossed to Lucius, who was crouched pensively over a pan of water, busily washing something with his clever, tiny paws.

Denny knelt beside him, glanced elaborately at Billy, then at Pudge, and finally got to his feet. Lucius looked up nervously, and Denny gave him a reassuring pat. "I'd go easy on washing that lemon drop, if I were you," he advised softly. "They melt."

Lucius looked pleased. Being a perfectly normal coon, he always washed his food with the utmost care, and his expression indicated that this was simply good, clean fun.

Denny shrugged. "Okay," he agreed. "It just means that I have to work fast."

He then crossed to Billy's side and flopped down on the bench.

"Cute coon," said Denny.

"Lucius is wonderful," Billy stated, casting a dark look at Pudge. "Just because Pudge is sore—"

This was the opening Denny had been waiting for like a cat at a mouse-hole, and he pounced. "Funny thing about Pudge," he said casually.

"Funny!" exclaimed Billy, nicely blending a sneer and a snarl.

342

"Well, yes. Take this Lucius business, for instance. Pudge pretends he hates him. And because why?"

"Because he does hate him," Billy supplied, "and because he's a great big overgrown hunk of cheese, that's why. Pudge, I mean, not Lucius."

"Then why," said Denny innocently, playing his trump card, "why does Pudge feed him lemon drops?"

Billy started like a stricken deer. "Lemon drops?"

Denny nodded toward Lucius, who was washing busily but with a perplexed air. The candy was getting progressively smaller, and Lucius' paws were getting correspondingly stickier. Lucius had the look of one who is not getting a square deal, and Denny felt sorry for him, but the cause was a good one.

"Pudge never gave him that," Billy stated firmly.

"He must have," Denny insisted. "He's got a whole bag of them in his coat pocket."

"Lucius has?" said Billy in a befuddled way.

Denny was very patient. "No. Pudge."

"Are you *sure?*" said Billy.

"Of course I'm sure." He was too. He had put them there himself, but there was no need for Billy to know that. "It's my opinion Pudge has been making up to Lucius on the sly. I think he really likes him, only he's too— Well, he'd naturally be a little embarrassed now about letting you know it."

A strange expression crossed Billy's face. He looked at Lucius, then across the room at Pudge. Finally he got to his feet, walked over to the coon and picked him up gently.

Lucius looked pathetically at his empty paws. The lemon drop had now disappeared entirely, and nothing but a thin candy coating remained. It just went to show—you should never trust people.

With Lucius under his arm, Billy crossed to Pudge's side and sat down beside him. Pudge gave both arrivals a cold glare and moved over. Billy, unchilled, thought of him feeding Lucius lemon drops in shy secret sessions, and the picture touched him deeply.

"Uh—Pudge—" he began discreetly.

343

"Take that animal away from here," Pudge growled. "I'm trying to dress."

Billy paused uncertainly, and Lucius interfered. Just beyond Pudge lay a coat. In the pocket of the coat was a bag of delicious ripe lemon drops, sweetly scented with sugar. Lucius' little nose began to twitch. Lucius' anxious, greedy paw reached out toward Pudge. He had to cross Pudge, or he could not reach the delicious lemon drops. It was all quite simple.

"He likes you," said Billy suddenly.

Pudge gazed in astonishment at the furry body, now hunched hopefully against his leg while a cold nose and cold paws scrabbled purposefully. In spite of himself Pudge felt vaguely flattered.

"Coons don't like many people," said Billy, still thinking of those lonely vigils with the lemon drops. "It's quite unusual."

Lucius got annoyed. This large obstruction between him and his goal was really most irritating. He gave a wiggle and a flop and landed squarely on Pudge's lap.

Pudge automatically grabbed at Lucius to steady him. His hands sank into the soft, warm fur, and Lucius nudged at them with his head.

"Well!" said Pudge with a self-conscious laugh. "He does

344

like me, at that." After all you could sort of see why Billy was so goofy about the creature—he had a way with him. "Well," said Pudge again.

"Well," echoed Billy. "That's really quite unusual." Good old Pudge—you never really knew about people.

Good old Lucius. Coons were pretty intelligent animals, when you come to think of it.

Good old Billy. . . . Lucius gave an annoyed heave upwards, then relaxed philosophically, his nose sniffing the lemon drops. Experience had taught him that humans always went away eventually, and then he would be left alone with that lovely paper bag, and one by one he could wash the lovely things inside it. Lucius snuggled down with a contented sigh.

"Quite pretty to watch, isn't it?" said Denny in an undertone. "Come outside, Ken. I want a word with you."

Ken staggered after him dazedly.

"Well," said Denny dreamily. "It worked, didn't it?"

"Glug," said Ken.

"I thought you'd like to know," Denny went on, "that I've invited Mr. Keeler down to watch the race. He's the most stubborn of the trustees. I figured seeing Harford win might change his mind about having a crew here."

"Gurk," said Ken.

"Anything wrong?" Denny inquired gently.

Ken got his voice back. "Listen, Denny," he said. "You're a wonder man. I admit it freely. You've practically accomplished four miracles, but you've overlooked just one little thing."

"Yes?" said Denny.

"Yes," said Ken. "The Bainbridge crew can row faster than the Harford crew. They—"

"You're going to try to beat them, aren't you?" Denny murmured.

"Well, of course we're going to try!" Ken snapped indignantly. "What do you think?"

"Then don't worry about anything, my little man," Denny told him with infuriating kindness, "and run along, or you'll be late." He watched him go, then smothered a lazy yawn.

345

"One of my most interesting cases," said Denny.

Having superintended the start, Denny, with Lucius Tarquinius Superbus protestingly curled in the basket, bicycled to the bridge at the end of the river course. On arrival he tucked Lucius firmly under one arm, borrowed a pair of field glasses from a sad-eyed freshman, and, spying Mr. Keeler near by, pushed his way to the trustee's side.

"A lot of nonsense, the whole thing," Mr. Keeler fumed, gazing distastefully at the bright water below them. "Never heard of anything so—"

Denny handed him the glasses. "Since you're here, sir," he suggested with becoming hesitancy, "you might as well watch the race. They'll be in sight around the bend in a moment."

"Humph," said Mr. Keeler bitterly, but took the glasses. "What's that thing under your arm?"

"A raccoon, sir," said Denny respectfully.

Mr. Keeler was about to touch on this additional symptom of congenital madness pertaining to rowing, when a shout rose suddenly from the watchers on the bridge.

"Here they come!"

The two narrow streaks sliding over the waves, with sixteen oars glittering as they bit into the green water, attracted the trustee's reluctant attention. He focused the glasses irritably.

"H'r'mph," he said with triumph, his worst suspicions confirmed. "Harford's behind. What'd I tell you? Lot of nonsense."

"They're coming up, sir," Denny murmured, leaning dangerously over the railing and nearly squashing Lucius.

Most of the audience were saving their lungs for the really serious shouting, and as the boats came nearer, Harford a length and a half behind, the coxswains' voices carried clearly.

"Eyes in the boat, Three," Ken warned. "Steady, Seven, steady. Swing into it." He had worked the beat up to forty and was wondering with a sick heart if they could possibly hold it.

"Hit her up! Hit her up! Come on, fellows."

Bainbridge oars sliced the water in rhythmic precision. The Harford stroke was steady but at its peak. They would have to

346

raise it for the final spurt, and they were strained to the limit now. It looked as though the Bainbridge lead would hold.

Harford crept up fractionally but too slowly. The eight oarsmen and the hoarse-voiced cox were making a terrific fight of it, and even the languid Denny straightened up. He also took time to glance sideways at Mr. Keeler.

Mr. Keeler's face was purple. His long arms were waving around in a storm. He was shaking his fist at Bainbridge and shouting threats at Harford, from which Denny gathered that he intended to jail the Harford crew wholesale if they didn't come in first. He also gathered that Mr. Keeler favored shooting the Bainbridge men on the spot. The sad-eyed freshman, who owned the field glasses, looked worried—Mr. Keeler didn't seem to be the responsible type.

"Wow-woof!" said Mr. Keeler.

The Harford shell was drawing abreast of their rivals. Sixteen men pulled like maniacs. Harford came into the stretch, a scant half-length behind.

"That's their limit," sighed a voice behind Denny. "They can't follow a faster beat. Ken knows it. We're done. Bainbridge's race by a length."

Denny gave a jerk and half turned his head. There was a shout from the spectators, an echo from the Harford boat.

Lucius Tarquinius Superbus fell from Denny's hands, spun through the air, and landed in the river with a splash, a plop, and considerable bad-tempered oratory.

Ken, facing the finish, saw the whole thing. "It's Lucius!" he wailed. "He's fallen overboard. He'll drown! Fellows," shrieked the coxswain, in the right spirit, but the wrong technical terms, "hurry up, for Pete's sake! He'll drown!"

To the startled onlookers on the bridge, the Harford crew appeared to have been hit suddenly by a typhoon, a brain storm, and a bolt of lightning. Eight dripping oars poised for a split second above the waves, then flashed swoopingly down in frantic but rhythmical haste. Eight pairs of arms strained and tugged back in the long pull as Ken, his voice a hoarse shriek, begged the crew to hit it up.

348

The shell plowed gallantly through the water, nosing ahead of its Bainbridge rival. Denny stopped breathing. Mr. Keeler made a noise like a desperate hen.

"Pull! Pull!" Ken shouted.

The Bainbridge cox snapped frantic orders at his men, but his "Let her run," as the boat slipped into the shadow of the bridge, was dejected and flat. Harford had won by a length.

It was Pudge who fished Lucius out, Billy who received him with open arms. But it was Mr. Keeler's earthquaking yell that brought them back to their surroundings.

"Whoopee!" said Mr. Keeler. "Whoop—" He stopped short, finding Denny's eye on him. "Humph," said Mr. Keeler, "I suppose you think you want rowing here now. Humph. Nonsense," he added doubtfully, and then, unable to resist the urge, said "Whoopee," in no uncertain terms.

"Jeepers," said Ken, "we won."

The Harford crew caught up with Denny on shore. Lucius was very wet and in a bitter mood. First there had been that tiresome business of the vanishing lemon drop, and now this. He gave Denny a hard look.

Billy also gave Denny a hard look.

"Listen," said Billy passionately, "when you hold Lucius, you be more careful, see? He might have drowned, that's what might have happened."

Denny shook his head. "Lucius was perfectly safe," he said without thinking. "Coons can swim—I looked it up in the encyclopedia. Besides, I tried him out in the bathtub first, and he swam like a—"

It suddenly struck him that he was being a trifle too chatty, and he closed his mouth with a snap. It also struck him that there was a menacing movement being made in his vicinity.

Denny McCall, Psychologist, applied the elementary principles of the well-known Instinct of Self-Preservation, and left.

349

RONALD PERRY, star player on the Academy eleven, could not forget how he had deliberately hurt Meyer Goldman of the Abraham Lincoln High School team in the season's biggest game. When he realized that the Academy team had ganged up on Meyer, Ronald left the team and the Academy and enrolled in the high school. He became friends with Meyer while Meyer was in the hospital recovering from his injuries, but made few friends at school until he himself went to the hospital after a fight with Jim Stacey. Before long, Jim, Meyer, and Ronald are buddies as well as teammates for Abraham Lincoln High.

John R. Tunis

THE PASS

ILLUSTRATED BY *Hans Walleen*

W HEN you win, when passes click, when the interference forms smoothly in front and you cut in for five, ten, twenty yards, when the sun shines and your girl's sitting up there in the High School stands and the score mounts, yes, then football's fun. That's grand, that's something like.

But this sort of thing wasn't fun; it was agony. For almost the first time since he began playing football he longed to hear the sound of the whistle.

Of all days to have it rain, the day of the Academy game, the one day we want a good dry field and firm footing! The rain pelted down his neck, oozed into his shoes, made each pad a sodden lump of lead. He looked around. The 16-yard line! One more touchdown and we'll be licked; surely, positively licked. Ruefully he remembered standing on the same spot and saying that same thing to himself before the second touchdown. And the third.

Then the whistle blew.

The team picked itself out of the mud and straggled across the mire into the gymnasium. Into the lockers and clean clothes; relief from that incessant pounding, a chance to rest, to stretch out quietly, to pull themselves together.

The familiar room was warm and dry; in one corner steam was hissing cheerfully from the pipes, and the sight of those little piles of fresh, clean clothes before every locker was comforting. They trooped in, sodden and dripping, saying nothing because there wasn't much you could say, chucking their headgears across the benches in disgust, despondent and disappointed. 19-0. What could anybody say about that kind of a score? To think this was the team that had been talked of as possibly playing an Intersectional game!

"O.K., boys." The coach brought up the rear, slamming the door on an especially severe gust of wind and rain. If he was distressed by the upset he showed no evidence of it. "O.K. now, boys, get those clothes right off. Mike! Give us a hand here. Goldman, I'll fix that cut up over your eye. Doc, take a look at Jake's leg."

They hauled off their clothes, wet, soggy, disagreeable to touch, and dropped them to the floor. A small pool of water immediately collected about each pile. Mike and the Doc and the assistant coaches went around rubbing them down, repairing them for the second half. Ah, that's good. Good to be stretched out and relaxed on the hard board while Mike assails you with the coarse, dry towel. But that score, 19-0. Gee, that's terrible, you can't laugh that off. And we were the team mentioned in the papers as going south to play Miami High. Sure, in all the newspapers!

Slowly they dressed once more. Dry socks, underwear, supporters, pads, pants, jerseys, and shoes. There. That's better. That's something like. The coach came past and slipped to the bench where Ronny was leaning over to tie his shoelaces.

351

"Ronald!" His voice was low. "What seems to be the trouble out there this afternoon?"

Ronny knew perfectly well what the trouble was but he didn't like to say. So he just kept leaning over his shoes. When he didn't answer, the coach continued in a low voice. "I know it's wet out there; this kind of weather hurts the T-formation the worst way. But from the bench it kinda looks as if the boys aren't together."

Nope, we surely aren't together. Of course we aren't together; how can we be together when some of the crowd are set on something besides winning a football game? That's what he wanted to say, tried almost to say as loud as he could; but it refused to come out. He mumbled something about the bad weather, the storm, the wet ball, the footing.

The coach rose. He clapped his hands. The squad gathered about, everyone's hair still wet and damp. Behind in the rear Mike passed with an armful of soaking uniforms and equipment.

"Boys, this weather is certainly tough. No use talking. I recognize what you are up against out there. The T-formation needs good firm ground to be effective. But I still feel somehow you're better'n what you've shown, and I've still got confidence in you to win, yes, even with this score. I have confidence, that is, if you'll only get going. Nineteen points a lot? Sure. But the test of a player is what he can do when he's tired. This half go out and play the kind of ball you can."

Then they were outside, out in that deluge once more. Across the way the Academy stands rose in a roar as Keith led his team at the same moment onto the field. Over the end zone was the scoreboard with those dreadful figures staring at them:

H. S. 0   Visitors 19.

The ball was low, and from his position Ronald could watch his teammates converge on the runner, on Keith, no, on Heywood. That big halfback, heavy, powerful, fast, had been slashing holes in their line all afternoon. In the mud and slime he seemed impossible to stop, and Ronny himself had tackled him half a dozen times.

352

The teams lined up. Heywood took the ball once more for a sizeable gain. But Ronald was noticing something else; he was watching Mike and two others break through and pile up on Keith. It was what they'd been doing ever since the kick-off. To his astonishment some of his teammates hadn't forgotten Goldman's injury of the previous season. They were still trying to pay Keith for his share in it.

There's a guy we don't like, so we'll bang him off at the start. This was their attitude. Ronny knew what they didn't seem to know, that Keith could take it. All the time they were attempting to bang him off, Steve Ketchum and Heywood had plowed through for those touchdowns.

Once again Heywood sliced into the line and out into the secondary. He was nearly clear before he slipped and fell. That's a break, that is. On the next play they made a first down, and then Keith got loose off tackle, his most dangerous run. It was Ronny who, seeing the danger on that sloppy field, managed to knock him outside after a thirty-yard gain. He picked himself up, now as wet and soggy as he had been at the end of the first half.

"C'mon, gang, get in there, get in there and play ball like you can, will ya? Block that end, Mike, watch him every minute; get in low, Jake."

But slowly, surely, steadily, the Academy came toward their goal, toward a fourth touchdown, toward the worst licking the High School had ever taken. Keith charged in low and hard between Vic and Don Westcott who alone seemed to be holding up the center of the line, playing a magnificent defensive game. Don slapped at him and threw him off his stride as Ronny came running up. The whole play was clear before him. Keith with one arm out, stumbling in the mud; Mike and Dave rushing in hard to fall on him so that if he wasn't knocked out he'd at least know he'd been hit. It made Ronald furious. He closed in, determined not to permit them to get away with it, to block off Dave anyway. He did block him off, and as he did so Mike accidentally slipped and hit him on the chin with the full force of his fist.

353

He saw stars. When he came to they were standing around in the mud. Doc Roberts was leaning over, wiping his face and holding smelling salts under his nose.

"I'm O.K., Doc." He rose unsteadily, feeling dizzy, tried to step out a little, managed to trot a few steps. "I'm O.K." But he was not O.K., and he was mad clean through. This had to end. One thing or the other. They'd have to quit and play ball —or he would.

"C'm here, gang. This way. Look. This has gotta stop. It's gotta stop or I quit. If you guys don't lay off that bird, I'll leave the field, here, right now, and I'll tell Coach why. C'mon, gang, what say, gang, let's go. Let's forget that stuff. Let's get together, let's play against that crowd there, not against each other."

"You're dead right, Ronald!" Jim Stacey, adjusting his headgear, stepped in toward the center. "Listen, you guys, lay off that fella from now on and play ball. I've been watching you, and Ronny's quite right. We've been playing against each other, not together. Let's all shoot together for the team."

"O.K., Jim."

"Sure, let's go, gang."

"Yeah, let's go."

"All right now, get in there, you guys."

The whistle blew. The teams lined up. Ronald looked around. He was standing on the 8-yard line!

It was raining harder than ever. The Academy leaned over the ball. It was snapped to Heywood, who for the first time started a fraction of a second too soon. The ball was over his shoulder, he stabbed at it, deflected it in the air. A wet figure dashed past and snatched at it in the mist. He had it. Never missing a stride he was five yards down the field before anyone turned.

"Go on, Ned, go on, Ned-boy, for Pete's sake, go on. Don't slip, Ned, go on, Ned!"

The two teams picked themselves up out of the mud and streamed along behind him, but the fleet colored boy gained with every stride.

354

"Yeah, team! Team, team, team. Yeah, team!" The cymbals clashed and clanged from the High School side of the field. The first chance they had had to cheer since the kick-off.

Now then, we're moving. We're really moving. For the rest of the third quarter the teams slithered up and down the center of the gridiron, both Keith and Ronald punting and handling that juicy sphere as if it were dry and easy to hold. Somehow they managed to cling to the thing.

Then toward the end of the quarter the High School team got moving. A quarterback sneak was good for a long gain. On the Academy 30-yard line, however, they were held for two plays. Third and six. They went into their huddle.

"O.K., gang. 39 on 5 count." He was winded, he puffed hard. This was Meyer's play. They went into formation.

"Hike. 27 . . . 38 . . . 40 . . . hike . . ." He leaned over, his hand on Don's wet rump. The ball came, and for once the play was perfectly executed. He faked with his empty left hand to Jake, the halfback, and then in the same motion tucked the ball in Meyer's stomach, continuing back himself as if he were about to throw a pass. Meyer roared off Roger Tread-way's end into the secondary, he bounced off Steve, straight-armed Rex Heywood, and carried Keith along on his back almost five yards. The High School stands were jumping, shriek-ing, yelling.

Then someone shouted. Over to the left in clear territory a figure lay in the wet. Jim had gone down on the play to fake catching a possible forward and draw in one of the defensive backs in their 5-4-2 alignment. Doing so he had turned, slipped, and fallen in the open. When Ronny reached him a group of players was huddled round and he was writhing in agony on the ground.

The Doc rushed up, shoving them aside. He knelt down in a puddle, began feeling of the thigh, the leg, the calf, the ankle.

"Ouch!" Jim jerked up. "Ow . . . that hurts . . . ow . . ."

The Doc beckoned to the sidelines. "You lay still, young man. Lay still now, don't move."

Silence came over the field, and Ronny could hear them

from the stands. "It's Jake . . . naw . . . it's Perry . . . no, he's up, there . . . it's Jim Stacey."

Two managers ran out with a stretcher. They rolled him over, protesting. Ronny saw he was in acute pain. On the bench Jack Train, his substitute, leaned over toward the coach. Then they were carrying Jim from the field.

The team stood disconsolately in the rain. Aw, shoot! Shucks, don't we get the breaks against us! How's that for rotten luck! First this stinking lousy weather. Then we lose our captain, the key of our passing attack, the man who was our best pass catcher.

Jack Train came running on, adjusting his dry headgear. His uniform was unsoiled, his hands were fresh and clean. Ronny looked at him almost with disguest. Heck! What good is he? Couldn't catch a dry ball at ten feet. What use is he on a day like this?

They tried a play. Then another. Something had gone, the mainspring of their nervous energy had snapped, there was no punch left. Baldy was a bear on scouting other teams, and Ronald well knew they'd been told that with Stacey out the High School's passing attack wasn't to be feared. He saw the defensive halfback in one zone slide up. Ideal for a pass if only he had a receiver.

Looking over the situation he called for a fake split buck-end run with Jake carrying the ball. But they were waiting, and although Meyer blocked out the defensive end, the half-backs smeared the play for a small gain. Third and nine! Shoot! Just as we were rolling, too. That's lousy luck all right. Then he heard a voice at his elbow as they went into the huddle. It was Ned, who never raised his voice, who never spoke unless you spoke to him first—Ned, who was the best defensive end in the State but never carried the ball.

"Ronny. Lemme have a look at that thing. Shoot me that flat pass up the center. I b'lieve I kin hang on to that thing."

Why not? They were stopped now. Why not have a try at it? "O.K., gang. Number 46 on 4. Got it, everyone?" He looked round at their muddy faces, heard their panting, saw their affirmative nods. "C'mon now. Formation T. 46 on 4. Hike. 27-38-40-39 . . . hike . . ." He leaned over, patting Don on his wet back. Here it comes!

Taking the ball, he turned and scuttled to the rear. Careful. Keep your balance. Watch your feet now. Both defensive half-backs anticipating a thrust at the line had sneaked up, and Ronald, as he'd been coached, shot the flat pass over their heads into empty territory. Like lightning Ned was there, cutting in with a swerve and taking that greasy thing in midair on the dead run. He had it! Doggone, he had it! He was off. Ronald could see nothing more, for he himself was buried under a swarm of resentful tacklers.

He didn't need to see. When he shook himself free and got the mud out of his eyes, Ned was standing beneath the goal posts, and the umpire had his hands high in the air.

Another touchdown. 19-13.

You can't keep a good gang down! The band blared, squeaky noises came from the brasses, but the cheering drowned everything. Yeah, team! Team, team! Watch it, Meyer. Watch it, boy; watch that kick, it's terribly important. He remembered the coach's words as the ball was snapped back to Bob who always held it for Meyer. Give Meyer a chance, and he'll come through. He's only missed two out of the last fourteen tries.

Swell! Atta boy, Meyer, great work, Meyer. 19-14. Great work for you too, Ned. Boy, you're hot! "C'mon now, gang, c'm here, c'm over here. Look. We got eight minutes to score. Let's get this one for Jim, gang. You bet, we'll get this one for Jim."

It was the longest eight minutes of his life. In that eight minutes he lived a hundred lives, died and was reborn a hundred times. In that space of time he suffered ages of agonies. For he was weary, beaten, his whole frame ached as it had never ached before, he seemed to be carrying around twenty pounds of heavy mud. Each step was a horrible effort. Every fall, every tackle, jarred him badly.

They kicked off, downed them close to their goal line, held them after several rushes, and got the ball near midfield.

358

"O.K., gang, here's our chance. Here's where we go. 48 on 3. Hip-hip. Hike." Get outa the way, Mike, get outa the way or I'll tattoo your backbone. No gain? Shoot! Third and eight to go.

He punted, poorly. But then their own line held, and once more the Academy was forced to kick back. Now he gave everything he had, a delayed straight buck, a short forward to Ned which was knocked down, a forward to Bob which was incomplete. Again he had to kick.

For the third time they held despite the fierceness of the Academy attack. Dusk was descending fast in the wet and mist. You could hardly see the opposite goal posts. He called for 80. It was one of the coach's favorites, a play in which he handed the ball to Meyer who tossed it to Bob, the man in motion. His play which had been stopped three times in the first half for no gain went for twenty yards. They were creeping along, well in enemy territory now; but time was running out fast.

A fumble! A fumble! The ball slithered through the mud. He could see it, in the open. Then a figure shot toward it almost parallel to the ground. How he ever managed to hold that greasy object Ronny never knew. There he was, however, with the ball in his stomach when six men piled on top.

Ned LeRoy! Good boy, Ned! You saved us that time. Gee, that's great work, Ned, that's really super. They went into the huddle. Why not? Sure it was growing dark. Sure the ball was wet and hard to handle. But why not try it?

The defensive backs were sneaking up again, so he called for a pass down the sidelines in which the left end ran down and cut over to take the ball. Number 86 on 3. He leaned over, panting. Whew! Gosh, I'm all in. The words of the coach came suddenly to mind.

The test of a player is what he can do when he's tired.

He looked at them. Meyer on his knees in a pool of water, Ned with his mouth open and his white teeth showing, Don hardly able to stand up, Mike with the gash in his forehead open and bleeding, everyone done in, beaten, exhausted. But

359

the test of a player is what he can do when he's tired.

"Look, gang, let's give 'em one good one for Stacey. What say, hey, gang . . . let's give 'em this one for Jim. One good play. Everyone in it. 86 on 3. Dave, watch that defensive half-back. Jake, fade out a little more. End around direct pass. Everyone got it? Remember, they're scared now. They're plenty worried. And they're just as tired as we are. O.K., gang, let's make this one a good one for Jim."

They went into formation. He leaned over, took the ball, and faded slowly back. Meyer and Bob and Jake ran out ahead to form interference; Ned slipped around and then, going ahead, cut toward the sidelines. Ronald saw a form rushing toward him, dodged, and then let loose. This time he had the whole panorama of the play before his eyes.

The pass was true and straight out to the side. This time Ned was there waiting. Gee, if he only holds it. Cool as ice, the end gathered the ball in, turned and cut across the field behind Jake and Meyer. Someone went down. Gosh, is that Ned? Nope, they're still after him. The pursuit continued. Running forward, Ronny could see scattered bodies writhing on the ground in the mud and mist up ahead. Ned was crossing over now, heading for the opposite sideline. He was in the clear.

A wild spontaneous cheer came from his side. From Abraham Lincoln High.

Howard M. Brier

YOGI'S DARK HORSE

ILLUSTRATED BY *Seymour Fleishman*

YOGI ZIMMERMAN, freshman at Laurel High School, sat in the fifth period study hall and gazed through the window. The sun was shining and the sky was blue. Yogi sat with his chin cupped in his hands, his eyes half closed. It was a pose that might have indicated daydreaming, but Yogi's mind was not wandering in flights of fancy. Instead, it was concerned with grim reality. Yogi Zimmerman had reached a momentous conclusion—political affairs at Laurel High School were in a deplorable state.

Quite likely other students at Laurel High had reached the same conclusion, but because of apathy they had brushed the thought aside. Not so, Yogi Zimmerman. Yogi's mind was made of different stuff. When an idea persisted, he kicked it around until it emerged as a master plan, boiling and bubbling with great social significance.

Physically, Yogi Zimmerman was not impressive. He had wide-spaced eyes, and freckles over the bridge of his nose. His hair was as unruly as a cocker spaniel's, and only a shade darker. He wore mouse-colored sweaters, and mouse-colored cords, and he scampered around the halls like a mouse, quiet, unnoticed.

Few students at Laurel High realized Yogi's great talent for management, but two or three of his classmates sensed his dynamic personality, his eventual date with destiny. One of this select group was Montgomery J. Smith.

At the moment, Montgomery J. Smith was putting the final touches on an algebra assignment. Problems that left Yogi

baffled and bewildered were duck soup for Montgomery J. Smith. Algebra was a breeze. That was why Montgomery was often referred to by his classmates as "The Brain."

His teachers knew him for a modest and shy individual with a keen, analytical mind. Socially, this was a handicap for Montgomery, because frantic instructors frequently turned to him for the correct answer when everyone else in the class had booted the question. Many of his fellow students frowned upon such demonstrations of intellectual superiority, but Yogi Zimmerman placed a high value on brains. Yogi was not sure how a mind like Montgomery's could be used to secure better school government and improved student relations, but he was giving it some serious thought when the study-hall door opened noisily, and in strode Hal Root.

Hal Root was a senior. He wore a letter sweater on his broad shoulders and a smirk on his thick lips. He waved to a group of his pals, and clumped up to the teacher's desk, making sure that his footsteps would attract the attention of the two hundred students in the room. They did. Every eye was on his entrance.

He handed a message to the teacher, and then stepped back out of her vision to grin at his appreciative audience. Hal Root was looking for votes, and like many successful politicians he sensed the value of a brief moment in the limelight.

Yogi Zimmerman leaned across the aisle and whispered to Montgomery J. Smith.

"See that big ham up there, Monte?"

"Yeah." Montgomery showed little interest.

"He's a stuffed shirt if there ever was one."

"What makes you think so?"

"Look at him mugging at the crowd. He's as good as saying, 'Vote for me for student-body president.'"

"But Tip Turner is running against him."

"Tip's just as bad. I tell you, Monte, we got to do something about this election."

Montgomery shrugged. "Don't be silly, Yogi. The freshmen can't do anything. The deal is all sewed up."

"That's where you're wrong." There was a determined gleam in Yogi's eyes. He was looking at Montgomery J. Smith with strange new appraisal. His gaze traveled from the short crew haircut to the highly polished shoes. Yogi's eyes narrowed. "I have an idea, Monte."

"No!" Montgomery said, shuddering. He had been present on other occasions when Yogi got ideas. "Don't do anything foolish, Yogi. It'll just lead to trouble."

"Hmmmmmm!" Yogi was saying.

The study-hall teacher rapped for attention.

"I have an announcement from the student council," she said. "The public address system is temporarily out of order, so I must read this. Please pay close attention. The deadline for filing for student-body offices is 3:00 P.M., tomorrow. All petitions must be in Mr. Parker's office by that time. That is all. Back to your studies, students, quickly."

Hal Root finally reached the door, but not without brushing against a girl's notebook, sending it clattering to the floor. That called for gallant aid in picking up the scattered papers and an apology that could be heard throughout the room. Hal was pleased with himself as he left the study hall.

Yogi settled back in his seat and gazed absent-mindedly at the ceiling. He was giving this new idea the treatment, batting it around, searching for bugs. When Yogi had an idea fraught with far-reaching consequences, he had to view it in a detached manner—he had to set up his objectives. Once his goal was determined, Yogi became a man of action. Montgomery Smith darted apprehensive glances at him. When the bell rang at 2:10, Yogi had made up his mind. He turned to Montgomery.

"What this school needs is a student-body president with brains," Yogi said. "We need a man in office with a constructive program. We need an independent thinker, with a mind of his own and the courage to fight for his convictions. We need a candidate who is free from political promises and the influence of a social club. We need new blood, Monte, and you're it."

"No!" Montgomery gulped, clutching for Yogi's sleeve, but Yogi had already darted for the door.

"See you later," he shouted over his shoulder.

Yogi headed for the office of Mr. Parker, vice-principal. He arrived out of breath.

"May I please have a petition blank, Mr. Parker?"

The vice-principal tilted back in his chair.

"Don't tell me you have a last-minute candidate for office."

"Yes, sir. There's still time, isn't there?"

"You have until tomorrow afternoon. Most of the candidates filed their petitions early this week. It calls for fifty signatures, you know."

"I understand. Could I also have a copy of the Student Association constitution?"

The vice-principal handed Yogi a mimeographed booklet.

"Thank you, sir," Yogi said, as he dashed out of the office. He had two minutes to make his sixth-period history class. The bell was ringing when he slid into his seat.

Yogi was not greatly concerned with history during that sixth period. It was fortunate that the teacher did not call on him for he was devoting his time to a detailed study of the Student Association constitution. The section on student elections held most of his attention, and he read the article on qualification of candidates several times to be sure of his ground. Nowhere could he find a statement that disqualified a freshman from running for president of the student body.

When the sixth period was over, Yogi made his way to the Boys' Club office. This den, across from the locker-room, was

364

a beehive of political activity. Hal Root was there, sounding off in his usual loud voice to a little huddle of loyal supporters. Tip Turner was plotting with his campaign manager in a cubbyhole off the adviser's office. Yogi drifted into the room, unnoticed, and listened quietly to the hubbub.

"It's in the bag," Hal Root was saying. "It'll be another landslide for the Panthers. We got strong candidates for every office."

"The Owls are organizin' the sophomores," one of Hal's henchmen reported. "Tip Turner is startin' a card file on 'em. He's goin' to work 'em over individually."

"Let 'im work 'em," Hal said. "The sophomores got good sense. They aren't going to be railroaded."

The Panthers! The Owls! Yogi Zimmerman knew that here was the sore spot in student elections at Laurel High. For several years these two social organizations had been running the school. There was bitter rivalry between them, and because most of the senior leaders belonged to one or the other of these groups no one dared compete against their candidates. Yogi was going to change the system.

Yogi left the Boys' Club office and wandered around the stage of the auditorium. He knew several fellows on the stage crew, and he was sure they were working on scenery for the junior farce. He also knew that the stage-crew gang were not considered important enough for membership in the Owls and Panthers.

Mike Donovan was head electrician on the stage. He was a good-natured fellow, big, raw-boned, and always looking for fun.

"Hiya, Yogi!" Mike shouted, when Yogi appeared. "Want a job?"

"I have a job, Mike," Yogi grinned. "Take a gander at this."

Mike looked at the petition blank.

"Politics?" he said.

"Yeah."

"Who in the Sam Hill is Montgomery J. Smith?"

"Next president of the student body."

365

"Are you crazy? Hal Root and Tip Turner got that job tied with ribbons."

"That's what you think, Mike. The Panthers and Owls have been running things too long. I'm entering a dark horse."

"Is this guy Smith a senior?"

"No. He's a freshman."

"Freshman! Haw! That's rich. Listen, gang, gather round." Mike's voice boomed so that all of the stage crew could hear him. "Yogi, here, is runnin' a freshman for president. He ain't a Panther. He ain't a Owl. He's a lone wolf. What a gag! Make those big shots look silly. I'm signin' this petition for Montgomery J. Smith. How about you birds? Get your pencils out. Smith for president."

When Yogi left the stage he had ten signatures on his petition. He went down to the athletic locker-room and found four assistant managers cleaning equipment. They were glad to sign. He found the Chess Club meeting on the third floor. No one had ever heard of the members but their names brought the list to twenty.

By that time word had reached the Boys' Club office. Someone had carried the message down for a laugh. Hal Root and Tip Turner came storming through the hall looking for Yogi.

366

They found him in the cafeteria where two student dishwashers were eagerly signing the petition.

"What's this about running a freshman for president?" Hal growled.

"You got it straight," Yogi said. "Montgomery J. Smith is the name. You'll hear plenty about him in the next week."

Tip Turner tilted his head, unbelievingly. "You can't do that. No freshman ever ran for president of the student body in Laurel High. It's just unheard of."

"It won't be unheard of for long," Yogi grinned.

"But the constitution—" Hal said. "The constitution makes it clear—"

"Have you read the constitution lately?" Yogi asked, producing his copy. "Show me where it says a freshman can't run for president."

Hal took the booklet. It was the first time he had seen a copy of the constitution.

Hal and Tip scanned the qualifications for candidates. There was no mention of freshmen being excluded.

"This must be an old constitution," Hal said.

"I got it today from Mr. Parker," Yogi said. "Maybe you fellows would like to keep that copy."

The following morning Yogi was one of the first to arrive at Laurel High. He had forty-two signatures on his petition before the 8:30 warning bell sounded. It was 8:32 when Montgomery J. Smith found Yogi in the center of a group near the woodshop.

"Yogi," he puffed. "I've been looking all over for you. I have to see you. Alone."

Yogi left the group and walked across the hall with Monte.

"You'll have to stop, Yogi," Montgomery said. "I can't run for president. I'm . . . I'm just a freshman. The whole idea is silly."

"Calm down, Monte," Yogi said, patting the taller boy on the shoulder. "Everything is going all right. You just leave the details to me. I'm managing your campaign, Monte."

"But Hal Root said I had to withdraw, or else. He was plenty burned up, Yogi."

367

"That big bag of wind! Think nothing of it, Monte. Once we get this petition signed, we're going to put you across in a whirlwind campaign. This school will be dizzy. Just think of it, Monte. You'll be famous. The first freshman ever elected president of the student body. All you have to do is keep your mouth shut and grin. Look like a big shot."

"But I don't want to be a big shot—"

"Montgomery!" Yogi's tone was severe. "Don't ever let me hear you say that again. When I decided to make you president of the student body, the die was castoff."

"Don't you mean cast?"

"Cast! Castoff! What's the difference? Now run along to class. I'll handle this situation, and when I handle a situation it stays handled."

The halls were thinning out, and the 8:40 bell sounded. Montgomery J. Smith heaved a deep, uncertain sigh, and looked helplessly at his manager.

"I—I hope you know what you're doing," he said.

Yogi Zimmerman knew what he was doing. At the end of third lunch he had seventy-two names on the petition—twenty-two more than was necessary. Ten minutes before the 3:00 P.M. deadline he presented the document to Mr. Parker.

"I presume you know this petition is a little out of the ordinary," the vice-principal said, with a slight twinkle in his eye.

Yogi nodded.

"After hearing of your action, the student council held a special meeting this morning to decide what should be done about it."

For a moment Yogi had a sinking feeling in his stomach.

"They studied the constitution," the vice-principal continued, "and decided you are entirely within your rights. It takes three months to amend the constitution. This has never happened before. I must admit you have created quite a stir in our school."

"You haven't seen anything yet, Mr. Parker," Yogi grinned. "Wait until next week when our campaign really gets under way."

Monday marked the start of the campaign. It was to last for four days and was to culminate with the election the following Friday.

Yogi spent the week end getting his machine organized. On Saturday ten boys spent the day painting signs in Yogi's basement. They were tacked to the bulletin boards early Monday morning, and they created a sensation.

Yogi's masterpiece occupied a prominent spot in the front hall, and even Yogi was pleased with the bold lettering. The sign said:

NOT SNUFFY SMITH . . .

NOT KATE SMITH . . .

NOT AL SMITH . . .

BUT

MONTGOMERY J. SMITH

FOR PRESIDENT

The "Smith for President" campaign was under way.

"We gotta keep Smith's name in front of the voters every minute this week," Yogi said. He had called a caucus during first lunch in the Beanery, across the street from the school. Before the lunch period was over, each man in the group was imbued with Yogi's enthusiasm.

"We're holding a mass meeting in front of the Beanery during second lunch tomorrow. You fellows have to tell twenty others, and get them to pass the word on to twenty more. This thing is going to snowball. Talk Smith, think Smith, vote Smith! Now how about phone numbers? We gotta have a telephone committee. How many of you guys will agree to call thirty people on the phone if I can get their numbers?"

"They won't let you use the office card file," one of the fellows said.

"We don't need the office file," Yogi replied. "I got it! A contest! We'll run it right here in the Beanery. Here's how it works. We'll get a box, see. We'll offer a prize. We'll have students put their phone numbers on a slip of paper. The phone

369

number that comes closest to the number of votes cast for Smith in Friday's election wins a camera, or a tennis racket, or something."

"Where you going to get a camera, or a tennis racket?"

"You leave that to me," Yogi said. "I got ideas. Bill, can you fix up a box tonight? Have it here tomorrow morning?"

Bill nodded. The "Smith for President" campaign was rolling.

On Tuesday every student was handed a telegram as he walked toward the doors of Laurel High. The telegram was mimeographed on an official Western Union blank. It read:

STUDENTS THE PANTHERS AND THE OWLS HAVE RUN LAUREL POLITICS LONG ENOUGH STOP YOU CAN PUT AN END TO THIS NEFARIOUS PRACTICE STOP VOTE FOR MONTGOMERY J SMITH AN INDEPENDENT LONE WOLF STOP SMITH WILL BREAK THE CLIQUES THAT CONTROL THE STUDENT OFFICES. YOGI ZIMMERMAN, CAMPAIGN MGR

SMITH FOR PRESIDENT

"How'd you get those Western Union blanks," Mike Donovan grinned when he met Yogi in the hall.

"That was easy," Yogi said. "I talked the manager into giving me two thousand blanks. All I had to do was point out the advertising value."

The mass meeting in front of the Beanery went off as scheduled. Yogi Zimmerman gave a speech that had never been equalled at Laurel High for its oratorical quality. He closed with, ". . . and now I give you the man who is going to sweep the election next Friday . . . the man who is going to upset the applecart for Root and Turner . . . the man who started this landslide, and who will see it through to a successful finish. I give you—Montgomery J. Smith."

There were cheers from the five hundred students who had gathered for the meeting.

Monte grinned, held his hands over his head like a boxer, but before he could say anything, Yogi's helpers had started a

370

serpentine with the chant *Smith for President,* and most of the crowd joined in the parade. It was timed nicely, and Yogi watched the results of his planning with deep satisfaction.

Yogi expected trouble from Hal Root and Tip Turner. It came Tuesday afternoon when Root and Turner cornered Yogi in the third-floor corridor.

"Listen, you little squirt," Hal said. "We don't like the way you're running this campaign."

"What are you going to do about it?" Yogi said, defiantly.

"We're going to make it tough for you. If you have dreams of ever being elected into the Panthers or the Owls, you're potted right now."

"And the same goes for you," Yogi said.

"What do you mean?" Tip said. "You're talkin' in riddles."

"We're starting a new club after this election. The Lone Wolves. You birds are dinged right now."

Yogi appeared Wednesday morning with an expensive new tennis racket for a prize in the phone-number contest.

"How'd you get that?" Donovan asked, when he displayed it backstage.

"Nothing to it," Yogi said. "I traded advertising space."

"What advertising space?"

"In the *Bulldog*. The school paper gives each presidential candidate ten inches of space in the Thursday issue before the election. They don't care what you put in the space. I'm putting in a ten-inch ad for Thompson's Sporting Goods Store. They gave me the racket for the space."

Telephone numbers were coming in by the hundreds, and when the tennis racket was displayed at the Beanery during lunch period, the box was jammed with slips of paper.

"Get that telephone committee working tonight," Yogi instructed his helpers. "Call each number. Get in a plug for Smith. Have 'em say, 'Keep Laurel politics clean. Vote for Smith.'"

On Thursday a new publicity stunt greeted the Laurel students. Pasted over the center of every clock in the building was a circular sheet of paper bearing the words: TIME TO VOTE FOR SMITH.

"How'd you think of that?" Montgomery Smith said during first lunch.

"I just figured more students looked at the clock more times during the day than anywhere else. Some of the fellows who work as part-time janitors pasted 'em up for me."

"I don't see where you get the ideas."

"Ideas! Man, I'm loaded with ideas. I'm going to be a public relations man when I get out of school. This stuff is just practice for me."

Yogi had ideas all right. The crowning climax of the campaign came during the first period on Friday morning. Classes had just quieted down when suddenly the loudspeaker blared into action. A loud voice, clear and deep, proclaimed:

372

"Students of Laurel High. Rise up! Overthrow the cliques. Vote for a capable Independent when you go to the polls today. There is only one Independent in the race for student-body president. His name is Montgomery J. Smith."

The loudspeaker system went dead. Students looked at one another, grinned. There was whispering in every classroom, talk in the study halls.

Suddenly, the intercom system started to buzz again. This time the excited voice of the head clerk came in.

"Students. That announcement you just heard was not official. It did not originate in the office. Both the principal and the vice-principal are out of the building. Someone cut in on this address system. We are trying to trace the origin of that unofficial announcement. That is all."

Yogi Zimmerman grinned to himself. He knew the unofficial announcement would be hard to trace. By now Mike Donovan had scurried out of the loft, high above the stage, and there would be no trace left on the wires where he had tapped the circuit. The mystery of that timely message would never be solved.

Students voted all day Friday. The ballots were counted during sixth period, and Montgomery J. Smith had won with 1006 votes. Hal Root was second with 320, and Tip Turner trailed with 113.

After school, students flocked around Monte Smith, shaking his hand, pounding him on the back, offering congratulations.

"How about a statement for the *Bulldog*?" a reporter asked.

"Sure," Monte said. "Just thank the voters who supported me. Tell them things are going to be different around here. From now on everybody gets a break."

Yogi smiled to himself. He had confidence in Monte Smith or he would never have put him in this office. He buttoned his jacket and left the building by a side door. As he walked along the familiar streets he felt a deep pride in Laurel High. There were a few things still wrong with the school, but nothing that couldn't be cleared up during his sophomore year.

Index